EXPERIMENT
IN AUTOBIOGRAPHY

Autobiographical works by H.G. Wells

EXPERIMENT IN AUTOBIOGRAPHY, 2 vols.

H.G. WELLS IN LOVE (edited by G.P. Wells)

EXPERIMENT
IN AUTOBIOGRAPHY

DISCOVERIES AND CONCLUSIONS
OF A VERY ORDINARY BRAIN
(SINCE 1866)

BY

H.G. WELLS

VOLUME I

faber and faber
LONDON · BOSTON

First published in 1934
by Victor Gollancz/Cresset Press, London
First published in paperback in 1969
by Jonathan Cape, London
Reissued in this edition in 1984
by Faber and Faber Limited
3 Queen Square London WCIN 3AU

Printed in Great Britain by
Butler & Tanner Ltd, Frome, Somerset
All rights reserved

British Library Cataloguing in Publication Data

Wells, H.G.
Experiment in autobiography.
Vol. 1
1. Wells, H.G.—Biography   2. Authors,
English—20th century—Biography
I. Title
823′.912   PR5776
ISBN 0-571-13330-4

CONTENTS

Chapter the First
INTRODUCTORY

Chapter the Second
ORIGINS

Chapter the Third
SCHOOLBOY

Chapter the Fourth

EARLY ADOLESCENCE

Chapter the Fifth

SCIENCE STUDENT IN LONDON

Chapter the Sixth

STRUGGLE FOR A LIVING

Chapter the Seventh
DISSECTION

Chapter the Eighth
FAIRLY LAUNCHED AT LAST

Chapter the Ninth
THE IDEA OF A PLANNED WORLD

LIST OF ILLUSTRATIONS

VOLUME I

CHAPTERS I – VI

CHAPTER THE FIRST

INTRODUCTORY

§ 1
PRELUDE (1932)

I NEED freedom of mind. I want peace for work. I am distressed by immediate circumstances. My thoughts and work are encumbered by claims and vexations and I cannot see any hope of release from them; any hope of a period of serene and beneficent activity, before I am overtaken altogether by infirmity and death. I am in a phase of fatigue and of that discouragement which is a concomitant of fatigue, the petty things of to-morrow skirmish in my wakeful brain, and I find it difficult to assemble my forces to confront this problem which paralyses the proper use of myself.

I am putting even the pretence of other work aside in an attempt to deal with this situation. I am writing a report about it—to myself. I want to get these discontents clear because I have a feeling that as they become clear they will either cease from troubling me or become manageable and controllable.

There is nothing I think very exceptional in my situation as a mental worker. Entanglement is our common lot. I believe this craving for a release from—bothers, from daily demands and urgencies, from responsibilities and tempting distractions, is shared by an increasing number of people who, with specialized and distinctive work to do, find themselves eaten up by first-hand affairs. This is the outcome of a specialization and a sublimation of interests that has become frequent only in the last century or so. Spaciousness and leisure, and even the desire for spaciousness and leisure, have so far been exceptional. Most individual creatures since life began, have been " up against it " all the time, have been driven continually by fear and cravings, have had to respond to the unresting antagonisms of their surroundings, and they have found a sufficient and sustaining interest in the drama of immediate events provided for them by these demands. Essentially, their living was continuous adjustment to happenings. Good hap and ill hap filled it entirely. They hungered and ate and they desired and loved ; they were amused and attracted, they pursued or escaped, they were overtaken and they died.

But with the dawn of human foresight and with the appearance of a great surplus of energy in life such as the last century or so has revealed, there has been a progressive emancipation of the attention from everyday urgencies. What was once the whole of life, has become to an increasing extent, merely the background of life. People can ask now what would have been an extraordinary question five hundred years ago. They can say, " Yes, you earn a living, you support a family, you love and hate, but—*what do you do ?* "

Conceptions of living, divorced more and more from immediacy, distinguish the modern civilized man from all former life. In art, in pure science, in literature, for instance, many people find sustaining series of interests and incentives which have come at last to have a greater value for them than any primary needs and satisfactions. These primary needs are taken for granted. The everyday things of life become subordinate to these wider interests which have taken hold of them, and they continue to value everyday things, personal affections and material profit and loss, only in so far as they are ancillary to the newer ruling system of effort, and to evade or disregard them in so far as they are antagonistic or obstructive to that. And the desire to live as fully as possible within the ruling system of effort becomes increasingly conscious and defined.

The originative intellectual worker is not a normal human being and does not lead nor desire to lead a normal human life. He wants to lead a supernormal life.

Mankind is realizing more and more surely that to escape from individual immediacies into the less personal activities now increasing in human society is not, like games, reverie, intoxication or suicide, a suspension or abandonment of the primary life ; on the contrary it is the way to power over that primary life which, though subordinated, remains intact. Essentially it is an imposition upon the primary life of a participation in the greater life of the race as a whole. In studies and studios and laboratories, in administrative bureaus and exploring expeditions, a new world is germinated and develops. It is not a repudiation of the old but a vast extension of it, in a racial synthesis into which individual aims will ultimately be absorbed. We originative intellectual workers are reconditioning human life.

Now in this desire, becoming increasingly lucid and continuous for me as my life has gone on, in this desire to get the primaries of life under control and to concentrate the largest possible proportion of my energy upon the particular system of effort that has established itself for me as my distinctive business in the world, I find the clue to the general conduct not only of my own life and the key not only to my present perplexities, but a clue to the difficulties of most scientific, philosophical, artistic, creative, preoccupied men and women. We are like early amphibians, so to speak, struggling out of the waters that have hitherto covered our kind, into the air, seeking to breathe in a new fashion and emancipate ourselves from long accepted and long unquestioned necessities. At last it becomes for us a case of air or nothing. But the new land has not yet definitively emerged from the waters and we swim distressfully in an element we wish to abandon.

I do not now in the least desire to live longer unless I can go on with what I consider to be my proper business. That is not to say that the stuff of everyday life has not been endlessly interesting, exciting and delightful for me in my time : clash of personalities, music and beauty, eating and drinking, travel and meetings, new lands and strange spectacles, the work for successes, much aimless play, much laughter, the getting well again after illness, the pleasures, the very real pleasures, of vanity. Let me not be ungrateful to life for its fundamental substances. But I have had a full share of all these things and I do not want to remain alive simply for more of them. I want the whole stream of this daily life stuff to flow on for me—for a long time yet—if, what I call my work can still be, can be more than ever the emergent meaning of the stream. But only on that condition. And that is where I am troubled now. I find myself less able to get on with my work than ever before. Perhaps the years have something to do with that, and it may be that a progressive broadening and deepening of my conception of what my work should be, makes it less easy than it was ; but the main cause is certainly the invasion of my time and thought by matters that are either quite secondary to my real business or have no justifiable connection with it. Subordinate and everyday things, it seems to me in this present mood, surround me in an ever-growing jungle. My hours are choked with them ; my thoughts are tattered by them. All my life I have been pushing aside intrusive tendrils, shirking discursive consequences, bilking unhelpful obligations, but I am more aware of them now and less hopeful about them that I have ever been. I have a sense of crisis ; that the time has come to reorganize my peace, if the ten or fifteen years ahead, which at the utmost I may hope to *a salvage operation* work in now, are to be saved from being altogether over- grown.

I will explain later what I think my particular business to be. But for it, if it is to be properly done, I require a pleasant well-lit writing room in good air and a comfort- able bedroom to sleep in—and, if the mood takes me, to write in—both free from distracting noises and indeed all unexpected disturbances. There should be a secretary or at least a typist within call and out of earshot, and, within reach, an abundant library and the rest of the world all hung accessibly on to that secretary's telephone. (But it would have to be a one-way telephone, so that when we wanted news we could ask for it, and when we were not in a state to receive and digest news, we should not have it forced upon us.) That would be the central cell of my life. That would give the immediate material conditions for the best work possible. I think I would like that the beautiful scenery outside the big windows should be changed ever and again, but I recognize the difficulties in the way of that. In the background there would have to be, at need, food, exercise and stimulating, agreeable and various conversation, and, pervading all my consciousness, there should be a sense of security and attention, an assurance that what was pro- duced, when I had done my best upon it, would be properly significant and effective. In such circumstances I feel I could still do much in these years before me, without hurry and without waste. I can see a correlated scheme of work I could do that would, I feel, be enormously worth while, and the essence of my trouble is that the clock ticks on, the moments drip out and trickle, flow away as hours, as days, and I cannot adjust my life to secure any such fruitful peace.

self-criticism

It scarcely needs criticism to bring home to me that much of my work has been slovenly, haggard and irritated, most of it hurried and inadequately revised, and some of it as white and pasty in its texture as a starch-fed nun. I am tormented by a desire for achievement that overruns my capacity and by a practical incapacity to bring about for myself the conditions under which fine achievement is possible. I pay out what I feel to be a disproportionate amount of my time and attention in clumsy attempts to save the rest of it for the work in hand. I seem now in this present mood, to be saving only tattered bits of time, and even in these scraps of salvage my mind is often jaded and preoccupied.

It is not that I am poor and unable to buy the things I want, but that I am quite unable to get the things I want. I can neither control my surroundings myself nor can I find helpers and allies who will protect me from the urgencies—from within and from without—of primary things. I do not see how there can be such helpers. For to protect me completely they would have, I suppose, to span my intelligence and possibilities, and if they could do that they would be better employed in doing my work directly and eliminating me altogether.

This feeling of being intolerably hampered by irrelevant necessities, this powerful desire for disentanglement is, I have already said, the common experience of the men and women who write, paint, conduct research and assist in a score of other ways, in preparing that new world, that greater human life, which all art, science and literature have foreshadowed. My old elaborate-minded friend, Henry James the novelist, for example, felt exactly this thing. Some elements in his character obliged him to lead an abundant social life, and as a result he was so involved in engagements, acknowledgments, considerations, compliments, reciprocities, small kindnesses, generosities, graceful gestures and significant acts, all of which he felt compelled to do with great care and amplitude, that at times he found existence more troubled and pressing than many a sweated toiler. His craving for escape found expression in a dream of a home of rest, *The Great Good Place*, where everything that is done was done for good, and the fagged mind was once more active and free. The same craving for flight in a less Grandisonian and altogether more tragic key, drove out the dying Tolstoy in that headlong flight from home which ended his life.

This fugitive impulse is an inevitable factor in the lives of us all, great or small, who have been drawn into these activities, these super-activities which create and which are neither simply gainful, nor a response to material or moral imperatives, nor simply and directly the procuring of primary satisfactions. Our lives are threaded with this same, often quite desperate effort to disentangle ourselves, to get into a Great Good Place of our own, and work freely.

None of us really get there, perhaps there is no *there* anywhere to get to, but we get some way towards it. We never do the work that we imagine to be in us, we never realize the secret splendour of our intentions, yet nevertheless some of us get something done that seems almost worth the effort. Some of us, and it may be as good a way as any, let everything else slide, live in garrets and hovels, borrow money unscrupulously, live on women (or, if they are women, live on men), exploit patronage, accept pensions. But even the careless life will not stay careless. It has its own frustrations and chagrins.

Others make the sort of effort I have made, and give a part of their available energy to save the rest. They fight for their conditions and have a care for the things about them. That is the shape of my story. I have built two houses and practically rebuilt a third to make that Great Good Place to work in, I have shifted from town to country and from country to town, from England to abroad and from friend to friend, I have preyed upon people more generous than myself who loved me and gave life to me. In return, because of my essential preoccupation, I have never given any person nor place a simple disinterested love. It was not in me. I have loved acutely, but that is another matter. I have attended spasmodically to business and money-making. And here I am at sixty-five (Spring 1932), still asking for peace that I may work some more, that I may do that major task that will atone for all the shortcomings of what I have done in the past.

Imperfection and incompleteness are the certain lot of all creative workers. We all compromise. We all fall short. The life story to be told of any creative worker is therefore by its very nature, by its diversions of purpose and its qualified success, by its grotesque transitions from sublimation to base necessity and its pervasive stress towards flight, a comedy. The story can never be altogether pitiful because of the dignity of the work ; it can never be altogether dignified because of its inevitable concessions. It must be serious, but not solemn, and since there is no controversy in view and no judgment of any significance to be passed upon it, there is no occasion for apologetics. In this spirit I shall try to set down the story of my own life and work, up to and including its present perplexities.

I write down my story and state my present problem, I repeat, to clear and relieve my mind. The story has no plot and the problem will never be solved. I do not think that in the present phase of human affairs there is any possible Great Good Place, any sure and abiding home for any creative worker. In diverse forms and spirits we are making over the world, so that the primary desires and emotions, the drama of the immediate individual life will be subordinate more and more, generation by generation, to beauty and truth, to universal interests and mightier aims.

That is our common rôle. We are therefore, now and for the next few hundred years at least, strangers and invaders of the life of every day. We are all essentially lonely. In our nerves, in our bones. We are too preoccupied and too experimental to give ourselves freely and honestly to other people, and in the end other people fail to give themselves fully to us. We are too different among ourselves to get together in any enduring fashion. It is good for others as for myself to find, however belatedly, that there is no fixed home to be found, and no permanent relationships. I see now, what I merely suspected when I began to write this section, that my perplexities belong to the mood of a wayside pause, to the fatigue of a belated tramp on a road where there is no rest-house before the goal.

That dignified peace, that phase of work perfected in serenity, of close companionship in thought, of tactfully changing scenery and stabilized instability ahead, is just a helpful dream that kept me going along some of the more exacting stretches of the course, a useful but essentially an impossible dream. So I sit down now by the reader, so to speak, and yarn a bit about my difficulties and blunders, about preposterous hopes and unexpected lessons, about my luck and the fun of the road, and then, a little refreshed and set-up, a little more sprightly for the talk, I will presently shoulder the old bundle again, go on, along the noisy jostling road, with its irritations and quarrels and distractions, with no delusion that there is any such dreamland work palace ahead, or any perfection of accomplishment possible for me, before I have to dump the whole load, for whatever it is worth, myself and my load together, on the scales of the receiver at journey's end. Perhaps it is as well that I shall never know what the scales tell, or indeed whether they have anything to tell, or whether there will be any scales by which to tell, of the load that has been my life.

age 66

§ 2
PERSONA AND PERSONALITY

THE PRECEDING SECTION was drafted one wakeful night, somewhen between two and five in the early morning a year or more ago ; it was written in perfect good faith, and a criticism and continuation of it may very well serve as the opening movement in this autobiographical effort. For that section reveals, artlessly and plainly what Jung would call my *persona*.

A *persona*, as Jung uses the word, is the private conception a man has of himself, his idea of what he wants to be and of how he wants other people to take him. It provides therefore, the standard by which he judges what he may do, what he ought to do and what is imperative upon him. Everyone has a *persona*. Self conduct and self explanation is impossible without one.

the jungian persona

A *persona* may be very stable or it may fluctuate extremely. It may be resolutely honest or it may draw some or all of its elements from the realms of reverie. It may exist with variations in the same mind. We may have single or multiple *persona* and in the latter case we are charged with inconsistencies and puzzle ourselves and our friends. Our *personas* grow and change and age as we do. And rarely if ever are they the whole even of our conscious mental being. All sorts of complexes are imperfectly incorporated or not incorporated at all, and may run away with us in the most unexpected manner.

So that this presentation of a preoccupied mind devoted to an exalted and spacious task and seeking a maximum of detachment from the cares of this world and from baser needs and urgencies that distract it from that task, is not even the beginning of a statement of what I am, but only of what I most like to think I am. It is the plan to which I work, by which I prefer to work, and by which ultimately I want to judge my performance. But quite a lot of other things have happened to me, quite a lot of other stuff goes with me and it is not for the reader to accept this purely personal criterion.

A *persona* may be fundamentally false, as is that of many a maniac. It may be a structure of mere compensatory delusions, as is the case with many vain people. But it does not follow that if it is selected by a man out of his moods and motives, it is necessarily a work of self deception. A man who tries to behave as he conceives he should behave, may be satisfactorily honest in restraining, ignoring and disavowing many of his innate motives and dispositions. The mask, the *persona*, of the Happy Hypocrite became at last his true face.

It is just as true that all men are imperfect saints and heroes as it is that all men are liars. There is, I maintain, a sufficient justification among my thoughts and acts from quite early years, for that pose of the disinterested thinker and worker, working for a racial rather than a personal achievement. But the distractions, attacks and frustrations that set him scribbling distressfully in the night, come as much from within as without ; the antagonisms and temptations could do nothing to him, were it not for that within him upon which they can take hold. Directly I turn from the easier task of posing in an Apology for my life, to the more difficult work of frank autobiography, I have to bring in all the tangled motives out of which my *persona* has emerged ; the elaborate sexual complexities, the complexes of ambition and rivalry, the hesitation and fear in my nature, for example ; and in the interests of an impartial diagnosis I have to set aside the appeal for a favourable verdict.

A biography should be a dissection and demonstration of how a particular human being was made and worked ; the directive *persona* system is of leading importance only when it is sufficiently consistent and developed to be the ruling theme of the story. But this is the case with my life. From quite an early age I have been predisposed towards one particular sort of work and one particular system of interests. I have found the attempt to disentangle the possible drift of life in general and of human life in particular from the confused stream of events, and the means of controlling that drift, if such are to be found, more important and interesting by far than anything else. I have had, I believe, an aptitude for it. The study and expression of *tendency*, has been for me what music is for the musician, or the advancement of his special knowledge is to the scientific investigator. My *persona* may be an exaggeration of one aspect of my being, but I believe that it is a ruling aspect. It may be a magnification but it is not a fantasy. A voluminous mass of work accomplished attests its reality.

The value of that work is another question. A bad musician may be none the less passionately a musician. Because I have spent a large part of my life's energy in a drive to make a practically applicable science out of history and sociology, it does not follow that contemporary historians, economists and politicians are not entirely just in their disregard of my effort. They will not adopt my results ; they will only respond to fragments of them. But the fact remains that I have made that effort, that it has given me a considerable ill-defined prestige, and that it is the only thing that makes me conspicuous beyond the average lot and gives my life with such complications and entanglements as have occurred in it, an interest that has already provoked biography and may possibly provoke more, and so renders unavoidable the thought of a defensive publication, at some future date, of this essay in autobiographical self-examination. The conception of a worker concentrated on the perfection and completion of a work is its primary idea. Either the toad which is struggling to express itself here, *has* engendered a jewel in its head or it is nothing worth troubling about in the way of toads.

This work, this jewel in my head for which I take myself seriously enough to be self-scrutinizing and autobiographical, is, it seems to me, a crystallization of ideas. A variety of biological and historical suggestions and generalizations, which, when lying confusedly in the human mind, were cloudy and opaque, have been brought into closer and more exact relations ; the once amorphous mixture has fallen into a lucid arrangement and through this new crystalline clearness, a plainer vision of human possibilities and the conditions of their attainment, appears. I have made the broad lines and conditions of the human outlook distinct and unmistakable for myself and for others. I have shown that human life as we know it, is only the dispersed raw material for human life as it might be. There is a hitherto undreamt-of fullness, freedom and happiness within reach of our species. Mankind can pull itself together and take that now. But if mankind fails to apprehend its opportunity, then division, cruelties, delusions and ultimate frustration lies before our kind. The decision to perish or escape has to be made within a very limited time. For escape, vast changes in the educational, economic and directive structure of human society are necessary. They are definable. They are practicable. But they demand courage and integrity. They demand a force and concentration of will and a power of adaptation in habits and usages which may or may not be within the compass of mankind. This is the exciting and moving prospect displayed by the crystal I have brought out of solution.

I do not set up to be the only toad in the world that has this crystallization. I do not find so much difference between my mind and others, that I can suppose that I alone have got this vision clear. What I think, numbers must be thinking. They have similar minds with similar material, and it is by mere chance and opportunity that I have been among the first to give expression to this realization of a guiding framework for life. But I have been among the first. Essentially, then, a main thread in weaving my autobiography must be the story of how I came upon, and amidst what accidents I doubted, questioned and rebelled against, accepted interpretations of life; and so went on to find the pattern of the key to master our world and release its imprisoned promise. I believe I am among those who have found what key is needed. We, I and those similar others, have set down now all the specifications for a working key to the greater human life. By an incessant toil of study, propaganda, education and creative suggestion, by sacrifice where it is necessary and much fearless conflict, by a bold handling of stupidity, obstruction and perversity, we may yet cut out and file and polish and insert and turn that key to the creative world community before it is too late. That kingdom of heaven is materially within our reach.

My story therefore will be at once a very personal one and it will be a history of my sort and my time. An autobiography is the story of the contacts of a mind and a world. The story will begin in perplexity and go on to a troubled and unsystematic awakening. It will culminate in the attainment of a clear sense of purpose, conviction that the coming great world of order, is real and sure ; but, so far as my individual life goes, with time running out and a thousand entanglements delaying realization. For me maybe—but surely not for us. For us, the undying us of our thought and experience, that great to-morrow is certain.

So this autobiography plans itself as the crystallization of a system of creative realizations in one particular mind—

with various incidental, good, interesting or curious personal things that happened by the way.

§ 3

QUALITY OF THE BRAIN AND BODY CONCERNED

THE BRAIN upon which my experiences have been written is not a particularly good one. If there were brain-shows, as there are cat and dog shows, I doubt if it would get even a third class prize. Upon quite a number of points it would be marked below the average. In a little private school in a small town on the outskirts of London it seemed good enough, and that gave me a helpful conceit about it in early struggles where confidence was half the battle. It was a precocious brain, so that I was classified with boys older than myself right up to the end of a brief school career which closed before I was fourteen. But compared with the run of the brains I meet nowadays, it seems a poorish instrument. I *Comparisons* won't even compare it with such cerebra as the full and subtly simple brain of Einstein, the wary, quick and flexible one of Lloyd George, the abundant and rich grey matter of G. B. Shaw, Julian Huxley's store of knowledge or my own eldest son's fine and precise instrument. But in relation to everyday people with no claim to mental distinction I still find it at a disadvantage. The names of places and people, numbers, quantities and dates for instance, are easily lost or get a little distorted. It snatches at them and often lets them slip again. I cannot do any but the simplest sums in my head and when I used to play bridge, I found my memory of the consecutive tricks and my reasoning about the playing of the cards, inferior to nine out of ten of the people I played with. I lose at chess to almost anyone and though I have played a spread-out patience called Miss Milligan for the

past fifteen years, I have never acquired a sufficient sense of
the patterns of 104 cards to make it anything more than a
game of chance and feeling. Although I have learnt and
relearnt French since my school days and have lived a large
part of each year for the past eight years in France, I have
never acquired a flexible diction or a good accent and I
cannot follow French people when they are talking briskly—
and they always talk briskly. Such other languages as Spanish, Italian and German I have picked up from a grammar
or a conversation book sufficiently to serve the purposes of
travel ; only to lose even that much as soon as I ceased to
use them. London is my own particular city ; all my life I
have been going about in it and yet the certitude of the taxi-
cab driver is a perpetual amazement to me. If I wanted to
walk from Hoxton to Chelsea without asking my way, I
should have to sit down to puzzle over a map for some time.
All this indicates a loose rather inferior mental texture,
inexact reception, bad storage and uncertain accessibility.

I do not think my brain has begun to age particularly
yet. It can pick up new tricks, though it drops them very
readily again, more readily perhaps than it used to do. I
learnt sufficient Spanish in the odd moments of three
months to get along in Spain two years ago without much
trouble. I think my brain has always been very much as it
is now, except perhaps for a certain slowing down.

And I believe that its defects are mainly innate. It was
not a good brain to begin with, although certain physical
defects of mine and bad early training, may have increased
faults that might have been corrected by an observant
teacher. The atmosphere of my home and early upbringing
was not a highly educative atmosphere ; words were used
inexactly, and mispronounced, and so a certain timidity
of utterance and a disposition to mumble and avoid doubtful or difficult words and phrases, may have worked back

into my mental texture. My eyes have different focal lengths
and nobody discovered this until I was over thirty. Columns
of figures and lines of print are as a result apt to get a little
dislocated and this made me bad at arithmetic and blurred
my impression of the form of words. It was only about the
age of thirteen, when I got away with algebra, Euclid's
elements and, a little later, the elements of trigonometry,
that I realized I was not a hopeless duffer at mathematics.
But here comes an item on the credit side ; I found Euclid
easy reading and solved the simple " riders " in my textbook with a facility my schoolmaster found exemplary. I
also became conceited about my capacity for " problems "
in algebra. And by eleven or twelve, in some way I cannot
trace, I had taken to drawing rather vigorously and freshly.
My elder brother could not draw at all but my other brother
draws exactly and delicately, if not quite so spontaneously
and expressively as I do. I know practically nothing of brain
structure and physiology, but it seems probable to me that
this relative readiness to grasp form and relation, indicates
that the general shape and arrangement of my brain is
better than the quality of its cells, fibres and bloodvessels.
I have a quick sense of form and proportion ; I have a brain
good for outlines. Most of my story will carry out that
suggestion.

A thing that has I think more to do with my general
build than with my brain structure is that my brain works
best in short spells and is easily fatigued. My head is small
—I can cheer up nearly every one of my friends by just
changing hats ; the borrowed brim comes down upon my
ears and spreads them wide—my heart has an irregular
beat and I suspect that my carotid arteries do not branch
so freely and generously into my grey matter as they might
do. I do not know whether it would be of any service after
I am dead to prepare sections of my brain to ascertain

that I have made an autopsy possible by my will, but my son Gip tells me that all that tissue will have decayed long before a post mortem is possible. " Unless," he added helpfully, " you could commit suicide in a good hardening solution." But that would be difficult to arrange. There may perhaps be considerable differences in mental character due to a larger or smaller lumen of the arteries, to a rapid or sluggish venous drainage, to variations in interstitial tissue, which affect the response and interaction of the nerve cells. At any rate there is and always has been far too ready a disposition in my brain to fag and fade for my taste.

It can fade out generally or locally in a very disconcerting manner. Aphasia is frequent with me. At an examination for a teaching diploma which involved answering twenty or thirty little papers in the course of four days I found myself on the last day face to face with a paper, happily not of vital importance, of which the questions were entirely familiar and entirely unmeaning. There was nothing to be done but go out. On another occasion I undertook to give an afternoon lecture to the Royal Institution. I knew my subject fairly well, so well that I had not written it down. I was not particularly afraid of my audience. I talked for a third of my allotted time—and came to a blank. After an awkward silence I had to say : " I am sorry. That is all I have prepared to-day."

Psycho-analysts have a disposition to explain the forgetting of names and the dissociation of faces, voices and so forth from their proper context as a sub-conscious suppression due to some obscure dislike. If so I must dislike a vast multitude of people. But why should psycho-analysts assume a perfect brain mechanism and recognize only psychic causes ? I believe a physical explanation will cover a number of these cases and that a drop in the conductivity of the associated links due to diminished oxygenation or some slight variation in the blood plasma is much more generally the temporarily effacing agent.

I was interested the other night, in a supper-room in Vienna, by a little intimation of the poor quality of my memory. There came in a party of people who sat at another table. One of them was a German young lady who reminded me very strikingly of the daughter of an acquaintance I had made in Spain. He had introduced himself and his family to me because he was the surviving brother of an old friend and editor of mine, Harry Cust, and he had heard all sorts of things about me. "That girl," I said, " is the very image of ——." The name would not come. " She is the daughter of Lord B——." I got as far as the " B " and stuck. I tried again ; " Her name is —— Cust," I protested, " But I have known her by her Christian name, talked to her, talked about her, liked and admired her, visited her father's home at ——." Again an absolute blank. I became bad company. I could talk of nothing else. I retired inside my brain and routed about in it, trying to recover those once quite familiar names. I could recall all sorts of incidents while I was in the same hotel with these people at Ronda and Granada and while I stayed at that house, a very beautiful English house in the midlands, I could produce a rough sketch of the garden and I remembered addressing a party of girl scouts from the front door and even what I said to them. I had met and talked with Lady B and on another occasion met her son within the past year. But that evening the verbal labels seemed lost beyond recovery. I tried over all the peers I had ever heard of whose names began with " B." I tried over every conceivable feminine Christian name. I took a gloomy view of my mental state.

Next morning, while I was still in bed, the missing labels all came back, except one. The name of the house had gone ; it is still missing. Presently if it refuses to come home of its own accord I shall look it up in some book of reference. And yet I am sure that somewhere in the thickets of my brain it is hiding from me now. I tell this anecdote for the sake of its complete pointlessness. The psychological explanation of such forgetfulness is a disinclination to remember. But what conflict of hostilities, frustrations, restrained desires and so forth, is here? None at all. It is merely that the links are feeble and the printing of the impressions bad. It is a case of second-rate brain fabric. And rather overgrown and pressed upon at that. If my mental paths are not frequently traversed and refreshed they are obstructed.

Now defects in the brain texture must affect its moral quite as much as its intellectual character. It is essentially the same apparatus at work in either case. If the links of association that reassemble a memory can be temporarily effaced, so can the links that bring a sense of obligation to bear upon a motive. Adding a column of figures wrongly and judging incorrectly a situation in which one has to act are quite comparable brain processes. So in my own behaviour just as in my apprehension of things the outline is better than the detail. The more closely I scrutinize my reactions, the more I find detailed inconsistencies, changes of front and goings to and fro. The more I stand off from the immediate thing and regard my behaviour as a whole the more it holds together. As I have gathered experience of life, I have become increasingly impressed by the injustice we do ourselves and others by not allowing for these local and temporary faintings and fadings of our brains in our judgment of conduct.

Our relations with other human beings are more full and intricate the nearer they are to us and the more important they are in our lives. So, however we may be able to pigeon-hole and note this or that casual acquaintance for treatment of a particular sort, when we come to our intimates we find

ourselves behaving according to immensely various and
complex systems of association, which in the case of such
brains as mine anyhow, are never uniformly active, which
are subject to just the same partial and irrational dissocia-
tions and variations as are my memories of names and
numbers. I can have a great tenderness or resentment for
someone and it may become as absent from my present
thought as that title or the name of that country house I
could not remember in Vienna. I may have a sense of obligation and it will vanish as completely. Facts will appear in
my mind quite clear in their form and sequence and yet
completely shorn of some moving emotional quality I know
they once possessed. And then a day or so after it will all
come back to me.

Everyone, of course, is more or less like this, but I am of
the kind, I think, which is more so.

On the other hand, though my brain organization is so
poor that connexions are thus intermittently weakened and
effaced and groups of living associations removed out of
reach, I do not find in this cerebrum of mine any trace of
another type of weakness which I should imagine must be
closely akin to such local failure to function, namely those
actual replacements of one system of associations by another,
which cause what is called double personalities. In the
classical instances of double personality psychologists tell of
whole distinct networks of memory and impulse, co-existing
side by side in the same brain yet functioning independently,
which are alternative and often quite contradictory one to
the other. When one system is in action ; the other is more
or less inaccessible and vice versa I have met and lived in
close contact with one or two individuals of this alternating
type ; it is, I think, more common among women than among
men ; I have had occasion to watch these changes of phase,
and I do not find that in my own brain stuff there are any

such regional or textural substitutions. There are efface-
ments but not replacements. My brain may be very much
alive or it may be flat and faded out or simply stupefied by
sleepiness or apathy ; it may be exalted by some fever in the
blood, warmed and confused by alcohol, energized, angered
or sexually excited by the subtle messages and stimuli my
blood brings it ; but my belief is that I remain always
very much the same personality through it all. I do not
think I delude myself about this. My brain I believe is
consistent. Such as it is, it holds together. It is like a central-
ized country with all its government in one capital, even
though that government is sometimes negligent, feeble or
inert.

One other thing I have to note about this brain of mine
and that is—how can I phrase it ?—an exceptional want
of excitable " Go." I suspect that is due not, as my forget-
fulnesses and inconsistencies may be, to local insufficiencies
and failures in the circulation, but to some general under-
stimulation. My perceptions do not seem to be so thorough,
vivid and compelling as those of many people I meet and
it is rare that my impressions of things glow. There is a
faint element of inattention in all I do ; it is as if white was
mixed into all the pigments of my life. I am rarely *vivid* to
myself. I am just a little slack, not wholly and continuously
interested, prone to be indolent and cold-hearted. I am
readily bored. When I try to make up for this I am inevitably
a little " forced " when dealing with things, and a little
" false " and " charming " with people. You will find this
coming out when I tell of my failure as a draper's assistant
and of my relations to my intimate friends. You will discover
a great deal of evasion and refusal in my story.

Nature has a way of turning even biological defects into
advantages and I am not sure how far what may be called
my success in life has not been due to this undertow of

indifference. I have not been easily carried away by immediate things and made to forget the general in the particular. There is a sort of journalistic legend that I am a person of boundless enthusiasm and energy. Nothing could be further from the reality. For all my desire to be interested I have to confess that for most things and people I don't care a damn. Writing numbers of books and articles is evidence not of energy but of sedentary habits. People with a real quantitative excess of energy and enthusiasm become Mussolinis, Hitlers, Stalins, Gladstones, Beaverbrooks, Northcliffes, Napoleons. It takes generations to clean up after them. But what I shall leave behind me will not need cleaning up. Just because of that constitutional apathy it will be characteristically free from individual Woosh and it will be available and it will go on for as long as it is needed.

And now, having conveyed to you some idea of the quality and defects of the grey matter of that organized mass of phosphorized fat and connective tissue which is, so to speak, the hero of the piece, and having displayed the *persona* or, if you will, the vanity which now dominates its imaginations, I will try to tell how in this particular receiving apparatus the picture of its universe was built up, what it did and failed to do with the body it controlled and what the thronging impressions and reactions that constituted its life amount to.

CHAPTER THE SECOND

ORIGINS

§ 1
47 High Street, Bromley, Kent

THIS BRAIN of mine came into existence and began to acquire reflexes and register impressions in a needy shabby home in a little town called Bromley in Kent, which has since become a suburb of London. My consciousness of myself grew by such imperceptible degrees, and for a time each successive impression incorporated what had preceded it so completely, that I have no recollection of any beginning at all. I have a miscellany of early memories, but they are not arranged in any time order. I will do my best however, to recall the conditions amidst which my childish head got its elementary lessons in living. They seem to me now quite dreadful conditions, but at the time it was the only conceivable world.

It was then the flaxen head of a podgy little boy with a snub nose and a long infantile upper lip, and along the top his flaxen hair was curled in a longitudinal curl which was finally abolished at his own urgent request. Early photographs record short white socks, bare arms and legs, a petticoat, ribbon bows on the shoulders, and a scowl. That must have been gala costume. I do not remember exactly what everyday clothes I wore until I was getting to be a fairly big boy. I seem to recall a sort of holland pinafore for everyday use very like what small boys still wear in

France, except that it was brown instead of black holland.

The house in which this little boy ran about, clattering up and down the uncarpeted stairs, bawling—family tradition insists on the bawling—and investigating existence, deserves description, not only from the biographical, but from the sociological point of view. It was one of a row of badly built houses upon a narrow section of the High Street. In front upon the ground floor was the shop, filled with crockery, china and glassware and, a special line of goods, cricket bats, balls, stumps, nets and other cricket material. Behind the shop was an extremely small room, the " parlour," with a fireplace, a borrowed light and glass-door upon the shop and a larger window upon the yard behind. A murderously narrow staircase with a twist in it led downstairs to a completely subterranean kitchen, lit by a window which derived its light from a grating on the street level, and a bricked scullery, which, since the house was poised on a bank, opened into the yard at the ground level below. In the scullery was a small fireplace, a copper boiler for washing, a provision cupboard, a bread pan, a beer cask, a pump delivering water from a well into a stone sink, and space for coal, our only space for coal, beneath the wooden stairs. This " coal cellar " held about a ton of coal, and when the supply was renewed it had to be carried in sacks through the shop and " parlour " and down the staircase by men who were apt to be uncivil about the inconveniences of the task and still more apt to drop small particles of coal along the route.

The yard was perhaps thirty by forty feet square. In it was a brick erection, the " closet," an earth jakes over a cesspool, within perhaps twenty feet of the well and the pump ; and above this closet was a rain-water tank. Behind it was the brick dustbin (cleared at rare intervals via the shop), a fairly open and spacious receptacle. In this a small boy could find among the ashes such objects of interest as egg-shells, useful tins and boxes. The ashes could be rearranged to suggest mountain scenery. There was a boundary wall, separating us from the much larger yard and sheds of Mr. Covell the butcher, in which pigs, sheep and horned cattle were harboured violently, and protested plaintively through the night before they were slaughtered. Some were recalcitrant and had to be treated accordingly ; there was an element of Rodeo about Covell's yard. Beyond it was Bromley Church and its old graveyard, full then of healthy trees, ruinous tombs and headstones askew—in which I had an elder sister buried.

Our yard was half bricked and half bare earth, and an open cement gutter brought the waste waters of the sink to a soak-away in the middle of the space. Thence, no doubt, soap-suds and cabbage water, seeped away to mingle with the graver accumulations of the " closet " and the waters of the well from which the pump drew our supply. Between the scullery and the neighbour's wall was a narrow passage covered over, and in this my father piled the red earthen-ware jars and pans, the jam-pots and so forth, which bulk so large in the stock of a crockery dealer.

I " played " a lot in this yard and learnt its every detail, because there was no other open air space within easy reach of a very small boy to play in. Its effect of smallness was enhanced by the erections in the neighbours' yards on either side. On one hand was the yard of Mr. Munday, the haber-dasher, who had put up a greenhouse and cultivated mush-rooms, to nourish which his boys collected horse-droppings from the High Street in a small wooden truck ; and on the other, Mr. Cooper, the tailor, had built out a workroom in which two or three tailors sat and sewed. It was always a matter of uneasiness to my mother whether these men could or could not squint round and see the necessary comings and goings of pots and pans and persons to the closet. The unbricked part of our yard had a small flower-bed in which my father had planted a bush of Wigelia. It flowered reluctantly, and most things grew reluctantly in that bed. A fact, still vividly clear in my mind across an interval of sixty years, is that it was the only patch of turned up earth accessible to the cats of Mr. Munday, Mr. Cooper and our own ménage. But my father was a gardener of some resolution and, against the back of the house rooting in a hole in the brickwork, he had persuaded a grape vine not only to grow but to flourish. When I was ten, he fell from a combination of short ladder, table and kitchen steps on which he had mounted to prune the less accessible shoots of this vine, and sustained a compound fracture of the leg. But of that very important event I will tell a little later.

I dwell rather upon the particulars about this yard, because it was a large part of my little world in those days. I lived mostly in it and in the scullery and underground kitchen. We were much too poor to have a servant, and it was more than my mother could do to keep fires going upstairs (let alone the price of coal). Above the ground floor and reached by an equally tortuous staircase—I have seen my father reduced to a blind ecstasy of rage in an attempt to get a small sofa up it—were a back bedroom occupied by my mother and a front room occupied by my father (this separation was, I think, their form of birth control), and above this again was a room, the boys' bedroom (there were three of us) and a back attic filled with dusty crockery stock. But there was stock everywhere ; pots and pans invaded the kitchen, under the dresser and under the ironing board ; bats and stumps crept into the " parlour." The furniture of this home had all been acquired second-hand at sales ; furniture shops that catered for democracy had still to appear in the middle nineteenth century ; an aristocratic

but battered bookcase despised a sofa from some housekeeper's room ; there was a perky little chiffonier in the parlour ; the chairs were massive but moody ; the wooden
bedsteads had exhausted feather mattresses and grey sheets
—for there had to be economy over the washing bills—and
there was not a scrap of faded carpet or worn oil-cloth in
the house that had not lived a full life of usefulness before
it came into our household. Everything was frayed, discoloured and patched. But we had no end of oil lamps
because they came out of (and went back into) stock. (My
father also dealt in lamp-wicks, oil and paraffin.)

We lived, as I have said, mostly downstairs and underground, more particularly in the winter. We went upstairs
to bed. About upstairs I have to add a further particular.
The house was infested with bugs. They harboured in the
wooden bedsteads and lurked between the layers of wall-
paper that peeled from the walls. Slain they avenge themselves by a peculiar penetrating disagreeable smell. That
mingles in my early recollections with the more pervasive
odour of paraffin, with which my father carried on an
inconclusive war against them. Almost every part of my
home had its own distinctive smell.

This was the material setting in which my life began. Let
me tell now something of my father and mother, what
manner of people they were, and how they got themselves
into this queer home from which my two brothers and I
were launched into what Sir James Jeans has very properly
called, this Mysterious Universe, to make what we could
of it.

§ 2
SARAH NEAL (1822–1905)

MY MOTHER was a little blue-eyed, pink-cheeked woman with a large serious innocent face. She was born on October 10th, 1822, in the days when King George IV was King, and three years before the opening of the first steam railway. It was still an age of horse and foot transit, sailing ships and undiscovered lands. She was the daughter of a Midhurst innkeeper and his frequently invalid wife. His name was George Neal (born 1797) and he was probably of remote Irish origin ; his wife's maiden name was Sarah Benham, which sounds good English. She was born in 1796. Midhurst was a little old sunny rag-stone built town on the road from London to Chichester, and my grandfather stabled the relay of horses for the stage coach as his father had done before him. An uncle of his drove a coach, and one winter's night in a snowstorm, being alone without passengers and having sustained himself excessively against the cold and solitude of the drive, he took the wrong turning at the entrance to the town, went straight over the wharf into the pool at the head of the old canal, and was handsomely drowned together with his horses. It was a characteristic of my mother's family to be easily lit and confused by alcohol, but never subdued to inaction by it. And when my grandfather died he had mortgaged his small property and was very much in debt, so that there was practically nothing for my mother and her younger brother John, who survived him.

The facts still traceable about my grandfather's circumstances are now very fragmentary. I have a few notes my elder brother made from my mother's recollections, and I have various wills and marriage and birth certificates and a diary kept by my mother. George Neal kept the Fountains Inn at Chichester I think, before he kept the New Inn at Chichester ; the New Inn he had from 1840 to his death in 1853. He married Sarah Benham on October 30th, 1817. Two infant boys died, and then my mother was born in 1822. After a long interval my uncle John was born in 1836, and a girl Elizabeth in 1838. It is evident my grandmother had very indifferent health, but she was still pretty and winning, says my mother's diary, at the age of fifty-three, and her hands were small and fine. Except for that one entry, there is nothing much now to be learnt about her. I suppose that when she was well she did her best, after the fashion of the time, to teach her daughter the elements of religion, knowledge and the domestic arts. I possess quite a brave sampler worked by my mother when she was in her eighth year. It says, amidst some decorative stitching :

" Opportunity lost can never be recalled ; therefore it is the highest wisdom in youth to make all the sensible improvements they can in their early days ; for a young overgrown dunce seldom makes a figure in any branch of learning in his old days. Sarah Neal her work. May 26, 1830. 1 2 3 4 5 6 7 8 9 10 11 12 13 14 15 16 17 18."

After which it breaks off and resumes along the bottom with a row of letters upside down.

When my grandmother was too ill to be in control, my mother ran about the inn premises, laid the table for my grandfather's meals, and, as a special treat, drew and served tankards of beer in the bar. There was no compulsory schooling in those days. Some serious neighbours seem to have talked to my grandfather and pointed out the value of accomplishments and scholastic finish to a young female in a progressive age. In 1833 he came into some property through the death of my great-grandfather and thereupon

my mother was sent off to a finishing school for young ladies
kept by a Miss Riley in Chichester. There in a year or so
she showed such remarkable aptitude for polite learning,
that she learnt to write in the clear angular handwriting
reserved for women in those days, to read, to do sums up to,
but not quite including, long division, the names of the
countries and capitals of Europe and the counties and
county towns of England (with particular attention to the
rivers they were " on ") and from Mrs. Markham's History
all that it was seemly to know about the Kings and Queens
of England. Moreover she learnt from Magnell's Questions
the names of the four elements (which in due course she
taught me), the seven wonders of the world (or was it
nine ?), the three diseases of wheat, and many such facts
which Miss Riley deemed helpful to her in her passage
through life. (But she never really mastered the names of
the nine Muses and over what they presided, and though
she begged and prayed her father that she might learn
French, it was an Extra and she was refused it.) A natural
tendency to Protestant piety already established by her
ailing mother, was greatly enhanced. She was given various
edifying books to read, but she was warned against worldly
novels, the errors and wiles of Rome, French cooking and the
insidious treachery of men, she was also prepared for confirmation and confirmed, she took the sacrament of Holy
Communion, and so fortified and finished she returned to
her home (1836).

An interesting thing about this school of Miss Riley's,
which was in so many respects a very antiquated eighteenth
century school, was the strong flavour of early feminism it
left in her mind. I do not think it is on record anywhere, but
it is plain to me from what I have heard my mother say, that
among schoolmistresses and such like women at any rate,
there was a stir of emancipation associated with the claim,

ultimately successful, of the Princess Victoria, daughter of the Duke and Duchess of Kent, to succeed King William IV. There was a movement against that young lady based on her sex and this had provoked in reaction a wave of feminine partisanship throughout the country. It picked up reinforcement from an earlier trouble between George the Fourth and Queen Caroline. A favourite book of my mother's was Mrs. Strickland's *Queens of England*, and she followed the life of Victoria, her acts and utterances, her goings forth and her lyings in, her great sorrow and her other bereavements, with a passionate loyalty. The Queen, also a small woman, was in fact my mother's compensatory personality, her imaginative consolation for all the restrictions and hardships that her sex, her diminutive size, her motherhood and all the endless difficulties of life, imposed upon her. The dear Queen could command her husband as a subject and wilt the tremendous Mr. Gladstone with awe. How would it feel to be in that position? One would say this. One would do that. I have no doubt about my mother's reveries. In her latter years in a black bonnet and a black silk dress she became curiously suggestive of the supreme widow. . . .

For my own part, such is the obduracy of the young male, I heard too much of the dear Queen altogether ; I conceived a jealous hatred for the abundant clothing, the magnificent housing and all the freedoms of her children and still more intensely of my contemporaries, her grand-children. Why was my mother so concerned about them? Was not my handicap heavy enough without my having to worship them at my own mother's behest? This was a fixation that has lasted all through my life. Various, desperate and fatiguing expeditions to crowded street corners and points of vantage at Windsor, at Chislehurst near Bromley (where the Empress Eugénie was living in exile) from which we might see the dear Queen pass ;—

" She's coming. Oh, she's coming. If only I could see ! Take off your hat Bertie dear,"—deepened my hostility and wove a stout, ineradicable thread of republicanism into my resentful nature.

But that is anticipating. For the present I am trying to restore my mother's mental picture of the world, as she saw it awaiting her, thirty years and more before I was born or thought of. It was a world much more like Jane Austen's than Fanny Burney's, but at a lower social level. Its chintz was second-hand, and its flowered muslin cheap and easily tired. Still more was it like the English countryside of Dickens' *Bleak House*. It was a countryside, for as yet my mother knew nothing of London. Over it all ruled God our Father, in whose natural kindliness my mother had great confidence. He was entirely confused in her mind, because of the mystery of the Holy Trinity, with " Our Saviour " or " Our Lord "—who was rarely mentioned by any other names. The Holy Ghost she ignored almost entirely ; I cannot recall any reference to him ; he was certainly never " *our* " Holy Ghost, and the Virgin Mary, in spite of what I should have considered her appeal to feminist proclivities, my mother disregarded even more completely. It may have been simply that there was a papistical flavour about the Virgin ; I don't know. Or a remote suspicion of artistic irregularity about the recorded activities of the Holy Spirit. In the lower sky and the real link between my mother and the godhead, was the Dear Queen, ruling by right divine, and beneath this again, the nobility and gentry, who employed, patronised, directed and commanded the rest of mankind. On every Sunday in the year, one went to church and refreshed one's sense of this hierarchy between the communion table and the Free Seats. And behind everyone, behind the Free Seats, but alas ! by no means confining his wicked activities to them, was Satan, Old Nick, the Devil, who accounted for so much in the world that was otherwise inexplicable.

My mother was Low Church, and I was disposed to find, even in my tender years, Low Church theology a little too stiff for me, but she tempered it to her own essential goodness, gentleness and faith in God's Fatherhood, in ways that were quite her own. I remember demanding of her in my crude schoolboy revolt if she really believed in a hell of eternal torment. "We *must*, my dear," she said. "But our Saviour died for us—and perhaps after all nobody will be sent there. Except of course the Old Devil."

And even he, being so to speak the official in charge, I think she would have exempted from actual torture. Maybe Our Father would have shown him the tongs now and again, just to remind him.

There was a picture in an old illustrated book of devotions, Sturm's *Reflections*, obliterated with stamp paper, and so provoking investigation. What had mother been hiding from me ? By holding up the page to the light I discovered the censored illustration represented hell-fire ; devil, pitchfork and damned, all complete and drawn with great gusto. But she had anticipated the general trend of Protestant theology at the present time and hidden hell away.

She believed that God our Father and Saviour, personally and through occasional angels, would *mind* her ; she believed that he would not be indifferent to her prayers ; she believed she had to be good, carefully and continually, and not give Satan a chance with her. Then everything would be all right. That was what her " simple faith " as she called it really amounted to, and in that faith she went out very trustfully into the world.

It was decided that she should go into service as a lady's-maid. But first she had four years' apprenticeship as a dressmaker (1836–1840) and she also had instruction in hair-dressing, to equip herself more thoroughly for that state of life into which it had pleased God to call her.

It was a world of other ladies'-maids and valets, of house stewards, housekeepers, cooks and butlers, upper servants above the level of maids and footmen, a downstairs world, but living in plentiful good air, well fed and fairly well housed in the attics, basements and interstices of great mansions. It was an old-fashioned world ; most of its patterns of behaviour and much of its peculiar idiom, were established in the seventeenth century ; its way of talking, its style of wit, was in an unbroken tradition from the *Polite Conversation* of Dean Swift, and it had customs and an etiquette all its own. I do not think she had a bad time in service ; people poked fun at a certain simplicity in her, but no one seems to have been malignant.

I do not know all the positions she filled during her years as a lady's maid. In 1845, when her diary begins, she was with the wife of a certain Captain Forde, I know, and in her company she travelled and lived in Ireland and in various places in England. The early part of this diary is by far the best written. It abounds in descriptions of scenery and notes of admiration, and is clearly the record of an interested if conventional mind. Ultimately (1850) she became maid to a certain Miss Bullock who lived at Up Park near Petersfield. It was not so gay as the Forde world. At Christmas particularly, in place of merriment, " Up Park just did nothing but eat," but she conceived a great affection for Miss Bullock. She had left the Fordes because her mother was distressed by the death of her sister Elizabeth and wanted Sarah to be in England nearer to her. And at Up Park she met an eligible bachelor gardener who was destined to end her career as a lady's maid, and in the course of time to be my father. He wasn't there to begin with ; he came in 1851. " He seems *peculiar*," says the diary, and offers no further comment. Probably she encountered him first in the Servants' Hall, where there was a weekly dance by candlelight to the music of concertina and fiddle.

This was not my mother's first love affair. Two allusions, slightly reminiscent of the romantic fiction of the time, preserve the memory of a previous experience.

" Kingstown railway," the diary remarks, " is very compact and pretty. From Dublin it is short but the sea appears in view, and mountains, which to one fond of romantic scenery, how dear does the country appear when the views are so diversified by the changes of scene, to the reflective mind how sweet they are *to one alas a voluntary exile* from her dear, her native land, to wander alone to brood over the unkindness, the ingratitude, of a faithless, an absent, but not a forgotten lover. Ah, I left a kind and happy home to hide from all dear friends *the keen, bitter anguish* of my heart. Time and the smiles of dear Erin's hospitable people had made a once miserable girl comparatively happy, but can man be happy who gains an innocent love and then trifles with the girlish innocent heart. May he be forgiven as I forgive him ! ! ! "

And again, some pages later : " I meet kindness everywhere, but there are moments when I feel lonely, which makes me sigh for home, dear England, happy shore, still I do not wish to meet again that *false wicked man*, who gained my young heart and then trifled with a pure love. I hope this early trial will work good in me. I feel it ordered for the best and time will, I trust, prove it to me how mercifully has Providence watched over me, and for a wise purpose taught me not to trust implicitly to erring creatures. Oh, can I ever believe man again ? *Burnt all his letters.* I shall now forget quicker I hope, and may he be forgiven his falsehoods."

So, but for that man's treachery, everything might have

been different and somebody else might have come into the
world in my place, and this biography have never seen the
light, replaced by some other biography or by no biography
at all.

I know nothing of the earliest encounter of my father and
mother. It may have been in the convolutions of Hands
Across and Down the Middle, Sir Roger de Coverley, Pop
Goes the Weasel, or some such country dance. I like to think
of my mother then as innocently animated, pretty and not yet
overstrained by dingy toil, and my father as a bright and
promising young gardener, son of a head gardener of repute,
the head gardener of Lord de Lisle at Penshurst. He was
five years younger than she was, and they were both still
in their twenties. Presently she was calling him " Joe " and
he had modified her name Sarah to " Saddie."

He probably came to the house every day to discuss
flowers and vegetables, and so forth, with the cook and the
housekeeper and steward and perhaps there was a chance
for a word or two then, and on Sundays, when everybody
walked downhill a mile and more through the Warren to
morning service in Harting Church, they may have had
opportunities for conversation. He was not a bad-looking
young man, I gather, and I once met an old lady in Harting
who recalled that he wore the " most gentlemanly grey
trousers."

My parents' relationship had its serious side in those days.
It was not all country dances and smiling meetings. I still
possess a letter from him to her in which he explains that she
has misunderstood an allusion he had made to the Holy
Sacrament. He would be the last, he says, to be irreverent
on such a topic. It is quite a well written letter.

§ 3
UP PARK AND JOSEPH WELLS (1827–1910)

THIS UP PARK is a handsome great house looking south-
ward, with beechwoods and bracken thickets to shelter the
dappled fallow deer of its wide undulating downland park.
To the north the estate overhangs the village of South
Harting in the triangle between Midhurst, Petersfield and
Chichester. The walled gardens, containing the gardener's
cottage which my father occupied, were situated three or
four hundred yards or more away from the main buildings.
There was an outlying laundry, dairy, butcher's shop and
stables in the early eighteenth century style, and a turfed-
over ice-house. Up Park was built by a Fetherstonhaugh,
and it has always been in the hands of that family.

In the beginning of the nineteenth century the reigning
Fetherstonhaugh was a certain Sir Harry, an intimate of the
Prince Regent who was afterwards George IV. Sir Harry
was a great seducer of pretty poorish girls, milliners, tenants,
singers and servant maids, after the fashion of the time. An
early mistress was that lovely young adventuress Emma,
who passed into the protection of Greville of the Memoirs,
married Sir William Hamilton, and became Romney's and
Nelson's Lady Hamilton. In his declining years Sir Harry
was smitten with desire for an attractive housemaid, Frances
Bullock, and after a strenuous pursuit and a virtuous resistance, valiant struggles on the back stairs and much heated
argument, married her. No offspring ensued. She brought
her younger sister with her to the house and engaged a
governess, Miss Sutherland, to chaperon her and it was
after Sir Harry's death that my mother became maid to this
younger Miss Bullock.

Queen Victoria and Society never took very eagerly to

this belated Lady Fetherstonhaugh, nobody married Miss
Bullock, and Sir Harry being duly interred, the three ladies
led a spacious dully comfortable life between Up Park and
Claridge's. They entertained house parties ; people came
to them for their shooting and hunting. They changed so
little of the old arrangements that I find in a list of guests
made by the housekeeper forty years after his death, that
" Sir H's bedroom " is still called by his name and assigned
to the principal guest. A Mr. Weaver, a bastard, I believe,
of Sir Harry's, occupied an ambiguous position in the household as steward and was said—as was probably inevitable—to be Lady Fetherstonhaugh's lover. It could not have
been much in the way of love-making anyhow, with everyone
watching and disapproving.

In a novel of mine, perhaps my most ambitious novel,
Tono Bungay, I have made a little picture of Up Park as
" Bladesover," and given a glimpse of its life below stairs.
(But the housekeeper there is not in the least like my mother.)
That is how I saw it in the 'eighties when the two surviving
ladies, Miss Bullock (who took the name of Fetherstonhaugh
after her sister's death) and Miss Sutherland, were very old
ladies indeed. But in the late 'forties when my mother came
down from her costumes and mending and hair-dressing to
her lunch or tea or supper in the housekeeper's room, or
peeped, as I am sure she did at times from some upstairs
window towards the gardens, or beamed and curtseyed and
set to partners in the country dance, everyone was younger
and the life seemed perhaps more eventful. If it was not so
gay and various as that now vanished life below stairs in
Ireland, it was bright enough.

My father, Joseph Wells, was the son of Joseph Wells,
who was head gardener to Lord de Lisle at Penshurst Place
in Kent. My father was one of several brothers and sisters,
Charles Edward, Henry, Edward, William, Lucy, Elizabeth

and Hannah, and although he bore his father's name, he was the youngest of the sons. There were uncles and cousins in the district, so that I suppose the family had been in Kent for at least some generations. My great-grandfather's name was Edward ; he had six children and forty grandchildren, and the family is lost at last in a mangrove swamp of Johns, Georges, Edwards, Toms, Williams, Harrys, Sarahs and Lucies. The lack of originality at the Christenings is appalling. The aunts and uncles were all as far as I can ascertain, of the upper-servants, tenant-farmer class, except that one set of my father's first cousins at Penshurst, bearing the surname of Duke, had developed an industry for the making of cricket bats and balls, and were rather more prosperous than the others.

My father grew up to gardening and cricket, and remained an out-of-doors, open-air man to the day of his death. He became gardener at Redleaf, nearby, to a Mr. Joseph Wells, who, in spite of the identical name, was no sort of relation, and in the summer, directly the day's work was over, my father would run, he told me once, a mile and more at top speed to the pitch at Penshurst to snatch half an hour of cricket before the twilight made the ball invisible. He learnt to swim and to handle a muzzle-loading gun and so forth as country boys do, and his schooling gave him reading and writing and " summing," so that he read whatever he could and kept his accounts in a clear well-shaped handwriting ; but what sort of school imparted these rudiments I do not know.

Joseph Wells, of Redleaf, was an old gentleman with liberal and æsthetic tastes, and he took rather a fancy to young Joseph. He talked to him, encouraged him to read, and lent and gave him books on botany and gardening. When the old man was ill he liked my father to take his arm when he walked in the garden. My father made definite efforts to improve himself. In our parlour when I was a small boy in search of reading matter there was still the *Young Man's Companion* in two volumes and various numbers of Orr's *Circles of the Science* which he had acquired during this phase. He had an aptitude for drawing. He drew and coloured pictures of various breeds of apple and pear and suchlike fruits, and he sought out and flattened and dried between sheets of blotting paper, a great number of specimen plants.

Old Wells was interested in art, and one of his friends and a frequent visitor at Redleaf was Sir Edwin Landseer, the "animal painter," who could put human souls into almost every sort of animal and who did those grave impassive lions at the base of the Nelson monument in Trafalgar Square. My father served as artist's model on several occasions, and for many years he was to be seen in the National Gallery, peeping at a milkmaid in a picture called *The Maid and the Magpie*. Behind him in the sunshine was Penshurst Church. But afterwards the Landseers were all sent to the Tate Gallery at Millbank and there a sudden flood damaged or destroyed most of them and washed away that record of my father altogether.

I do not know what employment my father found after he left Redleaf, which he did when his employer died, before he came to Up Park and met my mother. I think there was some sort of job as gardener or under-gardener at Crewe. In these days he was evidently restless and uneasy about his outlook upon life. Unrest was in the air. He talked of emigrating to America, or Australia. I think the friendliness of Joseph Wells of Redleaf had stirred up vague hopes and ambitions in him, and that he had been disappointed of a "start in life" by the old man's death.

I wish I knew more than I do of my father's dreams and wishes during those early years before he married. In his working everyday world he, like my mother, was still very much in the tradition of the eighteenth century when the nobility and gentry ruled everything under God and the King, when common men knew nothing of the possibility of new wealth, and when either Patronage or a Legacy was the only conceivable way for them out of humdrum and rigid limitation from the cradle to the grave. That system was crumbling away ; strange new things were undermining it, but to my mother certainly it seemed an eternal system only to be ended at the Last Trump, and I think it was solely in rare moments of illumination and transparency that my father glimpsed its instability. He and his Saddie walking soberly through the Up Park bracken on a free Sunday afternoon, discussing their prospects, had little more suspicion that their world of gentlemen's estates and carriage-folk and villages and country houses and wayside inns and nice little shops and horse ploughs and windmills and touching one's hat to one's betters, would not endure for ever, than they had that their God in his Heaven was under notice to quit.

But if such was the limitation of his serious talk in the daylight, there could be other moods when he was alone. I had one hint of that which was as good I think as a hundred explicit facts. Once when I was somewhen in my twenties and he was over sixty ; as I was walking with him on the open downs out beyond Up Park, he said casually : " When I was a young man of your age I used to come out here and lie oh ! half the night, just looking at the stars."

I hadn't thought of him before as a star-gazer. His words opened a great gulf of unsuspected states of mind to me. I wanted him to tell me more, but I did not want to bother him with a cross-examination. I hesitated among a number of clumsy leading questions that would tell me something more of the feelings of that vanished young man of forty years ago who had suddenly reappeared between us.

" What for ? " I ventured to ask rather lamely.

" Wondering."

I left it at that. One may be curious about one's father, but prying is prohibited.

But if he could look out of this planet and wonder about the stars, it may be he could also look out of his immediate circumstances and apprehend their triviality by stellar standards. I do not think my mother ever wondered about the stars. God our Father had put them there " for his glory," and that sufficed for her. My father was never at any time in his life, clear and set in that fashion.

My mother's diary is silent about the circumstances of her marriage. There is no mention of any engagement. I cannot imagine how it came about. She left Up Park to be with her mother who was very seriously ill in the spring of 1853. My father visited the inn at Midhurst, I should think as her fiancé, in the summer. He had left Up Park and was on his way to stay with his brother, Charles Edward, in Gloucestershire until he could find another place. Then suddenly she was in a distressful storm. Her father was taken ill unexpectedly and died in August, and her mother, already very ill, died, after a phase of dementia due to grief and dismay, in November. That happened on the 5th, and on the 22nd my mother was married to my father (who was still out of a situation) in the City of London at St. Stephen's Church, Coleman Street. He seems to have been employed a little later as an under gardener at Trentham in Staffordshire, and for a time they could live together only intermittently. She visited him at Trentham, she does not say precisely how ; and they spent a Sunday she did not like in " the gardener's cottage " at Crewe. " No church, nothing." She paid visits to relations in between and felt " very unsettled."

I guess they were married on his initiative, but that is only guessing. He may have thought it a fine thing to do.

There is nothing like extravagance when one is down. He may have had a flash of imperious passion. But then one should go on in the same key, and that he did not do. My mother may have felt the need of a man to combat the lawyers whom she suspected of making away with her father's estate. If so, my father was very little good to her. Presently he got a job and a cottage at Shuckburgh Park in the midlands. On April 5th, 1854, she is " very happy and busy preparing for my new home." It was to be the happiest and most successful home she ever had, poor little woman ! In the diary my father becomes " dearest Joe " and " my dear husband." Previously he had been " Joe " or " J. W." " The Saturday laborious work I do not like, but still I am very happy in my little home." And he did a little water-colour sketch which still exists, of his small square cottage, and I suppose one does not sketch a house unless one is reasonably happy in it. He kept this place at Shuckburgh Park until a daughter had been born to him (in 1855) and then he was at loose ends again.

There seems to have been no intimation of coming trouble until it came. My mother's diary records : " July 17th 1855. Sir Francis gave Joe warning to *leave* (trebly underlined). Oh what a sorrow ! It struck to my poor heart to look at my sweet babe and obliged to leave my pretty *home*. May it please God to bless us with another happy quiet home in His own Good Time."

But it did not please God to do anything of the sort at any time any more.

I do not know why my father was unsuccessful as a gardener, but I suspect a certain intractability of temper rather than incapacity. He did not like to be told things and made to do things. He was impatient. Before he married, I gather from an old letter from a friend that has chanced to be preserved, he was talking of going to the gold diggings

in Australia, and again after he left the cottage at Shuckburgh he was looking round for some way out of the galling
subordinations and uncertainties of " service." He thought
again of emigrating, this time to America ; there were even
two stout boxes made for his belongings, and then his schemes
for flight abroad, which perhaps after all were rather half-
hearted schemes, were frustrated by the advent of my
eldest brother, his second child.

Perhaps it was as well that he did not attempt pioneering
in new lands with my mother. She had been trained as a
lady's-maid and not as a housewife and I do not think she
had the mental flexibility to rise to new occasions. She was
that sort of woman who is an incorrigibly bad cook. By
nature and upbringing alike she belonged to that middle-
class of dependents who occupied situations, performed
strictly defined duties, gave or failed to give satisfaction and
had no ideas at all outside that dependence. People of that
quality " saved up for a rainy day " but they were without
the slightest trace of primary productive or acquisitive
ability. She was that in all innocence, but I perceive that
my father might well have had a more efficient helpmate in
the struggle for life as it went on in the individualistic
nineteenth century.

He was at any rate a producer, if only as a recalcitrant
gardener, but he shared her incapacity for getting and
holding things. They were both economic innocents made
by and for a social order, a scheme of things, that was falling
to pieces all about them. And looking for stability in a
world that was already breaking away towards adventure,
they presently dropped into that dismal insanitary hole I
have already described, in which I was born, and from
which they were unable to escape for twenty-four dreary
years.

Since it was difficult to find a situation as a gardener and still more tiresome to keep it, since there was no shelter or help in the world while one was out of work but the scanty hospitality of one's family, the idea of becoming one's own master and getting a home of one's own even on an uncertain income became a very alluring one. An obliging cousin, George Wells, with a little unsuccessful china and crockery shop in the High Street of Bromley, Kent, offered it to my father on extremely reasonable terms. It was called *Atlas House* because of a figure of Atlas bearing a lamp instead of the world in the shop window. My father anticipated his inheritance of a hundred pounds or so, bought this business and set up for himself. He spent all his available savings and reserves, and my mother with one infant in arms moved into 47 High Street, in time to bring my eldest brother into the world there. And so they were caught. From the outset this business did not " pay," and it " paid " less and less. But they had now no means of getting out of it and going anywhere else.

" Took possession," says the diary on October 23rd 1855. On the 27th, " very unsettled. No furniture sufficient and no capital to do as we ought. I fear we have done wrong." On November 7th she says, " This seems a horrid business, no trade. How I wish I had taken that situation with Lady Carrick ! " " November 8th. No customers all day. How sad to be deceived by one's relations. They have got their money and we their old stock."

They both knew they were caught.

And being caught like this was to try these poor things out to the utmost. It grew very plain that my father had neither imagination nor sympathy for the woman's side of life. (Later on I was to betray a similar deficiency.) He had been brought up in a country home with mother and sisters, and the women folk saw to all the indoor business. A man just didn't bother about it. He lived from the shop outward and

had by far the best of things ; she became the entire household staff, with two little children on her hands and, as the
diary shows quite plainly, in perpetual dread of further
motherhood. "Anxiety relieved," became her formula.
There is a pathetic deterioration in the diary, as infested,
impossible, exhausting Atlas House takes possession of her.
There were no more descriptions of scenery and fewer and
fewer pious and sentimental reflections after the best models.
It becomes a record of dates and comings and goings, of
feeling ill, of the ill health of her children, growing up, she
realized, in unwholesome circumstances, of being left alone,
of triter and triter attempts to thank God for his many
mercies. "J. W."—he is "J. W." again now and henceforth
—"playing cricket at Chislehurst." "J. W. out all day."
"J. W. in London." . . .

"August 23rd, 1857. Church, morning, had a happy day.
J. W. went to church with me ! ! ! "

"August 30th, 1857. Went to church. Mr. J. W. did not
go all day, did not feel quite so happy, how often I wish he
was more serious."

"Dec. 1st, 1857. Joe resolved on going to New Zealand.
Advertisement of business to let or sold. 3rd. Please God to
guide us whichever way is for the best."

"Dec. 31st, '57. This year ends with extreme anxiety about
the business. How I wish we had never taken it. How
unsuited for us. Not half a living and dear parents have all
gone. Oh Heavenly Father guide and direct me."

"Jan. 4th. J. W. put a second advertisement in."

"Jan. 6th. Had an answer to advertisement."

These advertisements came to nothing. A "letting notice
in the window" came to nothing. "Several enquiries but
nothing." More strenuous methods were needed and never
adopted. Day follows day in that diary and mostly they are
unhappy days. And so it went on. For twenty-four years

of her life, and the first thirteen years of mine, dingy old
Atlas House kept her going up and down its wearisome
staircases in her indefatigable hopeless attempt to recover
something of the brightness of that little cottage at Shuckburgh.

My mother used to accuse my father of neglecting the
shop for cricket. But it was through that excellent sport as
it was then, that the little ménage contrived to hold out, with
an occasional bankruptcy, for so long before it was finally
sold up. He was never really interested in the crockery trade
and sold little, I think, but jam-pots and preserving jars to
the gentlemen's houses round about, and occasional bedroom sets and tea-sets, table glass and replacements. But
he developed his youthful ability to play cricket which he
had kept alive at Up Park, he revived the local club and was
always getting jobs of variable duration as a professional
bowler and cricket instructor in the neighbourhood. He
played for the West Kent Club from 1857 to 1869 and bowled
for the County of Kent in 1862 and 1863. On June 26th,
1862, he clean bowled four Sussex batsmen in four successive
balls, a feat not hitherto recorded in county cricket. Moreover his cousin John Duke at Penshurst, whom he had once
got out of danger when they were swimming together, let
him have long and considerate credit for a supply of cricket
goods that ousted the plates and dishes from half the shop
window. Among the familiar names of my childhood were
the Hoares and the Normans, both banking families with
places near Bromley, for whom he bowled; and for some
years he went every summer term to Norwich Grammar
School as " pro."

§ 4
SARAH WELLS AT ATLAS HOUSE (1855–1880)

MY MOTHER drudged endlessly in that gaunt and impossible home and the years slipped by. Year after year she changed and the prim little lady's-maid, with her simple faith and her definite views about the Holy Sacrament, gave place to a tired woman more and more perplexed by life. Twice more her habitual " anxiety " was not to be relieved, and God was to incur her jaded and formal gratitude for two more " dear ones." She feared us terribly before we came and afterwards she loved and slaved for us intensely, beyond reason. She was not clever at her job and I have to tell it ; she sometimes did badly by her children through lack of knowledge and flexibility, but nothing could exceed the grit and devotion of her mothering. She wore her fingers to the bone working at our clothes, and she had acquired a fanatical belief in cod liver oil and insisted that we two younger ones should have it at any cost ; so that we escaped the vitamin insufficiency that gave my elder brother a pigeon breast and a retarded growth. No one knew about vitamin D in those days, but cod liver oil had been prescribed for my sister Fanny and it had worked magic with her.

My mother brought my brother Freddy into the world in 1862, and had her great tragedy in 1864, when my sister died of appendicitis. The nature of appendicitis was unknown in those days ; it was called " inflammation of the bowels " ; my sister had been to a children's tea party a day or so before her seizure, and my mother in her distress at this sudden blow, leaped to the conclusion that Fanny had been given something unsuitable to eat, and was never quite reconciled to those neighbours, would not speak to them, forbade us to mention them.

Fanny had evidently been a very bright, precocious and fragile little girl, an indoor little girl, with a facility for prim piety that had delighted my mother's heart. Such early goodness, says Dr. W. R. Ackroyd (in *Vitamins and other Dietary Essentials*) is generally a sign of some diet deficiency, and that, I fear is how things were with her. Quite healthy children are boisterous. She had learnt her " collect " every Sunday, repeated many hymns by rote, said her prayers beautifully, found her " place " in the prayer book at church, and made many apt remarks for my mother to treasure in her heart. I was born two years and more after her death, in 1866, and my mother decided that I had been sent to replace Fanny and to achieve a similar edification. But again Fate was mocking her. Little boys are different in constitution from little girls, and even from the outset I showed myself exceptionally deficient in the religious sense. I was born blasphemous and protesting. Even at my christening, she told me, I squalled with a vehemence unprecedented in the history of the family.

And later she was to undermine her own teaching with cod liver oil.

My own beginnings were shaped so much as a system of reactions to my mother's ideas and suggestions and feelings that I find some attempt to realize her states of mind, during those twenty-five years of enslavement behind the crockery shop, a necessary prelude to my account of my own education. We had no servants ; no nursemaids and governesses intervened between us ; she carried me about until I could be put down to trot after her and so I arose mentally, quite as much as physically, out of her. It was a process of severance and estrangement, for I was my father's as well as my mother's son.

I have tried to give an impression of the simple and confident faith with which my mother sailed out into life.

Vast unsuspected forces beyond her ken were steadily destroying the social order, the horse and sailing ship transport, the handicrafts and the tenant-farming social order, to which all her beliefs were attuned and on which all her confidence was based. To her these mighty changes in human life presented themselves as a series of perplexing frustrations and undeserved misfortunes, for which nothing or nobody was clearly to blame—unless it was my father and the disingenuous behaviour of people about her from whom she might have expected better things.

Bromley was being steadily suburbanized. An improved passenger and goods service, and the opening of a second railway station, made it more and more easy for people to go to London for their shopping and for London retailers to come into competition with the local traders. Presently the delivery vans of the early multiple shops, the Army and Navy Co-operative Stores and the like, appeared in the neighbourhood to suck away the ebbing vitality of the local retailer. The trade in pickling jars and jam-pots died away. Fresh housekeepers came to the gentlemen's houses, who knew not Joseph and bought their stuff from the stores.

Why didn't Joe do something about it?

Poor little woman! How continually vexed she was, how constantly tired and worried to the limits of endurance, during that dismal half-lifetime of disillusionment that slipped away at Bromley! She clung most desperately to the values she had learnt at Miss Riley's finishing school; she learnt nothing and forgot nothing through those dark years spent for the most part in the underground kitchen. Every night and morning and sometimes during the day she prayed to Our Father and Our Saviour for a little money, for a little leisure, for a little kindness, to make Joe better and less negligent—for now he was getting very neglectful of her.

It was like writing to an absconding debtor for all the answer she got.

Unless taking away her darling, her wonder, her one sweet and tractable child, her Fanny, her little " Possy," without pity or warning was an answer. A lesson. Fanny was well and happy and then she was flushed and contorted with agony and then in three days she was dead. My mother had to talk to her diary about it. Little boys do not like lamenting mothers ; Joe was apt to say, " There, there, Saddie," and go off to his cricket ; except for Our Lord and Saviour, whose dumbness, I am afraid, wore the make-believe very thin at times, my mother had to do her weeping alone.

It is my conviction that deep down in my mother's heart something was broken when my sister died two years and more before I was born. Her simple faith was cracked then and its reality spilled away. I got only the forms and phrases of it. I do not think she ever admitted to herself, ever realized consciously, that there was no consolation under heaven for the outrage Fate had done her. Our Lord was dumb, even in dreams he came not, and her subconsciousness apprehended all the dreadful implications of that silence. But she fought down that devastating discovery. She went on repeating the old phrases of belief—all the more urgently perhaps. She wanted me to believe in order to stanch that dark undertow of doubt. In the early days with my sister she had been able so to saturate her teaching with confidence in the Divine Protection, that she had created a prodigy of Early Piety. My heart she never touched because the virtue had gone out of her.

I was indeed a prodigy of Early Impiety. I was scared by Hell, I did not at first question the existence of Our Father, but no fear nor terror could prevent my feeling that his All Seeing Eye was that of an Old Sneak and that the

Atonement for which I had to be so grateful was either an imposture, a trick of sham self-immolation, or a crazy nightmare. I felt the unsoundness of these things before I dared to think it. There was a time when I believed in the story and scheme of salvation, so far as I could understand it, just as there was a time when I believed there was a Devil, but there was never a time when I did not heartily detest the whole business.

I feared Hell dreadfully for some time. Hell was indeed good enough to scare me and prevent me calling either of my brothers fools, until I was eleven or twelve. But one night I had a dream of Hell so preposterous that it blasted that undesirable resort out of my mind for ever. In an old number of *Chambers Journal* I had read of the punishment of breaking a man on the wheel. The horror of it got into my dreams and there was Our Father in a particularly malignant phase, busy basting a poor broken sinner rotating slowly over a fire built under the wheel. I saw no Devil in the vision ; my mind in its simplicity went straight to the responsible fountain head. That dream pursued me into the day time. Never had I hated God so intensely.

And then suddenly the light broke through to me and I knew this God was a lie.

I have a sort of love for most living things, but I cannot recall any time in my life when I had the faintest shadow of an intimation of love for any one of the Persons in the Holy Trinity. I could as soon love a field scarecrow as those patched up " persons." I am still as unable to account for the ecstasies of the faithful as I was to feel as my mother wished me to feel. I sensed it was a silly story long before I dared to admit even to myself that it was a silly story.

For indeed it is a silly story and each generation nowadays swallows it with greater difficulty. It is a jumble up of a miscellany of the old sacrificial and consolatory religions of the confused and unhappy townspeople of the early Empire ; its constituent practices were probably more soothing to troubled hearts before there was any attempt to weld them into one mystical creed, and all the disingenuous intelligence of generation after generation of time-serving or well-meaning divines has served only to accentuate the fundamental silliness of these synthesised Egyptian and Syrian myths. I doubt if one person in a million of all the hosts of Christendom has ever produced a spark of genuine gratitude for the Atonement. I think " love " for the Triune God is as rare as it is unnatural and irrational.

Why do people go on pretending about this Christianity ? At the test of war, disease, social injustice and every real human distress, it fails—and leaves a cheated victim, as it abandoned my mother. Jesus was some fine sort of man perhaps, the Jewish Messiah was a promise of leadership, but Our Saviour of the Trinity is a dressed-up inconsistent effigy of amiability, a monstrous hybrid of man and infinity, making vague promises of helpful miracles for the cheating of simple souls, an ever absent help in times of trouble.

And their Sacrament, their wonderful Sacrament, in which the struggling Believers urge themselves to discover the profoundest satisfaction ; what is it ? What does it amount to ? Was there ever a more unintelligible mix up of bad metaphysics and grossly materialistic superstition than this God-eating ? Was there anything more corrupting to take into a human mind and be given cardinal importance there ?

I once said a dreadful thing to my mother about the Sacrament. In her attempts to evoke Early Piety in me, she worked very hard indeed to teach me the answers in the English Church Catechism. I learnt them dutifully but I found them dull. In one answer (framed very carefully to guard me against the errors of the Church of Rome) I had to say what were the elements in the sacred feast. " Bread and Wine," it ran, " which our Lord hath ordained, etc., etc.

Bread and Wine seemed a strange foolish form of refreshment to me, the only wines I knew were ginger wine at Christmas and orange wine, which I took with cod liver oil, and port and sherry which were offered with a cracknel biscuit to housekeepers who came to pay bills, and so it occurred to me it would introduce an amusing element of realism into the solemnity of the recital if I answered " Bread and Butter " and chuckled helpfully. . . .

My mother knew she had to be profoundly shocked. She was shocked to the best of her ability. But she was much more puzzled than shocked. The book was closed, the audition suspended.

She said I did not understand the dreadfulness of what I had said, and that was perfectly true. And poor dear she could not convey it to me. No doubt she interceded with God for me and asked him to take over the task of enlightenment. " Forgive dear Bertie," she must have said.

And anyhow it was made evident to me that a decorative revision of the English Church Catechism was an undesirable enterprise. I turned my attention to the more acceptable effort to say it faster and faster.

My mother in my earliest memories of her was a distressed overworked little woman, already in her late forties. All the hope and confidence of her youth she had left behind her. As I knew her in my childhood, she was engaged in a desperate single-handed battle with our gaunt and dismal home, to keep it clean, to keep her children clean, to get them clothed and fed and taught, to keep up appearances. The only domestic help I ever knew her to have was a garrulous old woman of the quality of Sairey Gamp, a certain Betsy Finch.

In opulent times Betsy would come in to char, and there would even be a washing day, when the copper in the scullery was lit and all the nether regions were filled with white steam and the smell of soapsuds. My mother appears in these early memories, in old cloth slippers, a grey stuff dress or a print dress according to the season, an apron of sacking and a big pink sunbonnet—such as countrywomen wore in Old and New England alike before the separation. There was little sun in her life, but she wore that headdress, she explained, to keep the dust out of her hair. She is struggling up or down stairs with a dustpan, a slop-pail, a scrubbing brush or a greasy dishclout. Long before I came into the world her poor dear hands had become enlarged and distorted by scrubbing and damp, and I never knew them otherwise.

Her toil was unending. My father would get up and rake out and lay and light the fire, because she was never clever at getting a fire to burn, and then she would get breakfast while he took down the clumsy shop shutters and swept out the shop. Then came the business of hunting the boys out of bed, seeing that they did something in the way of washing, giving them breakfast and sending them off in time for school. Then airing and making the beds, emptying the slops, washing up the breakfast things. Then perhaps a dusty battle to clean out a room; there were no vacuum cleaners in those days; or a turn at scrubbing—scrubbing the splintery rotten wood of a jerry-built house. There was no O-Cedar mop, no polished floor; down you went to it on all fours with your pail beside you. If Joe was out delivering goods there might at any moment be a jangle of the shop bell and a customer.

Customers bothered my mother, especially when she was in her costume for housework; she would discard her apron in a hurry, wipe her wet hands, pat her hair into order, come into the shop breathless and defensive, and often my father had neglected to mark the prices on the things the customer wanted. If it was cricket goods she was quite at sea.

My father usually bought the meat for dinner himself, and that had to be cooked and the table laid in the downstairs kitchen. Then came a clatter of returning boys through the shop and down the staircase, and the midday meal. The room was dark and intermittently darker because of the skirts and feet going by over the grating. It wasn't always a successful meal. Sometimes there was not much to eat ; but there were always potatoes and there was too much cabbage for my taste ; and sometimes the cooking had been unfortunate and my father Pished and Tushed or said disagreeable things outright. My mother in those days was just the unpaid servant of everybody. I in particular was often peevish with my food, and frequently I would have headaches and bad bilious attacks in the afternoon. We drank beer that was drawn from a small cask in the scullery, and if it went a little flat before the cask was finished it had to be drunk just the same. Presently father lit his pipe and filled the kitchen air with the fragrance of Red Virginia, the boys dispersed quarrelling or skylarking or rejoicing, and there was nothing left to do of the first half, the heavier half, of my mother's daily routine but wash up the plates at the sink.

Then she could attend to appearances. Instead of the charlady ensemble of the morning, she changed herself into a trim little lady with a cap and lace apron. Generally she sat indoors. Perforce if my father was at cricket, but mainly because there was nothing to do abroad and much to do at home. She had a large confused workbasket—when I was small and exceptionally good it was sometimes my privilege to turn it out—and she had all our clothes to mend.

She darned my heels and knees with immense stitches. In addition she made all our clothes until such age as, under the pressure of our schoolfellows' derision, we rebelled against something rather naïve in the cut. Also she made loose covers for the chairs and sofa out of cheap chintz or cretonne. She made them as she cooked and as she made our clothes, with courage rather than skill. They fitted very badly but at least they hid the terrible worn shabbiness of the fundamental stuff. She got tea, she got supper, she put her offspring to bed after they had said their prayers, and then she could sit a little while, think, read the daily-paper, write a line or so in her diary, attend to her correspondence, before she lit her candle and went up the inconvenient staircase for the last time to bed. My father was generally out after supper, talking of men's affairs with men or playing a friendly game of Nap, by which I believe, generally speaking, he profited, in the bar parlour of the Bell

I know very little about the realities of my father's life at this time. Essentially he was a baffled unsuccessful " stuck " man, but he had a light and cheerful disposition, and a large part of his waking energy was spent in evading disagreeable realizations. He had a kind of attractiveness for women, I think he was aware of it, but I do not know whether he ever went further along the line of unfaithfulness than a light flirtation—in Bromley at any rate. I should certainly have learnt from my schoolfellows of any scandal or scandalous suspicion. He chatted a great deal at the shop door to fellow tradesmen in a similar state of leisure. The voices and occasional laughter came through the shop to my mother alone within.

He read diversely, bought books at sales, brought them home from the Library Institute. I think his original religious and political beliefs were undergoing a slow gentle fading out in those days. Evidently he found my mother, with her rigid standards and her curiously stereotyped mind, less and less interesting to talk to. She was never able to master the mysteries of cards or chess or draughts, so that alleviation of their evenings was out of the question. He felt her voluminous unspoken criticism of his ineptitude, he realized the justice of her complaints, and yet for the life of him he could not see what was to be done. I will confess I do not know what he could have done.

My mother's instinct for appearances was very strong. Whatever the realities of our situation, she was resolved that to the very last moment we should keep up the appearance of being comfortable members of that upper-servant tenant class to which her imagination had been moulded. She believed that it was a secret to all the world that she had no servant and did all the household drudgery herself. I was enjoined never to answer questions about that or let it out when I went abroad. Nor was I to take my coat off carelessly, because my underclothing was never quite up to the promise of my exterior garments. It was never ragged but it abounded in compromises. This hindered my playing games.

I was never to mix with common children, who might teach me naughty words. The Hoptons, the greengrocer's family over the way, were " rough " she thought ; they were really turbulently jolly ; the Mundays next door were methodists who sang hymns out of church which is almost as bad as singing songs in it, and the Mowatts at the corner she firmly believed had killed poor Possy and were not to be thought of. People who were not beneath us were apt to be stuck-up and unapproachable in the other direction. So my universe of discourse was limited. She preferred to have me indoors rather than out.

She taught me the rudiments of learning. I learnt my alphabet from a big sheet of capital letters pasted up in the kitchen, I learnt the nine figures from the same sheet, and from her, orally, how to count up to a hundred, and the first word I wrote was " butter," which I traced over her hand-writing against a pane of the window. Also I began to read under her instructions. But then she felt my education was straining for higher things and I went off with my brother Freddy (who was on no account to let go of my hand) to a school in a room in a row of cottages near the Drill Hall, kept by an unqualified old lady, Mrs. Knott, and her equally unqualified daughter Miss Salmon, where I learnt to say my tables of weights and measures, read words of two or more syllables and pretend to do summing—it was incompre-hensible fudging that was never explained to me—on a slate.

Such was my mother in the days when I was a small boy. She already had wrinkles round her eyes, and her mouth was drawn in because she had lost some teeth, and having them replaced by others would have seemed a wicked ex-travagance to her. I wonder what went on in her brain when she sat alone in the evening by the lamp and the dying fire, doing some last bit of sewing before she went to bed? I began to wonder what went on in her brain when I was in my early teens and I have wondered ever since.

I believe she was profoundly aware of her uncomfortable poverty-stricken circumstances, but I do not think she was acutely unhappy. I believe that she took refuge from reality in a world of innocent reverie. As she sewed, a string of petty agreeable fictions were distracting her mind from unpleasant fears and anxieties. She was meeting someone whom it was agreeable to meet ; she was being congratulated on this or that fancied achievement, dear Bertie was coming home with prizes from school, dear Frankie or dear Freddie was setting up in business and doing ever so well, or the postman was coming with a letter, a registered letter. It was a letter to

say she had been left money, twenty-five pounds, fifty pounds
—why not a hundred pounds ? All her own. The Married
Woman's Property Act ensured that. Joe couldn't touch it.
It was a triumph over Joe, but all the same, she would buy
him something out of it. Poor Possy should have that
gravestone at last. Mr. Morley's bill would be paid.

Should she have a servant ? Did she really want a servant
—except for what the neighbours thought? More trouble
than they are worth most of the time. A silly girl she would
have to train—and with boys about ! And Joe ? . . . The
boys were good as gold, she knew, but who could tell what
might not happen if the girl chanced to be a bad, silly girl ?
Better have in a serious woman, Betsy Finch for example,
more regularly. It would be nice not to have to scrub so
much. And to have new curtains in the parlour. . . . Doctor
Beeby coming in—just to look at Freddie's finger, nothing
serious. " Dear me, Mrs. Wells, dear me ! How *pretty* you
have made the room ! " . . .

Some such flow of fancy as that, it must have been.

Without reverie life would surely be unendurable to the
greater multitude of human beings. After all opium is merely
a stimulant for reverie. And reverie, I am sure, made the substance of her rare leisure. Religion and love, except for her
instinctive pride in her boys, had receded imperceptibly from
her life and left her dreaming. Once she had dreamt of re-
ciprocated love and a sedulously attentive God, but there was
indeed no more reassurance for her except in dreamland.
My father was away at cricket, and I think she realized more
and more acutely as the years dragged on without material
alleviation, that Our Father and Our Lord, on whom, to
begin with, she had perhaps counted unduly, were also away
—playing perhaps at their own sort of cricket in some remote
quarter of the starry universe.

My mother was still a good Churchwoman, but I doubt

if her reveries in the lonely evenings at Atlas House ever went into the hereafter and anticipated immortality. I doubt if she ever distracted herself by dreaming of the scenery of the Life to Come, or of anything that could happen there. Unless it was to have a vision of meeting her lost little " Possy " again in some celestial garden, an unchanged and eternal child, and hear her surprised bright cry of " Mummy Mummy ! " and hold her in her arms once more.

§ 5
A Broken Leg and Some Books and Pictures
(1874)

My leg was broken for me when I was between seven and eight. Probably I am alive to-day and writing this auto-biography instead of being a worn-out, dismissed and already dead shop assistant, because my leg was broken. The agent of good fortune was " young Sutton," the grown-up son of the landlord of the Bell. I was playing outside the scoring tent in the cricket field and in all friendliness he picked me up and tossed me in the air. " Whose little kid are you ? " he said, and I wriggled, he missed his hold on me and I snapped my tibia across a tent peg. A great fuss of being carried home; a painful setting—for they just set and strapped a broken leg tightly between splints in those days, and the knee and ankle swelled dreadfully—and then for some weeks I found myself enthroned on the sofa in the parlour as the most important thing in the house, consuming unheard-of jellies, fruits, brawn and chicken sent with endless apologies on behalf of her son by Mrs. Sutton, and I could demand and have a fair chance of getting anything that came into my head, books, paper, pencils, and toys—and particularly books.

I had just taken to reading. I had just discovered the art

of leaving my body to sit impassive in a crumpled up attitude
in a chair or sofa, while I wandered over the hills and far
away in novel company and new scenes. And now my
father went round nearly every day to the Literary Institute
in Market Square and got one or two books for me, and Mrs.
Sutton sent some books, and there was always a fresh book to
read. My world began to expand very rapidly, and when
presently I could put my foot to the ground, the reading
habit had got me securely. Both my parents were doubtful
of the healthiness of reading, and did their best to discourage
this poring over books as soon as my leg was better.

I cannot recall now many of the titles of the books I read,
I devoured them so fast, and the title and the author's name
in those days seemed a mere inscription on the door to delay
me in getting down to business. There was a work, in two
volumes, upon the countries of the world, which I think
must have been made of bound up fortnightly parts. It was
illustrated with woodcuts, the photogravure had still to
come in those days, and it took me to Tibet, China, the
Rocky Mountains, the forests of Brazil, Siam and a score of
other lands. I mingled with Indians and naked negroes ; I
learnt about whaling and crossed the drift ice with Esqui-
maux. There was Wood's *Natural History*, also copiously
illustrated and full of exciting and terrifying facts. I conceived a profound fear of the gorilla, of which there
was a fearsome picture, which came out of the book
at times after dark and followed me noiselessly about the
house. The half landing was a favourite lurking place for
this terror. I passed it whistling, but wary and then ran for
my life up the next flight. And I was glad to think that
between the continental land masses of the world, which
would have afforded an unbroken land passage for wolves
from Russia and tigers from India, and this safe island on
which I took my daily walks, stretched the impassable moat

of the English Channel. I read too in another book about
the distances of the stars, and that seemed to push the All
Seeing Eye very agreeably away from me. Turning over the
pages of the Natural History, I perceived a curious relationship between cats and tigers and lions and so forth, and to a
lesser degree between them and hyenas and dogs and bears,
and between them again and other quadrupeds, and curious
premonitions of evolution crept into my thoughts. Also I
read the life of the Duke of Wellington and about the
American Civil War, and began to fight campaigns and
battles in my reveries. At home were the works of Washington Irving and I became strangely familiar with Granada
and Columbus and the Companions of Columbus. I do not
remember that any story books figured during this first
phase of reading. Either I have forgotten them or they did
not come my way. Later on, however, Captain Mayne
Reid, Fenimore Cooper and the Wild West generally, seized
upon my imagination.

One important element in that first bout of reading was
the bound volumes of *Punch* and its rival in those days, *Fun*,
which my father renewed continually during my convalescence. The bound periodicals with their political cartoons
and their quaint details played a curious part in developing
my imaginative framework. My ideas of political and
international relations were moulded very greatly by the big
figures of John Bull and Uncle Sam, the French, the Austrian, and the German and Russian emperors, the Russian
bear, the British lion and the Bengal tiger, Mr. Gladstone
the noble, and the insidious, smiling Dizzy. They confronted
one another ; they said heroic, if occasionally quite incomprehensible things to one another. And across the political
scene also marched tall and lovely feminine figures, Britannia,
Erin, Columbia, La France, bare armed, bare necked, showing beautiful bare bosoms, revealing shining thighs, wearing

garments that were a revelation in an age of flounces and crinolines. My first consciousness of women, my first stirrings of desire were roused by these heroic divinities. I became woman-conscious from those days onward.

I do not wish to call in question the accounts the masters of psycho-analysis give us of the awakening of sexual consciousness in the children they have studied. But I believe that the children who furnished material for the first psychoanalysts were the children of people racially different, and different in their conceptions of permissible caresses and endearments from my family. What they say may be true of Austrian Jews and Levantines and yet not true of English or Irish. I cannot remember and I cannot trace any continuity between my infantile physical reactions and my personal sexual life. I believe that all the infantile sensuality of suckling and so forth on which so much stress is laid, was never carried on into the permanent mental fabric, was completely washed out in forgetfulness; never coagulated into subconscious memories; it was as though it had never been. I cannot detect any mother fixation, any Oedipus complex or any of that stuff in my make up. My mother's kisses were significant acts, expressions not caresses. As a small boy I found no more sexual significance about my always decent and seemly mother than I did about the chairs and sofa in our parlour.

It is quite possible that while there is a direct continuity of the sexual subconsciousness from parent to child in the southern and eastern Europeans, due to a sustained habit of caresses and intimacy, the psycho-sexual processes of the northern and western Europeans and Americans arise *de novo* in each generation after a complete break with and forgetfulness of the mother-babe reaction, and so are fundamentally different in their form and sequence. At any rate I am convinced that my own sexual life began in a naïve direct admiration for the lovely bodies, as they seemed, of those political divinities of Tenniel's in *Punch*, and that my first inklings of desire were roused by them and by the plaster casts of Greek statuary that adorned the Crystal Palace. I do not think there was any sub-conscious contribution from preceding events to that response ; my mind was inherently ready for it. My mother had instilled in me the impropriety of not wearing clothes, so that my first attraction towards Venus was shamefaced and furtive, but the dear woman never suspected the stimulating influence of Britannia, Erin, Columbia and the rest of them upon my awakening susceptibilities.

It is true that I worshipped them at first in a quasi infantile fashion, but that does not imply continuity of experience. When I went to bed I used to pillow my head on their great arms and breasts. Gradually they ceased to be gigantic. They took me in their arms and I embraced them, but nevertheless I remained fundamentally ignorant and innocent until I went to school after my accident. I found women lovely and worshipful before I was seven years old, and well before I came down to what we call nowadays the " facts of sex." But now that my interest was aroused I became acutely observant of a print or a statuette in a shop window. I do not think my interest at that time was purely heterosexual. My world was so clothed and covered up, and the rules of decency were so established in me, that any revelation of the body was an exciting thing.

Now that I had arrived at knickerbockers and the reading of books, I was sent to a little private school in the High Street, Bromley, for boys between seven and fifteen, and from my schoolmates I speedily learnt in the grossest way, imparted with guffaws and gestures, " the facts of sex," and all those rude words that express them, from which my mother had hitherto shielded me.

None of these boys came from bookish homes so that I had from the outset a queer relative wideness of outlook. I knew all sorts of things about lands and beasts and times of which they had never heard. And I had developed a facility for drawing, which in them was altogether dormant. So that I passed for an exceptionally bright and clever little boy and the schoolmaster would invoke " Young Seven Years Old," to shame the obtuseness of my elders. They were decent enough not to visit it upon me. Among boys from more literate homes I should have had none of these outstanding advantages, but I took them naturally enough as an intrinsic superiority, and they made me rather exceptionally self-conceited and confident.

The clash of these gross revelations about the apparatus of sex with my secret admiration for the bodily beauty of women, and with this personal conceit of mine, determined to a large extent my mental and perhaps my physical development. It imposed a reserve upon me that checked a native outspokenness. That a certain amount of masturbation is a normal element in the emergence of sexual consciousness was in those days almost passionately concealed by the English-speaking world. Yet probably no normal individual altogether escapes that response to the stir of approaching adolescence. To my generation it was allowed to come as a horrifying, astounding, perplexing individual discovery. Without guidance and recognition, and black with shame, it ran inevitably into a variety of unwholesome channels. Upon many boys and girls it became localized in the parts more immediately affected and exercised an overwhelming fascination. The school had its exhibitionist and ran with a dirty whispered and giggling undertow. Among the boarders, many of whom slept two in a bed, there was certainly much simple substitutional homosexuality. Personally I recoiled, even more than I cared to show, from mere phallicism. I did not so much begin masturbation as have it happen to me as a natural outcome of my drowsy clasping of my goddesses. I had so to speak a one-sided love affair with the bedding.

I never told a soul about it because I was ashamed and feared ridicule or indignant reproof. Very early I got hold of the idea, I do not know how, that Venus could drain away my energy, and this kept my lapses from ideal "purity" within very definite bounds indeed. There was also a certain amount of superstitious terror to restrain me. Maybe this was that sin against the Holy Ghost that could never be forgiven, that damned inevitably. That worried a brother of mine more than it did me, but I think it worried me also. I was eleven or twelve years old before religion began to fall to pieces in my consciousness.

So at the age of seven (and, to be exact, three quarters), when I went up the High Street to Morley's school for the first time, a rather white-faced little boy in a holland pinafore and carrying a small green baize satchel for my books, I had already between me and my bleak Protestant God, a wide wide world of snowy mountains, Arctic regions, tropical forests, prairies and deserts and high seas, cities and armies, Indians, negroes and island savages, gorillas, great carnivores, elephants, rhinoceroses and whales, about which I was prepared to talk freely, and cool and strange below it all a cavernous world of nameless goddess mistresses of which I never breathed a word to any human being.

CHAPTER THE THIRD

SCHOOLBOY

§ 1

MR. MORLEY'S COMMERCIAL ACADEMY
(1874-1880)

THIS MARCH up the High Street to Mr. Thomas
Morley's Academy begins a new phase in the story of the
brain that J. W. and his Saddie had launched into the world.
Bromley Academy was a school in the ancient tradition,
but the culmination of my schooling was to occur in the most
modern and advanced of colleges then in existence, the
science schools at South Kensington. It was a queer discontinuous series of educational processes through which
my brain was passed, very characteristic of the continual
dislocations of that time.

The germinating forces of that Modern World-State which
is now struggling into ordered being, were already thrusting
destructively amidst the comparative stabilities of the old
eighteenth century order before I was born. There was
already a railway station on the Dover line and this was
supplemented, when I was about twelve years old, by a
second line branching off from the Chislehurst line at Grove
Park. The place which had been hardly more than a few
big houses, a little old market place and a straggling High
Street upon the high road, with two coaching inns and a
superabundance of small " pull-up " beerhouses, was
stimulated to a vigorous growth in population. Steadily
London drew it closer and suburbanized it. No one foresaw

its growth except a few speculative jerry-builders ; no one in the world prepared for even the most obvious consequences of that growth. Shops and dwellings of the type of my home were " run up " anyhow. Slum conditions appeared almost at once in courts and muddy by-ways. Yet all around were open fields and common land, Bromley Common, Chislehurst Common, great parks like Sundridge Park and Camden, and to the south the wide heathery spaces about Keston Fish Ponds and Down.

The new order of things that was appearing in the world when I was born, was already arousing a consciousness of the need for universal elementary education. It was being realized by the ruling classes that a nation with a lower stratum of illiterates would compete at a disadvantage against the foreigner. A condition of things in which everyone would read and write and do sums, dawned on the startled imagination of mankind. The British and the National Schools, which had existed for half a century in order to make little Nonconformists and little Churchmen, were organized into a state system under the Elementary Education Act of 1871 and supplemented by Board Schools (designed to make little Unsectarian Christians). Bromley was served by a National School. That was all that the district possessed in the way of public education. It was the mere foundation of an education. It saw to the children up to the age of thirteen or even fourteen, and no further. Beyond that the locality had no public provision for technical education or the development of artistic or scientific ability whatever. Even that much of general education had been achieved against considerable resistance. There was a strong objection in those days to the use of public funds for the education of " other people's children," and school pennies were exacted weekly from the offspring of everyone not legally indigent.

But side by side with that nineteenth-century National School under the Education Act, the old eighteenth-century order was still carrying on in Bromley, just as it was still carrying on in my mother's mind. In the eighteenth century the lower classes did not pretend to read or write, but the members of the tenant-farmer, shopkeeper, innkeeper, upper servant stratum, which was then, relatively to the labourers, a larger part of the community, either availed themselves of the smaller endowed schools which came down from the mental stir of the Reformation, or, in the absence of any such school in their neighbourhood, supported little private schools of their own. These private schools were struggling along amidst the general dissolution, shuffling and reconstruction of society that was already manifest in the middle nineteenth century, and the Academy of Mr. Thomas Morley was a fairly well preserved specimen, only slightly modernized, of the departing order of things.

He had opened school for himself in 1849, having previously filled the post of usher at an old-established school that closed down in that year. He was Scotch and not of eminent academic attainments ; his first prospectus laid stress on " writing in both plain and ornamental style, Arithmetic logically, and History with special reference to Ancient Egypt." Ancient Egypt and indeed most of the History except lists of dates, pedigrees and enactments, had dropped from the school outlook long before I joined it, for even Bromley Academy moved a little with the times, but there was still great stress on copperplate flourishes, long addition sums and book-keeping. Morley was a bald portly spectacled man with a strawberry nose and ginger-grey whiskers, who considered it due to himself and us to wear a top hat, an ample frock-coat, and a white tie, and to carry himself with invariable dignity and make a frequent use of " Sir." Except for a certain assistance with the little ones from Mrs. Morley, a stout ringleted lady in black silk and a gold chain, he ran the school alone. It was a single room built out over a scullery ; there were desks round the walls and two, of six places each, in the centre, with a stove between which warmed the place in winter. His bedroom window opened upon the schoolroom, and beneath it, in the corner of the room, was his desk, the great ink bottle from which the ink-wells were replenished, the pile of slates and the incessant cane, with which he administered justice, either in spasmodic descents upon our backs and hindquarters, or after formal accusations, by smacks across the palm of the hand. He also hit us with his hands anywhere, and with books, rulers and anything else that came handy, and his invective and derision were terrific. Also we were made to stand on the rickety forms and hold out books and slates until our arms ached. And in this way he urged us—I suppose our numbers varied from twenty-five to thirty-five —along the path of learning that led in the more successful instances to the examinations, conducted by an association of private schoolmasters, for their mutual reassurance, known as the College of Preceptors, (with special certificates for book-keeping) and then to jobs as clerks.

About half the boys were boarders drawn from London public houses or other homes unsuitable for growing youth. There were a few day-boarders from outlying farms, who took their dinner in the house. The rest were sons of poorish middle-class people in the town. We assembled at nine and went on to twelve and again from two to five, and between these hours, except when the windows were open in warm weather, the atmosphere grew steadily more fœtid and our mental operations more sluggish and confused.

It is very difficult to give any facts about this dominie and his Academy which do not carry with them a quality of Dickens-like caricature. He ranted at us from his desk in the quaintest fashion ; he took violent dislikes and betrayed irrational preferences ; the educational tradition from which he arose and which is so manifest in that first prospectus already quoted, was in the same world with Miss Riley's school at Chichester which did so much to shape my mother ; it was antiquated, pretentious, superficial and meagre ; and yet there was something good about old Morley and something good for me. I have an impression that with a certain honesty he was struggling out of that tradition and trying to make something of us. That " College of Preceptors " was not only a confederation of private schools to keep up appearances ; it was a mutual improvement society, it was a voluntary modernizing movement. It ran lectures on educational method and devised examinations for teaching diplomas. Morley had learnt a lot between his start in 1849 and the days when I was his pupil. He had become an Associate, and then a Licentiate of this self-constituted college, by examination, and each examination had involved a paper or so on teaching method. I believe his teaching, such as it was, was better than that of the crudely trained mechanical grant earners of the contemporary National School which was the only local alternative, and that my mother's instinct was a sound one in sending us all to this antiquated middle-class establishment.

Yet if I describe a day's work in that dusty, dingy, ill-ventilated schoolroom, there will not be a qualified teacher in the world beneath the age of fifty who will not consider it frightful. A lifetime ago it would have seemed perfectly normal schooling.

Few people realize the immense changes that the organization and mechanism of popular teaching have undergone in the past century. They have changed more than housing or transport. Before that dawn of a new way of life, began that slow reluctant dawn in which we are still living, the vast majority of people throughout the world had no schooling at all, and of the educated minority, literate rather than educated, by far the larger proportion—in India and China and Arabia quite as much as in Europe—did their learning in some such makeshift place as this outbuilding of Morley's, in the purlieus of a mosque, for example, under a tree in India or beneath an Irish hedge, as members of a bunch of twenty or so ill-assorted pupils of all ages and sizes and often of both sexes, between six and sixteen. Schools large enough to classify were the exception, and there were rarely more than one or two teachers. Specially built school houses were almost unknown. A room designed and equipped for teaching and containing a manageable class of youngsters in the same phase of development, is comparatively a new thing in human experience, even for the young of the privileged orders. And necessarily under these old conditions teaching had to be intermittent because the teacher's mind could not confront all that diversity of reaction between childishness and adolescence at the same time ; necessarily he had to contrive exercises and activities to keep this group and that quiet while he expounded to another. He was like some very ordinary chess player who had undertaken to play thirty games of chess simultaneously. He was an unqualified mental obstetrician doing his work wholesale. Necessarily the phases and quality of his teaching depended on his moods. At times Morley was really trying to get something over to us ; at others he was digesting, or failing to digest, his midday meal ; he was in a phase of accidie ; he was suffering from worry or grievance ; he was amazed at life and revolted by his dependence upon us ; he felt the world was rushing past him ; he had got up late and omitted to shave and was struggling with an overwhelming desire to leave us all and repair the omission.

So the primary impressions left upon my brain by that

Academy are not impressions of competent elucidation and
guidance, of a universe being made plain to me or of skills
being acquired and elaborated, but of the moods of Mr.
Thomas Morley and their consequences. At times his attention was altogether distracted ; he was remote upon his
throne in the corner, as aloof almost as my mother's God,
and then we would relax from the tasks or exercises he had
set us and indulge in furtive but strenuous activities of our
own. We would talk and tell each other stories—I had a
mind suitably equipped by my reading for boyish saga
telling and would go on interminably—draw on our slates,
play marbles, noughts and crosses and suchlike games, turn
out our pockets, swap things, indulge in pinching and punch-
ing matches, eat sweets, read penny dreadfuls, do anything,
indeed, but the work in hand. Sometimes it would be
whispered in the drowsy digestive first hour of the afternoon, " Old Tommy's asleep," and we would watch him
sink slowly and beautifully down and down into slumber,
terminated by a snore and a start. If at last he got off completely, spectacles askew over his folded arms, a kind of
silent wildness would come upon us. We would stand up to
make fantastic, insulting and obscene gestures, leave our
places to creep noiselessly as far as we dared. He would
awaken abruptly, conscience awake also, inflict sudden
punishment on some belated adventurer ; and then would
come a strenuous hour of driving work.

Sometimes he would leave us altogether upon his private
occasions. Then it was our bounden duty to kick up all the
row we could, to get out of our places and wrestle, to " go
for " enemies, to produce the secreted catapult or pea-
shooter, to pelt with chewed paper and books. I can taste
the dust and recall the din as I write of it. In the midst of the
uproar the blind of the bedroom window would be raised,
silently, swiftly. Morley, razor in hand and his face covered

with soapsuds, would be discovered glaring at us through the glass, marking down sinners for punishment, a terrifying visage. Up would go the window. " You HOUNDS ! You Miserable Hounds ! " Judgments followed.

The spells of intensive teaching came irregularly, except for Friday afternoon, which was consecrated invariably to the breathless pursuit of arithmetic. There were also whole afternoons of " book-keeping by double entry " upon sheets of paper, when we pursued imaginary goods and cash payments with pen and ruler and even red ink, to a final Profit and Loss Account and a Balance Sheet. We wrote in copybooks and he came, peering and directing, over our shoulders. There was only one way in which a pen might be held ; it was a matter of supreme importance ; there was only one angle at which writing might slope. I was disposed to be unorthodox in this respect, and my knuckles suffered.

The production of good clerks (with special certificates for book-keeping) was certainly one of the objectives of Mr. Thomas Morley's life. The safety, comfort and dignity of Mr. and Mrs. Thomas Morley and Miss Morley were no doubt a constant preoccupation. But also there was interest in wider and more fundamental things. There was a sense in him that some things were righter than others, a disposition to assert as much, and a real desire for things to be done well. His studies for the diplomas of A.C.P. and L.C.P. (Associate and Licentiate of the College of Preceptors), low though the requirements were, absurdly low by our present standards, had awakened him to the pleasures of certain mental exercises ; a mathematical problem, a logical demonstration. When he found that I could be interested by the grammatical analysis of a complicated sentence or the solution of some elementary mathematical problem, he took a liking to me and showed me much more attention than he gave to the more obdurate material he had to deal with, minds stirred to a

high level of evasion and resistance by his clumsy, medieval,
impatient and aggressive methods of approach. He never
gave me a nickname and never singled me out for an abusive
tirade.

When I left his school at the age of thirteen (bracketed
with a fellow pupil first in all England for book-keeping,
so far, that is to say, as England was covered by the College
of Preceptors), whatever else I had missed, I had certainly
acquired the ability to use English with some precision and
delicacy, even if the accent was a Cockney one, and I had
quite as good a mathematical apparatus as most boys of the
same age get at a public school nowadays. I had read about
as much of Euclid as it was customary to read, made a fair
start with trigonometry and was on the verge of the calculus.
But most of the other stuff I got was bad. Old Tommy
taught French out of a crammer's textbook, and, in spite of
the fact that he had on several occasions visited Boulogne,
he was quite unable to talk in that elusive tongue; so I learnt
hardly anything about it except its conjugations and long
lists of " exceptions," so useful in written examinations and
so unimportant in ordinary life. He crippled my French for
life. He made me vowel-shy in every language.

I do not think he read much. He was not generally curious.
My reading habit I developed at home and do not recall that
Morley ever directed my attention to any book, unless it
was some cheap school textbook used in my work. But at
times he would get excited by his morning paper and then
we would have a discourse on the geography of the North-
West Frontier with an appeal to a decaying yellow map of
Asia that hung on the wall, or we would follow the search
for Livingstone by Stanley in Darkest Africa. He had traces
of early Radicalism and a Republican turn of mind; he
would discourse upon the extravagant Parliamentary grants
made in those days to the various members of the Royal

Family when they married, and about the unnecessary costliness of the army and navy. He believed that Mr. Gladstone really stood for " Peace, Retrenchment and Reform." All sorts of Radical principles may have filtered into my receptive mind from these *obiter dicta*.

Geoffrey West, in the exact and careful biography he wrote of me some years ago, is unjust to this old-world pedagogue because he measures him by his own twentieth-century standards with only the later nineteenth century as a background. Against the eighteenth-century background from which he derived, Thomas Morley was by no means so contemptible. West says he favoured a few willing boys with his instructions and let the rest drift. But that happened in all the schools ; it was an inevitable aspect of those small miscellaneous schools with single untrained teachers. To-day every teacher still " favours " the willing boy. That sort of favouritism will go on to the end of time. That old gentleman (A.C.P., L.C.P.) walking with a portly gravity that was all his own, hands clasped behind his back, at the tail of the crocodile of ill-assorted undrilled boys, steering them to the best of his ability into the future, taking them to church or for a walk or to the cricket field, is by no means such a dismal memory of inefficiency as West suggests. Bromley Academy had very little of the baseness which pervaded Dotheboys Hall.

But Geoffrey West, in that same book, called my attention to an interesting resemblance between Morley's school and the school of Charles Dickens, a third of a century earlier, of which I should otherwise be ignorant. There was a continual bickering between us and the boys of the National School, bickering which rose occasionally to the level of a pitched battle with staves and sticks upon Martin's Hill, at that time a waste and now a trim recreation ground. For some un-known reason we were called " Morley's Bull Dogs " and the elementary schoolboys were called, by us at any rate, "Bromley Water Rats" and "Cads." Now the Dickens parallel was "Baker's Bull Dogs" and "Troy Town Rats." Evidently this hostility between the boys of the old type of private schools and those of the new denominational schools, was of long standing, and widespread and almost stereotyped in its expression.

Geoffrey West thinks the antagonism was "snobbish," but that is a loose word to use for a very interesting conflict of divergent ideas and social tendencies. He probably considers the National Schools were "democratic" schools, like the common schools of the United States, "all class" schools, but that is a mistaken view. In spirit, form and intention they were inferior schools, and to send one's children to them in those days, as my mother understood perfectly well, was a definite and final acceptance of social inferiority. The Education Act of 1871 was not an Act for a common universal education, it was an Act to educate the lower classes for employment on lower-class lines, and with specially trained, inferior teachers who had no university quality. If Tommy Morley could not sport a university gown and hood, he could at least claim to wear a gown and hood as an L.C.P. (by royal charter), that was indistinguishable to the common eye from the real thing. He had all the dignity, if little of the substance, of scholarship. The more ancient middle-class schools, whatever their faults, were saturated with the spirit of individual self-reliance and individual dignity, with an idea, however pretentious, of standards "a little above the common," with a feeling (however vulgarized, debased and under-nourished) of *Noblesse oblige*. Certain things we could not do and certain things were expected of us because of our class. Most of the bickering of Morley's Bull Dogs was done against odds, and on the whole we held our own. I think it was a very lucky thing for me personally that I acquired this much class feeling.

I have never believed in the superiority of the inferior. My want of enthusiasm for the Proletarian ideal goes back to the Battle of Martin's Hill. If I was in almost unconcealed revolt against my mother's deferential attitude to royalty and our social superiors, it was because my resentful heart claimed at least an initial equality with every human being ; but it was equality of position and opportunity I was after, and not equality of respect or reward ; I certainly had no disposition to sacrifice my conceit of being made of better stuff, intrinsically and inherently, than most other human beings, by any self-identification with people who frankly took the defeated attitude. I thought the top of the form better than the bottom of the form, and the boy who qualified better than the boy who failed to qualify. I am not going to argue at this point whether such a state of mind is desirable or creditable to anyone ; my biographical duty is to record that so it was with me. So far as the masses went I was entirely of my mother's way of thinking ; I was middle-class,—" petty bourgeois " as the Marxists have it.

Just as my mother was obliged to believe in Hell, but hoped that no one would go there, so did I believe there was and had to be a lower stratum, though I was disgusted to find that anyone belonged to it. I did not think this lower stratum merited any respect. It might arouse sympathy for its bad luck or indignation for an unfair handicap. That was a different matter. My thought, as I shall trace its development in this history, has run very close to communist lines, but my conception of a scientifically organized class-less society is essentially of an expanded middle-class which has incorporated both the aristocrat and plutocrat above and the peasant, proletarian and pauper below.

Trotsky has recorded that Lenin, after his one conversation

with me, said that I was incurably middle-class. So far
Lenin was a sound observer. He, and Trotsky also, were of the
same vital social stratum ; they had indeed both started life
from a far more advantageous level than I had ; but the
discolouration of their stream of thought by Marxist pretences and sentimentalities, had blinded them to their own
essential quality. My conversation with Lenin turned entirely
on the " liquidation " of the peasant and the urban toiler—
by large-scale agriculture and power machinery. Lenin was
just as much for that as I was, we were talking about the
same thing in the same spirit ; but we said the same thing as
though it was a different thing because our minds were
tuned in different keys.

§ 2
PUERILE VIEW OF THE WORLD (1878–1879)

(AUGUST 4th, 1933). I have been trying, for a day or so, to
reconstruct my vision of the world as I had it in those days,
to restore the state of my brain as it was about 1878 or 9
when I was in mid-schoolboy stage. I find it an almost impossible task. I find it impossible to disentangle the things I
saw and read before I was thirteen, from the things that came
afterwards. The old ideas and impressions were made over
in accordance with new material, they were used up to make
the new equipment. This reconstruction went on from day to
day, and so, in order and detail, they are lost beyond
recovery. Yet impossible as it is to get any focussed clearness
and exactitude here, it is equally impossible to ignore this
phase of completed puerility. My formal education came to a
break at that date, was held up for two years and more before
it resumed, at a stage at which the brains of great multitudes of English people halted for good, and at which (or at

parallel levels) I believe multitudes still halt all over the world. This mass of human beings halting in puerility, is the determining factor in most of the alarming political and social processes of to-day.

In the universe in which my brain was living in 1879 there was no nonsense about time being space or anything of that sort. There were three dimensions, up and down, fore and aft and right and left, and I never heard of a fourth dimension until 1884 or thereabout. Then I thought it was a witticism. Space went on for ever in every direction, good Newtonian space. I felt it must be rather empty and cheerless beyond the stars, but I did not let my mind dwell on that. My God, who by this time had become entirely disembodied, had been diffused through this space since the beginning of things. He was already quite abstracted from the furious old hell-and-heaven Thunder God of my childish years. His personality had faded. My mind had been unobtrusively taking the sense of reality out of the Trinity and the Atonement and the other dogmas of official christianity. I felt there must be some mistake about all that, but I had not yet sat down to make any philosophy of my own by which these strange beliefs could be arraigned. I had simply withdrawn my attention. If I had had a catholic upbringing with intercessory individualized saints and local and special Virgins, that tacit withdrawal might have been less easy. Yes or no might have been forced upon me. I might have come earlier to positive disbelief.

Occasionally I would find myself praying—always to God simply. He remained a God spread all over space and time, yet nevertheless he was capable of special response and magic changes in the order of events. I would pray when I was losing a race, or in trouble in an examination room, or frightened. I expected prompt attention. In my first book-keeping examination by the College of Preceptors I could

not get my accounts to balance. I prayed furiously. The
bell rang, the invigilator hovered over my last frantic efforts.
I desisted reluctantly, " All right, God," I said, " catch me
praying again." I was then about twelve.

Through this universe with its diffused Space-God spun
the earth, moving amidst the stars along paths that were
difficult to understand and still more difficult to remember.
I was constantly reading that the earth was a mere pin point
in space ; that if the sun was as big as St. Paul's dome, the
earth would be a strawberry pip somewhere in the suburbs,
and many similar illustrative facts, but directly I took my
mind off these explicit statements, the pip grew bigger and
bigger and I grew even faster. St. Paul's dome stuck where
it was and the very Nebulæ came within range again. My
mind insisted on that. Just as it insisted that God was always
within range. Otherwise it had no use for them.

The earth, directly one let go of one's cosmic facts, expanded again like a vehemently inflated soap bubble, until
it filled the entire picture. One did not see all round it in
those days. It had mystery at its North and South Poles and
Darkest Africa on its equator. Poe's *Narrative of A. Gordon
Pym* tells what a very intelligent mind could imagine about
the south polar regions a century ago. The poor old earth in
those days had a hard crust and a molten interior and
naturally suffered from chronic indigestion, earthquakes,
rumblings, and eruptions. It has since solidified considerably.

Moreover it already had a past which was rapidly opening
out to men's minds in those days. I first became aware of
that past in the gardens of the Crystal Palace at Sydenham ;
it came upon me as a complete surprise, embodied in vast
plaster reconstructions of the megatherium and various
dinosaurs and a toadlike labyrinthodon (for at first laby-
rinthodons were supposed to have had toadlike bodies). I

was having one of those acute bilious attacks that always happened in the afternoons when I was taken to the Crystal Palace, and that made the impression none the less formidable. My mother explained that these were Antediluvian Animals. They had been left out of the ark, I guessed, on account of their size, but even then there seemed something a little wrong in the suggestion that the ichthyosaurus had been drowned in a flood.

Somewhen later I pored over Humboldt's *Cosmos* and began to learn something of geological time. But by means of accepting the gloss that the Days of Creation meant geological ages, nothing really essential was changed in the past of my universe. There was merely an extension. The Creation, though further off, remained still as the hard and fast beginning of time, before which there was nothing, just as a very pyrotechnic Day of Judgment " when time shall be no more " closed the vista at the other end. Ultimate emptiness bounded my universe in space and time alike. " Someday we shall know all," said my mother in response to my questions about what lay beyond, and with that for a time I had to be content.

Whatever else I doubted, I was incapable at that age of doubting my immortality. I had never known the universe without my consciousness and I could not imagine the universe without my consciousness. I doubt if any young things can really do so. The belief in immortality is tacit and formless in young animals, but it is there. The fear of death is not fear of extinction but a fear of something unknown and utterly disagreeable. I thought I was going on and on—when I thought of continuance at all. I had passed the College of Preceptors examination very well, so why shouldn't I get through the Day of Judgment ? But the world was just then so immediately full of interesting things, that I did not put in much time at the fundamental and eternal questions beyond.

It was made a matter of general congratulation about me that I was English. The flavour of J. R. Green's recently published (1874) History of the English People had drifted to me either directly or at second-hand, and my mind had leapt all too readily to the idea that I was a blond and blue-eyed Nordic, quite the best make of human being known. England was consciously Teutonic in those days, the monarchy and Thomas Carlyle were strong influences in that direction ; we talked of our " Keltic fringe " and ignored our Keltic infiltration ; and the defeat of France in 1870-71 seemed to be the final defeat of the decadent Latin peoples. This blended very well with the anti-Roman Catholic influence of the eighteenth-century Protestant training, a distrust and hostility that remained quite vivid when much else of that teaching had faded. We English, by sheer native superiority, practically without trying, had possessed ourselves of an Empire on which the sun never set, and through the errors and infirmities of other races were being forced slowly but steadily—and quite modestly—towards world dominion.

All that was quite settled in my head, as I carried my green-baize satchel to and fro between Morley's school and my dismal bankrupt home, and if you had suddenly confronted me with a Russian prince or a rajah in all his glory and suggested he was my equal, I should either have laughed you to scorn or been very exasperated with you about it.

I was taught no history but English History, which after some centuries of royal criminality, civil wars and wars in France, achieved the Reformation and blossomed out into the Empire ; and I learnt hardly any geography but British geography. It was only from casual reading that I gathered that quite a number of things had happened and quite a number of interesting things existed outside the world of

English affairs. But I looked at pictures of the Taj Mahal, the Colosseum and the Pyramids in very much the same spirit as I listened to stories about the Wonders of Animal Intelligence (beavers, bees, birds' nests, breeding habits of the salmon, etc.). They did not shake my profound satisfaction with the self, the township, the county, the nation, the Empire and the outlook that was mine.

In those days I had ideas about Aryans extraordinarily like Mr. Hitler's. The more I hear of him the more I am convinced that his mind is almost the twin of my thirteen year old mind in 1879 ; but heard through a megaphone and—implemented. I do not know from what books I caught my first glimpse of the Great Aryan People going to and fro in the middle plains of Europe, spreading east, west, north and south, varying their consonants according to Grimm's Law as they did so, and driving the inferior breeds into the mountains. But they formed a picturesque background to the duller facts of ancient history. Their ultimate triumphs everywhere squared accounts with the Jews, against which people I had a subconscious dissatisfaction because of their disproportionate share of Holy Writ. I thought Abraham, Isaac, Moses and David loathsome creatures and fit associates for Our Father, but unlike Hitler I had no feelings about the contemporary Jew. Quite a number of the boarders in the Bromley Academy were Jewish and I was not aware of it. My particular pal, Sidney Bowkett, was I think unconsciously Jewish ; the point never arose.

I had reveries—I indulged a great deal in reverie until I was fifteen or sixteen, because my active imagination was not sufficiently employed—and I liked especially to dream that I was a great military dictator like Cromwell, a great republican like George Washington or like Napoleon in his earlier phases. I used to fight battles whenever I went for a walk alone. I used to walk about Bromley, a small rather

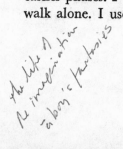

undernourished boy, meanly clad and whistling detestably
between his teeth, and no one suspected that a phantom
staff pranced about me and phantom orderlies galloped at
my commands, to shift the guns and concentrate fire on
those houses below, to launch the final attack upon yonder
distant ridge. The citizens of Bromley town go out to take
the air on Martin's Hill and look towards Shortland across
the fields where once meandered the now dried-up and
vanished Ravensbourne, with never a suspicion of the
orgies of bloodshed I once conducted there. Martin's Hill
indeed is one of the great battlegrounds of history. Scores of
times the enemy skirmishers have come across those levels,
followed by the successive waves of the infantry attack, while
I, outnumbered five to one, manœuvred my guns round, the
guns I had refrained so grimly from using too soon in spite
of the threat to my centre, to enfilade them suddenly from
the curving slopes towards Beckenham. " Crash," came the
first shell, and then crash and crash. They were mown down
by the thousand. They straggled up the steep slopes wavering.
And then came the shattering counter-attack, and I and my
cavalry swept the broken masses away towards Croydon,
pressed them ruthlessly through a night of slaughter on to the
pitiful surrender of the remnant at dawn by Keston Fish
Ponds.

And I entered conquered, or rescued, towns riding at the
head of my troops, with my cousins and my schoolfellows
recognizing me with surprise from the windows. And kings
and presidents, and the great of the earth, came to salute my
saving wisdom. I was simple even in victory. I made wise
and firm decisions, about morals and customs and particularly about those Civil Service Stores which had done so
much to bankrupt my father. With inveterate enemies,
monarchists, Roman Catholics, non-Aryans and the like I
was grimly just. Stern work—but my duty. . . .

In fact Adolf Hitler is nothing more than one of my thirteen year old reveries come real. A whole generation of Germans has failed to grow up.

My head teemed with such stuff in those days. But it is interesting to remark that while my mind was full of international conflicts, alliances, battleships and guns, I was blankly ignorant about money or any of the machinery of economic life. I never dreamed of making dams, opening ship canals, irrigating deserts or flying. I had no inkling of the problem of ways and means ; I knew nothing and, therefore, I cared nothing of how houses were built, commodities got and the like. I think that was because nothing existed to catch and turn my imagination in that direction. There was no literature to enhance all that. I think there is no natural bias towards blood-shed in imaginative youngsters, but the only vivid and inspiring things that history fed me with were campaigns and conquests. In Soviet Russia they tell me they have altered all that.

For many years my adult life was haunted by the fading memories of those early war fantasies. Up to 1914, I found a lively interest in playing a war game, with toy soldiers and guns, that recalled the peculiar quality and pleasure of those early reveries. It was quite an amusing model warfare and I have given its primary rules in a small book " for boys and girls of all ages " *Little Wars*. I have met men in responsible positions, L. S. Amery for example, Winston Churchill, George Trevelyan, C. F. G. Masterman, whose imaginations were manifestly built upon a similar framework and who remained puerile in their political outlook because of its persistence. I like to think I grew up out of that stage somewhen between 1916 and 1920 and began to think about war as a responsible adult should.

I recall no marked sexual or personal elements in my early reveries. Until my adolescence, sex fancies came to

me only in that dim phase between waking and sleeping. I
gave myself gladly and willingly to my warfare, but I was
shy of sex ; I resisted any urge I may have had towards
personal romancing and sensuous fantasies.

My sexual trend was, I think, less marked or more under
control when I was twelve and thirteen, than it was when I
was nine or ten. My primary curiosities had been satisfied
and strong physical urgencies were still unawakened.

My two brothers played only a very small part in this early
mental development, my Hitler phase. One was nine years
older than I and already bound apprentice to a draper ; the
other was four years my senior and presently suffered the
same fate. They were too far away from me. My elder
brother Frank was one of those mischievous boys who mix
much natural ingenuity with an aggressive sense of humour.
He was, said my mother, a " dreadful tease." He took a
lively interest in machinery and fireworks and making people
sit up. He fiddled with clocks and steam engines until some
accident ensued and with gunpowder until it exploded. He
connected all the bell wires in my Uncle Tom's hotel so that
with no great extra expenditure of labour, a visitor rang
not only his own bell, but every bell in the place. But Frank
gained nothing but unpopularity by this device. He haunted
the railway station, worshipping the engines and hoping
for something to happen. One day at Windsor he got on to
a shunting engine standing in a siding and pulled at a lever
and found great difficulty in pulling it back. By that time
he was half a mile down the line—and no longer a *persona
grata* upon the South Western Railway Company's premises.
The pursuing driver had to think first of his engine and so my
brother got clean away and survived the adventure. This
disposition to fiddle with levers made Frank a leader in his
generation. A gang followed him to see what would happen
next. He was always in trouble. But he found trouble was

less complicated if he kept me out of it. I did not share these escapades. Freddy was a more orderly youngster, but he was sent to a different private school for most of my time at Morley's.

Later on I grew up to my brothers, so to speak, and had great talks with them. With Frank, the eldest, indeed, I developed a considerable companionship in my teens and we had some great holiday walks together. But at the time of which I am writing all that had still to come.

Our home was not one of those where general ideas are discussed at table. My mother's ready orthodox formulæ were very effective in suppressing any such talk. So my mind developed almost as if I were an only child.

My childish relations with my brothers varied between vindictive resentment and clamorous aggression. I made a terrific fuss if my toys or games were touched and I displayed great vigour in acquiring their more attractive possessions. I bit and scratched my brothers and I kicked their shins, because I was a sturdy little boy who had to defend himself; but they had to go very easily with me because I was a delicate little fellow who might easily be injured and was certain to yell. On one occasion, I quite forget now what the occasion was, I threw a fork across the dinner table at Frank, and I can still remember very vividly the missile sticking in his forehead where it left three little scars for a year or so and did no other harm ; and I have an equally clear memory of a smashed window behind the head of my brother Freddy, the inrush of cold air and dismay, after I had flung a wooden horse at him. Finally they hit upon an effectual method of at once silencing me and punishing me. They would capture me in our attic and suffocate me with pillows. I couldn't cry out and I had to give in. I can still feel the stress of that suffocation. Why they did not suffocate me for good and all, I do not know. They had no way of checking what was going on under the pillow until they took it off and looked.

I got more mental stimulus from some of my school-fellows who were of an age with me. I felt the need of some companionship, some relief from reading and lonely reverie. I used to stay on at school after lesson time and go for walks or into the cricket field with the boarders, on holiday after-noons. My cricket was always poor because of my un-suspected astigmatism, but my participation was valued on account of my ready access to stumps and bats and used balls. I had a curious sort of alliance with the son of a London publican, Sidney Bowkett. We started with a great fight at the age of eight, in which we whacked at each other for the better part of an hour, and after that we conceived such a respect for each other that we decided not to fall out again. We became chums. We developed the tactics of combined attack upon bigger boys and so established a sort of joint dominance long before we were the legitimate seniors of the school.

We two talked a lot in and out of school, but what we talked about is not very clear in my mind now. There was probably a lot of bragging about what we meant to do with life. We were both very confident, because we both out-classed all the other boys we knew of our age, and that gave us an unjustified sense of distinctive ability. He was much better looking, more attractive, quicker witted and more aggressive and adventurous than I ; his verbal memory was better and his arithmetic quicker and more accurate, but he was quite out of the running with me when it came to drawing, elementary mathematics or that mass of par-tially digested reading which one may call general know-ledge. Sometimes we acted being explorers or great leaders in a sort of dramatized reverie, wherein I supplied most of the facts. Sometimes we helped each other out with long

sagas about Puss the Cat, a sort of puss-in-boots, invented
by my brother Fred and me, or Ally Sloper, the great comic
character of cockneydom at that time, or the adventures of
Bert Wells and the Boker Boy. They went to Central Africa,
to the Polar regions, down the Maelstrom and up the Him-
alayas ; they made much use of balloons and diving suits,
though aeroplanes were outside their imaginations. A great
deal of that romancing embodied our bright receptiveness
to things about us.

Bowkett's interest was more quickly aroused and livelier
than mine, but he had very little invention. He was one
of those who see quickly and vividly and say " Look,"
a sort of people to whom I owe much. Later on I was
to have a great friendship with Rebecca West who had
that quality of saying " Look " for me, in an even greater
degree. I never knew anyone else who could so light up and
colour and intensify an impression. Without such stimulus
I note things, they register themselves in my mind, but I do
not actively notice them of my own accord. Together
Bowkett and I could get no end of fun out of a casually
encountered rat or an odd butterfly, a stray beetle or an
easily climbed tree, which I alone would have ticked off at a
glance and passed. We would go through private gardens
and trespass together " for to see and to know."

I do not remember talking very much about sexual matters
with Bowkett and what we said was highly romanticized
and unimportant. We were decent and shy about all that.
Yet we knew all the indecent words in the language, we
could be astonishingly foul-mouthed in moments of exaltation and showing off ; and we were in no way ignorant. But
we were not at that time acutely interested. It is only, I
think, where small boys in the early teens are in close contact
with older youths, youths of sixteen or seventeen whose
minds are festering with desire, as they are in English

Public Schools, that they can be obsessed by gross sexuality. And then they are not pleasantly obsessed. Naturally boys in the earlier phase are instinctively afraid of intimate detail and avoid it. At any rate, whether we were typical or exceptional, we two avoided it. I have no doubt that Bowkett had his own secret incidental twilight Venusberg —I will not speculate about that—but sex did not loom large in our ordinary conversation.

At one time we organized a secret society. Unhappily we could never find a secret to put in it. But we had a tremendous initiation ceremony. Among other things the candidate had to hold his fore-finger in a gas jet for thirty seconds. Only two members ever qualified, Bert Wells and the Boker Boy. I still remember the smell of singed flesh and the hard painfulness of the scorched finger. We had a secret language of the " Iway aysay olday anman owhay areway ouyay " type. We warned a persistent sniffer in the school, by a cabalistic communication, to sniff no more or " incur the Vengeance of the Order " and we chalked up " beware " in the lavatory, in the interests of public morality. How gladly we would have adopted the swastika if we had known of it.

So much for the Hitlerite stage of my development, when I was a sentimentalist, a moralist, a patriot, a racist, a great general in dreamland, a member of a secret society, an immortal figure in history, an impulsive fork thrower and a bawling self-righteous kicker of domestic shins. I will now go on to tell as well as I can how this pasty-faced little English Nazi escaped his manifest destiny of mean and hopeless employment, and got to that broader view of life and those opportunities that have at last made this auto-biography possible.

§ 3
MRS. WELLS, HOUSEKEEPER AT UP PARK
(1880–1893)

I HAVE SAID that a cardinal stroke of good fortune was the breaking of my leg when I was seven years old. Another almost as important was the breaking of my father's leg in 1877, which made the dissolution of our home inevitable. He set himself to prune the grape-vine one Sunday morning in October, and, resolved to make a job of it and get at the highest shoots, he poised a ladder on a bench and came a cropper. We returned from church to find him lying in the yard groaning, and our neighbours, Mr. Cooper and Mr. Munday helped to carry him upstairs. He had a compound fracture of the thigh bone.

Before the year was out it was plain that my father was going to be heavily lame for the rest of his life. This was the end of any serious cricket, any bowling to gentlemen, any school jobs as " pro," or the like for him. All the supplementary income was cut off by this accident which also involved much expense in doctoring. The chronic insolvency of Atlas House became acute.

Things were more tight and distressful than ever, for two years. An increasing skimpiness distinguished our catering. Bread and cheese for supper and half a herring each with our bread and butter at breakfast and a growing tendency for potatoes to dominate the hash or stew at midday in place of meat, intimated retrenchment. Mr. Morley's bill had gone unpaid for a year. Frank who was earning £26 a year (and live in) came home for a holiday and gave my mother half a sovereign to buy me a pair of boots (at which she wept). I was growing fast and growing very thin.

And then suddenly the heavens opened and a great light shone on Mrs. Sarah Wells. Lady Fetherstonhaugh had been dead some years and Miss Bullock, to whom my mother had been maid, either inherited or was given a life tenure of Up Park, with not very plentiful means to maintain it. She took the name of Fetherstonhaugh. Presently arose trouble with the servants and about the household expenses, and Miss Fetherstonhaugh's thoughts turned affectionately towards her faithful maid, between whom and herself there had always been a correspondence of good wishes and little gifts. My mother went to Up Park on a visit. There were earnest conversations. It was still possible for her to find employment. But was it right to leave Joe alone in Atlas House ? What would become of the boys ? Frank's apprenticeship as a draper was already over and he was in a situation. Freddy's time as a draper's apprentice was up also. He could go out too. My five years of schooling were culminating in special certificates in book-keeping and hope. The young birds were leaving the nest. Father could rub along by himself for a bit. My mother became housekeeper at Up Park in 1880.

Now if this had not happened, I have no doubt I should have followed in the footsteps of Frank and Freddy and gone on living at home under my mother's care, while I went daily to some shop, some draper's shop, to which I was bound apprentice. This would have seemed so natural and necessary that I should not have resisted. I should have served my time and never had an idea of getting away from the shop until it was too late. But the dislocation that now occurred closed this easy path to frustration. I was awakened to the significance of a start in life from the outset, as my brothers had never been.

But before I tell of the series of starts in life that now began, I must say a little about my mother's achievements in housekeeping. Except that she was thoroughly honest, my mother was perhaps the worst housekeeper that was ever thought of. She had never had the slightest experience in house-keeping. She did not know how to plan work, control servants, buy stores or economize in any way. She did not know clearly what was wanted upstairs. She could not even add up her accounts with assurance and kept them for me to do for her. All this came to light. It dawned slowly upon Miss Fether-stonhaugh ; it became clearly apparent to her agent, who came up periodically from Portsmouth, Sir William King ; it was manifest from the first to the very competent, if totally illiterate, head housemaid Old Ann, who gave herself her own orders more and more. The kitchen, the laundry, the pantry, with varying kindliness, apprehended this inefficiency in the housekeeper's room. At length I think it dawned even upon my mother.

Not at first. She was frightened, perhaps, but resolute and she believed that with prayer and effort anything can be achieved. She knew at least how a housekeeper should look, and assumed a lace cap, lace apron, black silk dress and all the rest of it, and she knew how a housekeeper should drive down to the tradespeople in Petersfield and take a glass of sherry when the account was settled. She marched down to church every Sunday morning ; the whole downstairs household streamed down the Warren and Harting Hill to church ; and once a month she took the sacrament. The distressful Atlas House look vanished from her face ; she became rounder and pinker, she assumed a tranquil dignity. She contrived that we should have situations round about Up Park, and in our holidays and during phases of being out of a situation, we infested the house. My father came on a visit once or twice and at last in 1887 abandoned Atlas House altogether and settled down on an allowance she paid him, in a cottage at Nyewoods near Rogate Station about four miles away. So the servitude of Atlas House was avenged and J. W. found his level.

She held on to her position until 1893 and I think Miss Fetherstonhaugh was very forbearing that my mother held on so long. Because among other things she grew deaf. She grew deafer and deafer and she would not admit her deafness, but guessed at what was said to her and made wild shots in reply. She was deteriorating mentally. Her religious consolations were becoming more and more trite and mechanical. Miss Fetherstonhaugh was a still older woman and evidently found dealing with her more and more tiresome. They were two deaf old women at cross purposes. The rather sentimental affection between them evaporated in mutual irritation and left not a rack behind.

On several occasions Sir William was " very unpleasant " to my mother. Economy and still more economy was urged upon her and she felt that saving and pinching was beneath the dignity of a country house. The original elation of being housekeeper at Up Park had long since passed away. She began to gossip rather unwisely about some imaginary incidents in the early life of Miss Fetherstonhaugh and her sister, and it came to Miss Fetherstonhaugh's ears. I think that sealed her fate. My mother's downfall came, a month's notice and " much unkindness," in January 1893. The fallen housekeeper, with all her boxes and possessions, was driven to Petersfield station on February 16th, 1893, and the hospitable refuge of Up Park was closed to her and her needy family for ever.

A poor little stunned woman she must have been then, on Petersfield platform, a little black figure in a large black bonnet curiously suggestive now of Her Majesty Queen Victoria. I can imagine her as she wound mournfully down the Petersfield road looking back towards Harting Hill with tears in her blue eyes, not quite clear about why it had all occurred in this fashion, though no doubt God had arranged it " for some good purpose."

Why had Miss Fetherstonhaugh been so unkind?

But luckily, during my mother's thirteen years sway at Up Park and thanks largely to the reliefs and opportunity that came to me through that brief interval of good fortune in her life, I had been able to do all sorts of things. I was now twenty-six and a married man with a household and I was in a position to arrange a home for her and prevent the family bark from foundering altogether. I had become a Bachelor of Science in the University of London and a successful university crammer and I had published a textbook —a cram book to be exact—on biology as it was understood by the University examiners. I had begun to write for the papers. I had acquired a certain gravity of bearing, a considerable cascade of fair moustache and incipient side whiskers. How these changes had come about and what had happened to my brain and outlook in the process, I will now go on to tell.

§ 4

FIRST START IN LIFE—WINDSOR (SUMMER 1880)

MY FIRST START IN LIFE was rather hastily improvised. My mother had a second cousin, Thomas Pennicott, " Uncle Tom " we called him, who had always been very much in the margin of her world. I think he had admired her and been perhaps helped by her when they were young folk at Midhurst. He was one of the witnesses to her marriage. He was a fat, round-faced, clean-shaven, black-haired man, illiterate, good humoured and shrewd. He had followed the ruling tendency in my mother's family to keep inns, and he had kept the Royal Oak opposite the South Western

Railway Station at Windsor to such good effect, that he was able to buy and rebuild a riverside inn, called Surly Hall, much affected by the Eton wet-bobs, during the summer term. He built it as a gabled house and the gables were decorated with blue designs and mottoes glorifying Eton in the Latin tongue, very elegant and correct. The wet-bobs rowed up in the afternoons and choked the bar and swarmed over the lawn, vociferously consuming squashed flies and other strangely named refreshments. There was a ferry, a number of tethered punts and boats, green tables under the trees, a decaying collection of stuffed birds, ostrich eggs, wampum and sundries, in an outhouse of white plaster and tarred weather boarding, called the Museum, an eyot and a willow-bordered paddock for campers. Surly Hall has long since disappeared from the banks of the Thames, though I believe that Monkey Island, half a mile further up, still carries on.

It was Uncle Tom's excellent custom to invite Sarah's boys for the holidays ; it was not an invariable custom but it happened most years, and we had a thoroughly healthy and expansive three weeks or a month, hanging about his licensed premises in an atmosphere faintly flavoured by sawdust and beer. My brothers' times fell into the Royal Oak days, but my lot was to visit Surly Hall for the last three of my school years. There I learnt to punt, paddle and row, but the current was considered too swift for me to attempt swimming without anyone to teach me. I did not learn to swim until I was past thirty.

My uncle was a widower, but he had two grown-up daughters in their early twenties, Kate and Clara ; they shared the duties of the one or two barmaids he also employed. They all found me a very amusing temporary younger brother Kate was the serious sister, a blonde with intellectual aspirations, and she did very much to stimulate

me to draw and read. There was a complete illustrated set
of Dickens which I read in abundantly, and a lot of bound up
Family Heralds, in which I best remember a translation of
Eugene Sue's *Mysteries of Paris,* which seemed to me at the
time, the greatest romance in the world. All these young
women encouraged me to talk, because I said such unexpected things. They pretended to flirt with me, they used
me as a convenient chaperon when enterprising men customers wanted to gossip on the lawn in the twilight, and
Miss King, the chief barmaid, and Clara became competitive
for my sentimental devotion. It all helped to educate me.

One day there appeared on the lawn a delightful vision
in fluttering muslin, like one of the ladies in Botticelli's
Primavera. It was that great actress, Ellen Terry, then in her
full loveliness, who had come to Surly Hall to study a part
and presently be visited there by Mr. Henry Irving. I ceased
to consider myself engaged to Miss King forthwith ; I had
pledged myself heedlessly ; and later on I was permitted to
punt the goddess about, show her where white lilies were to
be found and get her a great bunch of wet forget-me-nots.
There was an abundance of forget-me-nots among the sedges,
and in a bend above us were smooth brown water surfaces
under great trees and a spread of yellow (and some white)
water-lilies in which dragon-flies hovered. It was far finer, I
thought, than the Keston Fish Ponds, which had hitherto
been the most beautiful place in my world, and at Keston
there was no boat with oars, paddle and boat-hook complete,
in which I could muck about for hours together.

Often when I was going for walks along the rather trite
and very pebbly footpaths about Bromley, thirty miles
away, I would let my imagination play with the idea that
round the next corner and a little further on and then a bit
more, I should find myself with a cry of delighted recognition
on the road that led immediately to Surly Hall in summer

and all its pleasantness. And how was I to suspect that Uncle Tom was losing money and his temper over the place, having borrowed to rebuild it rather too pretentiously, and that he was quarrelling with both his daughters about their lovers and that dark-eyed Clara, dreadfully bored and distressed temperamentally, was taking to drink? I knew nothing of all that, nor how greyly and dismally the Thames sluices by these riverside inns in the winter months.

But this is a mere glimpse of summer paradise on the way to my first start in life. My mother, I think I have made it clear, was within her limits a very determined little woman. Almost as unquestioning as her belief in Our Father and Our Saviour, was her belief in drapers. I know not whether that heartless trifler of her early years was a draper, but she certainly thought that to wear a black coat and tie behind a counter was the best of all possible lots attainable by man —at any rate by man at our social level. She had bound my brother Frank, resisting weakly, to Mr. Crowhurst in the Market Square, Bromley, for five years and she had bound my brother Freddy to Mr. Sparrowhawk of the Pavement for four, to obey those gentlemen as if they were parents and learn the whole art and mystery of drapery from them, and she was now making a very resolute attempt to incarcerate me and determine my future in the same fashion. It did not dawn upon her that my queer gifts of drawing and expression were of any value at all. But as poor father was to be all alone in Atlas House now—the use he made of his eight years of solitude does not concern this story—a Bromley shop was no longer a suitable soil in which to pop me in order to grow up the perfect draper. She did not like to send me away where there was no one to look after me, for she knew there are dangers that waylay the young who are not supervised. So she found a hasty solution to her problem by sending me on trial, with a view to apprenticeship, to

Messrs Rodgers and Denyer of Windsor, opposite the Castle. There my morals would be under the observation of Surly Hall. And from Messrs Rodgers and Denyer I got my first impressions of the intensely undesirable life for which she designed me. I had no idea of what I was in for. I went to my fate as I was told, unquestioningly, as my brothers had done before me.

I am told that for lots of poor boys, leaving school and going into employment about thirteen or fourteen is a very exhilarating experience. But that is because they get pay, freedom in the evening and on Sundays, and an enhanced dietary. And they are released from the irksomeness of lessons and school tasks. But I had rather liked lessons and school tasks and drapers' apprentices did not get pay. An immense fuss, entirely unjustifiable, was made about the valuable trade apprentices were going to learn, and in the past the parents of the victim, if he " lived in," usually paid a premium of forty or fifty pounds or so for his immolation. I knew that the new start meant a farewell to many childish things. I had seen both my brothers pass into servitude, and I can still remember my brother Freddy having a last game of " marble runs " with toy bricks on the tilted kitchen table, a game of which he was particularly fond, before he sub-mitted to the yoke of Mr. Sparrowhawk and began that ritual of stock-keeping, putting things away, tidying things up, bending over the counter, being attentive and measuring off, that lasted thereafter for forty-odd years of his life. He knew what he was going to, did my brother Fred ; and that game was played with sacrificial solemnity. " I enjoyed that game," said Freddy, who has always displayed a certain gentle stoicism. " It's supper time Bert. . . Let's put the things away "

Now it was my turn to put the things away, put the books away, give up drawing and painting and every sort of free delight, stop writing stories and imitations of *Punch*, give up all vain hopes and dreams, and serve an employer.

I hated this place into which I had been put from the outset, but I was far too childish, as yet, to make any real resistance to the closing in of the prison about me. But I would not, I could not, give myself satisfactorily to this strange restricted life. It was just by the luck of that incapacity that the prison rejected me.

I was set down from Uncle Pennicott's dog-cart, with a small portmanteau containing all my earthly goods, at the side door of the establishment of Messrs Rodgers and Denyer, I was taken up a narrow staircase to the men's dormitory, in which were eight or ten beds and four miserable wash-hand stands, and I was shown a dismal little sitting-room with a ground glass window opening on a blank wall, in which the apprentices and assistants might " sit " of an evening, and then I was conducted downstairs to an underground dining-room, lit by naked gas-jets and furnished with two long tables covered with American cloth, where the eating was to be done. Then I was introduced to the shop and particularly to the cash desk, where it had been arranged for the first year of my apprenticeship that I was to sit on a tall stool and receive money, give change, enter the amount on a sheet and stamp receipts. I was further instructed in a ritual of dusting and window cleaning. I was to come down at half past seven in the morning, I learnt, without fail, dust, clean windows, eat a bread-and-butter breakfast at half past eight, prepare my cash sheet and so to the routine of the day. I had to add up my cash at the end of the day, count the money in the till, make sheet and cash agree, help to wrapper-up and sweep out the shop, and so escape at half-past seven or eight to drink the delights of freedom until ten, when I had to be in. Lights out at half past ten. And this was to go on day after day—for ever it seemed to me—

a draper's apprentice

with an early closing day once a week at five, and Sunday free.

I did not rise to these demands upon me. My mind withdrew itself from my duties. I did my utmost to go on living within myself and leave my duties to do themselves. My disposition to reverie increased. I dusted abominably ; whenever I could manage it I did not dust at all. I smuggled books into my desk or did algebraic problems from my battered Todhunter's Larger Algebra ; I gave change absent-mindedly and usually I gave inaccurate change, and I entered wrong figures on the cash sheet out of sheer slovenliness.

The one bright moment during the day was when the Guards fifes and drums went past the shop and up to the Castle. These fifes and drums swirled me away campaigning again. Dispatch riders came headlong from dreamland, brooking no denial from the shopwalker. " Is General Bert Wells here ? The Prussians have landed ! "

I obeyed, I realize, all the impulses of a developing claustrophobia during that first phase of servitude. I would abandon my desk to sneak down into the warehouse, where I spent an unconscionable time seated in a convenient place of reflection, reading. Or I just stood about down there behind stacks of unpacked bales.

As the afternoon dragged on, the hour of reckoning when the cash sheet was added up drew near. It never by any chance corresponded with the money in the till. There had to be a checking of bills, a scrutiny of figures. Wrong sums had been set down. The adding had been wild work. At first the total error would be anything—more or less. After some weeks it became constantly a shortage. The booking clerk, and one of the partners who did the business correspondence and supervised things, would stay late to wrestle with the problem. They were impatient and reproachful.

I had to stay too, profoundly apathetic. Either I was giving change in excess, or in some way the money was seeping away. I did not care a rap. I had always hated money sums and long additions and now I detested them. I just wanted to get out of that shop before it was ten o'clock and time to return to the house. I did not realize the dreadful suspicions that were gathering above my head, nor the temptation my inaccuracies were offering to anyone who had access to my desk while I was at meals or otherwise absent. Nobody thought of that, unless perhaps it was the booking clerk.

Every early closing night, every Sunday, at every opportunity I had, I cut off to Surly Hall and took refuge with my cousins. I went with joy and returned with heavy feet. I did not want to talk about business there and when they asked me how I was getting on I said " Oh all right," and turned the talk to more agreeable topics. I did the long two miles from Windsor to and fro after dark for the one or two bright hours I spent there. My cousin Kate or Miss King would play the piano and sing. They would talk to me as though I was not the lowest thing on earth. There, I was still esteemed clever, and the queer things I said were applauded. My cousins, delighted at my appreciation, sang " Sweet Dreamland Faces," and " Juanita," to me and I sat on a little stool close to the piano in a state of rapt appreciation—of the music, the shaded lamp, the comfort and the ease of it.

In this world of gramphones, pianolas and the radio, it is worth noting that at the age of thirteen I had heard no music at all except an occasional brass band, the not very good music of hymn singing and organ voluntaries in Bromley Church and these piano songs at Surly Hall.

Rodgers & Dewsyers 25 High Street
Sunday July 4d 1880

My dear Mother
Here I am sitting in my bed
room after the fatigues of the day
etc   Cough slightly better & I
am tolerably comfortable
I give you an account of one days
work to give you an idea what
I have to do.
Morning
We sleep 4 together vez 3 apprentices
& 1 of the hands in one room (of
course in seperate beds)
We lay in bed until 7.30 when a
bell rings & we jump up & put
trousers slippers socks & jacket on over
nightgown & hurry down & dust
the shop etc
about 8.15 we hurry upstairs & dress
& wash for breakfast.
At 8.30 we go into a sort of vault
underground (lit by gas) & have

breakfast

After breakfast I am in the shop
& desk till dinner at 1
(we have dinner underground
as well as breakfast) & then
work till tea (which we
have in the same place) &
then go on to supper at 8 30
at which time work is done
& we may then go out
until 10·30 at which hour
the apprentices are obliged
to be in the house

I don't like the place much
food it is not at all
like home

Give love to Dad & give the
Cats my best respects

I'm rather tired of being indoors but

I went to Clewer Church & then on to Surley which I found much better than I used to think it in fact its a perfect heaven to R.D.E.

I'm rather tired so excuse further writing

yours
H G Wells

NB My washing will be 12/- a quarter

Then came a terrible inquisition at the shop. I was almost charged with pilfering. But my uncle Tom defended me stoutly. " You better not go saying *that*," said my uncle Tom, and indeed, except that there was now a continual shortage in the cash desk, there was no evidence against me. I had no expensive vices ; I had no criminal associates, I was extremely shabby and untidy ; no marked money—if they used marked money—or indeed any money except the weekly sixpence allowed me for pocket money, had ever been found upon me and my bearing was one of unconscious but convincing rectitude. Indeed I never realized fully what all the fuss was about until afterwards. Yet the fact remains that as a cash desk clerk I had leaked abominably and some-body—I suppose—had got away with the leakage.

It was plain also that I shirked all my other tasks. And while my start in life was thus already faltering, I had some sort of difference with the junior porter, which resulted in a conspicuous black eye for me. It was a gross breach of social conventions for an apprentice to fight a porter. I had great difficulty in explaining that black eye to my own satisfaction at Surly Hall. Moreover the clothes I had come to Windsor in were anything but stylish, and Mr. Denyer, the most animated of the partners, liked the look of me less and less. I wore a black velvet cap with a peak and that was all wrong. It became plain that my mother's first attempt to give me a start in life had failed. I was not starting. I was not fitted, said Messrs. Rodgers and Denyer, with perfect truth, to be a draper. I was not refined enough.

I do not recall that at Windsor from first to last I made more than the slightest effort to do what was expected of me. It was not so much a resistance as an aversion. And it is a queer thing about that place that though I stayed there a couple of months, I do not remember the name of a single individual except one assistant named Nash, who happened to be the son of a Bromley draper and wore a long moustache. But all the other figures who sat with him at the downstairs dinner table are now blank nameless figures. Did I look at them ? Did I listen to them ? Nor can I remember the positions of the counters or the arrangement of the goods in the shop. I made no friends. Mr. Denyer, young Mr. Rodgers and old Mr. Rodgers left impressions, because they were like great pantomime heads always looking for me and saying disagreeable things to me, and I was always engaged in getting away from them. They disliked me ; I think everybody in that place came to dislike me as a tiresome boring little misfit who made trouble and didn't do his share and was either missing when he was wanted or in the way when he wasn't. My self-conceit, I suppose, has blotted out all the other humiliating details from my memory. I do not even remember whether I felt any chagrin at my failure. All that seems effaced beyond recall. And yet that nocturnal tramp along the Maidenhead Road, which I took whenever I could, is real and living to me still. I could draw a map of the whole way down the hill and through Clewer. I could show where the road was wider and where it narrowed down.

Like most undernourished growing boys I was cowardly and I found the last stretch from Clewer to the inn terrifyingly dark and lonely. It was black on the moonless nights and eerie by moonlight and often it was misty from the river. My imagination peopled the dark fields on either hand with crouching and pursuing foes. Chunks of badly trimmed hedge took on formidable shapes. Sometimes I took to my heels and ran. For a week or so that road was haunted by a rumour of an escaped panther—from Lady Florence Dixie's riverside home, the Fisheries. That phantom panther waited for me patiently ; it followed me like a noiseless dog, biding its time. And one night on the other side of the hedge a sleeping horse sighed deeply, a gigantic sigh, and almost frightened me out of my wits.

But nothing of that sort kept me from going at every opportunity to Surly Hall, where there was something to touch my imagination and sustain my self-respect. I was hanging on subconsciously long before I held on consciously, to that life of books and expression and creative living from which the close exactions and economies of employment for private profit were sucking me down. And nothing that my mother and cousins could say to move and encourage me, could induce me to fix my attention on the little flimsy bits of paper with carbon duplicates, that were being slapped down at the guichet of the cash desk.

" One eleven half—two and six. Quick please."

§ 5
SECOND START IN LIFE—WOOKEY (WINTER 1880)

THE POOR little family commander-in-chief—for that she had become—in lace cap and apron in the housekeeper's room at Up Park had to deal with the situation as her lights and limitations permitted. Joe at Bromley, tied by the leg in insolvent Atlas House, had little to suggest. He had had an idea, in view of my remarkable special certificates for book-keeping that Messrs. Hoare's or Norman's, for whom he had bowled so often, ought to have welcomed me as a bank clerk, but when it became clear that Hoares and Normans were unresponsive, he made no further effort to assist my mother in her perplexities. Shelter and nourishment and justifying employment had to be found for the youngster somehow. And at this point Uncle Williams came in with what seemed a hopeful suggestion. He was going to be head of a little national school. I might become a pupil teacher under him.

In those days a great deal of the teaching, such as it was, in elementary schools was done by children scarcely older than the pupils. Instead of leaving school for work they became " P.T's." and, after four years, competent to enter a training college for a year or two, before they went on grant earning for the rest of their lives. If an elementary teacher in those days became anything more than a " trained " drudge, it was due to his or her own exertions. My Uncle Williams, hearing of my mother's difficulties, held out hopes that my College of Preceptors achievements might be used to shorten my pupil teacher stage and get me accepted as something which he called an " improver."

So I was packed off from Windsor to Wookey in Somerset, where my Uncle Williams was installed in the school house— but precariously. For he was never really qualified to teach in an English school. He had taught as a young man in Jamaica with qualifications that did not satisfy the Board of Education requirements. There had been a certain lack of explicitness in his application for the post and when that came to light, he had to get out of Wookey again. And the same lack of explicitness extinguished the scholastic career he proposed for me in the course of two or three months.

But it gave me the idea that there was something to be done in teaching and that it was pleasanter to stand in front of a class and distribute knowledge and punishments, than sit at a desk or hover behind a counter, at the beck and call of a hierarchy of seniors.

My Uncle Williams was not my uncle at all ; he had married the sister of that " Uncle Tom Pennicott," my mother's cousin who had rebuilt Surly Hall ; he had been a teacher in the West Indies, and he was a bright and adventurous rather than a truthful and trustworthy man.

a pupil teacher

He had invented and patented an improved desk for schools, with sunken inkpots that could not upset and could be protected by rotating covers, and he had left teaching to become the active partner of a firm of manufacturers of school appliances, including his desks, at Clewer near Windsor. A sanguine streak in his nature kept his expenses well above his income, and he presently sank to the position of clerk and manager in his own factory, and finally lost even that. Hence his attempt to establish himself in the school house at Wookey by means of inaccuracies.

As I knew him, he was an active centrally bald yellow-faced man with iron grey whiskers, a sharp nose, a chin like the toe of a hygienic slipper, and glasses. Extraordinary quantities of hair grew out of his ears. He had lost one arm, and instead he had a stump in which a hook was screwed, for which a dinner fork could be substituted. He held his food down vindictively and cut it up with a knife, and then put the knife down and ate snappily with another fork in the free hand. He instructed me in the arts and practices of his scholastic process and together, sometimes with a curtain to divide the children between us and sometimes in plenary session, we constituted the school staff. I found teaching heavy going but far more interesting than work in a cash desk. Discipline was difficult to maintain ; some of the boys were as big as myself and sturdier, and my cockney accent jarred on Somerset ears. But it had the prestige of being English. Except for occasional hints from Uncle Williams, I had to find out how and what to teach. I taught them dates and geographical lists and sums and tables of weights and measures and reading, as well as I could. I fought my class, hit them about viciously and had altogether a lot of trouble with them. I exacted a full performance of the penalties I imposed and on one occasion pursued a defaulter headlong to his home, only to be routed ignominiously by his indignant mother and chased by her and a gathering rabble of variously sized boys back to the school house.

My Uncle Williams said I was wanting in tact.

My Uncle Williams was a man of derisive conversation with a great contempt for religion and the clergy. His table talk was unrestrained. He talked to me frankly and as if I were an adult ; I had never in all my life before had that sort of talk with any grown-up person. It braced me up. He could talk very entertainingly about the church and its faith and about the West Indies and the world as he had seen it. He gave me a new angle from which to regard the universe ; I had not hitherto considered that it might be an essentially absurd affair, good only to laugh at. That seemed in many ways a releasing method of approach. It was a fresh, bright way of counter-attacking the dull imperatives of life about me, and taking the implacable quality out of them.

A daughter kept home for him. His wife had remained in Clewer, where two elder daughters had jobs as teachers. My cousin was only three or four years older than I and she was in a phase of great enterprise and curiosity about the business of sex. She pressed her investigations upon me. The urge to experiment was upon her. We went for walks together over the hills in our margin of time ; we went one Saturday into Wells and I saw my first cathedral ; and generally speaking our talk was instructive rather than what was then considered edifying. This phase in my education was interrupted before it was completed. I took my first lessons in sexual practice with a certain aversion. My mind was prepared with a different formula. The real thing as it was thus presented to me, seemed hot, uncomfortable, shamefaced stuff. But perhaps these conversations at Wookey did something to bring me back from an impracticable isolating dreamland.

the influence of 'Uncle' William

I was growing up now. I was past fourteen ; I was getting
sturdier in my body and less disposed to escape from reality
to reverie. The youngster who was returned rather apolo-
getically by Uncle Williams to my mother, may have looked
very much like the youngster who went in by the side door
of Rodgers and Denyer to try and be a draper, but in fact he
was something far more alert and solid. He had heard one or
two things which, hitherto, he had avoided facing, spoken of
very plainly and directly. And he had been interested by a
job. He had really tried to do something instead of merely
submitting to a boring routine in a business machine he did
not understand. He had come up against material fact with
a new nearness and vividness, and he had learnt that
laughter was perhaps a better way of dealing with reality
than were the evasions of reverie. He certainly owes a great
deal more to this second start in life than to the first. A facetious scepticism which later on became his favourite pose
may owe a great deal to Uncle Williams.

The collapse of the Wookey situation was so swift and
unexpected that it took me and my mother by surprise.
There was hasty letter-writing again. I do not know the
particulars. I was to go from Wookey to Surly Hall, either to
wait there until she could speak to Miss Fetherstonhaugh
about me, or because the entire journey from Wookey to
Harting was considered too much for me. Even the journey
to Windsor was a complicated one. My Uncle Williams
packed me off with instructions to catch a certain train, the
last possible train, at Maidenhead. There was a kink in the
journey between two railway systems. If I missed the
connexion I was to stay the night in a Temperance Hotel and
then go on the next morning. But the first train available on
the next day departed towards midday. (I may have got up
late and missed an earlier train ;—I cannot remember.) I
went for a walk in Maidenhead and came upon a marvellous

shop where one could be photographed and get a dozen
tintypes for a shilling or a shilling and sixpence. I had never
heard of such a thing and the temptation was irresistible.
Money had been given me to cover my bill at the Temperance Hotel and my fare on to Windsor, and I felt rich
beyond limit. But after the tintypes and a Bath bun and the
Temperance Hotel bill, I found myself at the booking-office
at half-past eleven with a dozen engaging portraits of myself
in my pocket but short of the fare demanded. I had to go
round by Slough and change trains ; it was a longer journey
than I had imagined. I emerged from the station, holding my
little portmanteau which had suddenly become very heavy
in my hand. " Please can you tell me the way to Windsor ? "
I asked.

I suppose the distance I covered was a little over four
miles, because Surly Hall was on the road between Windsor
and Maidenhead. But I still remember that walk as one of
the longest in the world. When I had gone fifty yards from
Maidenhead station I changed my portmanteau from one
hand to the other. Before I had gone a quarter of a mile I put
it down and reflected. My reflections were unfruitful. It is
muscle and not mind that must carry portmanteaus. Before
I had done a mile I was trying to carry that leaden valise on
my head for a change. It had to be carried somehow to
Surly Hall. I arrived after twilight with arms that felt like
limp strings of pain, extremely exhausted and sorry for
myself.

And when I got to Surly Hall, I found Surly Hall had
changed. It had become cheerless and almost sinister.

The shadow of approaching tragedy hung over it. Dreadful
things had happened already. In the interval since my departure from Windsor, my uncle had had a violent quarrel
with his daughter Clara about her lover, there had been
bitter recriminations and she had gone off to London. How

she lived in London nobody knew. Miss King, the barmaid, had gone. Cousin Kate was in a state of dismay and disapproval and threatening to marry a man she had been engaged to for some time and " get away from it all." The river was a swift flood of leaden silver ; there were no passing boats to pull up, the hotel was empty, the bar and taproom desolate and the lawn with its green tables sodden and littered with dead leaves. My uncle was greatly embittered at the swift darkening of life about him. I think too he was intensely worried financially. He had mortgaged himself deeply in his rebuilding of the place. He was distressed by the undutifulness of his daughters. He would sit in the taproom talking to a serious potman who had found religion. . . .

Music and song, moonlight on the lawn, forget-me-nots in the sedges and white water-lilies above the brown smooth water ; all had become incredible. My education was going on apace. . . .

I did not see Surly Hall again for many years after that visit. But cousin Kate married and went away and cousin Clara followed her destinies in London and came back at last after four years, a broken young woman. Her lover had abandoned her long ago. Uncle Tom, I fear, received her unkindly. All light and hope had gone out of life for her and late one night she flitted in her nightgown down the lawn from a sleepless bed to the river and drowned herself in a deep hole under a pollard willow. The old man died soon after. My cousin Kate died. The place was annexed to an adjacent property and ultimately its license was extinguished. The obliteration of Surly Hall was complete. I do not know of anything that survives of it now except my memories, a passing mention in some Old Etonian's Reminiscences and a fading photograph or so.

§6
INTERLUDE AT UP PARK (1880–1881)

I AM TRYING to recover the quality of those years between twelve and sixteen or seventeen with as many particulars as I can recall, because I think that the forces and
influences in operation then were of primary importance in
determining all my subsequent reactions. I am impressed as
I look over such documents and records as I can find to
revive these days, by the extraordinarily rapid growth of my
character and resolution during my fourteenth and fifteenth
years. I suppose this hardening and toughening and clearing
up of the will was the natural concomitant of puberty.
I was perhaps intellectually forward but morally I think I
followed an average curve.

But if I did, then I am convinced that this system of ter-
minating the education of an ordinary citizen before the age
of fourteen is a wrong one. I do not think that for the new
civilization ahead of us education will ever terminate, but
certainly thirteen or fourteen is premature for economic
citizenship. That age is not a natural turning point in the
development of either male or female—at any rate so far as
north European races are concerned. The transfer from
protected tutelage to quasi responsible employment is
premature. At earliest it should not occur until a year or so
later when the youngster has become able and willing to
take a directive interest in his or her own future. I was relatively precocious, yet clearly thirteen–fourteen was too soon
for me. And even if whole-time education is to be prolonged
for some years more—as may presently be the case all over
the world for everyone—there should still be a break,
not according to the present practice in England about
twelve or thirteen when a boy goes from a preparatory to a

public school, but about fifteen or sixteen. Then is the best time for a change over from instruction and guidance to an intelligent co-operation between teacher and disciple.

Both my brothers and myself, like nearly every boy in the British lower and lower middle classes of that time, were " put to a trade " and bound, before we could exercise any choice in the matter. In relation to any such issue we were children still. If this had been the case only with my brothers and myself, then this aspect of my story would hardly have been worth discussing. It would have been an individual misfortune. It would have been merely the story of three tadpoles who had chanced to be taken out of the water before their legs and lungs would act properly. But this transfer at the wrong age was and still is the common experience. It has therefore had far-reaching social consequences. Because of this premature termination of the primary educational phase in the closing years of the last century, a great proportion, perhaps a majority, of British men and women were (and are) employed upon their tasks against their will or at least without their willing assent. The nation almost as a whole is taken out of its tadpole stage too soon. Just as the civilizations of the ancients was based upon the labour of serfs and slaves, so this industrial civilization in which we are still living is based on the toil of masses of people mentally and morally arrested before fourteen. The bulk of the population is neither uneducated and quasi-animal as its servile predecessor was, nor educated as the whole mass should be in a soundly conceived mechanized civilization. It is incompletely metamorphosed; neither one thing nor the other.

One miserable result, though not by any means the only one, is this: that industrial life goes on in a spirit of boredom, with a demand therefore for shorter hours and higher wages as the main expression of the Labour mentality evoked under these conditions. An extraordinary indifference to the amount and quality of the product or service rendered is also manifest. Half Europe still watches the clock just as I watched the clock in Rodgers and Denyer's establishment, and by an inner necessity it tries in every possible way to scamp whatever tiresome task has to be done. Its labour is spiritless labour because it is essentially uninterested labour.

But our already highly mechanized and organized world community, if it is to develop further and sustain an efficient common life requires before everything else interested and participating workers. In this respect as in so many others it has got off from the mark too soon and started at too low a level.

It has taken three quarters of a century for this fact to dawn upon us. Responsible people have still to realize as a class that a happy, stably progressive human community can be made possible only if—among several other necessary primary conditions—the new generation is held back under education until it is at least sixteen years old, before its life rôles are determined and conscious specialized economic citizenship begins. Although, as I have said, relatively precocious I was not fit to have a decisive voice in my own destiny until I was sixteen. For want of a breathing time at this crucial phase, my eldest brother became a complete failure in life—for he did not stick to the shop—and my brother Fred wasted upon haberdashery a fine conscientiousness and an exceptional gift for sensitive meticulous artistic work. And I escaped from becoming a wretched employee in an entirely uncongenial trade not by any merit of my own but by sheer luck.

Against a background of such generalizations my little mother, you see, becomes a symbol of the blind and groping parental solicitude of that age, a solicitude which enslaved and hampered where it sought to aid and establish ; and my individual story merges into the story of the handicapped intelligence of our species, blundering heavily towards the realization and handling of vast changes and still vaster dangers and opportunities. My mother becomes a million mothers and my brothers a countless brotherhood. My life is a sample life and not an exceptional one ; its distinctive merit has been its expressiveness ; its living interest lies in that.

For some weeks after the retreat from Wookey, my mother did not know what to do with me. She asked all sorts of people for information and no doubt she took her troubles to her Heavenly Father, who remained, as ever, speechlessly enigmatical. She spoke to Miss Fetherstonhaugh about me and I was allowed to take refuge, from the gathering gloom of Surly Hall, at Up Park. And there a great snowstorm snowed me up for nearly a fortnight and I produced a daily newspaper of a facetious character, *The Up Park Alarmist* —on what was properly kitchen paper—and gave a shadow play to the maids and others, in a miniature theatre I made in the housekeeper's room.

Now it is one of my firmest convictions that modern civilization was begotten and nursed in the households of the prosperous, relatively independent people, the minor nobility, the gentry, and the larger bourgeoisie, which became visibly important in the landscape of the sixteenth century, introducing a new architectural element in the towns, and spreading as country houses and chateaux and villas over the continually more orderly countryside. Within these households, behind their screen of deer park and park wall and sheltered service, men could talk, think and write at their leisure. They were free from inspection and immediate imperatives. They, at least, could go on after thirteen thinking and doing as they pleased. They created the public schools, revived the waning universities, went on the Grand Tour to

see and learn. They could be interested in public affairs
without being consumed by them. The management of their
estates kept them in touch with reality without making
exhaustive demands on their time. Many, no doubt, degener-
ated into a life of easy dignity or gentlemanly vice, but quite
a sufficient number remained curious and interested to
make, foster and protect the accumulating science and
literature of the seventeenth and eighteenth centuries. Their
large rooms, their libraries, their collections of pictures and
" curios " retained into the nineteenth century an atmosphere of unhurried liberal enquiry, of serene and determined
insubordination and personal dignity, of established æsthetic
and intellectual standards. Out of such houses came the
Royal Society, the *Century of Inventions,* the first museums and
laboratories and picture galleries, gentle manners, good
writing, and nearly all that is worth while in our civilization
to-day. Their culture, like the culture of the ancient world,
rested on a toiling class. Nobody bothered very much about
that, but it has been far more through the curiosity and
enterprise and free deliberate thinking of these independent
gentlemen than through any other influences, that modern
machinery and economic organization have developed so
as to abolish at last the harsh necessity for any toiling class
whatever. It is the country house that has opened the way
to human equality, not in the form of a democracy of insurgent proletarians, but as a world of universal gentlefolk
no longer in need of a servile substratum. It was the experimental cellule of the coming Modern State.

The new creative forces have long since overflowed, these
first nests in which they were hatched and for the most part
the European country houses and chateaux that were so alive
and germinal, mentally, in the seventeenth and eighteenth
centuries, stand now mere empty shells, resorts for week-end
gatherings and shooting parties, but no longer real dwelling

The influence of the 'country house
— his view + his experience

places, gracefully and hospitably in decay. Yet there still
lingers something of that former importance and largeness
in outlook, on their walls and hangings and furnishings, if
not in their attenuated social life. For me at any rate the
house at Up Park was alive and potent. The place had a
great effect upon me ; it retained a vitality that altogether
overshadowed the insignificant ebbing trickle of upstairs
life, the two elderly ladies in the parlour following their
shrunken routines, by no means content with the bothered
little housekeeper in the white panelled room below.

During this visit and subsequent visits, when the weather
did not permit of my wandering in the park, I rummaged
about in an attic next to my bedroom which was full of odd
discarded things. I found several great volumes of engrav-
ings of the Vatican paintings of Raphael and Michael
Angelo. I pondered immensely over the mighty loveliness of
these saints and sibyls and gods and goddesses. And there
was a box, at first quite mysterious, full of brass objects that
clearly might be screwed together. I screwed them together,
by the method of trial and error, and presently found a
Gregorian telescope on a tripod in my hands. I carried off
the wonder to my bedroom. By daylight it showed everything
upside down, I found, but that did not matter—except for
the difficulty of locating objects—when I turned it to
the sky. I was discovered by my mother in the small
hours, my bedroom window wide open, inspecting the
craters of the moon. She had heard me open the window.
She said I should catch my death of cold. But at the time
that seemed a minor consideration.

Sir Harry Fetherstonhaugh, like many of his class and time,
had been a free-thinker, and the rooms downstairs abounded
in bold and enlightening books. I was allowed to borrow
volumes and carry them off to my room. Then or later, I
cannot now recall when, I improved my halting French

with Voltaire's lucid prose, I read such books as *Vathek* and *Rasselas*, I nibbled at Tom Paine, I devoured an unexpurgated *Gulliver's Travels* and I found Plato's *Republic*. That last was a very releasing book indeed for my mind. I had learnt the trick of mocking at law and custom from Uncle Williams and, if anything, I had improved upon it and added caricature to quaint words, but here was something to carry me beyond mockery. Here was the amazing and heartening suggestion that the whole fabric of law, custom and worship, which seemed so invincibly established, might be cast into the melting pot and made anew.

§ 7

THIRD START IN LIFE—MIDHURST (1881)

I DO NOT KNOW how my mother hit upon the idea of making me a pharmaceutical chemist. But that was the next career towards which I (and my small portmanteau) were now directed. I spent only about a month amidst the neat gilt-inscribed drawers and bottles of Mr. Cowap at Midhurst, rolled a few score antibilious and rhubarb pills, broke a dozen soda-water siphons during a friendly broom fight with the errand boy, learnt to sell patent medicines, dusted the coloured water bottles, the bust of Hahnemann (indicating homœopathic remedies) and the white horse (veterinary preparations), and I do not think I need here devote very much space to him and his amusing cheerful wife, seeing that I have already drawn largely upon this shop, and my experiences in it, in describing aunt and uncle Ponderevo in *Tono Bungay*. Cowap, like uncle Ponderevo, really did produce a heartening Cough Linctus, though he never soared to my hero's feat of commercial expansion.

But this time I gave satisfaction, and it was upon my initiative and not upon that of my prospective employer that pharmaceutical chemistry was abandoned as my calling in life. I enquired into the cost of qualification as an assistant and dispenser ; the details have long since escaped me ; but I came to the conclusion that the fees and amount of study required, would be quite beyond my mother's limited resources. I pointed this out to her and she saw reason in the figures I gave her.

I was reluctant to abandon this start because I really liked the bright little shop with its drawers full of squills and senna pods, flowers of sulphur, charcoal and suchlike curious things, and I had taken to Midhurst from the outset. It had been the home of my grandparents, and that gave me a sense of belonging there. It was a real place in my mind and not a morbid sprawl of population like Bromley. Its shops and school and post office and church were grouped in rational comprehensible relations; it had a beginning, a middle and an end. I know no country to compare with West Sussex except the Cotswolds. It had its own colour, a pleasant colour of sunlit sandstone and ironstone and a warm flavour of open country because of the parks and commons and pine woods about it. Midhurst was within three hours sturdy walking from Up Park. And I had recovered my self res-pect there very rapidly.

One manifest deficiency in my schooling came to light at the mere suggestion that I should be a chemist. I knew no Latin and much of the dignity of the qualified druggist at that time depended upon a smattering of that tongue. He had to read and to copy and understand prescriptions. Accord-ingly it was arranged that I should go to the Headmaster of the local Grammar School and have lessons in Latin. I had, I suppose, four or five hours of it before the project of my ap-prenticeship was abandoned, but in that time I astonished my instructor, accustomed to working against the resistances of Sussex tradesmen's and farmer's sons and the like, by rushing through the greater part of Smith's *Principia* Part I and covering more ground than he had been accustomed to get over with his boys in a year or more. I found this fine structural language congenial just as I had found Euclid's *Elements* congenial. It was a new way of saying things. It was like something I had been waiting for. It braced up my use of English immediately.

The Midhurst Grammar School was an old foundation which had fallen into decay and had been closed in 1859— after a fire which had destroyed the school house. It had been revived by the Endowed Schools Commissioners and the school had been re-opened in 1880, less than a year before my essay in pharmacy. Mr. Horace Byatt, M.A., the new headmaster, was a not very brilliant graduate of Dublin University, an animated and energetic teacher resolved to make a success of his first headmastership. He was a dark, semi-clerical man, plumply active, with bushy hair, side whiskers, a cleft chin, and a valiant rotund voice, and he was quartered with his wife and three small children in a comfortable old house near the South Pond, until the commissioners could rebuild the school house, which was still at that time a weedy heap of ruins.

I know nothing of Byatt's previous history and training, but I doubt if his Latin went very far and I stumped him completely when, some years later, I took some Greek quotation from Paley's *Evidences* to him for elucidation. He had evidently had a considerable experience in teaching elementary science, geometrical drawing and the like, and his rôle at Midhurst was to build up a secondary school on comparatively modern lines. At that time the British Education Department was spreading a system of evening class instruction from which the organized science schools of the next decade were developed. The classes ran through the winter and were examined in May and the teacher received pay according to his results, a pound or two pounds or four pounds for every pass, according to its class and grade. Byatt, who was a university M.A., was considered qualified to conduct classes and earn grants in any of the thirty odd subjects scheduled by the Department, and in addition to his day-time teaching, he was already running evening classes in freehand, perspective and geometrical drawing and in electricity and magnetism, to supplement his fundamental stipend. His interest in the classics was therefore relatively less keen. Latin in such schools as his had ceased to be a language ; there was no real thought of either reading it or writing it, much less of speaking it ; it was an exercise directed to the passing of various qualifying examinations.

Now Cowap had counted on my premium as an apprentice, and when he realized that I did not intend to go on with that, he betrayed considerable vexation and became urgent to clear me out to make way for a more profitable aspirant. My mother had nowhere for me to go and she arranged to put me as a boarder with the Grammar School headmaster until she could organize a fourth start in life for me. I became the first boarder of the renascent school. I spent about two months there, returning by special request to sit for the May examinations in all the subjects of Byatt's evening classes and so earn grants for him.

Now here again was a new phase in my very jumbled education, and one that I still look back upon with pleasure. I liked Byatt, and he formed an encouragingly high opinion of my grit and capacity. The amount of mental benefit I derived from those few weeks as his pupil, cannot be measured by the work actually done ; the stimulus I got was far more important. I went on with Latin but now at a reduced speed, for Byatt preferred to direct me rather towards grant-earning subjects and put textbooks in such subjects as physiology and physiography into my hands, realizing that I was capable of learning very rapidly by reading alone without any nursing in class. I could understand a book of my own accord and write, and if necessary illustrate, a good answer to a question, and that was something beyond the general capacity of his Midhurst material. I think it was extraordinary good fortune for me, that I had this drilling in writing things down at this time. It gave my reading precision and accustomed me to marshal my knowledge in an orderly fashion. There are many valid objections to a system of education controlled by written examinations ; it may tend very easily towards a ready superficiality ; but I am convinced that it has at any rate the great merit of imposing method and order in learning. It prevents the formation of those great cavities of vagueness, those preferential obsessions, those disproportions between detail and generalization which are characteristic of gifted people who have never been " examinees."

This broadening out, bucking up and confirmation of my mind by the flood of new experiences at Up Park and Midhurst, were immensely important in my development. I dwell upon this phase because when I look back upon 1880 and early 1881 it seems to me as though these above all others were the years in which the immediate realities about me began to join on in a rational way to that varied world with which books had acquainted me. That larger world came slowly within the reach of my practical imagination. Hitherto it had been rather a dreamland and legend than anything conceivably tangible and attainable. It had been no more credible to me than my mother's imaginative escape to Our Father, Our Saviour, celestial music and the blessedness of heaven. One let one's mind stray away to such things when the rigid uncomfortable imperatives of employment, the inescapable insufficiency and shabbiness of the daily round became insupportable. But one had no belief in any possible escape in fact, and sooner or later the mind had to return to its needy habitation and its fated limitations. Temporary escape and alleviation by reverie were the easier substitutes for positive effort to get out of the imprisoning conditions. But now I was abandoning reverie and working up towards a conscious fight for the positive enlargement of my life.

I wish I could set down with certainty all the main facts in this phase of my adolescence. Then I should be able to separate the accidental elements, the element of individual luck that is to say, from the normal developmental phases. I realize that I was almost beyond comparison a more solid, pugnacious, wary and alert individual in 1881 than I was in 1879, and as I have already suggested that a large factor in this may have been the nervous and chemical changes that are associated with puberty. So far my experience was the general experience. Puberty is certainly a change in much more than the sexual life. The challenge to authority, the release of initiative, the access of courage are at least equally important. But added to this normal invigoration was the escape from the meagre feeding and depressingly shabby and unlit conditions of Atlas House. There I had a great advantage over my two brothers and I think a quite unusual push forward. I was living in those crucial years under healthier conditions ; I was undergoing stimulating changes of environment, and, what is no small matter, eating a more varied and better dietary. Yet even when these more fortunate physical circumstances have been allowed for, there remains over and above them, the influence upon my perplexed and resentful mind for the first time, at its most receptive age, of a sudden irruption of new ideas, ideas of scientific precision and confirmation and ideas of leisure,

culture and social margin. If I had been the son of an
instructive-minded astronomer and had been bothered with
early lessons about the stars when I wanted to play with
mud pies, I might not have made my first contact with the
starry heavens in a state of exaltation, nor pursued Jupiter
with the help of *Whitaker's Almanack* until with my own
eyes, I saw him and his moons quivering in the field of my
telescope, as though I were Galileo come back to earth. Nor
should I have realized with anything like the same excitement, had geology been made easy for me in my childhood,
that when I stood on the brow of Telegraph Hill and looked
across the weald to the North Downs I was standing on the
escarpment of a denuded anticlinal, and that this stuff of the
pale hills under my feet had once been slime at the bottom
of a vanished Cretaceous sea. And again this definite estate
of Up Park and the sharply marked out farms, villages and
towns of the countryside below, caught me just in the proper
phase to awaken a sense of social relationship and history
that might never have been roused if I had remained in the
catastrophic multitudinousness of suburban development.

The stuff accumulated by the discursive reading of my
earlier years, fell rapidly into place in the wider clearer
vision of my universe that was coming into being before
my eyes. Science in those days insisted, if anything, over-
much upon the reign of law. The march of progress was
still being made with absolute assurance, and my emancipation was unqualified. It must be hard for intelligent people
nowadays to realize all that a shabby boy of fifteen could
feel as the last rack of a peevish son-crucifying Deity dissolved
away into blue sky, and as the implacable social barriers,
as they had seemed, set to keep him in that path unto which
it had pleased that God to call him, weakened down to temporary fences he could see over and presently perhaps hope
to climb over or push aside.

But before one breaks or climbs fences one must look over them or through them for a time, and just then I was merely in the stage of peeping with a wild surmise and daring nothing more. I was still a good ten years from the reality of personal freedom.

CHAPTER THE FOURTH

EARLY ADOLESCENCE

§ 1
FOURTH START IN LIFE—
SOUTHSEA (1881-1883)

WHILE I WAS MAKING my first systematic acquaintance
with modern science at the Midhurst Grammar School,
my mother was busy finding yet another start in life for me.
She had consulted Sir William King, who was Miss Fetherstonhaugh's Agent and an important man in Portsmouth
affairs, and he had recommended her to Mr. Edwin Hyde,
the proprietor of the Southsea Drapery Emporium in Kings
Road, Southsea. I learnt at Easter that I was destined once
again to try the difficult rôle of a draper, this time under
the tutelage of this Mr. Hyde. I was still unprepared with
any alternative scheme. I expressed dissent, but my mother
wept and entreated. I promised to be a good boy and try.

But this time I went recalcitrant, not indeed against my
mother, whose simplicity and difficulties I was beginning to
understand, but against a scheme of things which marched
me off before I was fifteen to what was plainly a dreary and
hopeless life, while other boys, no better in quality than
myself, were enjoying all the advantages—I thought they
were stupendous advantages in those days—of the public
school and university. I conveyed my small portmanteau
to Southsea with a sinking heart. I was left upstairs in the
dormitory for a time until someone could come to show me

round, and I leant upon the window-sill and looked out upon the narrow side street upon which the window gave, with no illusion about what had happened to me. I can still feel the unhappiness and dismay of that moment.

Retail trade, I thought, had captured me for good. I had now to learn to work and to work faithfully for the profit and satisfaction of my prospective employers to the end of my days. I had been at large for a year and found no other way of living. The last chance had gone. At that moment I could not discover in my mind or in my world, as represented by the narrow side street into which I was looking, the little corner pub or the blind alley below me or the strip of sky overhead, the faintest intimation of any further escape.

I turned round from this restricted outer world to survey my dormitory in much the same mood as a condemned prisoner surveying the fittings of the cell he is to occupy for his allotted term. . . .

It is an open question in my mind whether this dismay at the outset, is the common experience of modern youth of the less fortunate classes, or whether because of the enlightenment of my previous starts I happened to see further and more clearly than most of my fellows. A considerable number, I think, get that caught feeling rather later. My brother Frank, after fifteen years of being good, said he could endure the life no longer and broke away as I shall tell in due course. My brother Fred held to the religion of submission longer ; he was the good boy of the three of us, and he did subdue himself to the necessary routines for the best part of his life.

What percentage of those who are bound apprentices to drapers, go on to comparative success I do not know, nor what their vital statistics are, but it is beyond all question a meagre distressful life they lead and exceptionally devoid of hope. Caradoc Evans, like myself, has been a draper, and the *supportive evidence*

scene he draws of a draper's existence in the meaner shops of London in *Nothing to Pay* is, I know, true in all substantial particulars. He tells of the perpetual nagging and mutual irritation, the petty " spiffs " and fines, the intrigues and toadyism, the long tedious hours, the wretched dormitories, the insufficient " economized " food, the sudden dismissals, the dreadful interludes of unemployment with clothing growing shabby and money leaking away. There was no dole behind the " swapped " shop assistant in those days. You swam for as long as you could and then, if you could not scramble into some sort of shop, down you went to absolute destitution, the streets and beggary. Hyde was an exceptionally good employer ; the place, from an assistant's point of view, was infinitely superior to my previous " crib " at Rodgers and Denyer's, yet still I recall those two years of incarceration as the most unhappy hopeless period of my life. I was indentured for four years, but after nearly two years of it I took matters into my own hands. I rebelled and declared that come what might I would not go on being a draper.

Yet I never got to the worst experiences of an assistant's life. I never knew how it felt to be out of a crib or tasted the full sordidness of the Caradoc Evans type of shop. I learnt about such matters chiefly from my brothers and the assistants at Hyde's. What overwhelmed me immediately was the incessancy of this employment and its lack of compelling interest. I do not know how the modern state as it develops will solve the problem of service in the distributing trades, but I am convinced it will have to be made an employment for short periods, short hours or alternative weeks and months with relays of workers, and that such special education as may be provided for it will link up the mind of the employee with the methods and novelties of manufacture on the one hand and the ultimate use of the

vision of a job

goods sold on the other. Then the assistant would go behind the counter or into the stockroom with a sense of function instead of a sense of routine, there would be a minimum of shirking, resentment and lassitude, and he would do his job as a brisk terminable job worth doing and would find it the more interesting the better it was done. Nothing of that sort happened in my case.

It is remarkable how alien and incomprehensible the stuff I had to handle was to me. I was put first into the Manchester department, and there I found fixtures of wrappered blocks labelled incomprehensibly Hard Book or Turkey Twill or the like, rolls of grey and black silesia, flannels with a variety of names, a perplexing range of longcloths and calicoes, endless packages of diaper table-cloths, serviettes, and so forth, and rolls of crash, house cloth, ticking and the like. All that stuff had no origin and no purpose for me, except that it seemed to have been created to make my life burthensome. There were also in this Manchester department cotton dress materials, prints, ginghams and sateens, cretonne and kindred fabrics for covering furniture ; stuffs that were rather more understandable but equally irksome to handle. I had to straighten all this stock and pack it up after it had been shown and put it back into the proper fixtures ; I had to measure and refold it when the manufacturers delivered it, to block it or to roll it in rolls. This blocking, rolling and folding was skilled work that needed a watchful effort I gave grudgingly, and I never learnt to do it swiftly and neatly. You cannot imagine how maliciously a folded piece of sateen can get askew, how difficult it is to roll huckaback, how unruly a fat blanket is to pack up and how heavy and unwieldy pieces of cretonne can be when you have to carry a score or so of them up narrow folding steps and adjust them neatly on a rising pile. My department also included lace curtains. These had to be unfolded and held up by the junior apprentice while the salesman discoursed to the customer. As the heap of tumbled curtains grew and the customer still wanted to see something a little different, storms of hatred and revolutionary fervour went on behind the apathetic mask of the junior apprentice, doomed before closing time to refold them all and put them away.

Stock keeping, showing goods and clearing up, were the middle duties of the day. We apprentices were roused from our beds at seven, peremptorily, by one of the assistants ; he swept hortative through the dormitory and on his return journey pulled the bedclothes off anyone still in bed. We flung on old suits, tucking our nightgowns into our trousers, and were down in the shop in a quarter of an hour, to clean windows, unwrapper goods and fixtures, dust generally, before eight. At eight we raced upstairs to get first go at the wash basins, dressed for the day and at half-past eight partook of a bread and butter breakfast before descending again. Then came window dressing and dressing out the shop. I had to fetch goods for the window dresser and arrange patterns or pieces of fabric on the brass line above the counter. Every day or so the costume window had to be rearranged and I had to go in the costume room and fetch those headless effigies on which costumes are displayed and carry them the length of the shop, to the window dresser, avoiding gas brackets, chairs and my fellow creatures *en route*. Then I had to see to the replenishing of the pin bowls and the smoothing out and stringing up of paper for small parcels. The tediums of the day were broken for an hour or so while I went out to various other shops in Southsea, Portsmouth and Landport " matching " for the workroom, getting lengths of ribbon and material that were needed and could not be supplied out of stock, taking money from the cash desk to the bank or getting bags of small change. I loitered as much as I dared on these blessed errands, but by half-past eleven or twelve at latest, the shop swallowed me up again and there was no more relief until after closing time, which came at seven or eight according to the season. I had to stand by ready for any helpful job. There were a hundred small fussy things to do, straightening up, putting away, fetching and carrying. It was not excessively laborious but it was indescribably tedious. If there was nothing else to do I had to stand to attention at the counter, as though ready for a customer, though at first I was not competent to serve. The length of those days at Southsea were enormous until closing time ; then the last hour fell swiftly past me to " lights out " at half-past ten.

Half an hour before closing time we began to put away for the last time and " wrapper up," provided no customer lingered in the department. And as soon as the doors were shut and the last customer gone, the assistants departed and we junior apprentices rushed from behind the counters, scattered wet sawdust out of pails over the floor and swept it up again with great zest and speed, the last rite of the day. By half-past eight we were upstairs and free, supping on bread and butter, cheese and small beer. That was the ritual for every day in the week, thirteen hours of it, except that on Wednesday, Early Closing Day, the shop closed at five.

There was an interval of five minutes at eleven o'clock in the morning when we went upstairs in relays for bread and butter and—my memory is not quite clear here but I think we had a glass of beer. Or it may have been milk or tea. We had a mid-day meal about one for which we had half an hour and we had ten minutes for tea. The dining-room was airy, well lit and upstairs, far more agreeable than the underground cellar at Rodgers and Denyer's, and instead of the squalid rooms which characterised the Windsor place, with truckle beds and no accommodation for personal belongings, so that everyone had to keep his possessions in a trunk or valise, high partitions between the beds divided the dormitory into cubicles and everyone had a private chest of drawers, looking glass, pegs, a chair and so forth. For his time and trade, Mr. Edwin Hyde was a fairly civilized employer. He had even provided a reading room, with a library of several hundred books, of which I shall have a word to say in the next section.

Though I began this life of a draper's shopman at the best end, so to speak, I found it insupportable. The unendurable thing about it was that I was never master of my own attention. I had to be thinking continually about pins and paper and packages. If there was nothing for me to do then I had to find something to do and look sharp about it. But the excitement of successful learning, which had come to me at Midhurst, would not die down. For a time Latin was for me, as for Hardy's *Jude the Obscure*, the symbol of mental emancipation. I tried to go on with Latin ; I wanted to prepare for more examinations. My mind no longer escaped in reverie, but I was rarely without a book of some sort in my pocket which I would try to read when I should have been combing and grooming Witney blankets for the window, or when I was out of sight of the shopwalker, as I imagined, behind a pile of cotton goods.

It became evident to those who were set in authority over me that I was an inattentive and unwilling worker. This mattered most immediately to Casebow the head of the Manchester department, and the " improver " and senior apprentice who were between him and myself. Casebow was a good sort, but he had to keep up a rain of " Come up ! " " Oh, look *sharp* ! " " What in heaven are you doing now ? " " What on earth are you doing here ? " Over him and me ruled the shop walker, Mr. John Key, a stately and quasi-military figure with a good profile and a cherished

moustache, very gentlemanly and dreadfully brisk, who mar-
shalled all the forces of the shop together and did not for a
moment intend that I or anyone under his sway should sink
into sloth and insignificance. When I reflect upon him, I
marvel at his all-seeing energy. He lurked watchfully in a
little desk in the middle of the main shop, from which he
sallied to accost customers, lead them to the appropriate
department, summon the proper assistant, " Merton forward ! " " Ascough forward ! " " Miss Quilter forward ! "
hover to intervene if the sale did not go well, answer to the
cry of " Sign ! " and check each transaction, introduce
novelties to the departing client,—" We are showing some
very pretty sunshades just now Moddum. This for example"
(startlingly opened)—and see that no part of our organization
(and particularly, it seemed to me, myself) fell out of action.
He found me a responsibility, and after a time I got a little
on his nerves. He would remember me suddenly and in-
conveniently. " Wells ? " he would ask. " What is Wells
doing ? Where on earth is that boy now ? "

" Jay-Kay's after you," Platt or Rodgers would say.

Wells would become virtuously active at a counter where
he had been invisible five minutes before. " Here Sir. I've
just been straightening up the longcloths."

" Eugh ! "

My life went to the refrain of Mr. Key's disgusted " Eugh."

The proprietor, the "G.V.", I saw less of ; he was snappy
in his manner and very terrifying. But he came into the
department at irregular intervals ; he blew over. J.K. who
was always about, always keeping me up to the mark,
observant of every untidiness in my dress or any slackness
in my bearing, an ever present " Eugh " of disapproval, was
the living sting of my servitude. At the time I hated him
beyond measure. And yet now, when I can pass judgment
upon him across an interval of half a century, I see that he

was really an excellent man, most anxious to guide my feet into the path of successful drapering and without a grain of malice in his persecution. If he never let me alone for five minutes, then he did me the immense service of bringing home to me in time, just how slack, unsatisfactory and hopeless I was by nature for the calling that had been chosen for me. I could do nothing right for him from the moment when I came into the shop, with an unnecessarily careless slam of the door three minutes late after breakfast, to the time when, broom and pail in hand, I stared malevolently round the corner of a fixture at the lingering customer. The parcels in my department became more and more askew ; until they might have been packed, he said, by " old women."

He wasn't " finding fault." The faults obtruded. I wasn't doing things right. Although I tried hard and tried to school myself, the humiliating fact has to be faced by an honest autobiographer, I wasn't equal to the job.

Now it is all claptrap to say that this was so because I was meant for better things. But I was " meant," if I may use that expression, for different things. I don't think I ever had any snobbishness in me about the relative values of Latin and longcloth, but it was an immense consolation to me in those days of drab humiliations, that after all I had been able to race through Euclid's *Elements*, Smith's *Principia* and various scientific textbooks at a quite unusual speed. That consolation became brighter as my prospect of winning any of the prizes in the trade or even holding my own as a satisfactory assistant, darkened. Manifestly I had not the ghost of a chance of becoming a buyer, a shop walker, a manager, a traveller or a partner. I listened to the tales my seniors would unfold, of the long-drawn despair and hardships of " crib hunting " and rotten shops and what it meant to lose one's " refs," with a growing certitude that that was my part of it, that was the way I should go. And, meditating on my outlook, it was inevitable I should recall the nice authoritative feeling of dictating knowledge to a class and wonder whether even for me with such an appetite for learning as I possessed there might not be prizes and scholarships in the world and some niche of erudition for me to fill.

Possibly my mind would have run naturally towards such ideas, but Mr. Key's expostulating " I never saw such a boy ! What do you think will become of you ? " was undoubtedly thought-provoking. What *would* become of me ?

Might there not be some Wookey where the headmaster's certificates were in order ?

This question became more urgent in my mind as I got into my second year. A fresh apprentice came and I was no longer junior ; he took over those pleasant errands of matching and so forth that had hitherto fallen to me and I was kept more closely in the shop. (He had by the bye an amusing simplicity of mind, a carelessness of manner, a way of saying " Oo'er," and a feather at the back of his head that stuck in my memory, and formed the nucleus which grew into *Kipps* in my novel of that name.) Junior apprentices wear short black coats, but afterwards they go into black morning coats with tails, and now, at sixteen, I bore these evidences of my increasing maturity. I began to serve small and easy customers. I served them badly. Rodgers and Platt my immediate seniors were far sharper at the job. And the parcels I packed were damnable.

" Get on with it Wells." " Wells Forward." " Has anyone seen Wells ? " " Sign ! " " But you haven't shown the lady the gingham at six-three ! The young man has made a mistake Moddum ; we have exactly what you require." " A parcel like that will fall to pieces, man, before it gets home." And at the back of my mind, growing larger and more vivid, until it was like the word of the Lord coming to one of his

sources for his novels

prophets, was the injunction : " Get out of this trade before it is too late. At any cost get out of it."

For some time I did not tell anyone of this amazing urgency to disentangle myself. Then I tried the idea on my brother Frank, who had settled into a reasonably pleasant job at Godalming and was " living out " in lodgings. I used to go to him at Easter and Whitsuntide to spend hilarious friendly Bank Holidays. " But what else can you do ? " he asked. The second clerk in the booking desk, named West, was a man of some education who had had dreams of entering the church and who took a sympathetic interest in my spurts with the Latin grammar of an evening. I talked to him. I may have got suggestions from him. Finally I had the brilliant idea of writing to Mr. Horace Byatt at Midhurst. " Weren't there such things as ushers ? Might I not be useful in the school ? "

He answered that he thought I might be quite useful.

But I was indentured for four years and I had not yet served two. My mother had undertaken to pay a premium of fifty pounds and had already paid forty. She was dismayed beyond measure to find that once again, apparently, I was to come unstuck. She wept and prayed me to " try again " ; Freddy was " trying." If only I would " pray for help " in the right quarter. I explained I didn't want help of that sort from any quarter. I had discovered that the drapery business was a dismal trap and I meant to get out of it. My father was invoked and first he supported and then opposed my liberation.

Byatt made an offer. It was the salvation of my situation. It made my revolt reasonable. I might go as a student assistant in the Grammar School ; at first he suggested without pay and then decided that he would pay me twenty pounds a year and raise this to forty after a twelve-month. He had a faith in my grant-earning capacity that

I was to justify beyond expectation and this inspired him.

I had reached a vital crisis of my life, I felt extraordinarily desperate and, faced with binding indentures and maternal remonstrances, I behaved very much like a hunted rabbit that turns at last and bites. A hunted rabbit that turned and bit would astonish and defeat most ordinary pursuers. I had discovered what were to be for me for some years the two guiding principles of my life. " If you want something sufficiently, take it and damn the consequences," was the first and the second was : " If life is not good enough for you, change it ; never endure a way of life that is dull and dreary, because after all the worst thing that can happen to you, if you fight and go on fighting to get out, is defeat, and that is never certain to the end which is death and the end of everything."

Among other things, during that dismal two years, I had thought out some very fundamental problems of conduct. I had really weighed the possibilities of the life before me, and when I used suicide as a threat to shake my mother's opposition to my liberation, it was after a considerable amount of meditation along the Southsea sea front and Portsmouth Hard. I did not think suicide an honourable resort, but it seemed to me a lesser evil than acquiescence. The cool embrace of swift-running, black deep water on a warm summer night couldn't be as bad as crib hunting or wandering about the streets with the last of one's courage gone. There it was in reserve anyhow. Why should I torture myself to earn a living, any old living? If the living isn't good enough, why live ?

Not perhaps with that much virility did I think at the time, but in that fashion, I was beginning to think.

I do not remember now the exact order of events in my liberation nor when it was I wrote to Byatt. But I know things were precipitated by some row of which I have forgotten every particular. On some issue I had been insubordinate, deliberately disobeyed orders. There had to be trouble. The matter was something beyond J.K., and I should have to see the G.V. At any rate I got up early one Sunday morning and started off without breakfast to walk the seventeen miles to Up Park and proclaim to my mother that things had become intolerable and this drapery experiment had to end. I think that was the first intimation the poor little lady had of my crisis.

I have told just how that happened in *Tono Bungay* and how I waylaid the procession of servants as they were coming up Harting Hill from Harting Church. I appeared among the beeches and bracken on the high bank. " Cooee Mummy," said I, white-faced and tired, but carrying it off gaily.

The bad shilling back again !

I remember too an act of singular ungraciousness on my part. When at length it had been arranged that my indentures should be cancelled, Mr. Hyde bethought himself of the summer sale that was imminent, when every hand, however incompetent, was welcome. " Would I at least stay on for that ? " It meant another month of shop, just four weeks more. I refused obstinately, would not hear of it. There was no real need for me to go to Midhurst for a month yet ; the school would not reassemble until September, but I had already anticipated a month of perfervid reading. I felt I was already nearly two years behind those fellows who went to public schools. I had to be after them without any further delay.

Still more vivid is my memory of being alone in a railway compartment between Portsmouth and Petersfield junction, *en route* for Midhurst. My small but faithful portmanteau was on the seat before me. I could not keep still, and after flitting restlessly from one window to another and back again and trying to read, I found it necessary to express my feelings by a staggering dance and a song, a song consisting, I seem to remember, of disrespectful improvisations about the Southsea Drapery Emporium, and more particularly about "old J.K." (Which Emporium was, I insist, after all far above the average of drapers' shops and very decently run, and J.K. an excellent man.) But this chant and breakdown about my exodus from drapery, set to a railway rhythm, is now lost beyond recovery.

" Puff and rumble old J.K. old J.K. old J.K.

" Damn-the-boy has got away, *got* away, *got* away

" Damn-the-boy has got away, got away for ever."

Something in that fashion at any rate.

§ 2

The Y.M.C.A., the *Freethinker* ; a Preacher
and the Reading Room

THIS CHAPTER in the history of the adventures of a sample human brain in the latter phase of the Private Capitalist System, must go a little deeper than the story of a misfit, a discontent and an escape, if it is to do justice to the phases through which a clear and firm vision of a world renewed, and a plain satisfying and sustaining objective in life, were built up in it. The educational influence of Up Park was going on during these two years and during the subsequent student period at Midhurst and in London. And, in addition, this now hungry and excited cortex was seizing upon and annexing whatever was relevant to the matters that were becoming of primary importance in the scheme of things it was making for itself. There was a clerk in the office at

Southsea, named Field, who had found religion and showed a
certain interest in me. He introduced me to the Young
Men's Christian Association in Landport, where there was a
reading room and a circulating library. And another clerk
I have already mentioned, named West, prided himself upon
his theology and talked interestingly about religious services.
I would spend my Sunday evenings, especially in winter, in
attending the various religious services ; there was a fashion-
able high Anglican in Southsea, popular preachers to be
heard in the Catholic cathedral, duller but still tolerable
entertainment in other chapels and churches. There was
also a secularist society in an upstairs room where a number
of quiet men rejoiced discreetly when a church was struck
by lightning. My still vague and instinctive disbelief in
Christianity had now to be put through a closer scrutiny.

Except for a deep resentment of social inequality and
particularly of the unfairness of letting those other fellows
go to college, I had still hardly the rudiments of social,
economic or political ideas. I don't remember any Socialism
at this time. There was a " Parliament " which met in the
reading room of the Y.M.C.A. and I attended its sessions
regularly. It was one of those parodies of the House of
Commons, similar to the one in Camden Town wherein
figured the parental Harmsworth, the father of Northcliffe
and Rothermere. Ambitious barristers, local politicians and
embryo journalists, familiarized themselves with the current
phrases of politics and the methods of debate, but I found
the pedantries of procedure confusing and I could not make
head or tail of most of the issues of the time : "Leasehold
Enfranchisement " or Our Foreign Policy or Egypt, an Extra
Penny on the Income Tax, Licensing Laws and so forth. It
bothered me a lot to witness all this mental excitement and
not to have a clue to it. Where did it join on—to theology for
example ?

My mind was still exploring fundamentals in a profoundly dissatisfied mood, and it was working at a level that was too far down to establish any contact between these fundamentals and the political issues of the day. It still seemed to me to be of primary importance to find out if there was, after all, a God, and if so whether he was the Christian God and which sort of Christian God he was. In the absence of a God what *was* this universe and how was it run? Had it ever begun and had it any trend? I knew now something of geology and astronomy and I had a crude conception of Evolution. But the proposition that " somebody must have made it all," had been stuck into my mind early in life and it was only much later that I realized that there was a flaw in this assumption. Such questions seemed to me already of far more importance than satisfying J. K. or securing a satisfactory " ref." when my apprenticeship was up, and they drove that mock Parliament stuff completely off the stage.

I was still much exercised by what might happen when my earthly apprenticeship as a whole, was over. It seemed to me much more important to know whether or no I was immortal than whether or no I was to make a satisfactory shop assistant. It might be a terrible thing to be out of a crib on the Thames Embankment but it would be a far more terrible thing to be out of a crib for ever in the windy spaces of nothingness. Jeering at the Trinity did not dismiss the God idea, nor disbelief in hell the idea of immortality. I realized that unless my memory was very bad indeed I had had a comparatively recent beginning, but I found it difficult to suppose I should ever have an end. I tried to imagine how it would feel not to exist and my imagination failed me. I did all the queer things that everyone, I suppose, does at this stage. I would sit on my bed in my cubicle trying to withdraw my mind from all external things and think through the universe to the

Inner Reality. I would lie quite still in my bed invoking the Unknown to " Speak now. Give me a sign."

On my matching expeditions, when I had to go from Southsea to the Landport Drapery Bazaar, I passed through some side streets in which an obscure but spirited newspaper shop displayed a copy of a weekly called the *Freethinker*. Each week had a cheerful blasphemous caricature, which fell in very agreeably with my derisive disposition. I looked for this very eagerly and when I could afford it I bought a copy. In regard to the religions it confirmed my worst suspicions but it left me altogether at a loss for some general statement of my relation to the stars.

Field tried to save my soul. He was strongly evangelical. He took me home to cold supper with his family on several Sunday nights and I participated in some lusty hymn singing. He induced me as a personal favour to pray for faith, but I doubt if I put much power into my prayers. He induced me to read various theological books, but for the most part these deepened my scepticism, by " answering " unconvincingly various objections of which I had been previously unaware. The answer faded and the objection remained. One of those apologetic works stands out in my memory still ; I read it with peculiar delight and shared my glee with West. It was Drummond's *Natural Law in the Spiritual World*. Drummond tried to make various leading Christian dogmas more acceptable by instances drawn from natural history. The Virgin Birth for instance was sustained by a dissertation on parthenogenesis and the prolific summer generation of the green fly was invoked to justify the ways of the Holy Ghost to man.

Somewhen during my stay at Portsmouth my mother wrote to me about my confirmation as a Member of the Church of England. I did not take up the suggestion. Then I was summoned to the inner office by Mr. Hyde, who told me my mother had written to him about it, and that I was to go to the Vicar of Portsmouth to be prepared. I remember one interview. Perhaps it was towards the end of my truncated apprenticeship, because I recall only one. I told the vicar that I believed in Evolution and that I could not understand upon that hypothesis, when it was the Fall had occurred. The vicar did not meet my objections but warned me against the sin of presumption. But it seemed to me to be equally presumptuous to affirm a scheme of salvation as to deny it. And if it was presumptuous to set up my private judgment against all the divines of Christendom, it is surely even more presumptuous to set up one's judgment against all the philosophers of China, India, Islam and the Ancient World.

All of which points were subsequently argued with very great heat after " lights out " in the dormitory, until Rodgers the apprentice next above me, set up a great outcry and said he would listen to blasphemy no longer. " Smut," said Rodgers, " I can stand. There's no harm as I can see in a good smutty story. But this here Blasphemy ! . . . "

One picture of this last phase of critical suspense about the quality and significance of Christianity still stands out in my mind. It is a memory of a popular preacher preaching one Sunday evening in the Portsmouth Roman Catholic cathedral. It was in the course of a revivalist mission and I had been persuaded to go with one of the costume room assistants who played elder sister to me. The theme was the extraordinary merit of Our Saviour's sacrifice and the horror and torment of hell from which he had saved the elect. The preacher had a fluting voice and a faintly foreign accent, a fine impassioned white face, burning eyes and self-conscious hands. He was enjoying himself thoroughly. He spared us nothing of hell's dreadfulness. All the pain and anguish of life as we knew it, every suffering we had ever experienced or imagined, or read about, was as nothing to one moment in the unending black despair of hell. And so on. For a little while his accomplished volubility carried me with him and then my mind broke into amazement and contempt. This was my old childish nightmare of God and the flaming wheel ; this was the sort of thing to scare ten year olds.

I looked at the intent faces about me, at the quiet gravity of my friend and again at this gesticulating voluble figure in the pulpit, earnest, intensely earnest—for his effect. Did this actor believe a word of the preposterous monstrosities he was pouring out ? Could anyone believe it ? And if not, why did he do it ? What was the clue to the manifest deep satisfaction, the fearful satisfaction of the believers about me ? What had got hold of them ?

And from that my eyes and thoughts went, with all the amazement of new discovery, about the crowded building in which I was sitting, its multitudinous gas and candle flames, its aspiring columns, its glowing altar, the dim arched roof, which had been made to house this spouting fount of horrible nonsense. A real fear of Christianity assailed me. It was not a joke ; it was nothing funny as the *Freethinker* pretended. It was something immensely formidable. It was a tremendous human fact. We, the still congregation, were spread over the floor, not one of us daring to cry out against this fellow's threats. Most of us in some grotesque way seemed to like the dreadful stuff.

So far the revolt of my mind had been against the God of Hell in his most Protestant form, it had been as it were a duel ; but now I perceived myself in the presence of a different, if parallel attack upon my integrity, the Catholic Church, a mass attack, the attack of an organization, of a great following. I realized as if for the first time, the menace of these queer shaven men in lace and petticoats who had been intoning, responding and going through ritual gestures at me. I realized something dreadful about them. They were thrusting an incredible and ugly lie upon the world and the world was making no such resistance as I was disposed to make to this enthronement of cruelty. Either I had to come into this immense luminous coop and submit, or, I had to declare the Catholic Church, the core and substance of Christendom with all its divines, sages, saints and martyrs, with successive thousands of millions of believers, age after age, wrong.

In the mouth of the Vicar of Portsmouth " presumption " had seemed a light word, but now I saw it as a grave, immense defiance. To deny was to assert that error had ruled the world so far and wisdom was only beginning—with scared little chaps like me. How could I dare ?

That was the terrific alternative my friend presently put to me and which West of the booking desk, sitting eloquent on my bed in the dormitory after " lights out," enforced. I had not the wit to say then or the clearness of mind to see, that wisdom begins again with every birth and that there is no arrogance at all in perpetually putting the past on trial.

It was, I think, the illuminated figure of that mellifluous preacher which decided me in my recalcitrance. Cathedrals maintain their argument best when they are beautifully silent or when they echo to music and chanting in strange mysterious phrases. Catholicism should imply everything and assert nothing, and generally it does, but this missioner brought the issue down for me to concrete and personal terms. The beautiful hands haunted me with an immense unconvincingness. Face and voice appealed in vain. My perception was invincible ; the man was an actor ; he was making the most of a part. At best he had had the will to believe and not the will for truth.

Through him the Church and its authority, were laid bare to me. He had feared and acquiesced where I had not feared and acquiesced, he found a pleasure and excitement in imparting his fear and acquiescence, he had fitted himself into the incredible and I despised him. I had to despise him. I could no other. The thing he believed was so impossible to me that I could not imagine it being believed in good faith. Could anyone who had even tried for truth believe it? And if I despised him then it was natural to proceed to despise all these like-minded individuals and all who succumbed to him.

I found my doubt of his essential integrity, and the shadow of contempt it cast, spreading out from him to the whole Church and religion of which he with his wild spoutings about the agonies of hell, had become the symbol. I felt ashamed to be sitting there in such a bath of credulity.

It marks a new phase in mental development when one faces ideas not simply as ideas but as ideas embodied in architecture and usage and every-day material fact, and still resists. Hitherto I had taken churches and cathedrals as being as much a part of indisputable reality as my hands and feet. They had imposed themselves upon me as a necessary part of urban scenery just as I had taken Windsor Castle and Eton College as natural growths of the Thames valley. But somehow this Portsmouth Cathedral, perhaps because it had been newly built and so seemed more active than a time-worn building, took on the quality of an engine rather than an edifice. It was a big disseminator; it was like one of that preacher's gestures tempered and made into a permanent implement; it was there to put hell and fear and submission into people's minds. And from this starting apprehension, my realization that all religious buildings are in reality kinetic, spread out more and more widely to all the other visible things of human life. They were all, I began to see dimly, ideas,—ideas clothed and armed with substance. It was as impossible just to say that there was no hell and no divine Trinity and no atonement, and then leave these things alone, as to declare myself republican or claim a right to an equal education with everyone else, without moving towards a clash with Windsor and Eton. These things existed and there was no denying it. If I denied the ideas they substantiated then I proposed to push them off my earth; no less.

The ideas I had on my side to pit against these great realized systems seemed terribly bare and feeble from this point of view. But they possessed me. I felt small and scared but obdurate.

I was still half a lifetime away from the full realization that if one does not accept the general ideas upon which the existing world of men is based, one is bound to set about re-planning and reconstructing the world on the ideas one finds acceptable. Ultimately I was to come to a vision of a *anticipatia* possible state of human affairs in which scarcely one familiar landmark would remain. But revolution on that scale was beyond the courage of my youthful imagination. I was definitely in opposition to the structural concepts of this world into which I had come, and that is as far as I went. I was almost cowed into conformity by the realization of the magnitude of the structures involved. I was in rebellion, but it was still quite impotent rebellion.

I have already mentioned that the Emporium boasted a library for its assistants. This consisted mainly of popular novels. I had made a rule for myself which I kept for several years, never to read a work of fiction or play a game. This was not so priggish as it seems. I was greedy to learn, I had the merest scraps of time to learn in, and I knew the seduction of a good story and the disturbance of a game of skill. So the novels in the bookcase I left alone. But there were also one or two other books to which I owe a good deal. There was one of those compilations for the mentally hungry that have played so important a part in supplementing the deficiencies of formal education in the British communities in the nineteenth century. I cannot trace it now. It may have been Cassell's *Popular Educator*—I seem to have named that to Geoffrey West and he has jumped to the conclusion that I bought that in parts as it was issued. That was due to his natural desire for animating detail. I never did. I hadn't the pocket money to buy anything in parts. On the whole I think that the book I have in mind was more probably some compact encyclopædic production of that sound hardheaded Edinburgh firm, Chambers. It had long summaries of the views of various philosophical schools and of the physical and biological sciences, made I should imagine by competent and conscientious Scots.

I read these cautious and explicit summaries greedily. They cleared up and put my ideas in order. I acquired a number of mental tools at that time ; I exercised my mind upon words and phrases and forms of thought. I found myself balancing such oppositions as " subjective " and " objective " and " pessimism " and " optimism." I meditated (with magnificently insufficient data) upon the corpuscular and vibratory conception of a light ray. I asked, what is health ? It seems improbable that I did not then encounter the opposition of socialism and individualism, but oddly enough I cannot recall having thought at all about socialism until I read Henry George at Midhurst. I waived my temperamental scepticism before the Conservation of Energy and the sufficiency of Natural Selection. I drew fine distinctions of no practical value between pantheism and atheism.

I tried these new ideas upon West and Platt and others. West was always good for discussion but Platt was uncertain.

" God may be everywhere," said Platt, " or God may be nowhere. That's *His* look out. It doesn't alter the fact we've got to stack these bloody cretonnes before eleven."

My dear Mother.   3 Kings Road Southsea

By borrowing some money I was enabled to go to Midhurst
yesterday   Mr Byatt received me very kindly & gave me
a dinner & took me over his new house

He informs me that I am too old to enter the teaching
profession in the ordinary way as a pupil teacher in an elementary school   and that my only method would be   to
obtain a position as an assistant teacher in a middle class
school   In any case, for about nine or ten months
I should have to maintain myself

        He offers to take me in his own school after the next
holidays in September   I should have more instruction to receive than work to do for a little
while   and he could therefore give me no wages
and I should have to keep myself

        There is an assistant master there   and he
informs me that he pays an old lady 3/- a week
for a bed room share in her sitting room   and
to do his cooking   and he estimates his total
expenses (including this 3/-) washing & food
to be under 10/- a week

(Of course the cost of clothes for a schoolmaster is not half that of a draper)

Now I had a talk with this assistant master and he informs me that if I chose to come I can share his room & old lady for 2/6 a week

This in other words means that for a little while you would have to pay about 10/- a week for me or estimating clothes to cost £10 a year you would have to pay for me about £35 in the year for one year more

But then when the start is made there is every prospect of rising to a good position in the world while in my present trade I am a drapers assistant throughout life

But I must begin at once . if I start at all I must start next September
Which would you prefer ?

I leave the matter in your hands
I remain
Your aff son
H G Wells

Have you written to the GU about the holidays.

§ 3

FIFTH START IN LIFE—MIDHURST (1883–1884)

MIDHURST has always been a happy place for me. I suppose it rained there at times but all my memories of Midhurst are in sunshine. The Grammar School was growing, the school-house had been built and was now occupied by Byatt and his family and filled up with a score or more of boarders ; there was already an usher named Harris and presently came a third man Wilderspin who taught French and Latin. I lodged, and shared a bedroom with Harris, over a little sweetstuff shop next to the *Angel* Hotel. For a time, until the school reassembled I had this room alone.

In a novel of mine called *Love and Mr. Lewisham* which is about just such a Grammar School teacher as I was, I have described how he had pinned up on his wall a " Schema," planned to make the utmost use of his time and opportunities. I made that *Schema*, even to the pedantry of calling it that and not calling it plainly a scheme. Every moment in the day had its task. I was never to rest while I was awake. Such things—like my refusal to read novels or play games— are not evidence of an intense and concentrated mind ; they are evidence of an acute sense of the need for concentration in a discursive and inattentive brain. I was not attacking the world by all this effort and self-control ; I was making my desperate get-away from the shop and the street. I was bracing myself up tremendously. Harris and I would go for one-hour walks and I insisted on a pace of four miles an hour. During this pedestrianism we talked in gasping shouts.

Mrs. Walton my landlady who kept the sweetstuff shop, was a dear little energetic woman with a round friendly face, brown eyes and spectacles. I owe her incalculable things. I paid her twelve shillings a week and she fed me well. She liked cooking and she liked her food to be eaten. My meals at Midhurst are the first in my life that I remember with pleasure. Her stews were marvellously honest and she was great at junket, custard and whortleberry and blackberry jam. Bless her memory.

I taught in the main classroom with Byatt and he kept an eye on what I was doing and gave me some useful advice. He knew how to be lucid, persuasive and helpful. A system of neatly written out homework held his instruction together. I rather suspect he was a trained elementary teacher before he took his Dublin degree and anyhow I learned a lot from him in handling my class of small boys. I was disposed to be over strenuous with them as I was over strenuous with myself, and my discipline was hard at times ; I pushed and shoved them about because both I and they preferred that immediate treatment to impositions and detention, but I helped them whenever I grasped their difficulties and I got them along at a good pace.

The brightest and best of the bunch was " Master Horry," Byatt's eldest ; he was quick and plastic and my approval gave him just that confidence in his personal quality that sent him right up the school ahead of his age and won him an open scholarship at, I think, *Merchant Taylors*. Half a century later he came to see me at Easton, a dried-up ex-colonial official, Sir Horace Byatt, retired from Uganda and house-hunting in Essex. He had become terribly my senior and terribly an Imperialist, and though I knew Sir Harry Johnston and Sir James Currie well and had some general ideas about African colonial conditions, I could not penetrate his official reticence. It was all too evident that he thought the less that radical fellows of my stamp, knew, said or did about high Imperial matters the better. Mrs. Christabel McLaren had come down from London for lunch that day and she pulled his leg by expressing an extravagant admiration for Trotsky. Sir Horace seemed incapable of regarding a Bolshevik as anything more human than a cuttle fish and his deepening suspicion of her was very amusing. " And *that's* the sort of boy you made," said Mrs. McLaren when he had departed. We met once afterwards, before his death in 1933, at a city dinner to the Colonial Premiers. He still seemed puzzled about me. So far as I know, none of my other Midhurst boys made any notable success in life.

But half the work I did for Byatt was done not as a teacher but as a student. His university degree qualified him to organize evening classes in any of the thirty-odd subjects in the science scheme of the Education Department, and to earn grants on his examination results. Accordingly, in addition to the three or four normal classes of a dozen or so evening students which he had hitherto conducted, he now organized a number of others for my especial benefit. They were, to put it plainly, bogus classes; they included some subjects of which he knew little or nothing, and in none did he do any actual teaching. The procedure was to get me a good textbook, written for the examination in the subject in question, and to set me to read it in the schoolroom, while he at his desk attended to his correspondence. In this way I read up such subjects as physiography (Huxley's revival of the subject-matter of my old friend Humboldt's *Cosmos*), human physiology, vegetable physiology, geology, elementary " inorganic " chemistry, mathematics and so forth. In May came the examinations and, after that, if I got an " advanced " first class he earned four pounds, two pounds for a second " advanced " and so in diminishing amounts for a first or second " elementary."

The immediate result, so far as my mind was concerned, was to make me read practically the whole outline of physical and biological science, with as much care and precision as the check of a written examination imposes. I learnt a great deal very easily, but I also did a large amount of strenuous " mugging up." I remember for example toiling laboriously through the account of brain anatomy, illustrated by puzzling woodcuts of sections, in an old edition of Kirk's *Anatomy*. To understand the relations of ventricles, ganglion masses and commissures is not by any means difficult if the knowledge is built up in successive phases according to the embryonic development, but attacked at first from the point of view of adult structure, without the help of models and with no one to question upon the meaning of a difficult phrase, that was pretty hard going. And I also remember struggling with diagrams and paper models to grip the elusive demonstration of the earth's rotation by Foucault's pendulum experiment. And after a pretty slick introduction to electricity I got into heavy country, in Deschanel's textbook, where the tubes of force were gathered together. My realization that I knew a great deal more about things in general than most of the people about me, was balanced by another, that there were people in the world whose minds must be able to run and leap easily among these difficulties where mine wriggled and crawled most painfully.

But anyhow my reading was good enough to produce a cluster of A 1's when the examination results came to hand.

Unfortunately for my headmaster, who had hoped to repeat this exploit on a still larger scale next year, I passed these May examinations with such a bang, that I was blown out of Midhurst altogether.

The Education Department of that period was not completely satisfied with the quality of the science teaching it was disseminating about the country, and it was trying to develop its scattered classes into organized science schools and to produce a better type of teacher than the classical graduates, clergymen and so forth, on whom it had at first to rely. Accordingly it was circularizing its successful examinees, with the offer of a certain number of free studentships, at the Normal School of Science, South Kensington, carrying with them a maintenance grant of a guinea a week during the session and second class railway fare to the capital. I read the blue form with incredulity, filled it up secretly and with trepidation, and presently found myself accepted as a " teacher in training " for a year in the biological course under Professor Huxley—the great Professor Huxley, whose name was in the newspapers, who was known all over the world !

Byatt shared my surprise if not my elation.

I had come to Midhurst a happy but desperate fugitive from servitude ; I left it in glory. I spent my summer vacation partly at Up Park with my mother and partly with my father at Bromley, and I was hardly the same human being as the desperate, footsore, youngster who had tramped from Portsmouth to Up Park, breathing threats of suicide. My mother did not like to cast a shadow on my happiness, but yet she could not conceal from me that she had heard that this Professor Huxley was a notoriously irreligious man. But when I explained that he was Dean of the Normal School, her fears abated, for she had no idea that there could be such a thing as a lay Dean.

Later on my mother thought and learnt more about the Dean. I have described the quaint simple faith in Providence, Our Father and Our Saviour, by which to the best of her ability she guided her life and the lives of her family. I have guessed at a failure of belief in her after the trials of Atlas House and the loss of her " poor Possy." Whatever reality her religion had had for her ebbed away after that. She wept with dismay when I came blustering from Southsea to say I would not be confirmed, but I think it was social rather than religious dismay. I said I was an " Atheist," a frightful word for her to hear, as bad as swearing. " My dear ! " she cried. " Don't say such *dreadful* things ! " And then, good little Protestant that she was, she found consolation. " Better than being caught by those Old Priests," she said, " anyhow."

She could never talk about her religion except in set phrases, but slowly the last vestiges of faith faded out. Towards the end of her life her mind flattened and faded very much. She still went to church but I doubt if she prayed with her will and thought any more. Her phases of reverie flowed past with less and less circumstance and definition, ceasing to ripple at last, smoothing down towards a silvery stream of nothingness.

The idea of immortality lost its necessity for her and I think the prospect of a Resurrection began to seem rather an unnecessary and tiresome fuss ahead of her. And that is where Huxley came in. After her death I found this in her little brass-footed work-box, copied out in her old slow angular Italian handwriting on a browning piece of note-paper :

" These lines, once written by Mrs. Huxley, have been placed over the tomb of the late Professor Huxley at his own request :

> " And if there be no meeting past the grave,
> " If all is darkness, silence, yet 'tis rest ;
> " Be not afraid ye waiting hearts that weep,
> " For God still giveth his beloved sleep
> " And if an endless sleep He wills, so best."

§ 4
FIRST GLIMPSES OF PLATO—AND HENRY GEORGE

CRAMMING MYSELF with knowledge for examinations as my immediate objective, was by no means the sole occupation of my mind at Midhurst. Now that my theological turmoil was subsiding to a sort of Cause and Effect Deism, I was waking up to the importance of the strands of relationship that held me, though not inflexibly, in my place in the social web. Just as it had dawned upon me with an effect of profound discovery that the Roman Catholic cathedral at Portsmouth *need not be there*, so now it was to become apparent that Up Park need not be there, that the shops in the Midhurst street need not be there, nor the farmers and labourers on the countryside. The world would still turn on its axis, if all these things were replaced by different structures and arrangements.

I have already said that I cannot clearly remember when it was that I read Plato's *Republic*. But it was somewhen before I went to London and it was in summer time, because I remember lying on the grass slope before a little artificial ruined tower that, in the true spirit of the eighteenth century, adorned the brow of the Up Park Down overlooking Harting. The translation of the Dialogues, was all by itself in a single green bound volume, happily free from Introduction or Analysis. I must have puzzled over it and skipped and gone to and fro in it, before its tremendous significance came through. A certain intellectual snobbishness in me may have helped me to persevere. And associated with it, because of its fermenting influence upon my mind, is a book of a very different calibre, a sixpenny paper-covered edition of Henry George's *Progress and Poverty* which I bought in a newspaper shop in Midhurst. This last was, I suppose, published by some propagandist Single Tax organization. These two books caught up and gave substance to a drift of dispositions and desires in my mind, that might otherwise have dispersed and left no trace.

Plato in particular, as I got to the mighty intention behind his (to me) sometimes very tedious and occasionally incomprehensible characters, was like the hand of a strong brother taking hold of me and raising me up, to lead me out of a prison of social acceptance and submission. I do not know why Christianity and the old social order permitted the name of Plato to carry an intellectual prestige to my mind far above that of Saint Paul or Moses. Why has there been no detraction? I suppose because the Faithful have never yet been able to escape from a certain lurking self-criticism, and because in every age there have been minds more responsive to the transparent honesty and greatness of Plato and Aristotle than to the tangled dogmatism of the Fathers. But here was a man wearing the likeness of an Olympian God, to whom every scholarly mind and every clerical back bowed down in real or imposed respect, who had written things of a revolutionary destructiveness beyond my darkest mutterings. Hitherto there had always been something insurgent, inferior, doubtful and furtive in my objections to the religious, moral and social systems to which my life had, it seemed, to be adapted. All my thoughts leapt up now in open affirmation to the novel ideas he opened out to me.

Chief of these was the conception of a society in which economic individualism was overruled entirely in the common interest. This was my first encounter with the Communist idea. I had accepted property as in the very nature of things, just as my mother had accepted the Monarchy and the Church. I had been so occupied with my mental rebellion against the ideas of God and King, that hitherto I had not resented the way in which the Owner barred my way here, forbad me to use this or enjoy that. Now with Plato's picture of an entirely different social administration before me, to make a comparison possible, I could ask " *By what right*— is this for you and not for me?" Why are things monopolized? Why was everything appropriated and every advantage secured against me before I came into the world?

Henry George's book came in like a laboratory demonstration to revivify a general theory, with his extremely simplified and plausible story of the progressive appropriation of land, his attack upon the unearned increment of private rents and his remedy of a single tax to make, in effect, rents a collective benefit. His was an easy argument to understand, as he put it, and I was able to modify it and complicate it for myself by bringing in this or that consideration which he had excluded. It was like working kindred mathematical problems of progressive complexity under a common Rule. It was quite easy to pass from the insistence of Henry George upon the inalienable claim of the whole community to share in the benefit of land, to the simpler aspects of interest and monetary appreciation. I became what I may call a Socialist in the Resentful Phase, and what was happening to me was happening to millions of the new generation in Europe and America. Something—none of us knew how to define it but we called it generally the Capitalist System—a complex of traditional usage, uncontrolled acquisitive energy and perverted opportunities, was wasting life for us and we were beginning to realize as much. But at that time in the whole world there was really no explicit realization that this was due not to a system but to an absence of system.

Now it happened to me that the chances, by which one meets or escapes books, so worked at Midhurst that I scarcely heard the name of Karl Marx until I came to London. My socialism was pre-Marxian. I had read something about

Socialism

Robert Owen, I think, in that encyclopædic book in the Southsea Emporium reading-room, and I must have met with some summary of More's *Utopia*, though I do not remember reading it until much later, and essentially my ideas were built on the " primitives " of socialism. I was all for planning a new society. But it seemed plainly unnecessary to clear the old confusion out of the way before the new order came. As a planned order comes, the confusion disappears of itself. It was only after a year and more of biological work at the Normal School of Science, that I came full face upon Marxism and by that time I was equipped to estimate at its proper value its plausible, mystical and dangerous idea of reconstituting the world on a basis of mere resentment and destruction : the Class War. Overthrow the " Capitalist System " (which never was a system) was the simple panacea of that stuffy, ego-centred and malicious theorist. His snobbish hatred of the bourgeoisie amounted to a mania. Blame somebody else and be violent when things go wrong, is the natural disposition of the common man in difficulties all the world over. Marx offered to the cheapest and basest of human impulses the poses of a pretentious philosophy, and the active minds amidst the distressed masses fell to him very readily. Marxism is in no sense creative or curative. Its relation to the inevitable reconstruction of human society which is now in progress, is parasitic. It is an enfeebling mental epidemic of spite which mankind has encountered in its difficult and intricate struggle out of outworn social conditions towards a new world order. It is the malaria of the Russian effort to this day. There would have been creative revolution, and possibly creative revolution of a far finer type if Karl Marx had never lived.

Still happily unaware of the immense frustrations that awaited the urge towards a new social order, I walked about the russet lanes and green shaded paths of Midhurst, talking over the stuff that was in my mind with Harris, or dreaming of the new rational state that I supposed to be at hand when what was plain to me had become plain to everybody. We were a shabby-looking couple in ready-made clothes, going swiftly and talking volubly. Harris had a grave Red Indian profile and his share in the conversation was mostly nodding judiciously. Or he would say " That's all right ; that is," or " I don't see that." I was " shooting up " and growing a little out of my garments, but our generally unkempt appearance was redeemed by the fact that we wore " mortar boards " college caps like those worn by Oxford or Cambridge undergraduates, to maintain about the Grammar School a suggestion of erudition.

So, by way of Plato, I got my vision of the Age of Reason that was just about to begin. Never did anyone believe more firmly in the promptitude of progress than I. I had to learn even the elements of human behaviour in those days and I had no sense of the immense variety of mind-build and working conviction that was possible. I do not seem to have had a suspicion that there was such a force as social inertia to be reckoned with. I lived no longer in reverie, I looked at the world, but I saw it as yet with a divine simplicity ; all that was not simple about it was speedily going to be ; all its declensions and verbs were going to be made regular almost immediately and everything conjugated in the indicative mood. Socialism was plainly ahead of us all, when everyone would be active and happy.

It was not only with regard to Economics that my mind had become liberated and moved now with a sanguine simplicity. I was also filled with strange and stimulating ideas about sexual life. Sexual urgencies were becoming more insistent in me with enhanced health and courage. There had been a great amount of smutty and indecent conversation

again, the intellectual 'phase' and the sexual 'phase'

behind the counters at Southsea, but like the foul talk of my schoolfellows at Bromley, it was curious and derisive rather than amorous. It dissipated rather than stimulated desire. Almost completely disconnected in my mind from that stream of not very harmful uncleanness there had been a certain amount of superficial flirtatiousness with the girl apprentices and women assistants, rather after the fashion of the posturing politenesses and pretended devotions I had learnt from my cousins at Surly Hall. The costume hands were by profession young ladies with figures ; they attracted the apprentices and professed a sisterly affection for them in order to have them available as escorts and the like, but this relationship never came to kisses or caresses. So far as I was concerned the " good figure " of that period, with its tight long stays, its padded bustle behind, its single consolidated bosom thrust forward and its " Grecian bend " thrust back, had scarcely anything to recall the deep breasted Venuses and Britannias who had first awakened my sexual consciousness. The stark and easy generation of to-day can scarcely realize how completely, from the whalebone-assisted collar round its neck to the flounces round its feet, the body of woman was withheld from masculine observation, and how greatly this contributed to the practical effective resistance to " the nude " in art. Men went to the music halls simply for the rare joy of seeing feminine arms, legs and contours, but I had no money to go to a music hall.

Once, I suppose, that one had penetrated these complicated defences and got to the live body inside, one could think of individualized physical love, but at that I never arrived at Southsea or Midhurst. Mother Nature did what she could to egg me on, and stripped a girl apprentice I thought rather pretty and the costume lady who was my official Sister, in my dreams, but the old harridan accompanied this display with so many odd and unnecessary exaggerations and accessory circumstances, that it made me rather more shy and unreal and decorous than ever when I encountered her victims in my waking life. And moreover, at Southsea, the women were in one wing of the premises and we youths and men in another, inaccessible, dragons intervening. Short of a sort of rape of the Sabines and general social dissolution, little was possible. Once or twice at Southsea or Portsmouth a prostitute would make an alluring gesture to me, but a shilling a week of pocket-money gives no scope for mercenary love. At Midhurst I had no feminine associates at all. Mrs. Walton had two grown-up daughters, but she was always alert about her lodgers, and a playful scuffle with the eldest about a penny, sternly suppressed and reprimanded by mother, was as far as passion went in that direction. In vain did Nature intervene and amplify the scuffle in dreamland.

On one occasion, however, I reached a stage nearer the desired reality. It was at Christmas at Up Park and there was a dance in the Servants Hall and the upper and lower servants mingled together. There was a kitchen maid whom I suddenly discovered was pretty beyond words and I danced and danced again with her, until my mother was moved to find other partners for me. She was a warm-coloured girl with liquid brown eyes and a quick pretty flush of excitement. Her name was Mary and that is all the name I ever had for her. And afterwards in one of the underground passages towards the kitchen, where perhaps I was looking for her, she darted out of a recess and kissed and embraced me. No lovelier thing had ever happened to me. Somebody became audible down the passage and she made a last dash at me, pressed her lips to mine and fled. And that is all. Next morning I trundled off in the dog-cart on the frosty road to Rowlands Castle station for Portsmouth, before sunrise, and when next I went to Up Park for a holiday, Mary had gone. I never saw her again and I could not find

Mary

her name nor where she had gone. My mother who knew would not tell me. But I can feel her heart beat against mine now, I can recall the lithe body in her flimsy yellow dress, and for all I know I have driven my automobile past Mary —an alert old lady I am certain—on some Hampshire road within the last few weeks.

But after that I knew that love was neither filth nor flirtation and I began to want more of it.

As my mind filled up and broadened out at Midhurst I began to resent the state of sexual deprivation in which I was living, more and more explicitly. All over Europe and America youths and maidens fretted under the same deprivation. Not only were their minds being afflicted by that nightmare story of the Ogre-God and his Hell, not only were they being caught helplessly young and jammed for life into laborious, tedious, uninteresting and hopeless employments, but they were being denied the most healthy and delightful freedoms of mutual entertainment. They were being driven down to concealed and debilitating practices and shameful suppressions. Every year the age of marriage was rising and the percentage of marriages was falling, and the gap of stress and vexation between desire and reasonable fulfilment was widening. In that newspaper shop on the way to Landport where I saw and sometimes bought the *Freethinker*, I also found the *Malthusian* displayed, and one or two numbers had been the subject of a lively discussion with Platt and Ross. The Bradlaugh Besant trial had occurred in 1876 and the light of sanity was gradually breaking into the dark places of English sexual life. There was perhaps a stronger belief current then that births were completely controllable than the actual facts warranted. Now under the stimulus of Plato's Utopianism and my quickening desires I began to ask my imagination what it was I desired in women.

I desired and needed their embraces and so far as I could

understand it they needed and desired the embraces of men. It came to me as the discovery of a fresh preposterousness in life as it was being lived about me, that there were endless millions of young people in the world in the same state of sexual suspense and unrest as myself, quite unable to free themselves sweetly and honestly from these entangling pre-occupations. Quite enough, there was, of either sex to go round. But I did not want an epidemic of marriages. I had not the slightest wish for household or offspring at that time ; my ambition was all for unencumbered study and free movement in pursuit of my own ends, and my mind had not the slightest fixation upon any particular individual or type of individual. I was entirely out of accord with the senti-mental patterns and focussed devotions adopted by most people about me. In the free lives and free loves of the guardians of the *Republic* I found the encouragement I needed to give my wishes a systematic form. Presently I discovered a fresh support for these tentative projects in Shelley. Regardless of every visible reality about me, of law, custom, social usage, economic necessities and the unex-plored psychology of womanhood, I developed my adolescent fantasy of free, ambitious, self-reliant women who would mate with me and go their way, as I desired to go my way. I had never in fact seen or heard of any such women ; I had evolved them from my inner consciousness.

This was my preliminary fantasy of love, before I began love-making. It exerted a ruling influence on my conduct for many years. It is remarkable how much we frame our ex-pectations upon such secret fantasies and how completely we ignore the probability that the lovers we encounter may have quite other systems of imagination. The women of the " Samurai " in my *Modern Utopia* (1905), the most Platonic of my books, are the embodiment of these Midhurst imaginings.

So, before I was eighteen, the broad lines of my adult ideas about human life had appeared—however crudely. I was following a road along which at variable paces a large section of the intelligentsia of my generation was moving in England, towards religious scepticism, socialism and sexual rationalism. I had no idea of that general drift about me. I seemed to be thinking for myself independently, but now I realize that multitudes of minds were moving in precisely the same direction. Like forces acting upon like organizations give like results. I suppose when a flight of starlings circles in the air, each single bird feels it is moving on its own initiative.

One glaring omission from my outlook, as I have sketched it here, will be evident at once to the post-war reader. I had scarcely thought at all and I have nothing to tell of my thoughts concerning the problem of war and international relationship. My untravelled political mind was confined within the limits of the Empire. Flags and soldiers, battleships and big guns were already much in evidence in the European landscape and seascape but, until the Boer War at the end of the century, they had not challenged critical attention. I had no idea that the guns went off—except when pointing right away from civilization, in Afghanistan or Zululand or against remote inadequate batteries at Alexandria. They had an air of being in the order of things, much as mountains, earthquakes and sunsets were in the order of things. They made a background. In England they did not invade the common personal life until after 1914.

This was the most conspicuous blind patch in the English liberal outlook at the close of the nineteenth century, but it was not the only one. I was also blankly unaware of the way in which the monetary organization of the world reflected its general economic injustices and ineptitudes. But then I had never yet seen ten sovereigns together of my own in my life,

distant war

what he thought & what he didn't think

never touched any paper money except a five pound note, nor encountered a cheque. (Bank of England notes were dealt with very solemnly in those days ; the water-mark was scrutinized carefully and the payer, after a suspicious pene-trating look or so was generally asked to write his name and address on the instrument.) The bags of money and slips of paper I carried to the Portsmouth bank had not aroused me to any sense of significance. I did not suspect that there was anything more treacherous about money than there was about weights and measures. Either I did not know or it did not seem to matter to me that while a yard was always so much of a metre, the pound and the franc and the lira and the dollar were capable of slipping about in their relations to each other, and that prices could execute the most re-markable and disconcerting changes of level. They were not doing so at the time. In those days they were just sinking very gently, and everything was getting cheaper and cheaper.

There were, as I shall point out in due course, still other primary gaps and disproportions in the radical outlook at the close of the nineteenth century, but these were the chief among them. You will find them equally evident in the autobiography of any labour leader of my generation.

True?

§5

QUESTION OF CONSCIENCE

AT MIDHURST I had a queer little struggle between pride and practical wisdom. I did something that wounded my private honour very deeply. I knelt at the altar rail in the parish church and bowed my head to the bishop's hand and was confirmed, meekly and submissively, a member of the Church of England. You may regard that as a mere formality, but I did not see it in that light. I felt as an early Christian may have felt who for sound domestic and worldly reasons, had consented to burn a pinch of incense to Divus Cæsar.

But I had found myself in an extremely tight corner. Byatt realized that I had not yet been confirmed and that by the statutes of the Grammar School, every member of the teaching staff had to be a communicant. If I was to go on to our mutual benefit devouring and regurgitating scientific fact, the matter had to be put right forthwith. I suggested that I might have " doubts." " My dear Fel-low ! " boomed Byatt. " My dear Fel-low ! You mustn't talk like that. Let me lend you Paley's *Evidences*. That will put you all right about that. . . . And positively you know you *must*." . . .

Positively I knew I must. There was no visible job for me in the world if I did not stick now to the Midhurst adventure. To abandon it now would have been like jumping from a liner in mid-Atlantic. I ought to have thought of this confirmation business before. If I refused, the whole burthen of the situation would fall on my mother. The more I grew, the smaller and weaker she seemed and the less I cared to hurt her. I consented, to her great joy. For a time I am sure Our Father got some heartfelt thanks and praises again. Byatt arranged for me to be prepared specially and swiftly by the curate, for the approaching Confirmation Service.

Under happier circumstances I might have had a certain amount of fun out of that curate, but I was too mortified and bitter at my own acquiescence. We sat by lamplight opposite one another at a table in his lodgings. He was a fair aquiline sensitive young man, with a fine resonant service voice, who did his best to keep our conversation away from the business in hand as much as possible. But I was sullenly resolved to make him say—all of it. I asked a string of questions about the bearing of Darwinism and geology on biblical history, about the exact date of the Fall, about the nature of Hell, about Transubstantiation and the precise benefit of the communion service and so forth. After each answer I would say " So that is what I have to believe. . . . I see." I did not attempt to argue. He was one of those people whose faces flush, whose eyes wander off from you and whose voices get higher in pitch at the slightest need for elucidation.

" It's all a little *subtle* you know——," he would begin.

" Still, people might make difficulties afterwards. I want to know what to say to them."

" Oh—precisely." . . .

" I suppose it's all right if I just believe this in—er—a spiritual sense."

" It's much *better* that way. It's ever so much better that way. I'm so *glad* you see that."

The organ played, the service proceeded. Side by side with a real young gentleman of my own age I walked up the aisle and knelt. And afterwards I communicated and consumed a small cube presenting my Redeemer's flesh and had a lick of sweetish wine from the chalice which I was assured contained his blood. I was reminded of a crumb of Trifle. Later to please my mother I repeated this performance at Harting and after that I made an end to Theophagy. I derived neither good nor ill, so far as I could trace, from these homœopathic doses of divinity.

But the wound to my private honour smarted for a long time and it was many years before I could forgive the Church for setting these barriers of conformity in my way to social usefulness. I do not think that I have forgiven her altogether even now.

I record that shame and resentment about my confirmation because it seems to me that this queer little mood of obduracy was something very important in my development. I do not understand it at all clearly myself and still less can I explain it. What made me attach all that importance to that public lie? I wasn't particularly a George Washington for veracity. If I was never a fluent liar I could at any rate lie quite effectively on occasion. And indeed there was a great deal of material about in my conduct for an officious conscience to play upon, without so entire a concentration on this particular lapse. There was no alternative affirmation in mind. There was no sense of an onlooking divinity in protest. I had no other God. I can only explain my feelings by supposing that there was in my make-up a disinterested element, which attached more importance to the denial of Christianity than to my merely personal advantage. There was something in my brain, an impersonal self, that contested my prior right to welfare at the price of lowering my standard of veracity.

I did what I could to ease this conflict in my being by blasphemous facetiousness, until old Harris became a little scared of me. He did not " believe much " in God but he thought it well not to go too far with Him.

Harris had no self-conceit ; he had a prominent nose and a wary mouth and he went discreetly and ironically through a world which he had found by experience was apt to prove unexpectedly irascible. Something might be fired at me, some thunderbolt he felt, and it would be like his luck if it hit him. " Don't you *say* such things," he said. " Don't you say it." And presently came the distraction of the May examinations and the end of the school term and after a short stay at Up Park I went off to Atlas House to stay with my father until South Kensington was ready to receive me.

My raw mind was so busy at Midhurst with the scramble to get a comprehensive and consistent conception of the principal parts of the universe, in the place of the orthodox interpretations I was rejecting, that I paid very little

attention to another mind-and-purpose-drama that was
going on beside me. While I was making my thorny way out
of Protestantism in one direction, my senior colleague Wilderspin, who lived in the school house, so that I saw very little
of him, was *en route* for Rome. Midhurst is one of those places
in England which has retained a Catholic congregation from
pre-reformation times and a little proselytizing priest flitted
about it, very ready to be friendly with any casual young
men he might encounter. He had a slightly lewd streak in
his conversation that I found repulsive ; he pushed his joke
at you slily and laughed fatly first, he belonged to that
" jolly " school of propagandist which seeks to make it
clear that there is none of your damned Kill-Joy Puritanism
about the dear old, merry old church ; and after a walk and
a talk or so with him I avoided him. Among other things,
believing me to be a newly confirmed Anglican and having
no idea of my real state of mind, he wanted to dispute with
me about the validity of Protestant orders. But I did not
care a curse about either the Catholic or the Protestant
brand of sacerdotalism, except to dislike them both. I was
a universe away from that. I was hampered in my talks
with him because I did not know what disconcerting use
he might make of any sweeping disavowal of Christianity on
my part.

But he got Wilderspin and Wilderspin also vanished from
Midhurst at the same time as myself.

Years after, when I had a home at Woking, Wilderspin
flickered back into my life for a few days as a full fledged
itinerant priest. He called to see me and he seemed to be
needy, hungry and uncomfortable. Evidently he was working
in a sweated industry. He told me he had to go into the
oddest of quarters among the faithful, and that recently he
had found the nest of a mouse in a bed he had been given.
He gave me the impression of being still slightly astonished

at the life he was leading and the mental and material
disciplines to which he was subjected. We fixed for him to
come to dinner and he showed the keenest interest in planning the menu. We chose a day unrestricted by any fasts or
disciplines. He came ; we feasted, talked over Midhurst and
the school and the boys, laughed together more abundantly
than we had ever done before, drank, smoked and parted
cordially. It was evidently a spree for him. After which I
never saw nor heard of him again. Perhaps my cheerful
house upset him, and possibly I was hardly the sort of friend
a not very austere and devout priest would be encouraged
to frequent.

§ 6

WALKS WITH MY FATHER

I HAD NOT SEEN very much of my father for three
years and it was interesting to go back to him and stay with
him alone, practically on terms of equality. He had been a
large person far above me as a schoolboy, but now I was
growing up to him at a great pace. We became excellent
friends and companions. Atlas House was extensively un-
scrubbed and shabbier and more threadbare than ever, but
my father camped, so to speak, amidst its disorder very
comfortably. He cooked very well, far better than my mother
had ever done, in the underground kitchen, and made me
wash up and look after my own bedroom, and we did not
fuss about the other aspects of housekeeping. He was very
lame now and he was getting heavy ; he stumped about with
the help of a thick cabbage stick but he stumped about
actively. He was bald and blue-eyed, with a rosy cheerful
face and a square beard like King David. He admired my
certificates and ambitions frankly and took a lively interest

in the elementary science and philosophy I unfolded to him at second-hand.

The shop was in a sort of coma and gave us very little trouble ; the only trade left was the sale of cricket goods. He did more business by locking up the front door after teatime and going round to the cricket field. If people were taken with a craving to buy crockery in the evening they knocked and rattled at the door until the craving left them. On Sundays we were free for a long walk and a bread and cheese lunch—or even a cold meat lunch—miles away from home.

He had always been something of a reader and now he was reading widely and freely. He read the *Daily News*—the *Daily News* of Richard Jeffries and Andrew Lang—and *Longman's Magazine*—in the R. L. Stevenson and Grant Allen days ; he got books from the Library Institute and picked them up at sales. We gradually broke down the inhibitions about religion and politics natural between father and son, and had a fine various amount of talk and discussion.

In after years I grew away from my father mentally, though we always remained good friends, but during these last years of his at Bromley, we were very much on a level ; if I had a lot of knowledge of one sort, he had a lot of another sort and our conversation was a fair exchange. His was a mind of inappeasable freshness, in the strangest contrast to my mother's. I do not think my mother ever had a new idea after she left Miss Riley's school ; her ideas faded out, that was all. But my father kept going to the last. He was playing chess, by correspondence, with my mother-in-law when he was in the late seventies, and about that time he unearthed some old school books of mine and started in upon Algebra and the Elements of Euclid, an unknown world to him, acquiring considerable facility in the solution of quadratic equations and the working of " riders " before he desisted.

He began now at Atlas House under the stimulus of my studentship and the writings of W. H. Hudson and Grant Allen, to brush up his gardener's botany anew and his countryman's natural history.

Upon all sorts of counts my father was a better man than myself. He had all the delicate nervous and muscular skill and the rapid hardly conscious mental subtleties of a cricketer, he was an instinctive good shot, and at every sort of game he was ripe good wary stuff. We began chess together in these days but while he went on to a sound game I found it too exacting and irritating and gave it up. At draughts I battled with him incessantly, held my own at last but never established a thorough ascendency. About fields and green things and birds and beasts he had a real intimate knowledge that made my accumulation seem bookish and thin. The country round Bromley was being fast invaded by the spreading out of London ; eruptions of new roads and bricks and mortar covered lush meadows and, when I was about fifteen or sixteen, that brown and babbling Ravensbourne between its overhanging trees was suddenly swallowed up by a new drainage system, but my father managed to see and make me see a hundred aspects of the old order of things, a wagtail, a tit's nest, a kingfisher, an indisputable trout under a bridge, sun-dew in a swampy place near Keston, the pollen of pine trees drifting like a mist, the eagle in the bracken root (which I could tell him in return was *Pteris Aquilina*). " We'll be after them mushrooms at Camden," he'd say. " They'll be just about right now. We'll take a screw of salt for them, my boy, and eat them raw. Then we won't have any bother about saying where we found them." And when we got to Camden there were the mushrooms as though he had evoked them, white buttons straining up out of the turf for us.

He had the knack of reviving the countryside amidst the

deluge of suburbanism, just as he had had the knack of
growing a grape vine and making a Wigelia bush flourish
in that smutty backyard of ours.

One bank holiday, Whit-Monday no doubt, he took
advantage of a cheap fare to go back with me to his boyhood
at Penshurst. We walked across the park from Tonbridge.
He wanted me to see and feel the open life he had led before
the shop and failure had caught him. He wanted to see and
feel it again himself. " We used to play cricket here—well,
it was just about here anyhow—until we lost sight of the
ball in the twilight. . . . There's more bracken and less
turf about here now." He talked of a vanished generation of
our cousins, the Dukes, and of a half-sister I had never heard
of before. She and he had gone fishing together through the
dew-wet grass between sunrise and the beginning of the day's
work. She was a tall strong girl who could run almost as
fast as he could. He repeated that. So I guess his first dreams
of women were not so very unlike mine. He showed me where
she sat in Penshurst Church. Also he discoursed very
learnedly on the growing of willows to make cricket bats and
how long it took for a man to learn to make a first-class
cricket ball. That was a great day for my father and me.

All his days my father was a happy and appreciative man
with a singular distaste for contention or holding his own
in the world. He liked to do clever things with his brain
and hands and body, but he was bored beyond endurance
by the idea of a continual struggle for existence. So was my
elder brother Frank. My brother Fred and I may have the
same strain in us, but the world made such ugly, threatening
and humiliating gestures at us at the outset that we pulled
ourselves together and screwed ourselves up for self-repres-
sion and a fight, and we fought and subdued ourselves until
we were free. Was that a good thing for us or a bad ?

I am inclined to think bad. The disposition to acquire

and keep hold and accumulate, to work for a position, to secure precedences and advantages was alien to all four of us. It isn't in our tradition ; it isn't in our blood ; it isn't in our race. We can do good work and we are responsive to team play, we can " play cricket " as the phrase goes, but we cannot sell, bargain, wait, forestall and keep. In a world devoted to private ownership we secure nothing. We get shoved away from opportunity. It was distortion for us to keep our attention on that side of life. I was lucky, as I shall tell, because quite accidentally I suddenly developed extraordinary earning power, which I am still able to exercise, and for thirty years I had my business looked after for me by an extremely competent wife. But I think some very fine possibilities in my brother Fred were diverted to mere saving and shop-keeping.

In a social order where all the good things go to those who constitutionally and necessarily, watch, grab and clutch all the time, the quality of my father, the rich humour and imagination of my brother Frank, were shoved out of play and wasted altogether. In a world of competitive acquisitiveness the natural lot of my sort of people is to be hustled out of existence by the smarties and pushers. A very strong factor in my developing socialism is and always has been the more or less conscious impulses, an increasingly conscious impulse, to anticipate and disarm the smarty and the pusher and make the world safe for the responsive and candid mind and the authentic, artistic and creative worker. In the *Work, Wealth and Happiness of Mankind* I have written about " Clever Alec." He's " rats " to me and at the smell of him I bristle. I set the highest value on people of my own temperament, which is I suppose, a natural and necessary thing to do, and I believe in the long run our sort will do better than their sort, as men do better than rats. We shall build and what we build will stand at last.

But for thousands of generations yet, the bright-eyed, quick incessant rats will infest our buildings, eat our food, get the better of us in all sorts of ways and gnaw and scuttle and scamper. They will muck about with our money, misrepresent our purpose and disposition, falsify ownership and waste and frustrate millions of genial lives.

My father ended his days in a little house at Liss which I was able to rent and afterwards to buy for him, and my mother and my elder brother joined him there. As I began to prosper I was able to increase the income of that ménage until they were quite comfortable by their not very exacting standards ; my brother Fred too, away in South Africa, insisted upon paying his share. When I rebelled against the servitude of the draper's shop, my yawps of liberation had been too much for my elder brother and he had thrown up the yardstick also. He had conceived an ideal of country existence from reading Washington Irving's *Bracebridge Hall*, and he quartered himself with my father first at Rogate and then at Liss, and wandered about the country repairing clocks, peddling watches, appreciating character and talking nonsense. If it was not particularly profitable, it was amusing —and free. There is a touch of my brother about Mr. Polly, —the character I mean, not the story. My father played nap at times and billiards often in the Liss Club Room. My mother sat in reverie, peeped out of the window of the upstairs parlour at passers-by, wrote prim little letters to Freddie and me, dressed more and more like Queen Victoria and went to Church and Holy Communion. (But she did not go to evening service at Liss because she thought it rather " high," surplices, candles, intonation—" too much of it.") My brother peddled his watches and went off on his bicycle, sometimes for days together.

In 1905 my mother slipped and fell downstairs one evening and was hurt internally and died a few weeks later. In her last illness her mind wandered back to Midhurst and she would fuss about laying the table for her father or counting the stitches as she learnt to crochet. She died a little child again. In 1910 my father woke up very briskly one morning, delivered a careful instruction on the proper way to make suet pudding to his housekeeper Mrs. Smith, insisted that it should be chopped small, protested against " lumps the size of my thumb," glanced over the *Daily Chronicle* she had brought him and prepared to get up. He put his legs out of bed and slid down by the side of the bed a dead man. There is an irregularity in our family pulse, it misses a beat ever and again and sooner or later it misses more than one and that is the end of us. My grandfather had leant over a gate to admire the sunset and then ceased to live in the same fashion. This last spring as I write (1933) heart stoppage came also to my elder brother and as he got up from his breakfast, he reeled and fell down dead. But this was a little premature ; he was only seventy-seven and my father and grandfather were both eighty-two. I shall hate to leave the spectacle of life but go I must at last, and I hope when my time is fulfilled that I too may depart in this apparently hereditary manner. It seems to me that whatever other defects we have, we have an admirable way of dying.

CHAPTER THE FIFTH

SCIENCE STUDENT IN LONDON

§ 1

PROFESSOR HUXLEY AND THE SCIENCE OF BIOLOGY
(1884–1885)

THE DAY WHEN I walked from my lodging in Westbourne Park across Kensington Gardens to the Normal
School of Science, signed on at the entrance to that burly
red-brick and terra-cotta building and went up by the lift
to the biological laboratory was one of the great days of my
life. All my science hitherto had been second-hand—or third
or fourth hand ; I had read about it, crammed textbooks,
passed written examinations with a sense of being a long way
off from the concrete facts and still further off from the living
observations, thoughts, qualifications and first-hand theoriz-
ing that constitute the scientific reality. Hitherto I had had
only the insufficient printed statements, often very badly
and carelessly written, of the textbooks, eked out by a few
perplexing diagrams and woodcuts. Now by a conspiracy of
happy accidents I had got right through to contact with all
that I had been just hearing about. Here were microscopes,
dissections, models, diagrams close to the objects they
elucidated, specimens, museums, ready answers to questions,
explanations, discussions. Here I was under the shadow of
Huxley, the acutest observer, the ablest generalizer, the great
teacher, the most lucid and valiant of controversialists. I
had been assigned to his course in Elementary Biology and
afterwards I was to go on with Zoology under him.

In a very carefully done short story, *A Slip under the Microscope* (*Yellow Book*, 1893) and in an equally careful novel, *Love and Mr. Lewisham* (1900) I have rendered something of the physical and social atmosphere of that early biological laboratory. These descriptions were written so much nearer to the actual experience than I am now, that I will not even attempt to parody them here, and it seems hardly fair to quote them. But I must try, however unsuccessfully, to convey something of my realization of an extraordinary mental enlargement as my mind passed from the printed sciences within book covers to these intimate real things and then radiated outward to a realization that the synthesis of the sciences composed a vital interpretation of the world.

In those days both sides of descriptive biology, botany and zoology, were in a parallel phase ; they were passing on from mere classification to morphology and phylogeny. Comparative physiology and genetics had still to come within the scope of the ordinary biological student. It was perhaps inevitable that they should wait upon the establishment and confirmation of the phylogenetic tree, the family tree of life, before they in their turn could take the centre of the stage. The phylogeny of the invertebrata was still in a state of wild generalization, vegetable morphology concerned itself with an elaborate demonstration of the progressive subordination of the oophore to the sporophore, and even the fact of evolution as such was still not universally conceded. The mechanism of evolution remained therefore a field for almost irresponsible speculation. Weismann and his denial of the inheritance of acquired characteristics was in the ascendant. Our chief discipline was a rigorous analysis of vertebrate structure, vertebrate embryology and the succession of vertebrate forms in time. We felt our particular task was the determination of the relationship of groups by the acutest possible criticism of structure. The available fossil evidence was not a tithe of what has been unearthed to-day ; the embryological material also fell far short of contemporary resources ; but we had the same excitement of continual discoveries, confirming or correcting our con-clusions, widening our outlook and filling up new patches of the great jig-saw puzzle, that the biological student still experiences. The study of zoology in this phase was an acute, delicate, rigorous and sweepingly magnificent series of exercises. It was a grammar of form and a criticism of fact. That year I spent in Huxley's class was, beyond all question, the most educational year of my life. It left me under that urgency for coherence and consistency, that repugnance from haphazard assumptions and arbitrary statements, which is the essential distinction of the educated from the uneducated mind.

I worked very hard indeed throughout that first year. The scene of my labours was the upper floor of the Normal School, the Royal College of Science as it is called to-day, a floor long since applied to other uses. There was a long laboratory with windows giving upon the art schools, equipped with deal tables, sinks and taps and, facing the windows, shelves of preparations surmounted by diagrams and drawings of dissections. On the tables were our micros-copes, reagents, dissecting dishes or dissected animals as the case might be. In our notebooks we fixed our knowledge. On the doors were blackboards where the demonstrator, G. B. Howes afterwards Professor Howes, a marvellously swift draughtsman, would draw in coloured chalks for our instruction. He was a white-faced, black bearded, nervous man, a sort of Svengali in glasses ; swift and vivid, never still, in the completest contrast with the powerful delibera-tion of the master. Huxley himself lectured in the little lecture theatre adjacent to the laboratory, a square room,

surrounded by black shelves bearing mammalian skeletons
and skulls displayed to show their homologies, a series of
wax models of a developing chick, and similar material. As
I knew Huxley he was a yellow-faced, square-faced old man,
with bright little brown eyes, lurking as it were in caves
under his heavy grey eyebrows, and a mane of grey hair
brushed back from his wall of forehead. He lectured in a
clear firm voice without hurry and without delay, turning
to the blackboard behind him to sketch some diagram, and
always dusting the chalk from his fingers rather fastidiously
before he resumed. He fell ill presently, and after some delay,
Howes, uneasy, irritable, brilliant, took his place, lecturing
and drawing breathlessly and leaving the blackboard a
smother of graceful coloured lines. At the back of the
auditorium were curtains, giving upon a museum devoted
to the invertebrata. I was told that while Huxley lectured
Charles Darwin had been wont at times to come through
those very curtains from the gallery behind and sit and
listen until his friend and ally had done. In my time
Darwin had been dead for only a year or so (he died
in 1882).

These two were very great men. They thought boldly,
carefully and simply, they spoke and wrote fearlessly and
plainly, they lived modestly and decently ; they were mighty
intellectual liberators. It is a pity that so many of the younger
scientific workers of to-day, ignorant of the conditions of
mental life in the early nineteenth century and standing for
the most part on the ground won, cleared and prepared for
them by these giants, find a perverse pleasure in belittling
them. In a thousand respects their work was incomplete
and tentative and any little Mr. Whippersnapper who choses
to use the vastly greater resources of to-day against them
can find statements made by them that were insufficient or
slightly erroneous, and theoretical suggestions that have been

abandoned and disproved, and he can catch a bit of personal publicity from the pulpit or the reactionary press by saying that Darwin has been discredited or Huxley superseded. Great joy for Mr. (and Mrs.) Whippersnapper it is, naturally enough, to realize that he knows clearly things that Darwin never heard of, and is able to tatter some hypothesis of Huxley's. Little men will stand on the shoulders of giants to the end of time and small birds foul the nests in which they were hatched. Darwin and Huxley knew about one per cent of the facts about variation and mutation that are accessible to Mr. Whippersnapper. That does not alter the fundamental magnificence of Darwin's and Huxley's achievement. They put the fact of organic evolution upon an impregnable base of proof and demonstration so that even the Roman Catholic controversalists at last ceased to vociferate, after the fashion of Bishop Wilberforce of the Anglican Church on a memorable occasion, " Yah ! Sons of apes ! You *look* it," and discovered instead that the Church had always known all about Evolution and the place of man in Nature, just as it had always known all about the place of the solar system in space. Only it had said nothing about these things, because it was wiser so. Darwin and Huxley, in their place and measure, belong to the same aristocracy as Plato and Aristotle and Galileo, and they will ultimately dominate the priestly and orthodox mind as surely, because there is a response, however reluctant, masked and stifled, in every human soul to rightness and a firmly stated truth.

This biological course of Huxley's was purely and strictly scientific in its character. It kept no other end in view but the increase and the scrutiny and perfection of the knowledge within its scope. I never heard or thought of practical applications or business uses for what we were unfolding in that year's work, and yet the economic and hygienic benefits that have flowed from biological work in the past forty years have been immense. But these aspects were negligible by the standards of our study. For a year I went shabby and grew shabbier, I was under-fed and not very well housed, and it did not matter to me in the least because of the vision of life that was growing in my mind. I worked exhaustively and spent an even happier year than the one I had had at Midhurst. I was rather handicapped by the irregularity and unsoundness of my general education, but nevertheless I was one of the three who made up the first class in the examinations in zoology which tested our work.

A first-class in the Normal School meant over 80 per cent of the possible marks and the two others who took first-classes were Martin Woodward, a scion of a well-known family of biologists, who was afterwards drowned while dredging for marine zoological material on the west coast of Scotland, and A. V. Jennings, the son of a London private school-master, for whom I formed a considerable friendship. All the rest of the class tailed down through a second class to failure.

Jennings was the only close associate I made in that first year. He was a year or so older than I, a slender grey-clad, red-faced young man with close curly black hair ; he had had a sound classical education, and if he had not read as discursively as I he had read much more thoroughly. He was a well-trained student. He liked the strain of blasphemy and irreverence I had evolved for familiar conversational use, it startled him into appreciative chuckles, and once we had surmounted the obstacle of my shyness of sincere discussion, we got through an immense amount of talking about religious, political and scientific ideas. I learnt a great deal from him and polished much crudity and prejudice off my mind against his. For the first time in my life I was coming into touch at South Kensington with minds as lively as or livelier than my own and much better equipped, minds interested as much as I was interested in the significance of life. They saved me to a large extent from developing a shell of defensive reserve about my self conceit.

Once or twice Jennings showed a personal concern for me that still glows bright in my memory. The " Teachers in Training " at the Normal School were paid a maintenance allowance of a guinea weekly, which even in those days was rather insufficient. After I had paid for my lodgings, breakfasts and so forth, I was left with only a shilling or two for a week of midday meals. Pay day was Wednesday and not infrequently my money had run out before Monday or Tuesday and then I ate nothing in the nine-hour interval between the breakfast and the high-tea I had at my lodgings. Jennings noted this and noted that I was getting perceptibly thinner and flimsier, and almost by force he carried me off to a chop house and stood me an exemplary square meal, meat, two vegetables, a glass of beer, jam-roll pudding and a bit of cheese ; a memorable fraternal feast. He wanted to repeat this hospitality but I resisted. I had a stupid sort of pride about unrequited benefits or I know he would have done this frequently. " This makes competition fairer," Jennings insisted.

At the end of this invigorating year I had had a vague hope that I should be able to go right on with zoological work but there were no facilities for research available. I cared so much for the subject then that I think I could have sailed away to very sound and useful work in it. I could have built up the full equipment of a professor of zoology upon the basis I had secured, if I had been free to take my own where I could find it. I should have filled up my gaps. I am convinced that for college and university education, keenly interested students—and after all they are the only students worth a rap ; the others ought not to be there—should have much more freedom to move about and choose their own courses and teachers than is generally conceded them. However, my first year's performance had impressed the board of selection sufficiently to secure my reappointment as a Teacher in Training for a second and afterwards for a third year in other departments of the school where there were vacancies to be filled.

§ 2

PROFESSOR GUTHRIE AND THE SCIENCE
OF PHYSICS (1885–1886)

UNHAPPILY for me me there was only one Huxley in the Normal School of Science and the course into which I was now thrown had none of the stimulation and enlargement of that opening year. The process of interest and curiosity was broken, and my mind was unable to turn itself with any energy to the new work that was put before it. It suffered from disruption and shock. I found myself almost at once at cross purposes with my new professors and instructors.

I can see now much more clearly than I did at the time what it was that turned me abruptly from the extravagantly greedy and industrious learner I was in my first year, to the facetious, discontented, restless and tiresome rebel I now became. It is a phase of my life I am only now getting into perspective and seeing as a logical part of a whole.

There were extraordinary faults and inconsistencies in the teaching machinery that had got hold of me. I had no idea of these faults and inconsistencies when I blundered against them, I understood scarcely anything either of the clumsiness of the educatiqnal forces to which I was reacting or of the nature of my own reactions ; and it was altogether too much for my intelligence and will to get anything but perplexity and a series of partial frustrations and humiliations from the encounters that now lay before me. I am not complaining. Perplexity, frustration, humiliation and waste of energy are the common lot of human beings in a phase of blindly changing conditions, and what is exceptional in my story is not the clumsy struggling that now began but the previous luck of release and encouragement at Midhurst and under Huxley, that bright run of luck between 1883 and 1885, which had invigorated and given me self-confidence and a mulish persistence in the direction in which my feet were set.

The Normal School of Science and Royal School of Mines, to give it the full title it bore in these days, stood with an air of immense purposefulness four-square upon Exhibition Road. When I first took my fragile, unkempt self and my small black bag through its portals, I had a feeling of having come at last under definite guidance and protection. I felt as I think a civilized young citizen ought to feel towards his state education. If I worked hard, did what I was told and followed the regulations, then I thought I should be given the fullest opportunity to develop whatever fine possibilities were in me and also that I should be used to the best advantage for the world and myself. I thought that the Normal School of Science knew what it meant to do with me. It was only after my first year that it dawned upon me that the Normal School of Science, like most other things in the sliding, slipping civilization of the time, was quite unaware even of what it meant to do with itself. It was an educational miscellany. It had been hastily compiled. Only that big red-brick and terra-cotta building, in which it was then assembled, held it together.

It was a product of the irregular and convulsive thrusts

made by the embryonic modern world-state in its unconscious efforts to free itself from the aristocratic national
system of eighteenth-century Europe. Throughout the nineteenth century, one far-reaching dislocation after another had
emphasized the growing need for a general education of the
population and for a new type of education based upon the
enlightenment due to scientific discovery and a widening
range of experience. Already in the eighteen fifties Huxley
was hammering away at the importance of biology in education The drive of this need was resisted by the established
religions, the ruling aristocracies and whatever remained
over of the " scholarly " mediaeval universities. The new
educational organizations essential to the proper working of
the new order, had to grow against these resistances and
were greatly delayed, dwarfed, distorted and crippled in the
process.

The powers in possession conceded the practical necessity
for technical and scientific instruction long before they
would admit the might and value of the new scientific knowledge. Just as these conservative forces permitted elementary
education to appear only on the understanding that it was
to be a useful training of inferiors and no more, so they
sanctioned the growth of science colleges only on condition
that their technical usefulness was recognized as their sole
justification.

The great group of schools at South Kensington which is
now known as the Imperial College of Science and Technology, grew therefore out of an entirely technical school,
born of the base panic evoked in England by the revelation
of continental industrial revival at the Great Exhibition of
1851. The initial institution was situated in the Museum of
Practical Geology (note the minatory implication of that
"Practical") in Jermyn Street, and its original title was
" The Government School of Mines and Science applied to

the Arts." To this a chemical school, a lecturer on mineralogy and, later on, physical laboratories were added; it was
transferred to South Kensington bit by bit, and upon it a
Normal School, to train teachers for the science classes
that were being spread belatedly over the country, was
rather incongruously imposed (1873 and 1881). It has continued to expand and absorb ever since. It is to-day, a huge
fungoid assemblage of buildings and schools without visible
centre, guiding purpose or directive brain. It has become a
constituent of that still vaster, still more conspicuously
acephalic monster, the University of London.

The thumby wisdom of the practical man, with a conception of life based on immediate needs, unanalysed motives
and headlong assumptions, and with an innate fear of free
and searching thought, is still manifest at a hundred points
in the structure and working of this great aggregation. The
struggle to blend technical equipment with a carefully
cherished illiteracy, an intact oafishness about fundamental
things, has been well sustained. South Kensington will still
tell you proudly " we are not literary " and explain almost
anxiously that the last thing it wants to impart is a liberal
education. The ideal output of the Imperial College remains
a swarm of mechanical, electrical and chemical business
smarties, guaranteed to have no capacity for social leadership, constructive combination or original thought. There
is an ineradicable tendency in sound technology to go on to
purely scientific interest and breadth of social thought, the
higher centres will keep on breaking through, and South
Kensington, in spite of itself, does a great deal of real University
work and makes men of many of its technicians. But so far
the recognition of this tendency in any organized form has
been successfully resisted.

Happily for me it happened that the vigorous, persistent
far-reaching and philosophical mind of Huxley had become

very influential with the Department of Science and Art in the sixties and seventies and particularly at South Kensington, and he had been able not only to establish that general scientific survey, physiography, as a " subject " in the evening class curriculum throughout the country, but he had had also a practically free hand to teach the science of life in his own fashion in the Normal School. This freedom involved, however, a similar freedom for the other professors with whom he was associated and they too without any consultation with their fellows, developed their courses according to their own capacities and their ideas of what was required of them.

Now Professor Guthrie, the Professor of Physics, into whose course I toppled from the top floor to the ground floor of the Normal School building, was a man of very different texture from the Dean. He appeared as a dull, slow, distraught, heavily bearded man with a general effect of never having fully awakened to the universe about him. He seemed very old to me but as a matter of fact he was fifty-two. It was only after some years that I learnt what it was that made him then so slow and heavy. He was ill, within a year of his death, a still unsuspected cancer in his throat was dragging at his vitality, unknown to anyone. This greatly enhanced the leaden atmosphere of his teaching.

But quite apart from that he was not an inspiring teacher. The biological course from which I came had been a vivid, sustained attempt to see life clearly and to see it whole, to see into it, to see its inter-connexions, to find out, so far as terms were available, what it was, where it came from, what it was doing and where it was going. And, I take it, the task of a properly conceived elementary course in Physics, would be to do the same thing with non-living matter, to establish a fruitful description of phenomena, to clear up our common terminology, dating mostly from mediaeval times, about space, time, force, resistance, to explore the material universe with theory and experiment and so to bring us at last to the real living edge of the subject, the line of open questions on the verge of the unknown. But Guthrie's mind, quite apart from its present sickness, was devoid of the incessant interrogative liveliness necessary to a great man of science. He is best remembered as the initiator of the Physical Society. His original work was not of primary importance. The professorial scientist is by no means inevitably a man of science, any more than your common curate is inevitably a man of faith.

Guthrie, to put it plainly, maundered amidst ill-marshalled facts. He never said a thing that wasn't to be found in a textbook and his course of lectures had to be supplemented by his assistant professor C. V. Boys, then an extremely blond and largely inaudible young man, already famous for his manipulative skill and ingenuity with soap bubbles, quartz fibres and measuring mechanisms. Boys lectured on thermodynamics. In those days I thought him one of the worst teachers who has ever turned his back upon a restive audience, messed about with the blackboard, galloped through an hour of talk and bolted back to the apparatus in his private room.

His turn came late in the course when I had already developed to a very high degree the habit of inattention to these physics lectures. I lost him from the word Go. If Guthrie was too slow for me, Boys was too fast. If Guthrie gave me an impression that I knew already most of what constituted the science of physics and that, though pretty in places, on the whole it was hardly worth knowing, Boys shot across my mind and vanished from my ken with a disconcerting suggestion that there was a whole dazzling universe of ideas, for which I did not possess the key. I was still in a state of exasperation at this belated discovery when the course came to an end, and in spite of a considerable loss of marks for certain defects, to be described, in the apparatus I had made, I was put in the examination list at the top of the second class. That did not shake my newborn conviction that I had learnt practically nothing about physics.

I do not know how the science of matter is taught to-day, but there is no gainsaying the colossal ineptitude of that particular course of instruction. We had half a school year to devote to our subject day after day and that was none too much for the observations, the demonstrations and the graphic and other mathematical analyses, which would have built up a sound system of conceptions about physical processes in our minds. But I doubt if there was any such system in Professor Guthrie's mind, and if there was in the mind of Boys he was either unable or too indolent to take it out, have a good look at it and explain it to anyone else. And so, instead of being used in real work on the science of physics, the time of the class was frittered away in the most irrelevant and stupid " practical work " a dull imagination has ever contrived for the vexation of eager spirits. Let me try and convey something of my horror of that physics laboratory to the reader.

It would seem that Professor Guthrie, while he was incubating this course, had been impressed with the idea that most of his students were destined to be teachers or experimental workers and that they would find themselves in need of apparatus. Unaware of the economic forces that evoke supply in response to demand, he decided that it was a matter of primary necessity that we should learn to make that apparatus for ourselves. Then even upon desert islands or in savage jungles we should not be at a loss if suddenly an evening class surrounded us. Accordingly he concentrated our energies upon apparatus making. He swept aside the idea that physics is an experimental science and substituted a confused workshop training. When I had gone into the zoological laboratory upstairs, I had been confronted by a newly killed rabbit ; I had began forthwith upon its dissection and in a week or so I had acquired a precise and ample knowledge of mammalian anatomy up to and including the structure of the brain, based upon my dissections and drawings and a careful comparison with prepared dissections of other types. Now when I came into the physics laboratory I was given a blowpipe, a piece of glass tubing, a slab of wood which required planing and some bits of paper and brass, and I was told I had to make a barometer. So instead of a student I became an amateur glass worker and carpenter.

After breaking a fair amount of glass and burning my fingers severely several times, I succeeded in sealing a yard's length tube, bending it, opening out the other end, tacking it on to the plank, filling it with mercury, attaching a scale to it and producing the most inelegant and untruthful barometer the world has ever seen. In the course of some days of heated and uncongenial effort, I had learnt nothing about the barometer, atmospheric pressure, or the science of physics that I had not known thoroughly before I left Midhurst, unless it was the blistering truth that glass can still be intensely hot after it has ceased to glow red.

I was then given a slip of glass on which to etch a millimetre scale with fluorine. Never had millimetre intervals greater individuality than I gave to mine. Again I added nothing to my knowledge—and I stained my only pair of trousers badly with acid.

Then, if I remember rightly, I was required to make a specific gravity bottle, stopper and all, out of more glass tubing. It took days. But by that time I was convinced that Professor Guthrie was playing the fool with me and that he had no intention whatever of imparting whatever he might

know and think—if indeed he did know and think anything
—about the science of physics to me.

A wiser and more determined character than I, might
have held firmly to my initial desire to learn and know about
this moving framework of matter in which life is set, might
have sought out books and original literature, acquired
whatever mathematical equipment was necessary, and come
round behind the slow obstructive Guthrie and the swift
elusive Boys, outflanking them so to speak, and getting to the
citadel, if any, at the centre of the thickets and wildernesses of
knowledge they were failing to guide me through. I did not
realize it then, but at that time the science of physics was in a
state of confusion and reconstruction, and lucid expositions
of the new ideas for the student and the general reader did
not exist. Quite apart from its unsubstantial equipment and
the lack of time, my mind had not the strength and calibre
to do so much original exploration as was needed to get near
to what was going on. I made a kind of effort to formulate
and approach these primary questions, but my effort was
not sustained.

In the students' Debating Society, of which I will tell more
later, I heard about and laid hold of the idea of a four
dimensional frame for a fresh apprehension of physical
phenomena, which afterwards led me to send a paper, " The
Universe Rigid," to the *Fortnightly Review* (a paper which
was rejected by Frank Harris as incomprehensible), and
gave me a frame for my first scientific fantasia, the *Time
Machine,* and there was moreover a rather elaborate joke
going on with Jennings and the others, about a certain
" Universal Diagram " I proposed to make, from which all
phenomena would be derived by a process of deduction.
(One began with a uniformly distributed ether in the infinite space of those days and then displaced a particle. If
there was a Universe rigid, and hitherto uniform, the character

of the consequent world would depend entirely, I argued
along strictly materialist lines, upon the velocity of this
initial displacement. The disturbance would spread outward
with ever increasing complication. But I discovered no way,
and there was no one to show me a way to get on from such
elementary struggles with primary concepts, to a sound
understanding of contemporary experimental physics.

Failing that, my mind relapsed into that natural protest of
the frustrated—malicious derision of the physics presented
to us. I set myself to guy and contemn Guthrie's instructions
in every possible way, I took to absenting myself from the
laboratory and when I was recalled to my attendances by
the registrar of the schools, I brought in Latin and German
textbooks and studied them ostentatiously. In those days
the matriculation examination of the London University was
open to all comers ; it was a discursive examination involving among other things a superficial knowledge of French,
Latin and either German or Greek and I found German the
easier alternative. I mugged it up for myself to the not very
exacting standard required. I matriculated in January 1886
as a sort of demonstration of the insufficiency of the physics
course to occupy my mind.

My campaign to burlesque Guthrie's practical work was
not a very successful one, it was a feeble rebellion with the
odds all against me, but it amused some of my fellow students and made me some friends. Even had I been trying to
satisfy the requirements of the course, the inattentive clumsiness that had already made me a failure as a shop assistant,
would have introduced an element of absurdity into the
barometers, thermometers, galvanometers, demonstration
apparatus and so forth that I manufactured, but I added to this
by demanding a sound scientific reason for every detail in
the instructions given me and contriving some other, and
usually grotesque, way of achieving the required result if

such an imperative reason was not forthcoming. The laboratory instructor Mitchell was not a very quick-minded or intelligent man, bad at an argument and rather disposed to make a meticulous adhesion to instructions a matter of discipline. That gave me a great advantage over him because his powers of enforcement were strictly limited. After a time he began to avoid my end of the laboratory and when he found my bench littered with bits of stuff, a scamped induction coil or suchlike object in a state of scandalous incompleteness and myself away, he thanked his private gods and no longer reported my absence.

The decisive struggle which persuaded him to despair of me, turned upon the measurement of the vibrations of a tuning-fork giving the middle C of an ordinary piano. We had to erect a wooden cross on a stand with pins at the ends of the arms, and a glass plate, carefully blackened with candle smoke, was hung by a piece of silk passing over these arms in such a way as just to touch a bristle attached to a tuning-fork. This tuning-fork was thrown into sympathetic vibration by another, the silk thread was burnt in the middle, the plate as it fell rubbed against the bristle and a trace of the vibrations was obtained. A careful measurement of this trace and a fairly simple calculation (neglecting the buoyant effect of the atmosphere) gave the rate of vibration per second. I objected firstly to the neglect of the atmospheric resistance and I tried to worry Mitchell into some definite statement of the extent to which it vitiated the precision of the experiment. Poor dear ! all that he could say was that it " didn't amount to much." But we joined issue more seriously upon the cross-piece. I alleged that as a non-Christian I objected to making a cross if that was avoidable. I declared that as a Deist I would prefer to hang my falling plate from one single pin. Also I insisted that it was the duty of a scientific worker always to take the simplest course to his objective. This cross-piece with its two pins was, I argued, a needless elaboration probably tainted by the theological prepossessions of Professor Guthrie. In fact I refused to make it. I could get just as good results with a Monotheistic upright. Mitchell fell into the trap by insisting that that was " how it had to be done." Whereupon I asked whether I was a student of physical science or a convict under discipline. Was I there to learn or was I there to obey ?

Obviously Mitchell had no case and as obviously I was making a confounded nuisance of myself for no visible reason. He was acting under direction. My retrospective sympathies are entirely with him.

One example is as good as a score of the silly bickering resistances I put up to annoy my teachers during that futile course of instruction. In the end when my apparatus was assembled for inspection and marking, it was of such a distinguished badness that it drew an admiring group of fellow students and some of it was preserved in a cupboard for several years. As a comment on Professor Guthrie's conception of education it was worth preserving. But I pretended to be prouder of that collection than in my heart I was. Guthrie was taking life at an angle different from mine and I had been betrayed into some very ungracious and insulting reactions. Poor discipline goes with poor teaching. A lecture theatre full of impatient undergraduate students is the least likely of any audience to detect the presence of failing health. His husky voice strained against our insurgent hum. He was irritable and easily " drawn." There was a considerable amount of ironical applause and petty rowdiness during his lectures and in these disturbances I had made myself conspicuous.

I was bad and I was not able to explain why I was bad even to myself. I was not sufficiently mature about the pur- port of my resistance to make my case clear to anyone. I was not clear about it myself. It was plain I hated and despised the superficialities of that so-called physics course, but it was not at all plain that I was honestly fumbling about to get hold of some clue to a real science of physics. I was. Confusedly my mind was making an effort. I didn't realize that in that effort I was rather in the position of a dwarf who seeks a drinking horn in order to drink the ocean. The drinking horn was certainly not in the laboratory task. The general effect upon the authorities and my contemporaries was that after quite a brilliant start I lacked staying power. Nobody noted anything relevant about the Universal Diagram. My performance in the geological course to which I was now transferred did nothing to qualify that reputation for instability.

I return after fifty years to that old perplexing quarrel with my subject and my teachers. I plead guilty at once to bad manners and a lack of worldly wisdom. I admit I had neither understanding nor humanity for any of my instructors. On the other hand I maintain that my judgment on the kindergarten childishness of that practical course was fundamentally sound. But these are really very superficial and personal issues. There is more to be got out of that baffled phase in my mental development. If, to coin a phrase, we can " de-individualize " what happened, we are left with a fairly bright sample intelligence completely thrown out, in its attempts to grasp what physics was up to. To a certain point it had all been plain sailing, a pretty science, with pretty sub-divisions, optics, acoustics, electricity and magnetism and so on. Up to that point, the time-honoured terms which have crystallized out in language about space, speed, force and so forth sufficed to carry what I was learning. All went well in the customary space-time framework. Then things became difficult.

I realize now that it wasn't simply that neither Guthrie nor Boys was a good teacher. No man can be a good teacher when his subject becomes inexplicable. The truth, of which I had no inkling then, was that beyond what were (and are) the empirical practical truths of the conservation of energy, the indestructibility of matter and force, and so forth, hung an enigmatical fog. A material and experimental *meta-physics* was reached.

The science of physics was peering into this fog, aware that there was some very fundamental misapprehension, getting glimpses of elusive somethings and nothings, making trial guesses and gestures and not getting much further. So far it had travelled upon the common presumptions and now the common presumptions were failing it. Curiously paradoxical facts were coming to light and making those common presumptions seem unsubstantial. Why for instance should there be an absolute zero of temperature? What happened to matter when it got there? Our common presumption was that " more or less " went on for ever in either direction. Why again should there be an invariable relative velocity of light? The common presumption was that if one ran with the light it should go relatively slower. Why was there a limited material universe in apparently limitless space? In an infinitude of stars the whole sky should glow with nebulous light.

There are more of these paradoxical riddles to-day. They have indeed multiplied greatly. The science of physics is even more tantalizing than it was half a century ago, and, above the level of an elementary introduction, optics, acoustics and the rest, even less teachable. The more brilliant investigators rocket off into mathematical pyrotechnics and return to common speech with statements that are, according to the legitimate meaning of words, nonsensical. The fog seems to light up for a moment and becomes denser for these professorial fireworks. Space is finite, they say ! That is not space as I and my cat know it. It is something else into which they are trying to frame the vague imperfect concepts they labour to realize. The stars existed before the universe ! The universe is expanding into God knows what ; and will presently contract ! Being is a discontinuous stipple of quanta ! In normal everyday language this is sheer nonsense. Ordinary language ought not to be misused in this way. Clearly these mathematical physicists have not made the real words yet, the necessary words that they can hold by, transmit a meaning with and make the base of fresh advance.

How was I, only a year up from the country grammar school and elementary textbooks, to guess at that embarrassing fog on the other side of the professor and his assistant ?

Biological science can still get along because practically all its questions and phenomena lie within the scope of normal experience. Its subject matter is apparently confined to the earth and to a measurable sphere of time. It frames human history and human life and is itself in its turn completely framed. It can work on indefinitely within the common presumptions. It is only when biology comes into contact with physics and the question What is life ? demands an answer in terms of physics, that real mystery is broached. But physical science is far more comprehensive, and in every direction it recedes beyond the scope of experiential thinking and of language based on common experience. It has to misuse and overstrain one familiar term after another. Its progress becomes more and more departure until a degree of remoteness is attained whereat definite consistent statement gives place altogether to philosophical speculation.

Not only was Guthrie no Huxley, but in the whole world of physics at that time there was nobody with the grasp and power of exposition capable of translating the difficulties of material science into language understandable by the eager student or the un-specialized intelligent educated man. My subsequent occupations, interests and limitations, have all stood in the way of my studying physical science and my experience of it has remained that of an outsider trying to adjust his general ideas to what he can overhear. I have never been able to make that adjustment. I am still unable to realize what modern Physics is up to. I do not find myself interrogative *with* those who are conducting research and speculation, but I find myself interrogative about them. My impression is that the Darwin and Huxley of Physics have still to come. There is a gap which has still to be bridged between the ideology and phraseology of normal intelligent people and those specialists who go out from the normal world into this great region of experimental and mathematical exploration.

It is curious to find that to-day the professors of physics are, as a body, still failing to be unanimously lucid upon even such old-world questions as predestination and free-will. A number of them lunge back ambiguously as if towards theological and spiritualistic suggestions. Some have succumbed to the lure of journalism and, writing for the general reader, have become not so much explanatory as popular and sensational.

I have here lying on my writing desk a most interesting and a most significant book. It is called *Where is Science Going ?* It is translated from the German of that indisputably great physicist and innovator Max Planck ; it is reinforced by Einstein and very ably edited by a capable scientific journalist Mr. James Murphy. Its interest centres upon the fact that these two cardinal figures in the world of physical science are clearly so perturbed by the misrepresentation and romantic treatment of the trends of physical science by some of the less intellectually scrupulous of their contemporaries and colleagues, that they feel the necessity for a clear statement of the bearing of that work upon ordinary thought. Planck reiterates very clearly the inseparability of the idea of causation from scientific work. He restates the old distinction between the objective conception of events as *caused*, on which all science rests, and our subjective conception of our own personal actions (but not those of the people we observe about us) as wilful and free. So far as our own conduct goes we have free-will ; that does not alter the fact that to an external observer our acts are determinate.

But Planck is not as absolute in his insistence upon causation as a universal external fact, as a Victorian man of science would have been. He admits certain difficulties arising out of experimental experiences. A completely comprehended system of causation, which is what I was discussing in that paper the *Universe Rigid* and caricaturing in that Universal Diagram to which I have already alluded, should admit of exact prophecy. In certain cases exact prophecy does not work and consequences, until they occur, appear to be indeterminate. Here, says Planck, we must fall back on our Faith that ultimately finer measurements and a closer analysis will eliminate that quality of indeterminateness.

But *will* they ?

I will not add my small yes or no to Planck's decisive Yes, but since I am writing a mental autobiography there is no reason why I should not supplement his repudiation of indeterminateness by a word or so about a collateral line of thought of my own, which may help a little to explain why this scepticism about the adequacy of causation has reappeared in physical theory. I fell into this line of thought as the outcome of the question " What is a species ? " which is necessarily raised by the study of organic evolution and much emphasised by classification work in petrology and mineralogy. I happened to have to read a certain small amount of logic and mental science to secure two teaching diplomas (the L.C.P. 1889 and the F.C.P. 1891) and almost simultaneously I had to read some inorganic chemistry for my intermediate examination for the degree of B.Sc. (1889). The chemical, biological and logical conceptions of what constitutes a species were thus thrown into a fruitful juxtaposition. They fermented together.

The first result of this fermentation, was a very ill-written but ingenious paper, *The Rediscovery of the Unique*, which was published in the *Fortnightly Review* in July 1891. It insisted upon the idea that every phenomenon amenable to scrutiny was found to be unique ; that therefore there might be no such thing as an identical similarity among outer realities but only approximate similarities, and that though the mind found it necessary to classify in order to operate at all, there was nevertheless a marginal fallacy lurking even in the statement that two and two made four. One set of four would never be quite the same as another set of four ; no pair matched completely. Classification was a convenient simplification of realities that would otherwise be incomprehensible. We overlooked this in ordinary practice, though it was plain before our noses if we chose to see it, and we allowed a convenient habit of acquiescence in the identification of merely similar things to harden into a fixed assumption that they were identical repetitions of the same thing. This led us to make such unjustifiable assumptions as that atoms of the same element were identical and to confuse an average result with an unanimous result.

In 1891 this was an anticipation of what physicists now call " statistical causation." The identical similarity of atoms and most other physical units was then an almost universal persuasion. To concede individuality to atoms seemed unnecessary and unprofitable.

Nobody took much notice of this article of mine at the

time, but the idea kept alive in my mind ; I gave it another form in a *Saturday Review* article, *The Cyclic Delusion*, in 1893 ; and I revived it in a paper I read before the Oxford Philosophical Society (Nov. 8th, 1903) called *Scepticism of the Instrument*. This was reprinted in *Mind*, vol. XIII N.S., No. 51, and, after revision, in the first edition of my *Modern Utopia*, 1905. It insisted not only upon this loose play of the logical process upon which I had already laid stress ; " the forceps of our minds are clumsy forceps and crush the truth a little in taking hold of it " ; but dwelt also upon the dangerous facility with which such purely negative terms as " the absolute " and infinity could be used with an air of positive significance.

I dug up this old bone of mine and gnawed it again, without getting anything very fresh off it, in *First and Last Things* (1908).

Through this insistence upon the unique individuality of every event, it seems to me, you can arrive by another route at an understanding of that appearance of inexactitude and spontaneity in minute observations which has set some modern physicists talking about objective free-will—to the distress not only of Max Planck and Einstein but of a great number of other scientific workers. All phenomena escape a little from exact statement and logical treatment. Classification is always a little imprecise and every logical process slightly loose in its handle.

" The fact," says Sir James Jeans in a popular work, *The Mysterious Universe* quoted by James Murphy (*op. cit.*), " that ' loose jointedness ' of any type whatever pervades the whole universe, destroys the case for absolutely strict causation, the latter being the characteristic of perfectly fitted machinery." But if one starts out with a perception of the universality of uniqueness one never expects perfectly fitted machinery and one demands no more than a consistency in similarity. The fascinating thing about this material world outside our minds is that it is always harmonious with itself, never crazy and anyhow, and yet at the same time never pedantically exact. Like living individuals it has " character " ; it is at once true to itself and subtly unexpected. Every time it startles us by breaking away from the assumptions we have made about it, we discover in the long run that our assumptions have been premature and that harmony is still there. Hence every scientific generalization is tentative and every process of scientific reasoning demands checking and adjustment by experiment. The further you go from experimental verification the more sensible becomes the margin of error. The most beautifully reasoned deductions in the world, the most elaborate mathematical demonstrations collapse and must be made over again before the absolute veto of a single contradictory fact, however small this fact may be.

This pragmatical view of nature leaves a working belief in causation intact. We can still believe that exactly the same cause would produce exactly the same effect. We are sustained in that belief almost invincibly by the invariable experience that the more similar the cause the more similar the effect. Our minds seem to have been built up from the beginning of time upon such experiences. Nevertheless we can recognize that there is a quiver of idiosyncrasy in every sequence and that nature never repeats herself. There never has been, it seems, exactly the same cause and exactly the same effect.

Because the universe continues to be unique and original down to the minutest particle of the smallest atom, that is no reason for supposing it is not nevertheless after the pattern of the rational process it has built up in the human mind. But was it not to be expected that the whole of Being would be infinitely more subtle and intricate than any web of terms and symbols our little incidental brains could devise to express it?

We are compelled to simplify because of the finite amount of grey matter we possess. The direct adequate dynamic causation of every event, however minute, remains the only possible working hypothesis for the scientific worker. There is no more need to abandon it than to abandon counting and weighing because no two things are exactly alike. And we may so far agree with Max Planck as to believe that we shall continually approximate to it with increased precision of observation and analysis. But also we may add a conviction that we shall never get to it. We shall never get to it for the excellent reason that there is not the slightest justification, outside the presumptions of our own brain, to believe that it is really there.

This section on the elements of physics grows, I perceive, to an inconvenient length. You see at any rate in what fashion I paddled on the edge of the illimitable ocean of physical speculation and possible knowledge, leaving the glass and stuff on my laboratory bench to take care of itself. After a little paddling I came out of those waters again and dried my feet and ran about on the shore.

In my book, the *Work, Wealth and Happiness of Mankind* (1932) there are twenty pages (Chapter II., §§ 1–4 inclusive) which summarize all that I know about the relations of the human mind to physical reality. Those pages I wrote and rewrote with very great care, I got friends to scrutinize them and make difficulties about them, and I can add nothing to them as a general statement of what I believe. In brief I realize that Being is surrounded east, south, north and west, above and below, by wonder. Within that frame, like a little house in strange, cold, vast and beautiful scenery, is life upon this planet, of which life I am a temporary speck and impression. There is interest beyond measure within that house ; use for my utmost. Nevertheless at times one finds an urgency to go out and gaze at those enigmatical immensities. But for such a thing as I am, there is nothing conceivable to be done out there. Ultimately those remote metaphysical appearances may mean everything, but so far as my present will and activities go they mean nothing. The science of physics shrinks to the infinitesimal in a little sparkling flicker in a glass bulb or whirls away vastly with the extra-galactic nebulæ into the deeps of space, and after a time I stop both speck-gazing and star-gazing and return indoors.

§ 3

PROFESSOR JUDD AND THE SCIENCE OF GEOLOGY (1886–1887)

PERHAPS I had been spoilt by the soundness and beauty of the biological course, but in geology again, I failed to find the inspiration that had come to me under Huxley. Judd was a better teacher than Guthrie, but he was a slow, conscientious lecturer with a large white face, small pale blue eyes, a habit of washing his hands with invisible water as he talked, and a flat assuaging voice; and he had the same lack of militant curiosity as Guthrie in his make-up. His eye watched you and seemed to take no interest in what his deliberate voice was saying. These were superficial characteristics and I am told that not only was Judd's work in stratigraphy sound and patient and excellent but that he was a very good and pleasant man to know. But I never knew him and my antipathy was immediate.

Geology is a badly assembled subject, anyhow. It is rather a lore than a science. In the hands of no teacher who had to cover the whole ground, could it be made as consecutive and exciting as biology and physics, those two fundamental sciences, can be made.

doable?

Assuming that my mind is a fairly ordinary one it is worth while, from the point of view of educational theory, trying to state just why it was that while biology as it was taught to me interested and concentrated me and physics interested me and tormented me as something fascinatingly attractive (though withheld, inaccessible and unattainable), geology as a whole failed to interest me at all. The work attracted me acutely in bits but in such a way as to entangle and distract my attention from most of the stuff put before me.

The explanation, I think, is that geology after the passing of that great generation which included Lyell, Murchison and their peers, had been allowed to accumulate great masses of new material without any persistent intelligible application of this new material to its general idea, which was to scrutinize the earth as a whole, say what it is and what it was, ransack it for evidence of how it originated and what it has gone through, focus the superficial evidence available upon the condition of its inaccessible interior and so at last arrive at such a power of ordered knowledge, that the geologist would know of any sediment, rock, mountain or mineral, whence it came, where it was going and what could be done with it and about it.

There is really no point at which good teaching ends and original research begins. From first to last in a science the lash and spur of interrogation must keep the mind alive. But—if I may vary the image—that flame of interrogation which kept Huxley's biological course molten and moving, burnt not at all in the geological course, and, except for bright moments when our own individual curiosity lit up a corner—and went out again, we were confronted by a great array of dark cold assorted facts, lifelessly arranged and presented.

We had a course of stratigraphy ; we studied the succession of igneous rocks and of strata, more particularly as they occurred in the British Isles. Now this is a subject that bristles with interrogative possibilities. What is there in the composition of the rock to show the conditions under which it was consolidated ? What was the geography of the world when it was made ? What has happened to it since ? What tale do the organic remains in it tell of climate and change ? What is happening to it now ? Under such questions there is not a feature about a deposit which does not become significant and interesting.

But such questions were never followed up.

They were barely hinted at. We were confronted with a list of formations and series of beds, with some indications of their local exposures and with drawers of " characteristic " fossils which we had to sketch, handle and learn to recognize. It was about as interesting as learning the names of the streets, houses and residents, with their characteristic articles of furniture, in due order as they were found in a provincial town. That might be useful for certain business purposes, for delivery-van work for example, and no doubt it was useful to a prospector to know just where he was, geologically, and " spot " the formation he was dealing with. But all that could have been learnt *connectedly* with far more ease.

We did neatly tinted cross-sections of country showing faults that were never accounted for and thrusts of unknown origin. Then came mineralogy and petrology and day after day we lifted and looked at lumps of mineral and lumps of rock and put them down again. It was all rote learning ; the science that made the examination of a fragment of bone in the comparative anatomy course a beautiful exercise in inference, was entirely wanting. So far as we were taught, a lump of slate or a lump of pitchblende was like it was *because it was*, and that was that. What made the course so peculiarly exasperating was that we were pressed along this training in recognition—at a pace that made it disastrous to follow any incidental hares our own curiosity might start for us. Again I reiterate my profound persuasion that for successful science teaching the rule should be stimulation and a maximum of available information, with a minimum of prescription.

Among other frustrated and crumpled enquiries I remember the flash of excitement I found in crystallography. I learnt that in various series of minerals, the felspar group for example, there were subtle changes in the crystalline axis with changes of chemical composition. There were fluctuations in colour and crystalline form through most of the main mineral groups. What laws lurked in these fluctuations and why?

For petrography the school was at that date exceptionally well equipped. Every student had the use of a petrographical microscope, with polarizing prisms, and we examined a long series of representative rock sections. It would be difficult to exaggerate the beauty and fascination of some of these. They let one into the very heart of those specimen chunks of rock one found so boring in a drawer, they lit them up with a blaze of glorious colour. One saw the jumbled crystals thrust against each other, distorted by unknown pressures, clouded and stained by obscure infiltrations. In many there were odd inclusions of other crystalline substances, and still more entrancingly enigmatical there were often hollows in these crystals (although they had been formed under enormous pressures) and in these hollows there were drops of fluid and bubbles of gas. It was not simply an astounding loveliness, it was, one felt, a profoundly significant loveliness that these sections revealed. They were telling in this bright clear and glowing fashion, of tensions, solutions, releases, the steady creeping of molecule past

molecule, age after age. And in their interpretation lay the
history and understanding of the Earth as a whole. But the
geological course was not out to pursue significance. It would
tolerate no loitering for such discursive purposes. Each day
brought its drawer of specimens, its tale of slides. That was
and is my indictment of all that teaching.

I may perhaps be evolving all this adverse criticism of the
courses of science at South Kensington in an unconscious
attempt to solace myself for my manifest want of success
there as a serious student, after my first year. The reader is
better able than I am to judge of that. There can be no
doubt of my failure—which led to some painful subsequent
years. But when all possible allowance has been made for
such a bias on my part, the facts remain that Professor Judd
bored me cruelly and that in his course just as in the physics
course, my discontent preceded and did not arise out of my
failures.

Since those days I have given a reasonable amount of
attention to pedagogics and social organization generally. I
find it more and more remarkable that the old Normal
School and Royal School of Mines, the present Imperial
College of Science and Technology, although an important
part of its work still consists in preparing teachers of science,
has never had, has not now and never seems likely to have,
any chair, lecturer or course in educational science and
method. Much less is there any study of social, economic
and political science, any enquiry as to objectives, or any
attempt to point, control and co-ordinate the teaching in the
various departments. To the ruling intelligences of South
Kensington a course in geology is just a course in geology.
When you have gone through a course, any course, then you
know geology. Isn't that useful for mining and metallurgy?
Both Guthrie and Judd were amateurs in science teaching,
and neither of them had sound ideas of how to inveigle

students into their subjects. And there was in the organization no supervising pedagogic philosopher with the knowledge and authority to tell them as much.

The Imperial College, I realize in the retrospect, was and still is in fact not a college but a sprawl of laboratories and class rooms. Whatever ideas of purpose wrestled together in its beginnings are now forgotten. It has no firm idea of what it is and what it is supposed to do. That is to say it has no philosophy. It has no philosophical organization, no social idea, no rationalized goal, to hold it together. . . . I do not see how we can hope to arrest and control the disastrous sprawling of the world's affairs, until we have first pulled the philosophical and educational sprawl together.

I had come up to South Kensington persuaded that I should learn everything. I found myself at South Kensington lost and dismayed at the multitudinous inconsecutiveness of everything.

Judd had a disposition very common in conscientious teachers, to over-control his students. He wanted to mess about with their minds. Huxley gave us his science, but he did not watch us digesting it. He was watching his science. Judd insisted not merely on our learning but learning precisely in his fashion. We had to make note-books, after his heart. We had to draw and paint and write down our facts just as a Judd would have done. We had to go at his pace and in his footsteps. We had to send in satisfactory note-books at the end. If not we lost marks in the final examination. To be lopped and sketched to the mental proportion of Judd in this fashion was almost as agonizing as being a victim to Og, King of Bashan.

I made an effort to do what was required of me but an irresistible boredom wrapped me about and bore me down. The habit I had acquired during the physics course of vanishing from my place in the laboratory and resorting to the Education Library or the Dyce and Foster Reading Room presently returned with enhanced strength.

The still favourable opinion of the board of selection kept me at the geological course, elementary and advanced, for an academic year and a half. By that time my career as a science student was in ruins, and that favourable opinion had evaporated. The path to research was closed to me for ever. Academically I had gone to the bad. I had become notoriously unruly. I got a second class at the end of 1886, but I failed the final examination in geology in 1887.

But I carried something out of that geological course nevertheless, for when, after various vicissitudes I presented myself to the London University examiners in 1890 for my B.Sc. degree, I had still enough geology to supplement my first class honours in zoology by taking the first place in second class honours in geology. I doubt if I had read very much in the interim. I think Professor Judd must have mingled considerations of discipline with his estimate of any progress in that final test which killed my scientific career.

§ 4

DIVAGATIONS OF A DISCONTENTED STUDENT
(1884–1887)

THIS CRITICISM of the large indeterminateness of the educational bulks and thrusts through which my brain dodged its way, is the outcome of a life's experience. Such, I now realize, were the conditions about me. But at the time I had no grasp of the huge movements and changes that were going on in the world. I had no idea of how the Normal School or the Education Office or the teaching of science in any form had come about ; I did not understand the conflicting forces that had made that teaching as good and as

of author / subject

bad as it was, nor what it was had whipped me up out of servitude to be a learner, and was now rather alarmingly losing interest in me. I had been exalted at first and then I was puzzled and dismayed. I acquit myself of blame now much more completely than I acquitted myself at the time. Deep down in me a profound humiliation at my want of outstanding success in physics and geology struggled against the immense self-conceit I had brought up with me from Midhurst. My mind had to find compensating reassurance to save me from the conviction of entire inferiority. It found that reassurance in petty achievements and triumphs in other directions. Blasphemy and the bold and successful discussion of general ideas had already proved very sustaining to my self-respect in the drapery emporium. I now found the pose of a philosophical desperado a very present help against my depression under the teaching of Guthrie and Judd.

The startled guffaws of Jennings had already persuaded me that I was something of a wit, and my rather unconventional contributions to the discussions in the Debating Society were also fairly successful and attracted one or two appreciative friends. There were three men, Taylor and Porter and E. H. Smith in that early group, of whom I have lost sight ; there were also my life-long friends, A. T. Simmons and William Burton, Elizabeth Healey and A. M. Davies. We loitered in the corridors, made groups in the tea-shop at lunch-time, lent each other books and papers and developed each other's conversational powers.

Curiously enough, though I remember the Debating Society very vividly, I do not remember anything of the speeches I made. I did make speeches because my friends remember them and say they were amusing. The meetings were held in an underground lecture theatre used by the mining school. It was lit by a gas jet or so. The lecturers' platform and the students' benches were surrounded by big models of strata, ore crushers and the like which receded into a profound obscurity, and austere diagrams of unknown significance hung behind the chairman. The usual formula was a paper, for half an hour or so, a reply and then promiscuous discussion. Those who lacked the courage to speak, interjected observations, made sudden outcries or hammered the desks. The desks indeed were hammered until the ink jumped out of the pots. We were supposed to avoid religion and politics ; the rest of the universe was at our mercy.

I objected to this taboo of religion and politics. I maintained that these were primary matters, best beaten out in the primary stage of life. I did all I could to weaken and infringe those taboos, sailing as close to the wind as possible, and one or two serious-minded fellow students began to look out for me with an ever ready cry of " Or-der." One evening somebody read an essay on *Superstitions* and cited among others the thirteen superstitions. I took up the origin of that. " A certain itinerant preacher whom I am not permitted to name in this gathering," I began, " had twelve disciples. . . ."

The opposition was up in arms forthwith and we had a lovely dispute that lasted for the better part of an hour. I maintained that the phrase " itinerant preacher," was an exact and proper description of the founder of Christianity, as indeed it was. But the vocabulary of the ordinary Englishman is sticky with stereotyped phrasing and half dried secondary associations. It seemed that " itinerant preacher " connoted a very low type of minister in some dissenting bodies. So much the worse, I said, for the dissenting bodies. The sense of the meeting was against me. Even my close friends looked grave and reproachful. I was asked to " withdraw " the expression. I protested that it was based on information derived from the New Testament, " a most respectable compilation." This did not mend matters. Apparently they could not have it that the New Testament was "respectable" or "compiled." I was warned by the chair and persisted in my insistence upon the proper meaning of words.

I was carried out struggling. To be carried out of an assembly in full fight had recently been made splendid by Charles Bradlaugh. Irish members of parliament were also wont to leave that assembly by the same laborious yet exhilarating method of transport. Except that my hair was pulled rather painfully by someone, a quite momentary discomfort, that experience was altogether bright and glorious.

But I will not expand into this sort of anecdotage. That sample must serve. The Debating Society was a constant source of small opportunities for provocation and irreverence. And about the schools, in lecture theatres, I became almost an expert in making strange unsuitable noises, the wailing of a rubber blowpipe tube with its lips stretched, for example, and in provoking bursts of untimely applause. We, subsidized students, were paid every Wednesday by a clerk with a cash-box and a portfolio, at whose tone when calling out our names we saw fit to take offence. Mockery and ironical applause having failed to mend his manners, a tumult ensued and developed to such riotous behaviour that he fled to the registrar, professed to fear a raid on his tin box of sovereigns, and refused to proceed without police protection.

It seems to me that I must have been a thoroughly detestable hobbledehoy at this stage, a gaunt shabby candidate for expulsion, and it is not anything that I can remember to my credit, but only the constant friendship and loyalty of Jennings and these life-long friends I have named and of R. A. Gregory (now Sir Richard, the Editor of *Nature*) that makes me admit there may have been some qualification

Scientist manqué

of my detestableness which now escapes me. These faithful associates bolstered up my self-respect and kept me from becoming a failure absolutely. They stimulated me to make good in some compensatory way that would atone for my apathy in the school work.

The Education Department had paid all of us scholars, exhibitionists, teachers in training, to come to London, but it had no organization to look after us when we were there. There were no provisions to lodge us or see that we were properly lodged ;—it was only in my second year that provision was made in the form of a students' refreshment room to give us midday food at reasonable prices—and except for the registrar, an ex-army man, who noted when we " signed on " late repeatedly, and sent us red underlined copies of the rules when we were observed to be smoking, shouting or loitering in forbidden places, there was no effort to find out what we were doing or how things were with us. No one bothered to find out why I had got loose in my setting, much less did anyone attempt to readjust me in any way. I was not the only straggler from the steady pursuit of the ordained courses. I fainted only mentally, but twice in my time undernourished men fainted altogether in the laboratories. I paid in health for South Kensington all my life, as I shall tell. The schools, I repeat, ignored pedagogics and had no shadow of a general directive control even of our physical lives.

The natural pose to which I resorted to recover my self-esteem, was one of critical hostility to mechanical science and an affectation of literary ambition. I do not think I have ever had very much real literary ambition. And I found in the advancing socialist movement, just the congenial field for the mental energy that was repelled by those courses in physics and geology. After I had matriculated as an ex-collegiate student in London University, I did not go on at once to work for my Intermediate Examination in Science, but I became an active follower of the new propaganda.

I did not at first link the idea of science with the socialist idea, the idea, that is, of a planned inter-co-ordinated society. The socialist movement in England was under the aesthetic influence of Ruskin ; it was being run by poets and decorators like William Morris, Walter Crane, Emery Walker and Cobden Sanderson, brilliant intellectual adventurers like Bernard Shaw and Mrs. Annie Besant, teachers with a training in classical philosophy like Graham Wallas, advanced high churchmen like Stuart Headlam and a small group of civil servants like Sidney Webb and Sydney Olivier. These leaders were generally ignorant of scientific philosophy and they had been misled by Herbert Spencer's Individualism into a belief that biological science was anti-socialist. I do not recall any contributions on my part, in those early years, to correct that misunderstanding. Probably there was a certain amount of subconscious antagonism towards science, or at least towards men of science, on my own part during those two latter years at South Kensington.

William Burton, E. H. Smith and I declared ourselves to be out-and-out socialists and signified the same with red ties. The rest of our set came most of the way with us, but with a more temperate enthusiasm. We trailed off to open meetings of the Fabian Society, which reminded me not a little of that Parliament in Landport, and we went on Sunday evenings to Kelmscott House on the Mall, Hammersmith, where William Morris held meetings in a sort of conservatory beside his house. He used to stand up with his back to the wall, with his hands behind him when he spoke, leaning forward as he unfolded each sentence and punctuating with a bump back to position. Graham Wallas, a very good looking young man then with an academic humour, was much in evidence, and Shaw, a raw, aggressive Dubliner, was a frequent speaker. There was a sprinkling of foreigners, who discoursed with passion, and a tendency to length, in what they evidently considered was the English tongue. None of our little group had the confidence to speak at these gatherings, but our applause was abundant, and on our way back to the Underground Railway at Hammersmith, our repressed comments broke through.

My return to South Kensington, after the mediocre examination results of my second year, was rather uncertain. There is a letter from myself to Simmons in which I discuss the possibilities of getting a master's job in a school. This letter recalls something which otherwise I might have forgotten, how very definite my literary ambitions had already become. (In that letter I made a rude sketch of myself with my prospective "works" about me, including "All about God" and a " Design for a New Framework of Society.") My apprehensions though justifiable were not justified ; I was given another chance and I did not after all, at that time, write to the scholastic agents. My father arranged for me to stay for a month with my uncle Charles, a small farmer at Minsterworth near Gloucester. There, so soon as my anxiety about my return was dispelled, I set myself to write a paper on Socialism with which to open the autumn session of the Debating Society.

I made not the slightest attempt to get on with my geological reading. I remember I took enormous pains with that paper. I wrote in and altered until it became illegible and then I recopied it and started upon it all over again. I went for a day over to Cheltenham, where E. H. Smith was staying in the parental home, a greengrocer's shop, to plan a scheme for " capturing " the committee of the society " in the socialist interest " and to discuss the possibility of starting a college journal. We resolved that we were going to develop the literary and political consciousness of the Normal School whether the authorities liked it or not.

I do not know how far I may be considered to have cheated the Education Department by drawing my weekly guinea throughout that third year. I was at South Kensington to learn and I certainly learnt a lot, but I gave the very minimum of time and attention possible to the substance of Professor Judd's instructions. I had no sense of cheating at the time. I was certainly working most strenuously in the Education Library, the Art Library and the Dyce and Foster Reading Room, if not in the Advanced Geological Laboratory and the Mineral and Rock collections of the Natural History Museum. If I had relaxed in my efforts to learn about the past, present and implicit future of the planet earth, I was making the most strenuous efforts to get hold of all that was implicit in the idea of Socialism. I was reading not only a voluminous literature of propaganda but discursively in history, sociology and economics. I was doing my best to find out what such exalted names as Goethe and Carlyle, Shelley and Tennyson, Shakespeare, Dryden, Milton, Pope—or again Buddha, Mahomet and Confucius— had had to say about the world and what they mattered to me. I was learning the use of English prose and sharpening my mind against anyone's with whom I could start a discussion.

We got the *Science Schools Journal* going, finding an unexpected ally in A. E. Tutton, a tremendous swatter of chemistry, who hoped for a scientific publication and worked hard for us until he realized that our intentions were amateurish and literary and socialistic. I was the first editor, but in April 1887, the registrar, roused to concern by Professor Judd about the state of my work, made me resign control in favour of Burton. That did not win me back to systematic petrography. I made an effort to conform before it was too late and save my examination, but I could not fix my interest on that stuff, even for a final cram in the last fortnight.

I had just discovered the heady brew of Carlyle's *French Revolution* and the prophetic works of William Blake. Every day I went off with my note-books and textbooks to either the Dyce and Foster Reading Room or the Art Library. I would work hard, I decided, for two hours, abstracting notes, getting the stuff in order—and then as a treat it should be (let us say) half an hour of Carlyle (whose work I kept at my disposal in the Dyce and Foster) or Blake (in the Art Reading Room). Then, perhaps an observant stroll among the Chantry pictures—they were at Kensington for as yet there was no Tate Gallery to shelter those Victorian master-pieces—the Majolica, the metal work and so forth for ten minutes and then a renewed attack on those minerals. But long before the two hours were up a frightful lassitude, a sort of petrographic nausea, a surfeit of minerals, would supervene. Granite and gabbro and gneiss became all one to me. There seemed no sense in their being different. The extent to which I did not care what bases replaced what in the acid felspars and how an increasing dose of potassium affected their twinning, became boundless and uncontroll-able. There, ready to hand on the table, was a folder of Blake's strange tinted designs ; his hank-haired rugose gods, his *Blake* upward whirling spirits, his strained, contorted powers of light and darkness. What exactly was Blake getting at in this stuff about " Albion " ? He seemed to have everything to say and Judd seemed to have nothing to say. Almost sub-consciously, the note-books and textbooks drew themselves apart into a shocked little heap and the riddles of Blake opened of their own accord before me.

So I spent the last days that were left to me before the June examination made an end for ever to my career as a serious student of science.

§ 5

SOCIALISM (WITHOUT A COMPETENT RECEIVER)
AND WORLD CHANGE

IN MY OPENING CHAPTERS I have tried to put my
personal origins into the frame of human history and show
how the phases and forces of the education that shaped me,
Tommy Morley's Academy, old-fashioned apprenticeship,
the newly revived Grammar School at Midhurst, the multiplying colleges at South Kensington, were related to the
great change in human conditions that gathered force
throughout the seventeenth, eighteenth and nineteenth
centuries. World forces were at work tending to disperse the
aristocratic estate system in Europe, to abolish small traders,
to make work in the retail trades less independent and
satisfactory, to promote industrial co-ordination, increase
productivity, necessitate new and better informed classes,
evoke a new type of education and make it universal, break
down political boundaries everywhere and bring all men
into one planetary community. The story of my father and
mother and all my family is just the story of so many individual particles in the great mass of humanity that was driving
before the sweep of these as yet imperfectly apprehended
powers of synthesis. Our mental reactions were as remarkable
as our physical and in the end, they were more important.
What did my sort of people make of what was happening
to them ?

Nowadays most intelligent people are getting a grasp upon
the broad character of the changes and imperatives amidst
which we live. An outburst of discovery and invention in
material things and of innovation in business and financial
method, has, we realize, released so much human energy
that, firstly, the need for sustained toil from anyone has been

abolished, secondly, practically all parts of the world have been brought into closer interaction than were York and London three centuries ago and, thirdly, the destructive impulses of man have been so equipped, that it is no longer possible to contemplate a planet in which unconditioned war is even a remote possibility. We are waking up to the fact that a planned world-state governing the complex of human activities for the common good, however difficult to attain, has become imperative, and that until it is achieved, the history of the race must be now inevitably a record of catastrophic convulsions shot with mere glimpses and phases of temporary good luck. We are, as a species, caught in an irreversible process. No real going back to the old, comparatively stable condition of things is possible ; set-backs will only prolong the tale of our racial disaster. We are therefore impelled to reconstruct the social and economic organization until the new conditions are satisfied. The sooner all men realize that impulsion, the briefer our stresses and the better for the race. That is how an increasing number of minds are coming to see that things are shaping. It is, we perceive, as much a part of the frame in which our lives are set as the roundness and rotation of the earth, as the pressure of the atmosphere or the force of gravitation at the sea level.

But what is matter-of-fact to-day was matter of opinion yesterday and matter for guess and suggestion the day before. What is so manifest to-day was certainly not manifest to anyone in 1887 with the same clearness and completeness. I do not mean simply that it was not manifest to ordinary people, to people like me and my brothers and school-fellows and my fellow students and teachers ; it was equally beyond the perceptions of all these clever people who made it their rôle to discuss politico-social questions in and about the Socialist movement.

Perhaps these latter had a more vivid sense of the promise

and possibilities of change, some sort of change in our circumstances than the generality, but they were—it is plain to-day—extraordinarily blind to the shapes of whatever change they perceived. How blind they were to the true proportions of things and particularly to the pace of change in things, how blind we all were, I shall try to suggest in this section, although in doing so my comments will carry me in some particulars far beyond my mental states as a student.

I shall give the effect of Socialism as it impressed me at that time and then, as I point out its limitations, I shall tell in what order they dawned upon my own mind and how phase by phase they took the sense of completeness out of the original project.

It is curious to go back now with all that one has since learnt and thought in one's head, and sit in that little out-house at Hammersmith, a raw student again, listening to a lean young Shaw with a thin flame-coloured beard beneath his white illuminated face, or to Graham Wallas, drooping, scholarly, and fastidiously lucid. It is impossible alas ! to recover my original naïve participation. I can recall what I saw but not how I felt. I have in that memory a sense of watching people unawares. There they talked, unconscious of their destinies, and we younger outsiders listened and interjected a very occasional word. We were lively and critical disciples but we were disciples surely enough, intensely excited. We listened as they planned their policies. They seemed bold to us in spirit but they seemed extremely sage in method. Morris had his wild moments—of sympathy with the martyred Chicago anarchists for example—but then he was a poet. A vast revolution was going on swiftly and irresistibly all about us, but with perfect sincerity this Fabian group posed as a valiant little minority projecting a revolution reduced to its minimum terms. It was to permeate

See throughout, Wells on writing autobiography (i.e. theory)

the existing order rather than change it. There was no real hope in their revolutionary project. It was a protest rather than a plan.

There I think is the profoundest factor in my present sense of remoteness, that vanished persuasion that we were up against essentially immutable institutions. The prevalent sub-consciousness of the time was not a perception of change but an illusory feeling of the stability of established things. That Hammersmith gathering shared it to the full. It needed such a jolt as the Great War to make English people realize that nothing was standing still. There they all felt and spoke as if they were in an absolutely fixed world, even if they thought that it was a world in which stable social injustices called aloud for remonstrance, resistance and remedies.

The Socialist movement was, one may say, a group of mental reaction systems (with very great variations within the group) to the disconcerting consequences of the new change of scale, and it had appeared *pari passu* with that new change. It did not fully understand itself. Nobody troubled to ask why it had appeared when it did and not before. A new movement does not begin by scrutinizing its origins. Its various forms were all responsive adaptations disguised even in the projectors' minds, as heroically revolutionary innovations. It proceeded from men who did not realize they were being pushed towards adaptive effort. It looked to its projectors like a purely constructive proposal, a new thing altogether. Men asked fiercely why should things always be thus and thus when as a matter of fact they had only just become thus and thus and were bound to alter in any case. " Let us have a new world," they said and they called it Socialism. But they did not realize that *some* new world was bound to come and that a new world, new in scale and power, was coming all about them.

Socialism developed at first in England and then in France

because both the industrial and the mechanical revolution had hit first England and then France before it struck the rest of the world. From the time of Robert Owen onward, scattered people under the general banner of Socialism had been trying to make new plans for social and economic relationships in the place of those that were being distorted out of recognition or swept altogether away by blind new forces. But they had no real apprehension of the truth that those old social and economic relations would go anyhow without any pushing from them.

There was nothing essentially new in such pseudo-constructive efforts and social stress. England had been the theatre of very profound economic and social mutations from the Wars of the Roses onward, and the influence of these changes upon her social history and literature is very traceable. Long before Owen and the use of the word Socialism, there had been individual socialistic schemers responding to the stresses of the times. Sir Thomas More, for example, was such an early socialistic schemer, deriving from the city-communism of Plato, and the Elizabethan Poor Law was an important early essay in practical social reorganization. Defoe and Fielding were fully conscious of the need to set up new resistances and guiding embankments to the forces of social disintegration. All history is adaptation and the only essential difference between our time and past times is the immense difference in the scale and pace of adaptive urgency.

Socialism, from its christening stage onward, betrayed its incompleteness as a response to the social situation by a profound diversity in its proposals and by that readiness to acquire qualifying labels which is due to dissatisfaction with an original proposition. Here and there it was discovered to be " practical Christianity," and various outbreaks of Christian Socialism occurred, relapsing very readily into mere medieval charitableness towards the poor. Ruskin and Morris arrived at an anti-mechanical aesthetic socialism in recoil from the early degradation of popular art by crude machine processes. The early French socialisms were as partial and fragmentary as the early English, if somewhat more logical. The flight tendency in the new movement was strong : the tendency to get together a little band of the elect and start a new humanity somewhere well out of this apparently inflexible and incurable social system in which their discontents had been engendered. Strong as is my disposition to deflate the reputation of Marx I have to admit that he was the first to conceive of the contemporary social process not as a permanent system of injustice and hardship but as a changing and self-destroying order.

The organization for an effective interplay and criticism of social ideas has still to be invented, and what happened (and what does still to a considerable extent happen) was that each group of thinkers and often each individual thinker, started in on the general problem of readjustment in more or less complete unconsciousness or in contempt and disregard of whatever other nuclei existed. All of them began at some partial experience of the great change-complex in progress. None of them saw their problem whole.

The history of pre-Fabian beginnings is outside my story ; by the time I came to London Fabianism was Socialism, so far as the exposition of views and policy went. There was no other Socialist propaganda in England worth considering. But the Fabian Society had gathered together some very angular and incompatible fragments to secure its predominant position, and at every meeting it stirred with mutterings beneath its compromises. Some members denounced machinery as the source of all our social discomfort, while others built their hopes on mechanization as the emancipator of labour, some were nationalist and others cosmopolitan,

some were anti-Malthusian and others—with Annie Besant
—neo-Malthusian, some Christian and some Atheist (de-
nouncing religion as the opium of the people) some propos-
ing to build up a society out of happy families as units and
some wanting to break up the family as completely as did
Plato. Many were believers in the capacity of Everyman to
control his affairs by universal suffrage, while others had an
acuter sense of the difficulties of the task and talked of
oligarchies, toryisms and benevolent autocrats.

It was open to the movement either to think out and fight
out these differences or to let them cancel each other out and
take whatever was left. And since Fabianism was from the
first, politic rather than scientific, it adopted the latter
alternative. I will quote later on a paragraph in which this
deliberate renunciation of exhaustive thoroughness is stated
—aggressively. Foreign Socialism had little of our British
spirit of compromise. It did go on to think and fight out
differences. It rent itself with factions. But foreign Socialism
also, if it was less persuaded of the stability of the current
order, was under the sway of certain other obsessions which
I will presently discuss. It polished and elaborated doctrine
much more than the Fabian school, but unhappily not in a
practically constructive direction.

Our little group of eager youth from the Kensington
schools, going to the new Fabian Society for instruction in
this great movement of hope and effort that was to put the
world right again, discovered by degrees that this Socialism
of theirs was indeed as a whole, almost as planless as the
world outside. Anti-Socialists in those far off days used to
accuse the Socialists, just as pagans used to accuse the early
Christians, of having their wives in common. As a matter of
fact the Fabian Socialists did not even have their ideas in
common. With a solitary exception. There was one idea
which united them all and did indeed constitute them

Socialists. This was the idea that the motive of profit, which then dominated economic life, was wrong.

That condemnation of the profit motive was the G.C.M., the greatest common measure of Socialists. There Owen, Ruskin, William Morris, Marx, Webb, Shaw, Hyndmann, Maurice and Kingsley were unanimous. They were at open war with the contemporary theory that the search for gain, the desire to possess and to possess still more and the consequent competition to possess, constituted the main driving force of human association. Proudhon's *La propriété c'est le Vol* was typical. The main contribution made by Marx was a fairly convincing demonstration, that a system of competitive production for profit could not be a permanent system. Competition, he showed, argues the final victory of a dominating competitor (or group of competitors) which will own practically everything and attempt to hold all mankind in unendurable subjection. Unendurable—and hence, he argued, the revolution. All Socialists wished to eliminate profit from economic life and consequently all of them wished to abolish private property in any but the most immediately personal things. Following upon this arose the question, "And then how will the economic life of the community be run?" Thereupon they diverged (and continue to diverge) to all points of the compass.

That paper I prepared so elaborately at Minsterworth, and read to the Debating Society in 1886, was fairly representative of the common man's socialism at that period. It was a statement of the waste arising out of competition and the disproportionate development of what I called "distribution." I was too innocent still about the things of this world to develop any attack upon investment, stock-exchange gambling, speculation and the money-credit system, as the major interceptors and absorbers of "production" in the distributive system. I was thinking rather of the overlapping rounds of competitive milk carts and the needless multiplication of retail shops. I hailed the " stores," which had done so much to overwhelm Atlas House, as the precursors of a state distributing system. I had no use for the rôle of small retailer for my father or anyone else. I wanted distribution and production to be added to the existing functions of the state which I lumped together with a primitive simplicity under the word, " defence." " Production, Distribution and Defence," that was my artless trio of social functions. The state should control them all, I said, not simply confine itself to " defence." I made no definition of the State ; apparently I had not become critical of the contemporary state as such.

This primitive Socialism of mine, in spite of my hard narrowness of approach, was well received. In the subsequent debate Burton came in with some quotations from the angle of Ruskin, A. M. Davies raised some individualist objections and cited Herbert Spencer, while E. H. Smith sounded the democratic note (which I had left silent) with considerable emphasis. His sentimental belief in the masses was as near as anyone at South Kensington in these early days came to mystical democratic Marxism. This much I recall of that meeting ; E. H. Smith with his foot on a chair, rather harshly rhetorical, Davies slight and Iberian, recalling an early portrait of J. S. Mill, precise and hesitant already with that little cough of his, old Burton, Ruskinian, biblical, as became a man from John Bright's Manchester, and very eloquent and copious. Others spoke but I do not remember them so clearly.

We denounced individualism ; we denounced *laissez-faire*. The ownership of land and industrial capital was to be " vested in the community." We did not say what we meant by the " community " because none of us knew—or had even thought it might require knowing. But what we saw as in a vision was a world without a scramble for possession and without the motive of proprietary advantage crippling and vitiating every intellectual and creative effort. A great light had shone upon us and we could see no more.

Socialism was indeed a blinding thing then. It was so dazzled by the profound discovery of itself, in that age of scramble and go-as-you-please, that it seemed unable to get on with its job. It feared to dispel the lovely vision it had conjured up. It remained in a state of exalted paralysis refusing to think further—because that might split the movement—and waiting for the world to come up to it. A similar phase of exalted paralysis has occurred at times in various sciences. After the demonstration of Evolution, biology marked time for a generation, reiterating and elaborating that immense realization. Physics for a period poised at the indivisible atom and the conservation of energy. But Western Socialism has gone on poising, poising itself unprogressively for longer than any science has done. It has been marking time for the past half century.

There were special reasons for this exceptional unprogressiveness of Socialist ideology. In the Fabian Society the desire for politic compromise damped discussion, but there was more in it than that. It was not any dread of dissension that kept continental Socialism impracticable. It was the absence of an experimental and analytical spirit. There had been a conspicuous absence from about the cradle-side of Socialism, of men with the scientific habit of mind. Socialism was essentially a pre-scientific product and it had just that bad disposition to finality of statement which it is the task of experimental science to dispel. Nobody sighed and said " And *now* what ? " Nobody said, " Here is a great and inspiring principle which does in general terms meet the stresses of our time, let us go on at once to test it soundly and work out its necessary particulars and methods."

Instead Socialism was proclaimed as a completed panacea. It was announced in strange, mystical and dogmatic phrases. The " Proletariat " was to rise against the " Bourgeoisie " and " expropriate " them, etc., etc.

The old Calvinistic theologians, equally absolute and unprogressive, announced Salvation by the Blood, and they would never explain what exactly the Blood was, nor how Emmanuel's vein was to be identified, nor anything more about it. Don't argue, don't make difficulties, they said, believe in the Blood and repent. To take difficulties into consideration was to go half way back to apostasy. In exactly the same spirit the Bourgeoisie, industrial and financial leaders, contemporary statesmen, were now exhorted by the Socialists not to ask questions, make difficulties and so damn themselves further, but just repent and consent to " socialization."

No ! they were not to ask How.

Now the first difficulty in the way of expropriating the contemporary landowner and capitalist for the common good is the absence of what I have called (in a recent examination of the collectivist idea in the *Work, Wealth and Happiness of Mankind* 1931) a " competent receiver." The Fabian Socialists in their impatience for practical application, did their utmost to ignore this blank in their outlook. They strove to think that any contemporary administrative and governing body, a board of guardians, a bench of magistrates, Parliament, Congress, was capable of playing the rôle of " the community " and " taking over " the most intricate economic tasks. The Webbs (Beatrice and Sidney) whose unparalleled industry and insistence did so much to keep British Socialism in the narrow way, held apparently that almost any sort of administration could be stiffened up and controlled by an " expert " or so, to the required degree of specialized efficiency. They were quite prepared to accept and Fabianize the Tzardom or the tribal chieftainships of the Gold Coast.

The Webb mentality was a peculiar one and it imposed itself with paralysing effect upon the Socialist movement in Britain. Mrs. Webb had been brought up a brilliant girl among politicians, and it took her many years to realize that there could be any other sort of governing class than the class she had seen so closely and intimately. Webb, a clever civil servant by competitive examination, was all too disposed to accept that same governing class, provided it left matters of detail to trusted trained officials. But really the members of that governing class, with its social traditions, its commercial liberalism and its highly developed parliamentary technique of humbugging the new voting democracy, were the last people to submit to their own socialization by indefatigable little civil service officials. There was no autocratic indolence about them when it came to business. They had their own use for parliament. Still less were the existing public bodies elected by the haphazard methods then in use, practicable instruments for the Socialist. And as yet there was nothing else. But since no alternative directorate was at once forthcoming, the discussion of these difficulties seemed to many of the impatient and still exalted faithful, not so much a practical step forward, as a mischievous move to sabotage any progress towards an emancipated world.

There, it seemed to them, stood the aeroplane ready to soar and it was a terrible pity not to get off at once, simply because no one had as yet made even drawings of a possible controlling apparatus. It was hard to wait for that controlling apparatus. " At this rate we shall never get there " and so on. To complete the image, they tried therefore to use the reins from the old gig.

Now I happened to be detached by my circumstances

from political and administrative associations and so perhaps I was able to see this hiatus in the Fabian programme with more detachment than its more active members. This problem of direction in a socialist state, this *search for a competent receiver*, troubled my mind more and more throughout the nineties. I cannot now recall what first turned my attention to it. But as I shall tell in my concluding chapter it became at last a dominant idea in my social philosophy.

The failure to develop a conception of organized directive types, a development which is a necessary consequence of the primary socialist assumption, is I believe, due to the association, at once unreasonable and very natural, of Socialism with the opposition and insurrectionary politics of mere temporary social conditions. In 1886, in common with almost all Socialists at that time, I took that association for granted, and it was only as my experience enlarged and as I came to think out the theory of Socialism more thoroughly, that I realized how accidental and in some respects how unfortunate this alliance was.

There was extremely little "democracy" in the original patriarchal socialism of Robert Owen, and it was Marx who finally fettered the two ideas of Socialism and Democracy together. His imagination intensified the insurrectionary impulse in modern democracy and sought in the resentment and discomfort of the disinherited, a sufficient driving force for a revolutionary reconstruction of society. There was a certain plausibility in the suggestion that the mass-losers in the struggle for gain, would necessarily be in favour of the abolition of private property. But it did not follow at all that they would be able to grasp the idea of collectivized property and take an intelligent controlling interest in its collective administration. Over that thin ice the Marxists skated very swiftly and nimbly. Steadily and surely the idea of the class-war was imposed upon the Socialist idea, until for many

Socialism ceased to be a movement for a more comprehensive organization of economic life and took on the
quality of a violent restitution of stolen goods—to everybody
in general and nobody in particular.

Even Socialists who did not adhere textually to the
propositions of Marx were carried unconsciously in the
direction of his teaching. His misconceptions of the character
and possibilities of English Trade Unions had been profound
—and infectious. So in Britain and Russia and Germany and
everywhere Socialism was taken to the working masses as if it
were not simply their chance and hope but their vindication,
which is an altogether different matter; and it seemed the
most reasonable thing in the world for the Fabians to turn
to the Trade Union officials, exhorting them to enter Parliament as our natural leaders in the mighty task of reconstruction before mankind. Though if you only looked at and
listened to a few of them——!

I fell in with this prevalent error as readily as most people.
I am only being wise after the event. My theoretical dissent
from modern democratic theory was contradicted very flatly
by some of my actions. In practice at any rate I was not in
advance of my time. There was an interesting duplicity in
this matter between my persuasions which ran far ahead, and
my policy which lagged with the movement. It is only in the
retrospect that I perceive that in this matter I was like a
later-stage tadpole which has gills and lungs and legs and a
tail all at the same time. In 1906 I was responsible for a
Fabian report advocating, not indeed identification of the
Fabian Society with the new Labour Party, but " cordial
co-operation," and in the general elections of 1922 and 1923
I contested London University as an official Labour candidate. Later on in my story I will return to these lapses
towards the class-war conception of Socialism. But for the
present I am concerned only with my own inconsistencies in

so far as they are representative of this curious entanglement of two fundamentally divergent tendencies, which was everywhere apparent between 1880 and 1920. I am discussing the defects and misdirections of late nineteenth-century Socialism as a working project for world reconstruction.

In another closely associated direction also, the leaders and makers of Socialism misconceived the great problem before them. They did not realize that a change in the size and nature of communities was going on. They did not grasp that modern Socialism demands great administrative areas. To this day many professed Socialists have still to assimilate the significance of this change of scale. The local Socialist parish or town councillor who is the typical unit politician of the Labour Party, is the last person likely to understand and welcome enlargements that will abolish all those parochial intimacies to which he owes his position. Just as Mr. Ramsay MacDonald opposed proportional representation with large constituencies, because the practical impossibility of a poor adventurer working a constituency under such an electoral method would banish Ramsay Mac-Donalds from political life, so these Labour wardsmen, in close touch with the local builders and contractors, found insuperable subconscious difficulties to the substitution of any large scale administration for their local jobbery. Necessarily theirs was the Socialism of the parish pump and not the Socialism of a comprehensible control of water supply between watershed and watershed. How could it have been otherwise ?

I should probably have remained as blind as most other Socialists to this second aspect of the directive difficulty if I had not chanced to build myself a house in Sandgate in 1899 and 1900. I happened to choose a site upon the boundary line between the borough of Folkestone and the urban district of Sandgate, and the experiences I had in securing electricity for my house across that boundary worked upon certain notions I had picked up from Grant Allen about the sizes and distances between villages and towns upon a countryside (which are determined originally by the length of an hour's journey by horse or foot) and started me off thinking in an extremely fruitful direction. I hit upon the principle to which I had already given expression, that not only must a genuine Socialist government be in the hands of a much more closely knit body than were the party governments of our time, but that having regard to the fact that we were no longer in a horse-and-foot world, the proper administrative areas in a modern socialized community must be altogether different in extent and contour from existing divisions. I began to work out the now universally recognized truth that one of the primary aspects of this period of change, is a change in facility and speed of communications, and that among other things this had made almost every existing boundary too small and tight. This truth was not recognized thirty years ago. But it is of quite primary importance. The applications of this principle of change of scale, once it was stated, were, I discovered, unlimited. I was already making them in my *Anticipations* in 1900. Before I had done with this idea it had led me to the realization of the inevitability of a comprehensive world-state, overriding the sovereign governments of the present time.

In 1903, after I had joined the Fabian Society, I launched this disturbing suggestion of the incompatibility of our extensive projects for socialization with the existing local and municipal organizations, in a paper entitled *The Question of Scientific Administrative Areas in Relation to Municipal Undertakings*. (It was reprinted in an appendix to *Mankind in the Making* published in the same year.) I stated my case in the subdued and enquiring manner of a young learner bringing a thesis to his master for correction. I really thought I should tap a fount of understanding. But there I flattered my Fabian audience. The Fabian audience of that phase was not easily excited by ideas, it assembled for edification, and the paper was received as though it did not matter in the least. Graham Wallas made the most understanding comments. He thought that the Fabian disregard of political reform might have been carried too far.

Afterwards, at the Webbs' house in Grosvenor Road, I succeeded in emphasizing my point in relation to the elaborate studies they were making of local government in the eighteenth century. Finding them disposed to take up the attitude of specialists towards a vexatious pupil I was as rude as I could be about this work of theirs and insisted that so far as contemporary problems of local government were concerned, a study of the methods of Dogberry and Shallow was as likely to be as valuable a contribution to contemporary problems as a monograph on human sacrifice in Etruria. With the coming of electric trams and electric lighting and universal elementary education, every problem of local administration had been changed fundamentally.

And these changes were still going on. I became very emphatic for a time in these and other talks and writings, on the difference between " localized " and " delocalized " types of mind. I was quite sure I had come upon something important that had been previously overlooked. I had. Existing divisions, I argued, left everything in the hands of the " localized " types, and so long as we divided up our administrative areas on eighteenth-century lines, the delocalized man with wider interests and a wider range of movements, found himself virtually disenfranchised by his inability to attend intensively to the petty politics about his front door and garden. He might represent a strong body of opinion in the world, but he was in a minority in any particular constituency. We were in fact trying to modernize a world in which the modernized types were deprived of any influence.

Later on the Fabian Society in belated response to these more vivid personal representations of mine, produced the *New Heptarchy Series* (No. 1 at least of it), in which my idea was Fabianized in a tract, *Municipalisation by Provinces* by W. Stephen Sanders. The association of the rank and file of the Socialist movement with contemporary political hopes and ambitions was however too close to admit of any really bold and thorough pursuit of this idea, and after this sixteen page effort by Mr. Sanders and an attempt, by a sort of afterthought, to incorporate two earlier tracts, this *New Heptarchy Series* damped off and expired. It sank back to such obscurity that it is ignored in Pease's official history of the society's achievements, and the Socialist movement produced no further systematic enquiries either in administrative psychology or in political geography. Such enquiries were not " practical politics," the Webbs had administrative and not scientific minds, and the necessary interrogative spirit was lacking.

I was baffled for a time by this tepid reception of my bright idea by my Fabian teachers and perhaps rather too ready to be persuaded that there were sound practical reasons, outside the range of my experience, why my line of suggestion was not followed up with greater zest. I had many other things to occupy me and I did not press my criticism in the society beyond a certain point. When later I contrived a rebellion against the Old Gang (as I shall tell in the proper place), it was upon an entirely different score. Nevertheless the idea of a change in scale as a matter of quite vital importance in human experience had gained a footing in my brain and was stirring about there, and since it could find no adequate outlet in any modification of Fabian policy, it expressed itself in a fantastic story, *The Food of the Gods* (1903–4) which begins in cheerful burlesque and ends in poetic symbolism. And in my *Modern Utopia* (1905), I took the inevitability of a world-state for granted.

Now I think a sedulous examination of the optimum areas for government functions of various types leading up to a critical study of sovereignty, was a line of investigation which Socialism, if it had really shared with modern science the spirit of incessant research and innovation, would have welcomed and followed up with vigour. If this system of relationships had been worked out, it would now be of incalculable benefit. But it never was worked out. The craving for immediate political and practical application shortened the vision of our Socialist leaders. In the discussion of *Fabianism and the Empire* as early as 1900, lip service was paid to Tennyson's " Federation of the World," but it was the contemptuous lip service of men convinced of their own superior common-sense, and the tract itself, drafted by Shaw and evidently revised and patched a great deal by warier minds, assumed that the division of the whole planet amongst a small number of imperialisms, each under the leadership of a Great Power, was destined to be rapidly completed, that further synthesis was hopelessly remote, and that making " our Empire " efficient was a fit and proper limit to the outlook of British Socialism. Those were the days when " efficiency " was a ruling catchword. It implied both the business and military efficiency of the Empire regarded as a competing organization. Just as the Fabians of thirty-odd years ago could not or would not or did not dare see beyond parish councillors, parliaments, trade unions, constituencies of people hardly able to read, and all the obdurate anti-quated forms of contemporary law, so they would not and probably could not see beyond the Competing Great Empires of 1900–1914. The *New Statesman*, which was started by the Webbs and their friends in 1913, as a Socialist weekly, remained sedulously disdainful of the " World-State " up to the outbreak of the Great War. . . . Then came rapid changes of opinion about the permanence and desirability of those " Great Powers " and their imperial systems, and the *New Statesman* of to-day is as much for the World-State as I am.

Let me turn now to another major item in my account-rendered of the essentials that made the Socialism of the eighties and nineties so deficient and ineffective as a key to human frustration.

Socialism was primarily a criticism of private possessiveness in the common weal, and yet in no part of the Socialist movement in Britain or abroad, was there any evidence of an awareness, much less an examination of the connexion between proprietary claims and monetary inflation and deflation. The Socialist movement floated along in a happy unconsciousness of the possible effect of inflation in releasing the debtor and worker from the claims and advantage of ownership. Nowhere was monetary control linked with the process of expropriating the landowner and private capitalist. Yet many of our minds were playing about quite close to that topic. In my *Modern Utopia* (1905) I even threw out the idea of a currency based on energy units. I could do that and still be unaware that I was touching on another vital deficiency in the Socialist project. The normal Fabian gathering had a real horror of the " currency Crank," as it termed anyone who ventured to say that money has ways and tricks of its own which no serious student of social welfare can ignore. Platform and audience rose in revolt together at the mere whisper of such disturbing ideas.

It was not merely that the Fabians refused to think about money ; they pushed the thought away from them. A paragraph from *Tract* 70 published in 1896, dealing with the

" Mission of the Fabians " is probably unequalled in all literature for self-complacent stupidity. " The Fabian Society . . . has no distinctive opinions on the Marriage Question, Religion, Art, abstract Economics, historic Evolution, Currency, or any other subject than its own special business of practical Democracy and Socialism." As one reads one can almost hear a flat voice, with a very very sarcastic stress on the capitals, reciting this fatuous declaration.

The same intellectual conservatism, the same refusal to expand its interests beyond the elementary simplicity of its original assumptions, is to be seen in the attitude of the Fabian Society towards education and the instruction of people generally in the aims of the Socialist reconstruction. In 1906 indeed I was already protesting to the Fabian Society that in order to bring about Socialism we must " make Socialists," but the still more searching and difficult proposition that in order to carry on a Socialist state you must make a Socialist population, was beyond even my imaginative courage. In *Mankind in the Making* (1902), I showed myself alive to the interdependence of general education and social structure but my projected curriculum was extremely sketchy and the political and educational propositions do not interlock clinchingly. I attacked the monarchy as a centre of formalism and insincerity. It was a mask and disguised the actual facts of government. It is however only in quite recent works of mine such as the *Work, Wealth and Happiness of Mankind* (1932) and *The Shape of Things to Come* (1933), that I recognize that public education and social construction are welded by the very nature of things into one indivisible process.

Finally, as a fifth great imperfection of our nineteenth-century Socialism, and one that seems now the most incredible, was the repudiation of planning. Socialism sought to make a new world and yet resisted any attempt to scheme or even sketch what the world was to be. In the retrospect this seems the most extraordinary of all the defects of the movement and yet perhaps it was inevitable at the time. Providentialism was in the spirit of the age. Belief in the necessity of progress anyhow, was almost universal. Even Atheists believed in a sort of Providence. The self-complacency of the Wonderful Century has already become incredible to our unsafe, uneasy and critical generation. But the nineteenth-century Individualist said in effect, " give everybody the maximum of personal initiative short of permitting actual murder and robbery, and then free competition will give you the best possible results for mankind." And the nineteenth-century Socialist answered him, "Destroy the capitalist system, take property out of the hands of individuals and vest it in any old governing body you find about, and all will be well." This belief in the final indulgence of fate was universal.

But the influence of Marx had greatly intensified that general disposition to a fundamental belief in immanent good luck. Marx was an uninventive man with, I think, a subconscious knowledge of his own uninventiveness. He collected facts, scrutinized them, analysed them and drew large generalizations from them. But he lacked the imaginative power necessary to synthesize a project. His exceptionally intense egotism insisted therefore on a pose of scientific necessitarianism and a depreciation of any social inventiveness. He fostered among his associates a real jealousy of the creative imagination, imaginative dullness masqueraded among them as sound common-sense, and making plans, " Utopianism " that is, became at last one of the blackest bugbears in the long lists dictated by Marxist intolerance. Any attempt to work out the details of the world contemplated under Socialism was received by the old Marxists with contemptuous hostility. At the very best it was wasting time, they

critique / Marx

declared, on the way to that destructive revolution which would release the mechanical benevolence latent in things. Then we should see. They were all (before the Russian revolution knocked practical sense into them) embittered anti-planners. The Faithful may try to deny this nowadays, but their vast dull abusive literature, stored away in the British Museum and elsewhere, bears it heavy witness. Salvation could come only by the Class War and in the Class War, itself inevitable, was all that sufficed for salvation. And their vehemence, their immense pretensions to scientific method, overawed many a Socialist who stood far outside their organization. They sterilized Socialism for half a century. Indeed from first to last the influence of Marx has been an unqualified drag upon the progressive reorganization of human society. We should be far nearer a sanely organized world system to-day if Karl Marx had never been born.

Contact with reality has since insisted upon the most remarkable adjustments of his theories and the completest repudiations of his essential intellectual conservatism and finality. It has obliged Communist Socialism to become progressive and scientific in method, in complete defiance of its founder and of its early evangelical spirit. Lenin conjured government by mass-democracy out of sight, " vanished " it as conjurors say, by his reorganization of the Communist Party so as to make it a directive élite, and by his organization of the soviets in successive tiers. The ultimate adoption of the Five Year Plan and its successor has been the completest change over from the providentialism of Marx to the once hated and despised method of the Utopists. Russia, as we are all beginning to realize nowadays, is now no longer a Communism nor a democratic Socialism, it has come out of these things as a chick comes out of its egg and egg membranes. It is a novel experimental state capitalism, growing more scientific in its methods every year. It is the supposititious child of necessity in the household of theory. Steadily now throughout the world the Socialist idea and its communist intensification sink into subordination to the ampler proposition of planning upon a planetary scale thrust upon mankind by the urgent pressure of reality. World planning takes Socialism in its stride, and is Socialism plus half a dozen other equally important constructive intentions.

If anyone wants a real measure of the essential unfruitfulness of the Socialist movement, if he wants to realize how like it was to the bag of a hopeful but easily diverted collector into which nothing worth-while was ever put, let him turn his mind for a moment to the adventure of flying. Let him compare the amount of hard work and detailed invention, the patient gathering and development of knowledge and experience, the generous mutual help and mental exchange, that have brought flying in a third of a century, from a dream infinitely less hopeful than the original Socialist project, to the world animating reality it is to-day. Side by side with that vigorous contemporary thrust of the human mind, the literature of Socialism is a pitiful repetition of passing remarks and ineffective promises. Is it any wonder that its name ceases to kindle and its phrases are passing out of use?

But in the late eighties and for us students it was different. Socialism was then a splendid new-born hope. How were we to tell it would decline to grow up, become self-centred and self-satisfied and end as a pervasive, under-developed, unconvincing doctrine? Wearing our red ties to give zest to our frayed and shabby costumes we went great distances through the gas-lit winter streets of London and by the sulphurous Underground Railway, to hear and criticize and cheer and believe in William Morris, the Webbs, Bernard Shaw, Hubert Bland, Graham Wallas and all the rest of them, who were to lead us to that millennial world.

The students of to-day know that the way is harder and the road longer than we supposed. But for one of us in those old days, there are now dozens of keen youngsters in the world, more adventurous, better inured to the habit of incessant enquiry, more obstinately industrious and more persistent. The constructive movement to-day has no such picturesque, brilliant and perplexing leaders as we had. It has no Shaw, no William Morris, no galaxy of decorators and poets and speakers, it cannot evoke such exciting meetings, but that is because it has far greater breadth and self-reliance. Nineteenth-century revolutionism was intellectual ragging and boys'-play in comparison with the revolutionary effort now required of us. The great changes continue and will yield to the control only of adequately organized directive forces. It is only as I look back to what we thought and knew at South Kensington half a century ago that I realize the greatness of the world's imaginative expansion.

§ 6

BACKGROUND OF THE STUDENT'S LIFE
(1884–1887)

SO FAR I have been telling of my life in London entirely from the student's end, for that, during these crucial years, was the vitally important end. A vision was being established, in the grey matter of my brain, of the world in which I was to live for all the remainder of my years. Every weekday we students converged from our diversified homes and lodgings upon the schools in Exhibition Road to learn what the gigantic dim beginnings of the new scientific world-order,

which had evoked those schools, had, gropingly and confusedly enough, to tell us. That new world-order was saying
immensely important things to us, however indistinctly it
was saying them as yet, fundamental things about life and
its framework of matter and about our planet ; and among
ourselves we were awakening to our first perceptions of the
drama of human politics and economic affairs. The beds we
slept in, the meals we ate, the companionships we formed
outside the college limits were necessarily individual and
secondary things.

They were not so secondary that they did not exercise a
profound influence on our personal destinies. In those days
the organization of the South Kensington student's life hardly
extended beyond the class rooms and laboratories ; there
were no students' hostels and our times before ten and after
five were entirely in our own hands. We dispersed in the
evening to the most various lodgings and the oddest of
marginal experiences.

My account of the systematic foundation I was given in
biological and physical science, of how that foundation was
revised, strengthened and extended in subsequent years,
and of how I developed a system of social and political concepts upon the framework of the socialism of the period, has
carried my story forward in these last respects far beyond my
student days. And indeed far away from myself. I must now
bring the reader back to the raw youngster of seventeen up
from the country, because there are still several things I
want to tell of his particular adolescence and of adolescence
in general.

Neither my father, my mother nor I, had had the slightest
idea of how I could be put up in London, and we knew of
no competent adviser. I had to live on my weekly guinea,
that was a primary condition. My mother had perhaps an
exaggerated idea of the moral dangers of the great city and

too little confidence in my innate chastity and good sense. She had had an ancient friendship, dating from the Midhurst days, with the wife of a milkman in the Edgware Road. They had carried on an intermittent and pious correspondence until her friend died. The friend had had a daughter who was married to an employee of a wholesale grocery firm and to her my mother wrote, seeking a lodging for me, a dry pure spot, so to speak, above the flooding corruption of London. She was happy to entrust me to someone she knew—and she did not reflect how little she knew of this daughter of the elect. As a matter of fact my landlady had relapsed with great thoroughness from the austere standards of her Evangelical upbringing. Piety was conspicuously absent from the crowded little house in Westbourne Park to which I was consigned. The establishment was, indeed, another of those endless petty jokes, always, I think in the worst possible taste, which my mother's particular Providence seemed to delight in playing upon her.

The house, though small, was extensively sublet. On the ground floor was a lower-division civil service clerk and his wife, whose recent marriage was turning out badly. On the first floor and upward one were my landlady and her husband, two boys on the top floor, and I and another man lodger each of us in a room of his own. I think my fellow lodger was some sort of clerk, but I cannot now remember very much about him. We got all our food out except breakfast and, in my own case, a meat tea on week-days, and we shared a common Sunday repast. There was no servant. I do not remember that there was any bathroom—a statement which is perhaps best left in that simplicity.

From this lodging I set off with my little bag of books and instruments by way of Westbourne Grove and Kensington Gardens to the vast mental expansions of the schools and in

the evening, before the gardens closed at dusk, I hurried
back, often having to run hard through the rustling dead
leaves, as the keepers whistled and shouted " All out."
South of the green spaces and heavy boughs of the Gardens
were laboratories, libraries, museums and astronomical
observatories; north were the shops of Queen's Road and
Westbourne Grove, the gas-lit windows of Whiteley's stores
and the intensely personal life of this congested houseful of
human beings to which my mother had consigned me. Never
was there so complete a transition from the general to the
particular. There was a small living-room on a half-landing
which I shared with the two boys, and where I wrote up my
notes or read my textbooks, on an American-cloth-covered
table by the light of a gas jet, while they did their school
homework or scuffled with each other.

Both the wives in this double ménage were slatternly
women entirely preoccupied with food, drink, dress and sex.
They were left alone in the house during the day and during
that middle period they " cleaned things up " or gave way to
lassitude or, when they were in the mood, dressed themselves up in their smartest to go off to some other part of
London, to wander in the shops and streets and seek vague
adventures. It was a great triumph to be picked up by a man,
perhaps treated to refreshment, to play the great and mysterious lady with him, make a rendezvous with him, which might
or might not be observed, and talk about it all afterwards
excitedly—with anyone but one's husband. The sayings
and doings of the gallant were recalled minutely and searched
for evidence as to whether he was a gentleman or what manner
of man he was. The prize in this imaginative game was an
ideal being, the clubman, the man about town; but it always
seemed uncertain whether he had been found. He might
have been just a chap up from the country on holiday, or
some salesman out of work.

Things livened up for these wives in the evening and at the week-end. There were no " pictures " then but there were music-halls where drinks were served in the auditorium and there they went with their husbands. On Saturdays there was shopping for the Sunday dinner and most of the two households went in a sort of band to the shops and stores and stalls in the Edgware Road. I was invited to join in these rounds on several occasions. We mingled in the human jam between the bawling shopkeepers and the bawling barrow vendors. We stopped and stared, crowding up, at any amusing incident. We bought shrewdly. We saluted acquaintances. We refreshed ourselves in some saloon bar. I stood treat in my turn, condemning myself to go lunchless on the following Monday and Tuesday.

Sunday had a ritual of its own. The men were given clean linen in the morning and driven out to walk along the Harrow Road until by doing three miles they could qualify as " travellers " for refreshment at an inn. This they did with a doggish air. " Whaddleye-*ave* Guv'ner ? " Thence home. Meanwhile the wives prepared a robust joint Sunday dinner. This was consumed with cheerfulness and badinage. Then the boys were packed off to Sunday school, and dalliance became the business of the afternoon. The married couples retired to their apartments ; the lodger went off to a lady. I was left to entertain a young woman, who was I think, a sister of my landlady's husband. I do not know how she came in, but she was there. I have forgotten almost everything about her except that she was difficult to entertain. I sat on a sofa with her and caressed and was caressed by her, attempting small invasions of her costume and suchlike gallantries which she resisted playfully but firmly. Her favourite expressions were " Ow ! *starp* it " and " Nart that." I remember I disliked her and her resistances extremely and I cannot remember any definite desire for her.

I am quite at a loss now to explain why it was I continued to make these advances. I suppose because it was Sunday afternoon, and I was too congested with unusual nourishment to attempt any work, and there was nothing else to be done with her. Or if there were I did not know how to set about doing it.

This manner of life was presently grossly animated by a violent quarrel between the two wives. The Sunday dinners were divided ; all co-operations ceased. The precise offence I never knew, whether it centred round the lodger, one or both of the husbands or some person or persons unknown. But it involved unending recriminations in the common passage and upon the staircase, and attempts to involve the husbands. The husbands showed themselves lacking in the true manly spirit and came home late with a hang-dog look. My landlady was very insistent upon some defect in the health of her sub-tenant. " She's in a state when no man ought to go near her," is an enigmatical sentence delivered from the half landing, that has survived across the years.

One day my landlady came into my room to change the pillow-case while I was there and provoked me into a quasi-amorous struggle. She was wearing a print dress carelessly or carefully unhooked at the neck. Then she became reproach-ful at my impudence and remarked that I might be a man already, the way I behaved. And afterwards the lodger who seems to have been hovering in the passage, observed at supper in the tone of a warning friend, that if she thought I was too young to bring trouble upon her she might find herself mistaken.

Suchlike small things on the far side, the individual life side, of Kensington Gardens, excited me considerably, bothered me with contradictory impulses, disgusted me faintly and interfered rather vexatiously with the proper copying out of my notes of Professor Huxley's lectures.

It was certainly not the sort of pure safe life away from home that my mother had desired for me, but it did not occur to me to tell her anything about it and I should probably have begun my actual sexual life very speedily, clumsily and grossly and slipped into inglorious trouble if it had not been for the sensible action of a cousin on my father's side, whom he had asked to keep an eye on me.

My father was the sort of man to like, admire and cultivate a friendly niece and his opinion of Janie Gall was a particularly high one. She was an assistant in the costume department at an establishment in Kensington High Street which I see still flourishes, Messrs. Derry & Toms, and she made me call upon her and take her out on several occasions. It was like old times at Southsea to be the escort of an elegant lady from the costumes ; I knew the rôle and we got on very well together. In response to her frank enquiries I described to her the more seemly and impersonal defects of my lodgings, considered as quarters for a studious spirit, and she grasped the situation and acted with great promptitude.

A sister-in-law of my father's was letting lodgings in the Euston Road ; the situation at Westbourne Park was explained by my father to my mother, who had perhaps allowed the natural jealousy of relations-in-law to blind her to the merits of my Aunt Mary, and I and my small portmanteau were promptly transferred—probably in a four-wheeled " growler "—to my new quarters. A mile was added each way to my daily journey to the schools, but now it was no longer necessary to run at twilight because the new route lay diagonally across Hyde Park—and Hyde Park stands open to our bolder citizens night and day.

It is queer that I do not remember the particulars of that move, nor can I recall the address of that house in which I lodged in Westbourne Park, nor the names of either my landlady, her sub-tenant or her lodger. The few facts I have given and one or two other slightly salacious details remain in my memory, but all the rest of that interlude is forgotten beyond all recalling. It links to nothing else. I disliked it and put it out of my mind. I cannot remember how long it was, whether it was a matter of weeks or months that I lodged there before I went to Euston Road. I looked, so to speak, through a hole in my life of some weeks more or less, into a sort of humanity, coarser, beastlier and baser than anything I had ever known before. None of the other people in my experience before or since were quite so like simmering hot mud as that Westbourne Park household. I cannot recall really pleasant things about anybody in it, whereas there is scarcely any other group of people in my past which had not its redeeming qualifications. I think the peculiar unpleasantness of that episode lies in the fact that we were all too close together. We were as congested as the Zoo monkeys used to be before the benign reign of Sir Chalmers Mitchell. Crowded in that big cage they seemed in those days the nastiest of created things. Now, distributed spaciously under happier and less provocative conditions even the baboons have become—practically—respectable.

I can recall very little about Janie Gall beyond this timely intervention. She was a tall, blonde, sedate young woman whose life had been divided hitherto between England and her father's ship in the far east. She told me once that she was the first white woman ever to visit the Pelew Islands, but she had nothing very much to tell me about those distant scenes. She passed out of my world and afterwards I learnt she had gone to Sweden and had married a Swede named Alsing. I have a perfectly clear picture of myself walking along Knightsbridge and talking with her, and nearly everything else about her is obliterated. Did she

go first, or afterwards, to a well-known mourning warehouse in Regent Street? I cannot remember any of these
details. They are after all very trifling details.

But 181 Euston Road stands out very bleak and distinct
in my memories. In the eighties Euston Road was one of
those long corridors of tall gaunt houses which made up a
large part of London. It was on the northern boundary of
Bloomsbury. Its houses were narrow and without the
plaster porticos of their hinterland and of Bayswater,
Notting Hill, Pimlico, Kilburn and suchlike regions. They
had, however, narrow strips of blackened garden between
them and the street, gardens in which at the utmost grew a
dying lilac or a wilted privet. One went up half a dozen steps
to the front door and the eyebrows of the basement windows
were on a level with the bottom step.

So far as I can puzzle out the real history of a hundred
years ago, there was a very considerable economic expansion
after the Napoleonic war, years before the onset of the
railways. The steam railway was a great stimulus to still
further expansion, its political consequences were tremendous, but it was itself a product of a general release of energy
and enterprise already in progress. Under a régime of
unrestricted private enterprise, this burst of vigour produced
the most remarkable and lamentable results. A system of
ninety-nine year building leases was devised, which made
vast fortunes for the ground landlords and rendered any
subsequent reconstruction of the houses put up almost
impossible until the ground lease fell in. Under these conditions private enterprise spewed a vast quantity of extremely
unsuitable building all over the London area, and for four
or five generations made an uncomfortable incurable stress
of the daily lives of hundreds of thousands of people.

It is only now, after a century, that the weathered and
decaying lava of this mercenary eruption is being slowly

replaced—by new feats of private enterprise almost as greedy and unforeseeing. Once they were erected there was no getting rid of these ugly dingy pretentious substitutes for civilized housing. They occupied the ground. There was no choice ; people just had to do with them and pay the high rents demanded. From the individualistic point of view it was an admirable state of affairs. To most Londoners of my generation these rows of jerry-built unalterable homes seemed to be as much in the nature of things as rain in September and it is only with the wisdom of retrospect, that I realize the complete irrational scrambling planlessness of which all of us who had to live in London were the victims.

The recklessly unimaginative entrepreneurs who built these great areas of nineteenth-century London and no doubt made off to more agreeable surroundings with the income and profits accruing, seem to have thought, if they thought at all, that there was an infinite supply of prosperous middle-class people to take the houses provided. Each had an ill-lit basement with kitchen, coal cellars and so forth, below the ground level. Above this was the dining-room floor capable of division by folding doors into a small dining-room and a bureau ; above this again was a drawing-room and above this a floor or so of bedrooms in diminishing scale. No bathroom was provided and at first the plumbing was of a very primitive kind. Servants were expected to be cheap and servile and grateful, and most things, coals, slops, and so forth had to be carried by hand up and down the one staircase. This was the London house, that bed of Procrustes to which the main masses of the accumulating population of the most swiftly growing city in the world, including thousands and thousands of industrial and technical workers and clerks, students, foreigners upon business missions, musicians, teachers, the professional and

artistic rank and file, agents, minor officials, shop employees
living out and everyone indeed who ranked between the
prosperous householder and the slum denizen, had to fit their
lives. The multiplying multitude poured into these moulds
with no chance of protest or escape. From the first these
houses were cut-up by sub-letting and underwent all sorts
of cheap and clumsy adaptations to the real needs of the
time. It is only because the thing was spread over a hundred
years and not concentrated into a few weeks that history
fails to realize what sustained disaster, how much massacre,
degeneration and disablement of lives, was due to the
housing of London in the nineteenth century.

(But the autobiography of any denizen of any of the
swelling great cities of the nineteenth century who wished
to place his story in regard to the historical past and the
future would have, I suppose, a similar story to tell of housing
conditions ; the same tale of growth without form—like a
cancer. New York was almost as bad and St. Petersburg far
worse. There is a dreadful flavour of mortality about these
city growths of the past hundred years, so that one wonders
at times whether the world will ever completely recover from
them. Nowhere was there, nowhere is there yet, an intelligent
preparation of accommodation for the specialized civilians
in the endless variety rendered inevitable by the enlarging
social body. Nowhere was there protection from those Smart
Alecs, the primary poison of the whole process, who piled
up the rents. Even when the tenants were people who did
work of vital importance to the community, the ground had
been so sold under their feet that they came back from work
to needlessly restricted and devitalizing quarters for their
sleep and leisure.)

My uncle William had been no better business man than
my father and he had had no skill in cricket or any other
earning power to fall back upon. He had been a draper and,

my mother said, extravagant. I had seen him on one occasion, a dark shabby unhappy man clad in black, who came to Atlas House one wintry afternoon, ate with us, talked apart with my father, borrowed a half sovereign from our insufficiency and departed—to die not long afterwards in a workhouse infirmary. He had married one of two sisters named Candy, daughters of a small Hampshire farmer ; the other had remained unmarried and, after their father's death, with a van load of furniture and a few pounds, she and my widowed aunt had come to London to live by letting lodgings. They planned to occupy the basement, cooking in the back kitchen and living in the front and doing all the work up and down the house ; the dining-room floor to be let to one tenant and the drawing-room floor to another and all the rest of the bedrooms to nice young men or respectable young ladies ; and thus they would get a living. They made no provision in their estimates for the wear and tear of their furniture nor the wear and tear of themselves, and so, year by year, their rooms and their services became less and less attractive and desirable. That was what happened to countless widows, old servants with a scrap of " savings," wives of employees who wanted to help their husbands a bit and all that vast miscellany of dim and dingy women, the London landladies, who were guyed so mercilessly in the popular fiction of the time. The larger, more successful, lodging houses had a " slavey," a poor drudge to do the heavier carrying and scrubbing, but people like my aunt and her sister, had to be their own slaveys.

When my cousin Janie Gall took me to tea at Euston Road the Saturday afternoon before my removal, my aunt and her sister were in company costume with caps and small aprons, like my mother at Up Park. But even then I thought them grimy, and, poor dears ! they *were* grimy. They were far grimier than my mother had ever been in the worst days at

Atlas House. How could they have been anything else, seeing
that the house was warmed throughout by coal-fires and that
they were perpetually carrying up scuttles of coal (at sixpence a scuttle) to their various lodgers, and dusting and
scrubbing and turning out rooms and dealing with slops and
ashes ? My aunt Mary was a little bright-eyed woman and
very affectionate and lovable from the beginning ; her sister
was larger, with a small eye and profile faintly suggestive of
a parrot, judicious in her manner and given to moods of
gloom and disapproval. As we sat talking politely, a dark-eyed
girl of my own age, in the simple and pretty " art " dress that
then prevailed came shyly into the room and stood looking
at us. She had a grave and lovely face, very firmly modelled,
broad brows and a particularly beautiful mouth and chin
and neck. This was my cousin Isabel whom later I was to
marry.

It was arranged that I should have a room upstairs and
work at my notes in the evening by the gas light in the underground front room. This was a rather crowded room with
hanging shelves for books, a what-not and a piano upon
which at times my cousin played not very skilfully the few
pieces of music she had learnt. My aunt would darn stockings
and her sister fret over accounts, or sometimes we would
play whist, at which Miss Candy, aunt Arabella, was as
precise as Lamb's Mrs. Battle. She found the way her sister
Mary played particularly trying. " I'm silly," said my aunt
Mary anticipating her reproof. " You *shouldn't* be silly,
Mary," said auntie Bella. They had been saying that over
and over again since they were girls—far back in the eighteen
fifties.

On occasion, when the upstairs lodgers were away or the
rooms unlet, we transferred our evenings to the drawing-
room or dining-room. If I wanted to concentrate I went
to my own bedroom and there I would work by candle-light,

often in an overcoat, with my feet wrapped about with my clean underlinen and stuck into the lowest drawer of my chest of drawers to keep them out of the draught along the floor.

I forget most of the lodgers. There was a woman student at University College who had the drawing-room floor for some years, and a German woman in the dining-room whose visitors roused Auntie Bella's censorious curiosity. Some of them were men, and foreigners at that. " We mustn't come to that sort of thing," said Aunt Arabella darkly, but went no further in the matter.

On the top floor was a poor old clergyman and his wife, who presently died one after the other, the wife first. He had either never had a vicarage or he had lost one, and he earned a precarious income by going off to churches for a week-end or a week or so on " supply," to relieve the regular incumbent. Until, one wintry week-end, some careless person sent an open dog-cart to meet him at the railway station and gave him pneumonia. Apparently he had no surviving friends or if he had they did not come forward; he died intestate and practically penniless, and I escorted my aunt one wet and windy morning to Highgate cemetery where we were the only mourners at his funeral. Another old clerical derelict, with a dewdrop at his nose-tip, hurried through the service. It was my first funeral. I had never dreamt that a clergyman could end so shabbily, or that the Establishment could discard its poor priests so heartlessly. It was quite a new light on the Church. My little aunt was his sole creditor and executor and I doubt if, when the doctor was satisfied, there was much left to set against the arrears of the poor old fellow's bill.

I lodged at 181 Euston Road for all the rest of my student life. Every day in the session, unless I got up too late, I walked to South Kensington. I would go through the back

streets as far as the top of Regent Street with Isabel ; she
worked in Regent Street as a retoucher of photographs ;
there we said good-bye for the day and I went on for all the
length of Oxford Street to the Marble Arch and thence
across the Park to Exhibition Road. If I was late however
I left my cousin unescorted and went by train from Gower
Street Station (Euston Square they call it now) to Praed
Street at a cost of three half-pence, and then ran across the
Gardens. And as I went down Exhibition Road, Euston
Road passed out of my mind and my student life resumed
again as if it were a distinct and separate stream of experience. I thought again upon the scale of astronomical
distances and geological time and how, when presently
Socialism came, life would be valiant and spacious and there
would be no more shabbiness or darkness in the world.

§ 7

HEART'S DESIRE

I WANT to make my physical presence at the time I left
South Kensington, as real as possible to the reader. I have
given five sections to tell how my picture of life in the universe
was built up in my brain ; I now want to show what sort of
body it was that carried this brain about and supplied it
with blood and obedient protection. By 1887, it had become
a scandalously skinny body. I was five foot five and always
I weighed less than eight stone. My proper weight should
have been 9 st. 11 lbs., but I was generally nearer to seven,
and that in my clothes. And they were exceedingly shabby
clothes. It did not add to the charm of my costume that
frequently I wore a waterproof collar, an invention now
happily forgotten again. It was a glossy white rubber-covered

thing that cost nothing for laundry. That was the point of it. You washed it overnight with soap and a sponge, and then it was ready in the morning. But after a time it accumulated something rather like the tartar that discolours teeth. It marks one difference that is worth noting between the eighties and the present time, that never a Kensington student, however needy, would have dreamed of appearing in the classroom or laboratory without what could at least be considered a white collar. Now, I suppose, a good half of the Kensington crowd wear open-necked shirts. A certain proportion of us in those days, and all the staff, wore top hats.

I was as light and thin as I have said, because I was under-nourished. I ate a hastily poached egg and toast in the morning before going off for my three mile tramp to the schools and I had a meat tea about five when I got back— and a bread and cheese supper. Most of my time I was so preoccupied with my studies and my intellectual interests that I did not observe what was happening to me, but occasionally and more especially in my third year, I would become acutely aware of my bad condition. I would survey my naked body, so far as my bedroom looking-glass permitted, with extreme distaste, and compare it with the Apollos and Mercuries in the Art Museum. There were hollows under the clavicles, the ribs showed and the muscles of the arms and legs were contemptible. I did not realize that this was merely a matter of insufficient food and exercise. I thought it was an inferior body—perhaps past hope of mending.

To me, in my hidden thoughts, the realization that my own body was thin and ugly was almost insupportable—as I suppose it would be to most young men or women. In the secret places of my heart I wanted a beautiful body and I wanted it because I wanted to make love with it, and all the

derision and humour with which I treated my personal
appearance in my talking and writing to my friends, my
caricatures of my leanness and my unkempt shabbiness, did
not affect the profundity of that unconfessed mortification.
Each year I was becoming much more positively and urgently sexual and the desire to be physically strong and
attractive was intense. I do not know how far my psychology
in these matters is exceptional, but I have never been able
to consider any sort of love as tolerable except a complete
encounter of two mutually desirous bodies—and they have
to be reasonably lovely bodies. The circumstances must be
beautiful or adventurous or both. I believe this is how things
are with nine people out of ten ; as natural as hunger and
thirst.   *always the comparisons or justifications*
    The fact that I was slovenly to look upon and with hollows
    → the retreat to 'the general'.
under my collar-bones and with shoulder-blades that stuck
out, could not alter these insistent demands of the life in me.
No doubt these realizations reinforced those balancing inhibitions and that wariness and fastidiousness which are as
natural as the primary cravings, and made me more than
normally secretive ; but to hold down an urgency is not to
diminish it. I had quite another set of motives, ambition, a
desire for good intellectual performance and that vague
passion for service which expressed itself in my socialism, and
I tried, not always successfully, to take refuge in these from
my more vital and intimate imperatives.

Beautiful girls and women do not come the way of poor
students in London. One was nearer to such beings among
the costume hands and counter assistants of the draper's
shop. There were a few friendly women fellow-students in
the laboratories, but they deliberately disavowed sex in their
dress and behaviour. Sex consciousness broke out to visibility
only among the Art students, and these we saw but rarely
during brief promenades in the Art Museum, which made a

kind of neutral territory between the Art Schools and ourselves. On my long march back to Euston Road I would see women walking in the streets, especially along Oxford Street and Regent Street, and sometimes in the light of the shops, one would shine out with an effect of loveliness and set my imagination afire. I would be reminded of Ellen Terry walking in the sunshine upon the lawn at Surly Hall. Or I would see some handsome girl riding in the Row or taking a dog for a run in the park. They were all as inaccessible as the naked women in the Chantry pictures.

It was practically inevitable that all this suppressed and accumulating imaginative and physical craving in me should concentrate upon the one human being who was conceivable as an actual lover ; my cousin Isabel. She and I had from the outset a subtle sense of kindred that kept us in spite of differences, marriage and divorce, friendly and confident of one another to the end of her days, but I think that from the beginning we should have been brother and sister to each other, if need, proximity and isolation had not forced upon us the rôle of lovers, very innocent lovers. She was very pleasant to look upon, gentle mannered, kind and firm, and about her I released all the pent up imaginations of my heart. I was devoted to her, I insisted, and she was devoted to me. We were passionate allies who would conquer the world together. In spite of all appearances, there was something magnificent about us. She did her best to follow me, though something uncontrollable in her whispered that this was all nonsense. And whenever we could avoid the jealous eye of Auntie Bella, we kissed and embraced. Aunt Mary did not embarrass us because she had taken to me from the beginning.

Across a gulf of half a century I look with an extreme detachment and yet with an intense sympathy upon these two young Londoners, walking out together, whispering in a darkened staircase, hugging in furtive silence on a landing. Isabel wore simple dresses after the Pre-Raphaelite fashion. We should think them graceful to-day except that the sleeves would seem big and puffy to us and the pretty neck unaccountably hidden. Abroad she wore a cloak in winter and her hats were usually those velvet caps that also came out of the Cinquecento.

Having stripped my youthful self for your edification I will now cover up my worst physical deficiencies with my clothes again. They were rather shabby but very respectable, a grey " mixture " suit and a grey overcoat in winter. The collar was white even if it was waterproof and the hat was a hard bowler. There were no soft felt hats until much later and a cap, in London, would have been disgraceful behaviour. And we lived in an age when everyone had best clothes. On Sunday we two walked out together with a certain added seriousness; we walked in Regent's Park or we went to a church or a picture gallery, when there was a picture gallery open, or to some public meeting, and then I wore a morning coat and a top hat.

In my desire for correct particulars in this autobiography, I have spent some time trying to trace the beginnings, the rise and fall of my successive top hats. They mark periods in human history as surely as do the ramshackle houses in which I spent the first half of my life and the incoherent phases of my upbringing and education. In the mind of a febrile psycho-analyst, these top hats might be made to show the most curious and significant phases in the upward struggle of the human intelligence. They were more voluntary and so more subtle in their fluctuating intimations than were turbans, fezes, pigtails and the like which outlasted whole generations. But that history of the rise and fall of the top hat has yet to be written. When I was born it had already passed its zenith ; cricketers no longer played the game in top hats—though my father had begun in that fashion ; but it still seemed the most natural thing in the world for me to take out my cousin on Sundays in this guise. Half the young men I met on that day sported similar glossy cylinders. In the City and West End, on a week-day, you rarely saw a man wearing anything else. The streets below repeated the rhythms of the clustering chimney-pots on the roofs above. I must have acquired my first specimen, when I acquired my morning coat and its tails, during the second year of my apprenticeship at Southsea. But was that the one I wore in London ? I think it was and if so it went right on with me to 1891, when it died a natural death—as I shall tell in its place—in the presence of Mr. Frank Harris, the editor of the *Fortnightly Review*. After that I think I bought another to attend a funeral and a third seems to have marked a phase of social acquiescence before the War. I went to Bond Street picture shows, and the Academy, in the latter. It ended as a charade property for my sons at Easton Glebe. Since then I have had no more top hats.

But it is just that indication of social acquiescence which justifies this digression and makes the top hat of my student days so significant. It was the symbol of complete practical submission to a whole world of social conventions. It was not, in my case at any rate, just a careless following of the current fashion, for peace and quietness. That early top hat in particular had been economized for, it expressed an effort, it had *had* to be worn.

Now as my cousin and I walked along the broad path between the flower beds of Regent's Park—bright and gay they were then but not nearly so beautiful as they are now—I would be talking very earnestly of atheism and agnosticism, of republicanism, of the social revolution, of the releasing power of art, of Malthusianism, of free love and such-like liberating topics. In a tail coat and top hat. My mind was twenty years ahead of my visible presence. It was indeed making already for the gardens of Utopia.

But my cousin who was as direct and simple as she was sane, honest and sweet, was just walking in her Sunday best in Regent's Park.

In my eagerness to find in her the mate of my imaginings, I quite overlooked the fact that while I had been reading and learning voraciously since the age of seven, she had never broken a leg and so had never been inoculated with the germ of reading. While I had gone to school precociously equipped, she had begun just the other way about as a backward girl, and she had never recovered from that disadvantage. It was a purely accidental difference to begin with, I am sure her brain was inherently as good as or better than mine, but an inalterable difference in range and content was now established. Her world was like an interior by a Dutch master and mine was a loose headlong panorama of all history, science and literature. She tried valiantly to hang on to what I was saying, but the gap was too wide. She thought I must be dreadfully " clever " to talk such nonsense and she comforted her mind with the reflection that it had not the slightest relation to things about us. She liked me by nature and she did not like to irritate me, but sometimes something I said was too much for her, and she "stood up for " the old Queen, or the landlords, or business men, or Church ; whatever it was I happened to be abolishing. It was a fixed principle in her broad and kindly mind that they were all " doing their best " and that in their places we should do no better. Then, since what she said spoilt the picture I wanted to make of her in my imagination, I would become rude and over-bearing.

I tried to get her to read books and particularly the books of Mr. John Ruskin, but like so many people who have had the benefit of a simple English education she was book-shy.

The language she met in books was not the language of her speech and thoughts. I doubt if she read a hundred books in all her life.

I was far too much in a ferment myself to reduce my ideas to terms that would have persuaded her. I hadn't that much grasp of my own views. " Everybody doesn't think alike," said my cousin. " But that's no earthly reason why you shouldn't think at all," I bit, and after that the young couple would go on their way in a moody silence, dimly aware that there was something unjust and wrong about it all, but quite unable to find out what was wrong or in any way set it right. Why was I always talking of these queer and out-of-the-way things ? Because otherwise and particularly in my silk hat and so forth, I was quite a nice boy. And again why was I sometimes so pressing about love-making— in a way that one ought not to think about until one was in a position to marry ? And that might not be for years. A little love-making there might be, no doubt, but one must not go too far.

My mind in those days refused absolutely to recognize the incompatibility that is so plain as I state it here. I had laid hands on Isabel, so to speak, to love her and I would not be denied. She was to be my woman whether she liked it or not. I tethered my sexual and romantic imagination to her so long as I was in London—and that, quite as much as my poverty, saved me from the squalor of the street-walker. With a devotion that was more than half jealousy, whenever work did not hold me at South Kensington I used to devour my meat tea and then set off out again down to Regent Street to meet her and bring her home, and always when she was working in the evening at some art classes at the Birk-beck Institute, I made my way through the dark Bloomsbury squares to meet her. These evening assiduities kept me ex-ercised physically but they made grave inroads upon the time I should have given to my proper work. And I loved her smile, I loved her voice, I loved her feminity, I loved to feel that—provided I did not go too far—she was mine. And someday, somewhen, I should do something fine and successful and the world would be at my feet ; her tacit reservations would vanish and she would realize that everything I said, did and wanted, was right.

I was always wanting to board and storm and subjugate her imagination so that it would come out at last of its own accord to meet mine. It never came out to meet me.

Through some mysterious instinct my little Aunt Mary understood and believed in my heart's desire, but Auntie Bella was sterner stuff, with a more sceptical disposition and an acuter sense of reality. She thought it a pity that Isabel and I were so much together.

That was the naïve intensely personal other side of my life, to which I walked back daily across Hyde Park from that interplay of lectures room, laboratory, debating society and student talk described in the earlier sections of this chapter.

One of the queer things about us human beings is the way the obvious consequences of our actions take us by surprise. I will not now apply this to the large scale instances of the great wars of 1914 and, shall we say ?—1940. But I do remember very vividly how unprepared I was to walk the plank as a condemned science student in the summer of 1887. I had done practically everything necessary to ensure failure and dismissal, but when these came they found me planless and amazed. I suppose that is the way of youth— and all animals. Foresight is among the latest and incompletest of the acquisitions of mankind.

Abruptly the self confidence which had never really failed

me since my escape from the Southsea Drapery Emporium, collapsed like a pricked bladder. I had no outlook, no qualifications, no resources, no self-discipline and no physique.

" And what is to become of me *now* ? " I asked, in a real panic for the first time since my triumphant exodus from the draper's shop.

CHAPTER THE SIXTH

STRUGGLE FOR A LIVING

§ 1

Sixth Start in Life or Thereabouts (1887)

I HAVE TO THANK my lucky stars—and a faithful friend or so—that I did not sink as a result of my insubordinations, inattentions, digressions and waste of energy at South Kensington into absolute failure. Most of the orderly students in my generation made good as professors and fellows of the Royal Society, as industrial leaders, public officials, heads of important science schools ; knighthoods and the like are frequent among them ; I am probably the only completely unsatisfactory student turned out by the Normal School, who did not go the pace there and who yet came up again and made a comparative success in life. I was now nearly of age and able to realize the dangers of my position in the world, and I put up a fight according to my lights. But it was a wild and ill-planned fight, and the real commander of my destinies was a singularly facetious Destiny, which seemed to delight in bowling me over in order to roll me through, kicking and struggling, to some new and quite unsuspected opportunity. I have already explained how I became one of the intelligentsia and was saved from a limited life behind a draper's counter by two broken legs, my own first, and then my father's. I have now to tell how I was guided to mental emancipation and real prosperity by a

The plot

smashed kidney, a ruptured pulmonary blood vessel, an unsuccessful marriage and an uncontrollable love affair.

My very obstinate self-conceit was also an important factor in my survival. I shall die, as I have lived, the responsible centre of my world. Occasionally I make inelegant gestures of self-effacement but they deceive nobody, and they do not suit me. I am a typical Cockney without either reverence or a sincere conviction of inferiority to any fellow creature. In building up in my mind a system of self-protection against the invincible fact that I was a failure as a student and manifestly without either the character or the capacity for a proper scientific career, I had convinced myself that I was a remarkable wit and potential writer. There must be compensation somewhere. I went on writing, indeed, as a toy-dog goes on barking. I yapped manuscript, threateningly, at an inattentive world.

With every desire to be indulgent to myself I am bound to say that every scrap of writing surviving from that period witnesses that the output was copious rubbish, imitative of the worst stuff in the contemporary cheap magazine. There was not a spark of imagination or original observation about it. I made not the slightest use of the very considerable reservoir of scientific and general knowledge already accumulated in my brain. I don't know why. Perhaps I was then so vain that I believed I could write *down* to the public. Or so modest that I thought the better I imitated the better I should succeed. The fact remains that I scribbled vacuous trash. The only writing of any quality at all is to be found in the extremely self-conscious letters I wrote to my friends. Here I really did try to amuse and express myself in my own fashion. These letters are adorned with queer little drawings and A. T. Simmons and Elizabeth Healey among others, seem to have found them worth keeping so that a number of them have been preserved to this day. There is fun in them.

I doubt if I could possibly have carried on and become a writer without the support of those two people. They were my sole "public" for years. No letters I wrote to my cousin Isabel survive. I cannot remember writing to her though certainly I must have done so. I doubt if I wrote to her with the same zest and certainty of appreciation.

My plans for a rally against my richly-deserved disaster as student, had a certain reasonableness. I was now in a shocking state of bodily unfitness, very thin, under-exercised and with no muscular dexterity, loose in gesture, slow on the turn and feeble in the punch; and it seemed to me that if I got a job as an assistant in a school deep in the country, with good air, good food and good games (I had my previous invigoration at health-giving Midhurst in my mind), I might pick up the neglected beginnings of my bodily manhood and at the same time get a little leisure to learn, by the method of trial and error, what was the elusive vital thing I didn't yet know about this writing business. I had had, by the bye, one small success and earned a guinea. I had sent a short story, now happily untraceable, to the most popular fiction weekly of those days, the *Family Herald*. It was a very mis-leading success. It was a sloppy, sentimental, dishonest, short story and its acceptance strengthened me in my delusion that I had found the way to do it.

Meanwhile I had to live by teaching. In spite of my rather wilted qualifications, there were plenty of residential school jobs at forty or fifty pounds a year to be got ; I had matriculated as an ex-collegiate in London University, I was qualified to earn grants in a number of subjects, and I had had teaching experience. The Holt Academy, Wrexham seemed, on paper, the most desirable of all the places offered me by the agencies. It was a complex organization. A boys' school plus a girls' school plus a college for the prepara-tion of young men for the Calvinistic Methodist ministry, promised variety of teaching and possibilities of talk and exercise with students of my own age. I expected a library, playing fields, a room of my own. I expected fresh air and good plain living. I thought all Wales was lake and mountain and wild loveliness. And the Holt Academy had the added advantage of re-opening at the end of July and so shortening the gap of impecuniosity after the College of Science dispersed.

But when I got to Holt I found only the decaying remains of a once prosperous institution set in a dismal street of houses in a flat ungainly landscape. Holt was a small old town shrunk to the dimensions of a village, and its most prominent feature was a gasometer. The school house was an untidy dwelling with what seemed to be a small whitewashed ex-chapel, with broken and dirty windows and a brick floor, by way of schoolroom. The girls' school was perhaps a score of children and growing girls in a cramped little villa down the street. The candidates for the ministry were three lumpish young men apparently just off the fields, and the boys' school was a handful of farmers' and shopkeepers' sons. My new employer presented himself as a barrel of a man with bright eyes in a round, ill-shaven face, a glib tongue and a staccato Welsh accent, dressed in the black coat, white tie and top hat dear to Tommy Morley, the traditional garb of the dominie. He was dirty,—I still remember his blackened teeth—and his wife was dirty, with a certain life-soiled prettiness. He conducted me to a bedroom which I was to share, I learnt, with two of the embryo Calvinistic ministers.

My dismay deepened as I went over the premises and discovered the routines of the place. The few boarders were crowded into a room or so, sleeping two and three in a bed with no supervision. My only colleague was a Frenchman, Raut, of whom I heard years afterwards, because he claimed to have possessed himself of the manuscript of a story by me which he was offering for sale. (I found myself unable to authenticate that manuscript.) Meals were served in a room upon a long table covered with American cloth and the food was poor and the cooking bad. There was neither time-table nor scheme of work. We started lessons just anyhow. Spasmodic unexpected half-holidays alternated with storms of educational energy, when we worked far into the evening. Jones had a certain gift for eloquence which vented itself in long prayers and exhortations at meals or on any odd occasion. He would open school with prayer. On occasions of crisis he would pray. His confidence in God was remarkable. He never hesitated to bring himself and us to the attention of an Avenging Providence. He did little teaching himself, but hovered about and interfered. At times, the tedium of life became too much for him and his wife. He would appear unexpectedly in the schoolroom, flushed and staggering, to make a long wandering discourse about nothing in particular or to assail some casual victim with vague disconcerting reproaches. Then for a day or so he would be missing and in his private quarters, and Raut and I and the theological students would keep such order as we found practicable and convenient.

These theological students aimed at some easy, qualifying examination for their spiritual functions. The chief requirement for their high calling was a capacity for intermittent religious feeling and its expression in Welsh, and that they had by birth and routine. They were instructed in " divinity " (poor God!) and the elements of polite learning when it seemed good to Jones that this should happen. They were not without ambitions. Their hopes, I learnt, were not bounded by their own sect. A qualified minister of the Calvinistic Methodists might sometimes be accepted as a recruit and further polished by—I think it was—the

Wesleyans. A Welsh-speaking Wesleyan again might have scruples of conscience and get into the Anglican priesthood. The Anglican priesthood had always openings for Welsh speakers and so, far up the vistas of life, a living in the established church beckoned to my room-mates. I know not how far this process of ratting might be carried. An unmarried Anglican can, I believe, become a Roman Catholic priest. In Christendom all roads lead to Rome, and so my room-mates were potential, if highly improbable, popes.

I improvised lessons in the boys' school and in the girls' school, I taught scripture on Sunday afternoons, played cricket and Association football to the best of my ability, and made my first attendances at a Calvinistic Methodist service. It was more vivid and personal than the Anglican ritual and Rouse, the minister, was more copiously eloquent even than Jones. I found some of the hymns very effective. I was particularly fond of that frequent favourite which begins :

> *Not all the blood of goats*
> *Shall for my sins atone*

I liked the lusty voices singing together all out, and there was a satisfying picturesqueness about the spiritual geography of Beulah Land and Jordan's Stream, Hermon and Carmel, that let one out, in imagination at least, from Holt.

> *Christian, dost thou see them*
> *On the Holy ground,*
> *How the Hosts of Midian*
> *Prowl and prowl around ?*
> *Christian, up and SMITE them. . .*

But it was very plain to me, as a surviving letter to Miss Healey testifies, that I realized my career had got into a very awkward cul-de-sac. There was no getting away from this place that I could see, however much I disliked it. I had no money to get away with. There was nothing for me now but to stick it for at least a year, get some better clothes, save a few pounds, hammer away at my writing, and hope for some chance of escape. For a few weeks the weather was very good and I developed a tendency to let things drift. I seem to have forgotten my romantic devotion to my cousin very easily ; I suppose her inability to carry on a correspondence had something to do with that. For a time she just went out of the scheme of happenings. I met the daughter of the minister of an adjacent parish, Annie Meredith, a mistress in a high school on holiday, we liked each other at sight and we carried on a brisk and spirited flirtation. I find I boast about this in my letters—not to Miss Healey but to A. M. Davies—say she is well read and talk of spending " whole hours by shady river banks where I talk grotesquely to her and she very intelligently to me." Had that summer weather and my returning health and vigour lasted for ever, I suppose I should have slackened slowly from my futile literary efforts and reconciled myself altogether to the rôle of a second-rate secondary teacher. I should have awakened one day to find myself thirty and still in a school dormitory.

But this is where the peculiar humour of my Guardian Angel came in. Annie Meredith went off to her school work leaving Holt remarkably dull again, and the football season began. I played badly but with a desperate resolve to improve. The lean shock-headed intellectual doing his desperate tactless best in oper-air games is never an attractive spectacle. I had a rough time on the field because that was where the bigger louts got back upon me for my English accent and my irritating assumption of superior erudition. One bony youngster fouled me. He stooped, put his shoulders under my ribs, lifted me, and sent me sprawling.

I got up with muddy hands and knees to go on playing. But a strange sickness seized upon me. There was a vast pain in my side. My courage failed me. I couldn't run. I couldn't kick. " I'm going in," I said, and returned sulkily to the house regardless of the game, amidst sounds of incredulous derision.

In the house I was violently sick. I went to lie down. Then I was moved to urinate and found myself staring at a chamber-pot half full of scarlet blood. That was the most dismaying moment in my life. I did not know what to do. I lay down again and waited for someone to come.

Nothing very much was done about me that evening, but in the night I was crawling along the bedroom on all fours, delirious, seeking water to drink. The next day a doctor was brought from Wrexham. He discovered that my left kidney had been crushed.

He was a good doctor but he made one mistake which did very much to restore my prestige at Holt. I had been shocked and sickened but I had had no acute pain at all. He declared however that I must have suffered and still be suffering the greatest agony. I did not care to dispute his ruling. After all he was a specialist and I was an amateur. As it impressed Jones and Mrs. Jones and seemed likely to raise the low standard of nursing and sympathy in the place, I adopted the bearing of a stoical Red Indian under torture, very successfully. I gave the whole school a most edifying and inexpensive lesson in patient lip-biting heroism.

I lay in bed in that bleakly furnished bedroom for as long as I could, meditating on my future. I spent my coming of age in bed. I had, I decided, to carry on at Holt. I had no money and practically nowhere to go. My father at Bromley was being sold up. Up Park was wearying of Mrs. Wells's family.

At intervals Mr. Jones came and looked at me and I

regarded him with that serenity which comes to men who
know no alternatives. At first, being afraid that I might die
and under the spell of my heroic self-control, he was effusive
for my comfort. " Would I like some books ? " He was going
in to Wrexham. I said I had never read *Vanity Fair*. I had
always wanted to read *Vanity Fair* and this might be my last
chance. " But in your state," protested Jones, sincerely
shocked. " The vera name of the book ! It must be a vera
vera baaad book."

I didn't get it.

In a few days his attentions faded away. I began to be
hungry. The doctor said I ought to lie some days longer and
be kept warm and well fed. Jones came to suggest I should
go home to my friends—unpaid. I explained that I proposed
to get up and resume my duties. The weather was turning
cold and Jones would have no fires until the first of October,
but with a stiffness and ache in my side I got up and went on
with my classes in the brick-floored schoolroom. Presently
I had a bad cough which grew rapidly worse. Then I discovered that my lungs were imitating my kidney and that
the handkerchief into which I coughed was streaked with
blood. The Wrexham doctor, calling to see how I was getting
on, pronounced me consumptive. But consumptive or not,
I meant to see the half year out at least and pocket Jones's
twenty pounds. I had a faint malicious satisfaction in keeping
Jones to that.

§ 2

Blood in the Sputum (1887)

In those days we knew very little about tuberculosis.
People talked of consumption. 'It was not understood to be
infectious and since it produced no symptoms of importance

below the diaphragm, it was found particularly suitable for the purposes of sentimental fiction. The fragile sympathetic consumptive with his (or her) bright eyes, high colour and superficially hopeful spirits, doomed to an untimely end— for it was also supposed to be incurable—had unlimited encouragement to brave self-pity and the most unscrupulous demands, for toleration and sacrifice, upon the normal world. So even the intimations, as everyone supposed them to be, of an early death, were not without their compensations.

To a certain extent I fell in with the pattern of behaviour expected of me. I played the interesting consumptive to the best of my ability. But there were forces in both my body and mind that resented this graceful cutting down of my sprawling expectations of life. I don't know how a modern specialist would define my case but it certainly traversed all the accepted medical science of the eighties. No tuberculous germs were ever detected, but there was certainly some degenerative process at work in my lung, breaking down tissue and breaching the walls of blood vessels. This process went on for about five years, rising to a maximum and then being arrested and ceasing, leaving a scarred lung. There was an attack and there were resistances that finally won. But in my case, as in so many cases, there was (and is) no medical science adequate to define the evidently very complex tangle of stimulations and pro and anti functional forces at work. A degenerative adjustment of my damaged kidney began in 1898 to complicate the hidden business still further. Consequently, beginning with my condemnation by the Wrexham doctor as a consumptive, there were a series of misleading diagnoses, each one creating expectations and holding out prospects to which I tried to adjust my plans of life, and each diagnosis failing in its turn to come true. As late as 1900, I was building a house at Sandgate specially facing towards the sun, with bedrooms, living rooms, loggia and study all on one floor, because I believed I should presently have to live in a bath-chair and be wheeled from room to room. And all the while an essential healthiness was doing its successful utmost to bring me back to physical normality.

Not only were my blood and tissues resisting the suggestion that I was one of those transitory gifted beings too fine and fragile for ordinary life, but my mind also was in active revolt against that idea. I had, I will admit, some beautiful moments of exquisite self-pity, tender even to tears, but they were rare. In my bones I disliked the idea of dying, I disliked it hotly and aggressively. I was exasperated not to have become famous ; not to have seen the world. Still more deeply exasperated was I at the nets of restraint about me that threatened that I should die a virgin. I had an angry insurgence of sexual desire. I began to accumulate a curious resentment against my cousin Isabel because she had had no passion for me. I wanted to go out and pursue strange women. I reproached myself with my discretion about the street walkers of London during my student days. I make no apology for these moods ; that is how the thought of enfeeblement and death stirred my imagination. This resentment at being cheated out of a tremendous crowning experience was to survive into my later sexual life, long after the obsession with death, from which it had arisen, had lifted. My imagination exaggerated the joy of embracing a woman until it became maddeningly desirable.

There was also a considerable amount of pure fear in my mind, a sort of claustrophobia, for though I disbelieved intellectually in immortality I found it impossible to imagine myself non-existent. I felt I was going to be stifled, frozen and shut up, but still I felt I should know of it. I had a nightmare sense of the approach of this conscious nothingness.

In no respect I think does the mature mind differ so

widely from the youthful mind as in its fear of death. I
doubt if a young mind is really capable of grasping the
idea of a cessation of experience, although it may be acutely
alive to defeat and deprivation. But as life unfolds into
realization, death loses that sting. For the past quarter of a
century at any rate my death, as death, has had no terror or
distress for me. It does not, I realize, concern me. I want to
complete certain things, but if death sees fit to come before
I have done them, I shall never know of it. Maybe I do not
speak for all oldish men here. When I talked with Sigmund
Freud in Vienna this spring, he did not seem to feel as I do
about death. He is older than I and he was in bad health,
but he seemed to be clinging to life and to his reputation
and teaching much more youthfully than I do to mine. But
then perhaps he was just drawing me out.

Quite apart from the general fear of death, disappointment
and frustration which weighed so heavily upon my imagination at times during my consumptive phase, there were
unpleasant minor fears and anxieties that I can still recall
acutely. Every time I coughed and particularly if I had a
bout of coughing, there was the dread of tasting the peculiar
tang of blood. And I can remember as though it happened
only last night, the little tickle and trickle of blood in the
lungs that preceded a real hæmorrhage. Don't cough too
soon ? Don't cough too much ? There was always the question how big the flow was to be, how long it would go on,
what was to be the end of it this time. And as one lay exhausted, dreading even to breathe, there was still the doubt
whether it was really over.

I can tell of these disagreeable and dismaying things now
that they lie so far behind me, but at the time I did not
confess my states of dread and dismay to any human being.
Here again I can thank my Fate for my sustaining vanity. I
posed consistently as the gay consumptive. Indeed I carried

it off with Holt to the end that I was the invincible Spartan. My letters to those loyal correspondents of mine, were cheerfully fatalist and more blasphemous than ever.

My fellow student William Burton, who had followed me as editor of the *Science Schools Journal*, had got a good job as chemist with Wedgwoods the potters. The firm had lost many of its old recipes and his work was to analyse old potsherds and rediscover how the original Wedgwoods used to mix their more famous wares. He had just married, and he came out of his honeymoon way with his brightly new little wife to see me. I had a meal with them in the Holt Inn. It was a good and sustaining thing for me to have them thus concerned about me. They excited me and cheered me up, but they were secretly distressed to find me more fragile and emaciated than ever. They departed, bless their friendly hearts ! scheming helpfully about me.

The magic word consumptive softened the heart of Up Park towards me. The defences erected against any further invasions by Mrs. Wells's family were lowered. I came to what I considered a fair arrangement with Jones and set out upon my journey to Harting. I think I must have stopped the night at 181 Euston Road but I cannot remember. I was installed in a room next to my mother's at Up Park and celebrated my arrival by a more serious hæmorrhage than any I had had hitherto.

It chanced that a certain young Dr. Collins was staying in the house and he was summoned to my assistance. I was put upon my back, ice-bags were clapped on my chest and the flow was stopped. I was satisfying all the conventional expectations of a consumptive very completely. I lay still for a day or so and then began to live again in a gentle fashion in a pleasant chintz-furnished, fire-warmed, sunlit room. My previous few weeks at Holt assumed the quality of a bad dream, a quality it has never quite lost. A few days later came a box of books from Burton, an unforgettable kindness.

I must have stayed at Up Park for nearly four months. It was an interlude not only of physical recovery but mental opportunity. I read, wrote and thought abundantly. I got better and had relapses, but none were so grave as the breakdown on arriving. Collins was a brilliant young heretic in the medical world of those days, altogether more modern than my Wrexham practitioner, and he rather dashed my pose as a consumptive and encouraged my secret hope of life by refusing to recognize me as a tuberculous case. He held—and events have justified him—that with a year or so of gentle going I might make a complete recovery. But he was rather distrustful of the stability of my damaged kidney and there again he was right. And he spoke of the possibility of diabetes and now I am diabetic. We had one or two interesting talks about things in general. He was a leading Comtist and an Individualist, as his father was before him, and a valiant man in the affairs of London University. He is now Sir William Job Collins, as obstinately Positivist as ever and only a few weeks ago I reminded him of his excellent diagnosis in our Reform Club.

Geoffrey West, my indefatigable biographer, knows more about these months I spent at Up Park in 1887–88 than I do, for he has exhumed quite a remarkable number of letters written by me during that time. I seem to have had alternations of recovery and hope with relapse and stoicism. I seem to have hoped very readily and taken risks forthwith. At one time I am confined to my room, at another I boast of a sunlit seven-mile walk in thawing snow. But that was followed by a " rustling lung." Up Park below stairs was gay at Christmas and I was gay with it. My father had been sold up and had come with the vestiges of that old furniture in Atlas House to a small cottage at Nyewoods by Rogate

deferring to the biographer.'

station, three miles from Up Park. He had relinquished the idea of earning anything, modestly but firmly. My elder brother, who had fretted as a draper's assistant from the glorious days of my revolt, had joined him there. He proposed to make a new start in life as a watch and clock peddler and repairer. Freddie came to this Rogate cottage for his Christmas holiday and the whole family was shockingly in evidence for the Christmas feast in the Servants Hall, in excellent appetite and the most shameless and unjustifiable high spirits. A letter to Davies, quoted by West, makes it apparent that I danced abundantly and larked about and amused the company by some sort of performance with my brother Frank; but what it was about I cannot now remember. I am sure my mother chuckled with happiness to see her four menfolk so happy. I seem to have been concealing from my mother the fact that there was still blood in my sputum either to spare her feelings or else to escape excessive coddling, but Heaven knows how much posing and exaggeration there is in these letters to my friends.

What is however very plain in them is the gradual transition from the forced courage of a genuine invalid to the restlessness and irritability of a convalescent. I began to find my very comfortable quarters irksome and unstimulating. I had no one to talk to except the Harting curate, and that probably accounts for the voluminousness of these letters West unearthed. Other frustrations were becoming more and more vexatious. I fretted for some lovely encounter that never occurred. Yet, though I did not realize it, I was getting through something of very great importance in my education during these months of outward inaction. I was reading and reading poetry and imaginative work with an attention to language and style that I had never given these aspects of literature before. I was becoming conscious of the glib vacuity of the trash I had been writing hitherto. When I look back upon my life, there is nothing in it that seems quite so preposterous as the fact that I set about writing fiction for sale, after years of deliberate abstinence from novels or poetry. Now, belatedly, I began to observe and imitate. I read everything accessible. I ground out some sonnets. I struggled with Spenser ; I read Shelley, Keats, Heine, Whitman, Lamb, Holmes, Stevenson, Hawthorne, and a number of popular novels. I began to realize the cheapness and flatness of my own phrasing. I went on indeed with the " novel " I had worked upon at Wrexham, but with a growing distaste. I hadn't the vigour to scrap it forthwith and begin all over again. And I dislike leaving things unfinished. But I began to write other stuff, I aired the most extraordinary critical opinions in my letters to Miss Healey and apparently I sent her some verse. Because I find West quoting me to her : " You say my lines are lacking in metre—metres are used for gas, not the outpourings of the human heart. You say my poem has no feet ! The humming bird has no feet, the cherubim round the Mater Dolorosa have no feet. The ancients figured the poetic afflatus as a horse *winged* to signify the poet was sparing of his feet."

Later on in the year, with a quickened sense of what writing could be and do, I read over with shame and contrition all that I had written and I burnt almost all of it. That seemed the only proper way of finishing it. I realized that I had still to learn the elements of this writing business. I had to go back to the beginning, learn to handle short essays, short stories and possibly a little formal verse, until I had acquired the constructive strength and knowledge of things in general demanded for any more ambitious effort. I had not, I saw, been *writing* so far. I had just been playing at writing. I had been scribbling and assuring myself and my friends that it signified something. I had been covering my failure at South Kensington with these unfounded literary pretensions. But it is very illuminating to note that I never showed these copious scribblings to anyone. No human being, not even myself, knows now what *Lady Frankland's Companion* was supposed to be about. I remember only sheets and sheets of boyish scrawl. I saw myself at last with a rare and dreadful plainness. Should I always be too conceited to learn? I knew I had a gift, a quality, but apparently I was too vain and confident about that quality ever to make use of it. I chewed the bitter cud of these reflections as I prowled through the beech-woods and bracken-dells of Up Park or over the yew-dotted downs by Telegraph House.

Every bit of strength I recovered, every ounce of weight I added, deepened my dissatisfaction with the indolent life I was leading, and the feebleness of my invalid efforts. I wanted to resume my attack upon the world, but on a broader basis now and with more soundness and deliberation. My idea of getting a job to keep me while writing had been a sound one, even if it had chanced upon disaster at Holt. I realized that I must insert in the place of " while writing " a preliminary stage " while learning to write " but otherwise the plan of campaign was sound. Better luck next time—if I was to have a next time.

And presently the Burtons, installed in a newly furnished new little house conveniently close to the Wedgwood pot-bank at Etruria, wrote to say that they had a visitor's room quite at my disposal. It was a most enticing invitation and I accepted very eagerly. I found the Burtons and their books and their talk, and the strange landscape of the Five Towns with its blazing iron foundries, its steaming canals, its clay whitened pot-banks and the marvellous effects of its dust and smoke-laden atmosphere, very stimulating. As I went about the place I may have jostled in the streets of Burslem against another ambitious young man of just my age who was then clerk to a solicitor, that friendly rival of my middle years, Arnold Bennett.

There is a letter I wrote in February 1888, to Dr. Collins, which shows very clearly my conception of my position at that time. I lift it in its entirety from West's book. It is interesting as a sample of my early prose. There is something more than a little suggestive of Babu English in the phrasing. I had not yet fused my colloquial with the literary language which was still slightly foreign to me.

" You pointed out when you last did me the favour of examining my chest, how difficult it would be to get any employment compatible with my precarious health, without special concessions and personal influence. Miss Fetherston-haugh holds out very small hope of assisting me in this way, and Sir William King, her agent, to whom she mentioned the matter, spoke in an exceedingly depreciating way of the prospects of obtaining anything of the kind required. I am very ignorant of social conditions above my own level, but it appears to me that you, moving, as you are, among people who as a class are engaged in more vigorous intellectual employments and who are more intricately involved in the business of life than those with whom Miss Fetherstonhaugh comes chiefly into contact, would be far more influential in this present matter than she is. A very large portion of the visitors here is of the three orders of military gentry, clerical dignitaries, or that fortunate independent class whose only business is to live happily, and it seems to me that the only employment that such a connexion could offer above the rank of an unmitigated menial, is a private tutorship, for which I should, even after a very unwholesome meal of my principles, be vastly less suitable than the most rejected young gentleman that ever behaved himself at Oxford. You, on the other hand, are acquainted with men like Harrison, Bernard Shaw, the Huxleys, who must from the

Here he quotes his biographer quoting him!

active and extensive nature of their engagements of necessity
employ numerous fags to assist in the more onerous and less
responsible portions of their duties. It was this that I had
especially in view when I mentioned my desire for employment to you, but I am afraid that I failed to express myself
with sufficient definiteness on that occasion, and that I led
you to understand that I appreciated wine and oil above a
consistent position and the prospects of self-advancement.
My constitutional tendencies all incline me to prefer staking
the preservation of my life on my utility, to imperilling, as
everyone counsels, my utility to preserve my life ; I would
rather do what I wanted and felt was right to be done, and
retire soon with some faint irradiation of human dignity and
self-applause, than survive for a long period to my own
discontent and the general impoverishment. (This is applied
Socialism.) This is my second and more powerful reason for
coming upon you in this way to help me to some work,
because I consider you are not only more able to assist me,
but that you are the only person who is willing and in a
position to bring me into contact with that world of liberal
thought in which alone the peculiar circumstances of my
education render me capable of attaining to any degree of
success."

Collins replied kindly but nothing further ensued and I
stayed at Etruria for nearly three months waiting for
opportunity to come and find me. I think I must have been
a handful as a guest though neither my host or hostess
betrayed any impatience. I was always on hand. I was very
untidy. I had a teasing habit of luring Burton after his day's
work into exasperating discussions. But, they say—for they
are still alive and good friends of mine—that I used to amuse
them greatly by wild caricatures of life at Holt and Up Park,
and by sudden flights of fantasy. And at Etruria my real
writing began. I produced something as good at least as my

letters, something I could read aloud to people I respected without immediate shame. It was good enough to alter and correct and write over again.

I projected a vast melodrama in the setting of the Five Towns, a sort of Staffordshire *Mysteries of Paris* conceived partly in burlesque, it was to be a grotesque with lovely and terrible passages. Of this a solitary fragment survives in my collected short stories as *The Cone*. Moreover I began a romance, very much under the influence of Hawthorne, which was printed in the *Science Schools Journal*, the *Chronic Argonauts*. I broke this off after three instalments because I could not go on with it. That I realized I could not go on with it marks a stage in my education in the art of fiction. It was the original draft of what later became the *Time Machine*, which first won me recognition as an imaginative writer. But the prose was over-elaborate and with that same flavour of the Babu, to which I have called attention, in my letter to Dr. Collins. And the story is clumsily invented, and loaded with irrelevant sham significance. The time traveller, for example, is called Nebo-gipfel, though manifestly Mount Nebo had no business whatever in that history. There was no Promised Land ahead. And there is a lot of fuss about the hostility of a superstitious Welsh village to this Dr. Nebo-gipfel which was obviously just lifted into the tale from Hawthorne's *Scarlet Letter*. And think of " Chronic " and " Argonauts " in the title ! The ineptitude of this rococo title for a hard mathematical invention ! I was over twenty-one and I still had my business to learn. I still jumbled both my prose and my story in an entirely incompetent fashion. If a young man of twenty-one were to bring me a story like the *Chronic Argonauts* for my advice to-day I do not think I should encourage him to go on writing.

But it was a sign of growing intelligence that I was realizing my exceptional ignorance of the contemporary world and exploring the possibilities of fantasy. That is the proper game for the young man, particularly for young men without a natural social setting of their own.

Spring passed into summer and I grew stronger every day. It became manifest that I could not go on living upon the Burtons indefinitely. One bright afternoon I went out by myself to a little patch of surviving woodland amidst the industrialized country, called " Trury Woods." There had been a great outbreak of wild hyacinths that year and I lay down among them to think. It was one of those sun-drenched afternoons that are turgid with vitality. Those hyacinths in their upright multitude were braver than an army with banners and more inspiring than trumpets.

" I have been dying for nearly two-thirds of a year," I said, " and I have died enough."

I stopped dying then and there, and in spite of moments of some provocation I have never died since.

I went back to Burton. I had got the two halves of a five-pound note from my mother against such an eventuality. (People sent divided five-pound notes in separate letters in those days, for safety.) I told Burton I was going to London the day after to-morrow.

" What for ? " said Burton.

" To find a job."

" My dear chap ! " cried Burton, but I think it must have been an immense relief to him.

I posted letters to various scholastic and employment agencies that night, and said I would call upon them in two or three days' time. I was astonished that I had not done so a couple of months before.

§ 3
SECOND ATTACK ON LONDON (1888)

I HAVE GIVEN UP COUNTING my starts in life. This return to London was, I suppose, about the seventh or eighth in order.

When I read over my biography by Geoffrey West, I realize the peculiar advantages of an autobiographer. For a year between June 1887 and June 1888 I had been an active volcano of letters—and letters that chanced to be kept. Geoffrey West set about collecting these letters with great ability and industry. He got more matter than he bargained for and it is only the mercy of Heaven and my timely holocaust, that saved him from the manuscript of *Lady Frankland's Companion* (35,000 words) and other unpublished outpourings. But in 1888 the eruption died down. Except for a sketch I sent Simmons of myself very lean and unkempt standing at a street corner considering an advertisement for sandwichmen, with the pithy announcement, "I am in London seeking work but at present finding none," there is very little documentation of the next six months, at the end of which I turn up suddenly, with my epistolary vigour much restored, as an assistant master in Henley House School, Kilburn. I even find myself at a loss now to fix the dates and circumstances of that intervening period. I have nothing to go upon but patchy memories with the connecting events forgotten.

I did not want to bother my friends or be bothered by them until I got that job. I knew that in the last resort I could get money from my mother, but she had now to support my father at Nyewoods with very little assistance from brother Frank, and I was ashamed to press on her too heavily. It is doubtful if she had anything much in hand just at that time. It was possible I might not find a job because among other things I was extremely shabby. I arrived, with that old small portmanteau of mine, at St. Pancras and found a lodging that night in Judd Street, which I considered to be just within my means ; a rather disconcerting lodging. The room had three beds and one of my fellow occupants, the lodging-house keeper told me, was " a most respectable young man who worked at a butcher's." I forget him and I forget if the third bed was occupied that night. I went to bed early because the journey up had tired me. The next morning I breakfasted in a coffee house—one could get a big cup of coffee, a thick slice of bread and butter and a boiled or fried egg for fourpence or fivepence—and then set out to find a room of my own in the streets between Gray's Inn Road and the British Museum.

I got one for four shillings a week, in Theobald's Road. It was not really a whole room but a partitioned-off part of an attic ; it had no fireplace, and it was furnished simply with a truckle bed, a wash-hand-stand, a chair and a small chest of drawers carrying a looking-glass. The partition was so thin, that audibly I was, so to speak, in the next room. My neighbours were a young couple on whom I never set eyes, but their voices became very familiar to me and I learnt much about their intimate lives. When the intimacy seemed to be rising to a regrettable level, I would cough vigorously, make my bed creak or move my chair about, and the young couple would instantly sink out of existence into a profound silence like a frightened fish in a deep pool.

In this lair I tried to do some writing and my correspondence, and from it I sallied out to find that job that was to carry me and all my fortunes until I had really mastered this writing business. I went the round of the scholastic agents, I put myself on the lists of any employment agency that did not attempt to exact a fee for registration, and I answered many impossible and some possible advertisements. I ate at irregular intervals and economically. There were good little individual shops where sausages or fish sizzled attractively over gas jets in the windows ; the chops in chop houses were not bad, tea shops were multiplying ; a " cut from the joint and two vegs " in a public house cost eightpence or nine-pence. In Fleet Street I tried a very cheap vegetarian res-taurant once or twice, but it left me hungry in the night. The scholastic agents said I was late in the field for a per-manent job that year, but they put me down for possible visiting teaching in science. I did get a little special coaching in geology and mineralogy, with an army crammer, but that was all. My first substantial employer was my old fellow-student Jennings.

Jennings was trying to build up a position as a biological coach. He found his pay as a junior demonstrator in geology at the Science Schools insufficient, and he was using some of his capital to assemble teaching equipment. He was also lecturing in biology at the Birkbeck Institute in Chancery Lane. For these purposes he needed a collection of wall diagrams and, knowing me to be a sufficient draughtsman for the purpose, he commissioned me, so soon as he learnt I was in want of work, to make him a set. His idea was to have these copied from textbooks and high priced series of diagrams, mostly German, which I could sketch in the British Museum Reading Room. He bought a piece of calico and paints for me, I procured one of those now superseded, green, reader's tickets of very soft card, which lasted a life-time, or until they fell to pieces, and I made my sketches under the Bloomsbury dome and enlarged them as diagrams in a small laboratory Jennings shared with a microscopist named Martin Cole in 27 Chancery Lane. Cole, at the window, prepared, stained and mounted the microscope slides he sold, while I sprawled over a table behind him and worked at my diagram painting. Cole's slides were sold chiefly to medical students and, neatly arranged upon his shelves were innumerable bottles containing scraps of human lung, liver, kidney and so forth, diseased or healthy, obtained more or less surreptitiously from post-mortems and similar occasions.

My job with Jennings came none too soon, for my original five pounds had ebbed away to nothing. Before I could draw upon him, I came to the bottom of my resources. I had a sporting wish to carry the thing through if I possibly could, without a further appeal to my mother. I did some very fine computations outside small fried-fish shops and the like during these last days before Jennings and I struck our bargain. At last I came to an evening when I turned out my pocket and found a small piece of indiarubber, a pocket knife and a halfpenny. Even in that cheaper time there was nothing in the way of supper to be done on a halfpenny. And since even a post-card cost three farthings I had cut myself off from writing to anyone. I had cut it altogether too fine. I went to bed to reflect upon the problem. Since I had no watch nor rings or anything of that sort I had not yet discovered the routines of the pawnshop, and it was difficult to fix upon anything in my possession that I felt would appeal to a pawnbroker's appetite. I imagined in my innocence he would only consider "valuables." I had a bone-handled cane that had originally cost two and sixpence, some fine vestiges of surplus underclothing, socks all worn into holes at the heel, two waterproof collars, discoloured, and half a dozen normal linen ones, frayed, and so forth.

As I got up next morning I looked by chance at that halfpenny and something unusual in the design and colour caught my eye. It was a shilling, blackened by contact with the lump of ink eraser ! You cannot imagine the difference that sudden windfall of eleven pence ha'penny, made to my world. And first I broke my fast.

My week-days during that period of stress were fully occupied by small activities. The British Museum Reading Room and the Education Library at South Kensington were good places for light, shelter and comfort. You could sit in them indefinitely so long as they were open. And the streets and shops were endlessly interesting. I loitered and watched the crowds. It was encouraging to see how many people seemed able to get food and clothing. But I found the Sundays terrible. They were vast, lonely days. The shuttered streets were endless and they led nowhither but to chapels and churches which took you in and turned you out at inconvenient hours. Except in St. Paul's Cathedral there was nowhere to sit and think. In the smaller places of worship one had to be sitting down or standing up or kneeling and pretending to participate. Loneliness weighed upon me more and more. I began to wonder what my cousin Isabel was doing and whether I might not chance to meet her in the street. At last she seemed round every corner.

When I got an advance from Jennings I gave way to a growing desire for companionship and wrote to ask if I might come to tea with her on Sunday afternoon. My cousin was now earning good money by retouching photographs. The gaunt house in Euston Road had been abandoned, Auntie Bella had found a situation as housekeeper to a Wiltshire farmer, and my cousin and her mother were installed on the drawing-room floor of a little house in Fitzroy Road near Regent's Park. Thither I went and over the tea-cups and hot buttered toast my aunt Mary, who loved me like a son, rated me soundly in her earnest thin little voice for coming to London without telling her, and pointed out the economies and advantages of joining forces with them. There was a little bedroom on the landing to let. She was longing to look after me.

Within a week I had left Theobald's Road and transferred most of my paints and rolls of calico to Fitzroy Road, and something like the old pattern of my life with Isabel was restored. Directly I was in her presence again I forgot whatever I had forgotten about her. We were less children than we had been and she was more self-reliant than in Euston Road under the distrustful sway of Auntie Bella, but she had the same restrained sweetness and gentleness, the same sound and limited wisdom, the same withheld feminity to which my emotional life had been adjusted during my student days. We resumed our old familiarity as though there had been no interval. We went about again side by side with our thoughts and reveries worlds apart.

The restored sense of home and care at the back of me gave fresh vigour to my hunt for work and money. I went on with Jennings and his diagrams, did a bit of coaching, arranged to share Cole's room and steer Simmons, who had become an assistant schoolmaster, during his Christmas vacation through the dissections for the biology of his Intermediate Science examination, and also I picked up small but useful sums of money, if not by journalism at least in the margin of journalism. At that time a number of new penny weeklies were coming into existence to challenge the ascendancy of the old *Family Herald* with the new board-school public. There were *Tit Bits*, *Answers* and a little later *Pearson's Weekly*. I think it was *Tit Bits* which first devised a page called " Questions worth Answering " open to outside contributors. A dozen or so questions appeared one week and the best answer to each question was published the next. It was a popularization of *Notes and Queries*. For a question accepted, one got half-a-crown ; for an answer one was paid according to length. If one were lucky, one might send in an acceptable answer to one's own question. My copious reading and my special biological lore came in very usefully here. Every week I contrived in this way to add anything between two and sixpence and fourteen or fifteen shillings to the Fitzroy Road budget.

My lungs stood the onset of winter fairly well. My aunt Mary kept her bird-like eye upon me and knew I had a cough before I did, and did something about it. By the end of the year I had arranged to begin a job in Kilburn after Christmas, that was more like firm ground under my feet than anything I had been upon for a year and a half.

§ 4
HENLEY HOUSE SCHOOL (1889–1890)

FROM MY DEPARTURE from Southsea in 1883 to my return to London in 1888, the history of this brain of mine was mainly a story of growth and learning things. It acquired as much, decided as much and was exercised as much as if it had been inside the skull of a university scholar. It developed a coherent picture of the world and learnt the use of the English language and the beginnings of literary form. But from my emergence from St. Pancras Station to find lodgings and a job, this brain, for the better part of a year, was so occupied with the immediate struggle for life, so near to hunger and exposure and so driven by material needs, that I do not think it added anything very much to either its content or power. It was only after a term or so at Henley House School, that it began to take notice of external things again and resume its criticism of, and its disinterested attack upon, existence in general.

This Henley House School was, financially, a not very successful private school in Kilburn. It was housed in a brace of semi-detached villas, very roughly adapted to its educational needs. It drew its boys from the region of Maida Vale and St. John's Wood ; the parents were theatrical, artistic, professional and business people who from motives of economy or affection preferred to have their sons living at home. There were only a few boarders. It was a privately owned school and J. V. Milne, the proprietor, was responsible to no earthly authority for what he did or did not teach. In one of the houses he lived with his family and in the other were the various class-rooms and the assistants' room of the school. The playground was a walled gravelly enclosure that had once been two back gardens. It was too small for anything but the most scuffling of games. Equipment was little better than it had been in Morley's school ; the desks were not so age-worn and there were more blackboards and maps. But it remained—skimpy. When I entered upon my duties, J. V. came to me and pressed a golden sovereign into my hand. " Get whatever apparatus you require for your science teaching," he said.

" And if there is any change ? " I asked with this fund, this endowment, in my hand.

" You can give me an account later."

I had to administer this grant very carefully. The existing apparatus was huddled into what had once been a small bedroom cupboard on the second floor, and was in an extremely ruinous condition. My predecessor had been a Frenchman and very evidently a man of great persistence of character. His chemical teaching had apparently reached a climax in the production of oxygen by heating potassium permanganate in a glass flask. Young Roberts, the son of Arthur Roberts, the comedian, said it had been a very great lesson indeed. Those were primitive times in glass manufacture and the ordinary test-tube or Florentine flask was not of a special refractory glass as it is now, and it cracked and flew at the slightest irregularity in its heating. My predecessor had put his permanganate in a flask, put the flask on a tripod, set a Bunsen burner beneath it and made all the necessary arrangements for collecting his oxygen. But before there was any oxygen worth mentioning to collect, the flask flew with a loud crack and its bottom descended upon the flame. My predecessor rallied his forces and put a second Florentine flask into action, with exactly the same result. A certain joyousness invaded the class as, with the spirit of the French at Waterloo, a third flask was thrown into the struggle. And so on, *da capo* ; joy increased and open demonstrations had to be repressed. At the end there were no more Florentine flasks and the applause broke out unhindered. The cupboard was chiefly occupied by these shattered flasks neatly arranged, each over its own proper detached bottom.

I meditated upon these vestiges of experimental science and upon what seemed to me to be the evidence of an attempt to make carbon-dioxide out of blackboard chalk—an attempt fore-ordained to failure because blackboard chalk is not chalk and contains no carbon dioxide. And I considered my still intact sovereign.

I discussed the matter with J. V. " Mr. Milne," I said, " I think experimental demonstrations before a class are a great mistake."

" They certainly have a very bad effect on discipline," he remarked.

" I propose," I said, " with your permission, to draw all my experiments upon the blackboard—in coloured chalks which I shall buy out of this pound—to explain clearly and fully exactly what happens and to make the class copy out these experiments in a note-book. I have never known an experiment on a blackboard go wrong. On the other hand, these attempts at an excessive realism——"

" I am quite of your mind," he said.

" Later on, however, I may dissect a rabbit bit by bit and make them draw that. I may dissect it under water because that is cleaner and prettier than a heap of viscera on a board, and I shall have to buy a large baking-dish and cork and lead and pins."

" It will not be—indelicate ? "

" It need not be. I will show them what to see on the blackboard."

" One never knows what parents will find to object to. However—if you want to do it . . ."

In this way I contrived, without extravagance, to train my classes to draw, write and understand about a great many things that would have been much more puzzling for them if they had encountered them in all the rich confusion of actuality. I never attempted to use the chemical balance, for example ; chemical balances, especially if they have been left to brood in the darkness of bedroom cupboards, will seize upon the slightest pretext to confute the hasty experimentalist ; and moreover my predecessor had lost most of the weights. My boys therefore missed the usual stinks and bangs of scientific instruction and acquired instead a real grasp of scientific principles and scientific quantities, together with a facility in illustrating examination answers that stood them in good stead in the years immediately before them.

I found Milne a really able teacher, keen to do his best for his boys and with a curious obstinate originality, and I learnt very much from him about discipline and management. Finance, I knew, was worrying him a good deal, but he watched his boys closely and would slacken, intensify or change their work, with a skilled apprehension of their idiosyncrasies. He would think of them at night. The boys had confidence in him and in us and I never knew a better mannered school. He was friendly and sympathetic with me from the outset. He was a little grey-clad extremely dolicho-cephalic man with glasses, a pointed nose and a small beard, rather shy in his manner; he had a phantom lisp and there was a sort of confidential relationship between his head and his shoulders. His original proposal was that I should be resident English, science and drawing master at £60 a year. But I wanted to go on living with my aunt and cousin at Fitzroy Road, I detested Sunday duty and I wanted to write or to work at my preparation for the Intermediate Examination in the London University, in all the spare time I could get. So I offered to forgo my residence and all my meals except the midday one, if I could come at nine and vanish at or before five. And I stipulated that I should do no scripture teaching, as I felt I could not do it in good faith. The arrangement worked very well for us both. He liked my putting in that conscience clause at the risk of not getting a job I evidently wanted.

The midday meal was an excellent one, attended by a number of the day-boys. With memories of Holt in my mind, I wrote to Simmons effusively, praising the cleanliness, the table napkins and particularly the flowers on the table. In my world hitherto there had been no flowers on the meal table anywhere. And at the end of the table, facing me, sat Mrs. Milne, rather concerned if I did not eat enough, because I was still, she thought, scandalously thin.

I suppose the day is not so very remote when the last of these private schools will have vanished from the earth. Fifty years ago they were still responsible for the education, or want of education, of a considerable fraction of the British middle-class. They were under no public control at all. Anyone might own one, anyone might teach in one, no standard of attainment was required of them; the parents dipped their sons into them as they thought proper and took them out when they thought they were done. Certain university and quasi-public bodies conducted examinations to which a number of the brighter pupils were submitted in order to enhance the prestige of the establishment, and these examining bodies exerted a distinct influence upon the choice of subjects. For the most part these private schools passed the middle-class youth of England on to business or professional life incapable of any foreign language, incapable indeed of writing or speaking their own except in the clumsiest manner, unable to use their eyes and hands to draw or handle apparatus, grossly ignorant of physical science, history or economics, contemptuous of the board-school boy and with just enough consciousness of their deficiencies to make them suspicious of, and hostile to, intellectual ability and equipment.

It is only when the nature of the English private school education is grasped that it becomes possible to understand why the enormous possibilities of world predominance and world control, manifest in the British political expansion during the nineteenth century, wilted away so rapidly under the stresses of the subsequent years. Its direction was dull, ignorant, pretentious and blundering. I have given a glimpse of the British private school at its worst in my brief account of Holt Academy ; J. V. Milne and Jones were almost at opposite poles of conscience and intelligence ; Milne was a man who won my unstinted admiration and remained my friend throughout life ; nevertheless it is useless to pretend that Henley House was more than a sketch of good intentions or that we stirred up a tithe of the finer possibilities of the boys who passed under our hands. We taught them a few tricks, we got them a few " certificates," we did something for their manners and personal bearing, we dropped some fruitful hints into them, but we gave them no coherent and sustaining vision of life. One or two of the Henley House boys were destined to play a fairly conspicuous rôle in English affairs. Our prize boy, our whale so to speak, was Lord Northcliffe, who did so much to create the modern newspaper and died controlling owner of *The Times*. He can very well be studied as a sample of the limitations of the English private school education—and indeed of English education generally.

In making these criticisms I am not blaming J. V. Milne. In view of his conditions and resources he did wonderfully. He could hardly pay his way ; the two rather battered villas and that one golden sovereign for all the apparatus required for science teaching, give the measure of his means. When later on an opportunity offered, he got out of Kilburn and ran a more spaciously equipped school, Streete Court at Westgate-on-Sea. But for Henley House, he could not pick and choose his assistants ; economies and compromises cramped his style, and in endless respects the school made itself in spite of all his efforts to mould and direct it.

Nevertheless he had in operation an honour system of discipline that was far in advance of the times. It is a little too complex to explain here, but it was decidedly better than the discipline under Sanderson of Oundle, which I was to study later. A cane hung in Milne's study, a symbol of force as the ultimate sanction, but it was never used in my time and I do not think it had been used for some years before. He was understandingly interested by my abandonment of the worst pretences of ". practical " demonstration in my science teaching, he watched and discussed my use of the note-book system of binding work together that I had picked up from Byatt and seen misapplied by Judd, and when later I innovated in the mathematical work, threw out all the muddling-about with money sums, weights and measures, business " practice " and so forth that cumbered the teaching (and examining) of arithmetic, and took a class of small boys between six and eight straight away from the first four rules to easy algebra, he was delighted. In those days that was a new and bold thing to do. We got to fractions, quadratics and problems involving quadratics in a twelvemonth and laid the foundations of two or three university careers by way of mathematics. A. A. Milne, the novelist and playwright, was one of that band of young hopefuls, and his brother Ken and Batsford the publisher.

The sense of Milne's observation and interest quickened my teaching greatly. I would prepare little stunts for him and the boys. It was amusing to stroll up to the blackboard in an off-hand way and draw the outline of England or Scotland or North America from memory. (One had to be particularly wary about the relative latitude of the east and west coasts and the rest followed.) One could stand with one's back to a whole class and yet have every boy still and interested. The wickedest would be following the chalk line and comparing it with his Atlas if only in the hope of saying, " Please Sir," and making a correction.

Where Henley House was most defective from a modern point of view was in its failure to establish any social and political outlook. But there J. V. suffered not only from the limitations of a poorly financed private adventurer who had to make his school " pay," but also from the lax and aimless mentality of the period in which he was living. The old European order, as I have pointed out already in the chapter on my origins, was far gone in decay, and had lost sight of any conception of an object in life. The new order had still to discover itself and its objectives. In the eighteenth century, a school in Protestant England pointed every life in it, either towards hell-fire or eternal bliss ; its intellectual and moral training was all more or less relevant to and tested by the requirements of that pilgrimage ; for that in the long run you were being prepared. That double glow of gold and red had faded out almost completely from the school perspectives of 1890, but nothing had taken its place. The idea of the modern world-state must ultimately determine the curriculum and disciplines of every school on earth, but even to-day only a few teachers apprehend that, and in my Henley House days the idea of that social and political necessity had hardly dawned. The schools and universities just went on teaching things in what was called the " general education "—because they had always been taught. " Why do we learn Latin, Sir ? " asked our bright boys. " What is the good of this chemistry, Sir, if I am to go into a bank ? " Or, " Does it really matter, Sir, now, *how* Henry VII was related to Henry IV ? "

We were teaching some " subjects," as the times went, fairly well, we were getting more than average results in outside examinations. But collectively, comprehensively we were teaching nothing at all. We were completely ignoring the primary function of the school in human society, which is to correlate the intelligence, will and conscience of the individual to the social process. We were unaware of a social process. Not only were Henley House, and the private schools generally, imparting this nothingness of outlook, but except for a certain gangster esprit-de-corps in various of the other public schools and military seminaries, " governing class " sentiment and the like, the same blankness pervaded the whole educational organization of the community. We taught no history of human origins, nothing about the structure of civilization, nothing of social or political life. We did not make, we did not even attempt to make participating citizens. We launched our boys, with, or more commonly without, a university " local " or matriculation certificate, as mere irresponsible adventurers into an uncharted scramble for life.

And this is where our big specimen of output, our whale, Northcliffe, comes in. His story is a very illuminating

demonstration of the effects of private school insufficiencies upon social development.

He was eldest of the numerous family of an adventurous
barrister, Harmsworth, from Dublin, who came to London
with a capable and energetic wife, to make a great career,
and did not do so. He won only a moderate measure of
success ; he was " Counsel to the Great Northern Railway "
and so forth ; and his political activities never advanced
beyond one of those mock parliaments, the Camden Town
equivalent of the Parliament of the Landport Y.M.C.A.,
mentioned earlier in this book, in which politically
minded men displayed their quality and tempered themselves for real political activities. Camden Town, like Landport, never got down to any social or economic principles. It
was a training in saying " Mr. Speaker, Sir, the right honourable member for Little Ditcham," in moving " the
previous question " and such-like necessary superficialities
of the political game. He died in 1889 when his eldest son
was twenty-four years old, but the mother, a woman oddly
reminiscent in her vitality and character of Laetitia Bonaparte, survived to 1925, three years after the death of
Northcliffe.

Alfred was born in 1865, a little more than a year before
me, and he seems to have entered Henley House School
when he was nine or ten years old. He made a very poor
impression on his teachers and became one of those unsatisfactory, rather heavy, good-tempered boys who in the usual
course of things drift ineffectively through school to some
second-rate employment. It was J. V.'s ability that saved
him from that. Somewhen about the age of twelve, Master
Harmsworth became possessed of a jelly-graph for the
reproduction of MS. in violet ink, and with this he set
himself to produce a mock newspaper. J. V. with the
soundest pedagogic instinct, seized upon the educational

possibilities of this display of interest and encouraged young Harmsworth, violet with copying ink and not quite sure whether he had done well or ill, to persist with the *Henley House Magazine* even at the cost of his school work. The first number appeared in 1878 ; the first printed number in 1881 " edited by Alfred C. Harmsworth," and I possess all the subsequent issues up to the end of 1893, when Milne transferred his school to Streete Court. During my stay at Henley House, I contributed largely, and among others who had a hand in the magazine was A. J. Montefiore, who was later to edit the *Educational Review* and A. A. Milne (" aged six " —at his first appearance in print) the novelist, essayist and playwright.

Now neither Milne nor anyone in the Harmsworth family, as they scanned the early issues of this little publication, had the faintest suspicion of the preposterous thrust of opportunity that it was destined to give its youthful editor. But in the eighties the first school generation educated under the Education Act of 1871 was demanding cheap reading matter and wanting something a little easier than *Chambers Journal* and a little less simply feminine than the *Family Herald*. A shrewd pharmaceutical chemist named Newnes tried to make a modest profit out of a periodical, originally of cuttings and quotations, *Tit Bits*, and made a great fortune. Almost simultaneously our Harmsworth, pursuing print as if by instinct, tried to turn a modest hundred or so, by creating *Answers to Correspondents* (1888) which, among other things, provided me as I have told, with a few useful shillings a week during its first year of issue. He had been ill for a brief period after leaving school in 1882 and he had worked not so very successfully at outside journalism. *Answers* hung fire for a time until it dropped its initial idea and set out to imitate and beat *Tit Bits* at its own game, with the aid of prize competitions.

Neither Newnes nor Harmsworth, when they launched these ventures, had the slightest idea of the scale of the new forces they were tapping. They thought they were going to sell to a public of at most a few score thousands and they found they were publishing for the million. They did not so much climb to success ; they were rather caught by success and blown sky high. I will not even summarize the headlong uprush of Alfred C. Harmsworth and his brother Harold ; how presently they had acquired the *Evening News*, started the *Daily Mail* and gone from strength to strength until at last Alfred sat on the highest throne in British journalism, *The Times*, and Harold was one of the richest men in the world.

Only one item in this rocket flight is really significant here. The second success of the Harmsworth brothers was a publication called *Comic Cuts*. Some rare spasm of decency seems to have prevented them calling this enormously profitable, nasty, taste-destroying appeal for the ha'pence of small boys, *Komic Kuts*. They sailed into this business of producing saleable letterpress for the coppers of the new public, with an entire disregard of good taste, good value, educational influence, social consequences or political responsibility. They were as blind as young kittens to all those aspects of life. That is the most remarkable fact about them from my present point of view and I think posterity will find it even more astonishing. In pristine innocence, naked of any sense of responsibility, with immense native energy, they set about pouring millions of printed sheets of any sort of trash that sold, into the awakening mind of the British masses. The " instantaneous success " of *Comic Cuts* was hailed by J. V. in *Henley House Magazine* (May 1890) without a word of criticism or a sign of disapproval. He tells the " Short History of A Henley House Boy " and writes that *Answers* returns to its proprietors close upon £10,000 per annum.

" Mr. Alfred Harmsworth is now only twenty-four years of age," he writes. " He has written two successful books, *A Thousand Ways of Earning a Living*, of which 25,000 were sold, and *All About our Railways*. He attributes most of his success to—what do you think ?—*downright hard work*. ' I usually spend twelve hours a day on the paper,' he writes me. I wanted him to give me some facts showing the magnitude of the work—the staff, the management, etc., of his paper—and some facts about himself, but he writes, ' I really do not like biography. You can say this (what I have said to many other people), that the generous and thoughtful way in which I was educated at Henley House must have had a very great influence on my career. Though I was never much of a student, I did manage in those three years to pick up a vast amount of reasoning and fact, which often, even now, are useful. But there ! I am ashamed to say any more. You can say what you like about my opinion of Henley House, and you cannot put it too strongly. Yours affectionately, Alfred C. Harmsworth.'

" Now that you have just been reading of an old Henley House School boy, may I get in a word. If there is an idle boy in the school, let him take this lesson to heart—that sheer hard work is the magician's wand. Should there be any of you drifting along, and hoping, like Mr. Micawber, that something may turn up, let me tell you that the things that generally ' turn up ' are disappointments, failure, poverty and remorse. May the last never be yours."

J. V. Milne could write like that and teach like that—in a vein of pure competitive individualism. His own conscience and practice were happily better than his theories.

In twenty years these two young ruffians (ruffians so far as any sense of social obligations goes), these creators of *Comic Cuts*, had been flung up to the working ownership of *The Times*, and peerages; they had become immense factors in the chaos of English affairs, and with them and under the controlling counsels of their magnificent mother, they had carried their bunch of brothers to positions of importance and opulence in our social disorder. My friend

Geoffrey Harmsworth, the son of Northcliffe's brother Lester, has planned to tell the story under the title of the *Harmsworth Adventure*. It is absurdly like the Bonaparte adventure. During my time at Henley House School, one last Harmsworth of the original vintage remained, a sturdy and by no means brilliant youngster, St-John. A year or so ago before he died I met him at Cannes, a princely invalid, the proprietor of *Perrier*, preposterously wealthy, surrounded by obsequious valets, male nurses, maîtres d'hôtel and so forth.

With Northcliffe I maintained an intermittent friendship ; I co-operated with him for a time at Crewe House during the war and afterwards he came over to Easton to lunch and talk with me when I returned from Russia in 1920. But my articles were already ear-marked for the *Daily Express*. He was then in the grip of an obscure malady that distressed his mind, arrested its development and prevented sustained work. The doctors advised him to go for long wandering excursions by automobile or afoot, watching the world go by him. He must learn to be idle. I met him for a last encounter, walking alone in Westminster, " just looking at the shop windows." That must have been in 1920 or 1921. Finally these doctors sent him wandering round the world and he wandered right out of sanity. I saw enough of him to see the extraordinary mental and moral conflict created by the real vastness of the opportunities and challenges that crowded upon him on the one hand and, on the other, the blank inadequacy of his education at Henley House School for anything better than a career of push and acquisition.

In an autobiography it is permissible to compare his mind with my own. Mine—peace to its defects !—was a system of digested and assimilated ideas ; it was an assembled mind ; his was a vast jumble into which fresh experiences were for ever tumbling. I was educated—self-educated. He was uneducated. He was blown up so rapidly that he was never free to think out his rôle in the world. He never had the chances for weeks and months of reflection and readjustment given me by my various disablements and set-backs. When he was ill—and ever and again he was ill and took refuge with his mother at Totteridge—he was mentally disordered and lost grip altogether. And he was prone to the easy flattery of women. Nevertheless a certain admirable greatness of mind appeared eventually and he travelled far from the mere headlong vulgarity of his first drive into prosperity. He realized with a mixture of astonishment, exaltation and dismay, that a big newspaper proprietor, whether he liked it or not and whether or no the fact met with any formal recognition, was an immensely responsible figure in the world. He had vivid intimations that amidst the catastrophic shifts and changes of Western life, a new social order was finding its way into existence.

He never had the time nor the mental coolness to get this clear. But long before the Great War jolted the intelligence of Europe into a new system of aims and understandings, he was trying to fill up the gap that Henley House School—and all that went with it in tone and period—had left in his equipment. He had an almost pathetic belief that somewhere, just outside his world, were a lot of clever fellows who had better knowledge and ideas than his. He did not understand the breadth and slowness of the process by which the modern world-state has been and is still coming to self-realization. It had not dawned upon him what a heaving pretentious mess economic, social and educational science still was, because he had never come to grips with the stuff as I had done. But he felt the looseness and insecurity of things about him and he tried in his impatient way to get something constructive and stabilizing. He "ran" Norman Angell for a time and the question of world peace and, after my

Anticipations and *Modern Utopia*, he wanted very much to organize a following for me. He found me at once stimulating and disappointing. I did not want to be organized ; I did not even want to be hurried. His experience had been that you only had to advertise a thing well or offer a prize about it, to get all you wanted. And when you had got it you rushed on to something else. If you wanted world peace, or a cure for cancer or tuberculosis, or a machine to fly round the world, you offered a prize for it, you made an enormous fuss about it and then, he thought, some of those clever fellows at the back of things would set to work upon it, as he had set to work upon the *Daily Mirror*, and win it. He wanted to attack the economic riddles of the world long before any diagnosis had been made, in precisely the same energetic fashion. I shall mention later the articles upon "The Labour Unrest " that I wrote for him in this phase.

The World War and the world peace was a tremendous strain upon him. It was a forcible education for all of us and for him it brought both growth and disorganization. A really intimate record of Northcliffe's brain processes, his ambitions, his likes and dislikes, his general motivation, is impossible ; but in regard to his period it would be the most illuminating historical document in the world. It would be as typical a story as anyone could find of the stresses of transition from that blind confidence in Providence, that implicit confidence in the good intentions of the natural order of things, no matter what were our mistakes and misdeeds, characterizing the human mind in the nineteenth century, to that startled realization of the need for men to combine against the cold indifference, the pitiless justice, if you will, of nature, which is our modern attitude. The effort to achieve an adult behaviour under the stresses of ulcerative endocarditis and after forty odd years of triumphant puerility, shattered and killed him. Confounded by the catastrophe of

the Great War and its still more terrifying sequels, spun
giddily into the vortex of leadership and responsibility
without the restraints of a tradition or the preparation of a
philosophy, embittered into a clumsy personal feud by the
way in which he was jostled by Lloyd George out of any
honourable participation in the War Settlement—and so
abruptly stranded, Northcliffe's mind was shattered very
much, indeed, as was Woodrow Wilson's. It was burst
by opportunity.

I shall have more to say of him when I tell at the proper
time how my sample mind, and the English mind of which it
was a part, were put through the mill of the Great War. But
after this brief excursion forward into consequences, let me
return for the present to that little ill-equipped private
school in Kilburn from which it started, that little school in
which, with the best intentions in the world, Milne and his
staff taught neither human history, economics nor social
duty, and from which they launched boys into the gathering
disaster of civilization as though they were sending them
into a keen but merciful prize competition, in which " sheer
hard work " was the " magician's wand," and so forth
and so on.

Only now are we beginning to suspect there should be
more in education than that.

§ 5

THE UNIVERSITY CORRESPONDENCE COLLEGE
(1890–1893)

DURING 1889 my efforts to " write," so far as I can
remember or trace them now, died down to hardly anything
at all. My hope of an income from that source had faded,

and it seemed to me that such prospects in life as remained open to me, lay in school teaching. They were not brilliant prospects anyhow, because I was quite obstinately resolved not to profess Christianity, but my self-conceit was in a phase of unwholesome deflation and a mediocre rôle seemed a good enough objective for my abilities. Milne had interested me in teaching method, and I decided that if I secured a teaching diploma and took up my degree in the London University, I might, in spite of my religious handicap, get a sufficiently good position to marry upon. I wanted to marry ; I had indeed a gnawing desire to marry, and my life in close proximity to my cousin was distressing and humiliating me in a manner she could not possibly comprehend. I was keen and eager and she was tepid and rational. Plain risks dismayed her. It seemed the most obvious thing in the world to her that I should first win my way to a fairly safe place and the status of a householder before my devotion was rewarded. In pursuance of this intensely personal objective, I took my Intermediate Science Examination in July '89 with only second-class honours in zoology, and I got the diploma of licentiate of the College of Preceptors at the end of the year.

I have already said a word or two about this College of Preceptors in my account of Morley's Academy. Its requirements were not very exacting, and its diplomas were sought chiefly by teachers without university degrees. It offered papers in a number of subjects, and it allowed candidates to pass in one subject at one time and another later on, so that the grade of competing examinee was a lowly one. I took the whole range of subjects at a swoop, got what was called honours—80 per cent of the maximum marks—in most of the subjects and secured the three prizes for the theory and practice of education (£10), mathematics (£5) and natural science (£5). That itself was a useful accession of money, but the greater benefit of this raid upon the college was that I was obliged to read something of the history and practice of education, some elementary psychology (a mere rudiment of a science at that date), and logic. I was greatly interested in these subjects and, superficial though the standard was, they cleared up my mind upon various issues and started some valuable trains of thought. I planned to go on with mental and moral science and to take that, with zoology and geology, for my degree examination in London University in 1890, but I did not do so because I found that botany would be a more immediately marketable commodity and so I went back to botany.

Armed with this L.C.P. diploma and my second-class intermediate honours, I became exacting with J. V. Milne. He raised my salary £10 a year and agreed to cut down the hours I had to spend at Henley House. I looked about for supplementary employment and presently found myself in correspondence with a certain William Briggs, M.A., the organizer of a University Correspondence College at Cambridge, an institution which I still think one of the queerest outgrowths of the disorderly educational fermentations of that time. It flourishes still. Briggs was able not only to offer me just the additional work I wanted to keep me going until I took my degree of B.Sc., but his peculiar requirements enabled him to set a premium upon my taking honours in that examination. I went down to Cambridge to see him ; we fixed up an immediate arrangement for me to earn at least £2 a week by doing his correspondence tuition in biology which was in urgent need of attention, and we further agreed that if I took my degree in October, I should leave Henley House School and have a permanent appointment with him in a Tutorial College he was developing in London, at a rate of pay to be determined by my class in honours. He was to give me at least thirty hours' work a week all over the year at 2s. 2d., 2s. 4d. or 2s. 6d. an hour, according to whether I obtained third-, second- or first-class honours. Honours were very important to him from the prospectus point of view. His list of tutors displayed an almost unbroken front of Cambridge, Oxford and London "firsts." High honours men in biology were rare in those days, and it was characteristic of Briggs that he should decide to make one out of me for himself.

I left Henley House at the end of the summer term, I took my degree with first-class honours in zoology and second-class honours in geology. I had already been working for some months in my surplus time with Briggs, and I carried on first with classes in a small room above a bookshop in that now vanished thoroughfare Booksellers Row, and afterwards in a spacious well-lit establishment in Red Lion Square. There I had a reasonably well furnished teaching laboratory, with one side all blackboards and big billiard-room lamps for night teaching. Briggs gave me enough work to make an average of nearly fifty hours a week, on a system of piecework that enabled me at times to compress a number of nominal half-crown hours into a normal one and so, by the middle of 1891, I found myself in a position to satisfy my cousin's requirements, take a small house, 28, Haldon Road in East Putney, and release her from her daily journey to that Regent Street workroom. She intended, however, to retouch at home and to take pupils.

A word about our budget will be interesting to-day. We paid £30 a year rent for our house, an eight-roomed house (the eight included a kitchen, a bathroom and a box-room) ; we estimated 10s. a head as a maximum expenditure for food, and in January 1893 I opened a banking account in Wandsworth, which endures to this day, with a cheque from Briggs for £52 10s. 5d. Until then we had carried only a small reserve of twenty pounds or less in the Post Office Savings Bank.

This Post Office Savings Bank account had been opened in the Fitzroy Road days with my first instalment of salary from Milne. Before then our only reserve for emergency money had been a few pawnable articles of silver and an old watch belonging to my Aunt Mary. . . .

We were married very soberly in Wandsworth Parish Church on October 31st, 1891. My cousin was grave and content but rather anxious about the possibility of children, my aunt was very happy and my elder brother Frank, who had come up for the ceremony, was moved by a confusion of his affections and wept suddenly in the vestry.

But I will tell what matters about my domestic life later. What is of much more general interest, is the peculiar organization of that University Correspondence College of which I had now become a tutor. Briggs in his way was as accidental and marvellous as Northcliffe, and as illustrative of the planless casualness of our contemporary world.

To write an autobiography as the history and adventures of a brain, involves the unfolding of an educational panorama in the background. In what has gone before I have tried to display the strain upon and the disorganization of the petty educational organizations of the small-scale horse-foot, hand-industry civilizations that culminated in the seventeenth and eighteenth centuries, by the change of pace and scale due to mechanical invention. In two swift centuries the material structures of a single modern world-state came into being. Without any correlated mental structure. Social and political adaptation dragged further and further behind that headlong advance. Our world to-day is at the climax of that discord. And not only were the illiterate traditionalism of the general mass and the private schools and tutoring of the better sort, exhibited as wildly inadequate to the demands of the new occasions, but all the organization of professional training and the colleges, universities, academies and so forth, which had served the old order, were also tossed about, dwarfed and pressed upon by the huge dumb necessities of a world metamorphosis.

Nowhere yet was there a really comprehensive apprehension of what was happening. The gist of my individual story is the growth of that apprehension, belatedly, in one fairly quick-witted but not very powerful brain. But a partial and reluctant disposition to adaptation became more and more operative in the nineteenth century and produced a structure of universal elementary education throughout Europe, a great multiplication of technical and secondary schools, a growth in the numbers upon existing university rolls and the foundation of a great number of new universities. This adaptation was more quantitative than qualitative. The need for more and more widely extended education was realized long before the need for a new sort of education. Schools and universities were multiplied but not modernized. The spirit of the old educational order was instructive and not constructive ; it was a system of conservation, and to this day it remains rather a resistance than a help to the growing creative will in man.

So to the multitudinous demand of the advancing new generations for light upon what they were, upon what was happening to them and whither they were going, the pedagogues and professors replied in just as antiquated and unhelpful forms as possible. They remained not only out of touch themselves with new knowledge and new ideas, but they actually intercepted the approach to new knowledge and new ideas, by purveying the stalest of knowledge and the tritest, most exhausted ideas to these hungry swarms of a new age groping blindly for imperfectly conceived mental food. It is illuminatingly symbolical that everywhere the new universities dressed themselves up in caps and gowns and Gothic buildings and applied the degrees of the medi-aeval curricula, bachelor, master, doctor, to the students of a new time. I have already pointed out the oddity—seeing that I had little Latin and no Greek—of my calling my early plan of study at Midhurst a " Schema " and my first draft of the *Time Machine*, the " Chronic Argonauts." But this snobbish deference to the pomps, dignities and dialects of a vanishing age, ran through the whole world of education. There was no possibility of teaching (profitably and successfully), or indeed of practising any profession, without a university degree embodying great chunks of that privileged old learning. And when by means of clamour from without, such subjects as physical science and biology were thrust into the curricula, they underwent a curious standardization and sterilization in the process.

Now the urge to spread new knowledge of the modern type widely through the community, was so imperative, and the resistance of the established respectable educational organiz-ation, the old universities and the schools with prestige and influence, to any change and any adequate growth, was so tough, that a vast amount of educational jerry-building went on, precisely analogous to that jerry-built housing of London in the nineteenth century on which I have already expatiated. London was jerry-built because the ground landlords were in possession : English national education was jerry-built because Oxford and Cambridge were in possession. The British elementary teacher was an ex-tremely hasty improvisation and I have already given a glimpse of Horace Byatt, Esq., M.A. (Dublin) earning grants for teaching me " advanced " sciences of which he knew practically nothing. Equally jerry-built and provisional were the first efforts to create an urgently needed supply of teachers and university graduates beyond the expensive limits of Oxford and Cambridge. New degree-giving universities were brought into existence with only the most sketchy and loosely connected colleges and laboratories, or with evening classes or with no definite teaching arrangements at all. Most typical of these was our London University. This at first was essentially an examining board. It aimed primarily at graduating the students in the great miscellany of schools and classes that was growing up in London, but its examinations and degrees were open to all comers from every part of the world. I for instance was examined by my own professors in the South Kensington Science Schools, but the examinations I passed to take my degree in London University, were entirely independent of these college tests.

And this is where the great work of Mr. (afterwards Dr.) William Briggs comes in. It was at once preposterous and necessary. The practice of general examination boards is almost bound to be narrow and rigidly stereotyped. They must never do the unexpected because that might be unfair. The outside student working without direction or working under teachers who had no regard for the requirements of an examining board, was all too apt to wander into fields of interest that were not covered by the syllabus or to fail to get up prescribed topics because his attention had not been drawn to them. His tendency was to be as variable as the examining board was invariable. All the more to the credit of the intelligent student, you will say, but that is beside the present explanation. The ambitious new outsider had to be standardized—because for a time there was no other way of dealing with him. At that early stage in the popularization of education and the enlargement of the educational field, it is hard to see how the stimulus and rough direction of these far flung Education Department, school certificate and London University examinations could have been dispensed with. It was the only way of getting any rapid diffusion of learning at all. Quality had to come later. It was a phase of great improvisations in the face of much prejudice and resistance.

Waste and absurdity stalk mankind relentlessly, and it is impossible to ignore the triumphs of waste and absurdity occurring in that early struggle to produce an entirely educated community. It was the most natural thing for the human mind to transfer importance from the actual learning of things, a deep, dark, intricate process, to the passing of examinations, and to believe that a man who had a certificate in his hand had a subject in his head. With only the facilities for teaching at the utmost a few thousand men to experience chemical fact and know chemical science, there were produced hundreds of thousands with certificates in chemistry. When I matriculated in London University my certificate witnessed that I had passed in Latin, German and French and nevertheless I was quite unable to read, write or speak any of these tongues. About a small and quite insufficient band of men who knew and wanted to teach, seethed everywhere an earnest multitude of examinees. Briggs began life as an examinee. He was a man of great simplicity and honesty. To the end of his days I do not think he realized that there was any possible knowledge but certified knowledge. He became almost a king among examinees. All his life he was adding letters to the honourable cluster at the end of his name ; LL.D., D.C.L., M.A., B.Sc., and so forth and so on. He was a thick-set, shortish, dark, round-faced earnest-mannered man with a tendency to plumpness. I never knew him laugh. He was exactly five years older than myself, to a day. Having passed some sort of teachers' examinations—I believe in Yorkshire—he coached a few other candidates for the same distinction. But unlike most coaches he was modest about his abilities and honest in delivering the goods, and for some of the subjects he called in help. He employed assistant tutors. He had organizing power. Presently he turned from little teachers' qualifying examinations, to the widely sought after London University Matriculation. His pupils multiplied and he engaged more tutors. No doubt, like Northcliffe, he began with the ambition of making a few hundred pounds and like Northcliffe he was blown up to real opulence and influence. When I went down to Cambridge to interview him about his biological work, he already had a tutorial staff with over forty first-class honours men upon it, and he was dealing with hundreds of students and thousands of pounds.

The Briggs tutorial method was broadly simple. It rested upon the real absence of any philosophy or psychology in the educational methods of the time. The ordinary professor knew hardly anything of teaching except by rule of thumb and nothing whatever of the persistent wickedness of the human heart and, when this poor specialized innocent became an examiner in the university, almost his first impulse was to look over the papers of questions set in preceding years. These questions he parodied or if they had not turned up for some years he revived them. Rarely did he ever look at the syllabus of his subject before setting a paper, and still more rarely did he attempt any novelties in his exploration of the way in which that syllabus had been followed. Accordingly in almost every subject the paper set repeated various combinations and permutations of a very finite number of questions. Meditating upon these phenomena, Briggs was struck by the idea that if his pupils were made to write out a hundred or so model answers and look over these exercises freshly before entering the examination room, they would certainly be fully prepared and trained to answer the six or seven that would be put to them.

Accordingly he procured honours-men already acquainted with the examination to be attacked, and induced them to divide the proper textbook into thirty equal pieces of reading and further to divide up a sample collection of questions previously set, so as to control the reading done. The pupil after reading each of his thirty lessons sat down and answered the questions assigned to that lesson in a special copy-book supplied for the purpose and sent it in to the tutor, who read, marked, criticized and advised in red ink. " You must read § 35 again " he wrote or " You have missed the v.i. (vitally important) footnote on p. 11." Or " the matter you have introduced here is not required for a pass." This was a systemization of the note-book style of teaching I have already described as a success at the Midhurst Grammar School, and as, under circumstances of wider opportunity, a mental torture in Professor Judd's geological work. A few University Correspondence students, I believe, became insane, but none who pursued the thirty lessons to the end, failed to pass the examination for which they had been prepared. It was merely their thirty-first paper and differed from its predecessors merely by containing no novel questions.

Now " elementary biology " had long been regarded as a difficult subject. It was required for the Intermediate examination of all Bachelors of Science and for the Preliminary Scientific examination for the medical degrees, and it stood like a barrier in the way of a multitude of aspirants to the London B.Sc., M.B. and M.D. There were no textbooks that precisely covered the peculiar mental habits of the university examiners, and the careless student ran very grave risks of learning things outside the established requirements and becoming an intellectual nomad. Moreover there was a practical examination which proved an effectual " stumper " to men who had merely crammed from books. I set to work under Briggs to devise the necessary disciplines and economies of effort for making both the written and the practical examinations in biology safe for candidates.

That was an absolutely different thing from teaching biological science. I took over and revised a course of thirty correspondence instruction papers and later on expanded them into a small *Textbook of Biology* (my first published book for which I arranged to charge Briggs four or five hundred hours, I forget which), and I developed an efficient drilling in the practical work to cover about forty hours or so of intensive laboratory work. These forty odd hours could be spread over a session of twenty or more evening classes of two hours each, or compressed, for the convenience of students coming to London for the vacation or a last re-vision, into a furious grind of five or six hours a day for a fortnight. We met the demand for biological tutoring as it had never been met before and if it was a strange sort of biology we taught, that was the fault of the university examinations.

My classes varied in numbers from half a dozen to our maximum capacity of about thirty-two. For the bigger classes I had an assistant, who was my understudy in case of a breakdown. My students sat with their rabbits, frogs, dog-fish, crayfish or other material before them and I stood at the black-board, showed swiftly and clearly what had to be done and then went round to see that it was done. I had to organize the supply and preparation of material and meet all sorts of practical difficulties. For instance it was impossible in those days to buy a student's microscope in London for less than five pounds ; this was a prohibitive price for many of our people until we discovered and imported a quite practicable German model at half the price, and arranged for its resale at second-hand after it had done its work for

STRUGGLE FOR A LIVING 345

its first owner. I carried the books of answers of my correspondence students in buses and trains to and from the Red Lion Square laboratories and marked them in any odd time, with a red-filled fountain pen. Each book was a nominal twenty minutes work for me, but I became very swift and expert with them, swifter indeed than expert. My notes and comments were sometimes more blottesque than edifying, but on the whole they did their work.

I must confess that for a time I found this rapid development of an examiner defeating mechanism very exciting and amusing, and it was only later on that I began to consider its larger aspects. Briggs had a bookshop in Booksellers Row, which also dealt with those microscopes, his Tutorial College in Red Lion Square and a little colony of small villas for his resident tutors and students, and postal distribution in Cambridge. Later, I think, in the order of things was his printing plant at Foxton and the workers' cottages and gardens. I liked the persistent vigour with which he expanded his organization. My exploit with the L.C.P. diploma and my success in honours for the B.Sc. had made me an amateur examinee of some distinction and won his sympathetic respect. At the end of 1891 I raided the College of Preceptors again, took its highest diploma of Fellow and carried off a Doreck scholarship of £20.

Briggs hailed my marriage with warm approval. He liked his tutors to marry young and settle down to his work. I cannot estimate how much the early marriage of university honours men made his constellation of first-classes possible, but it was indisputably a factor of some importance. These prize boys, these climbers of the scholarship ladder, trained to lives of decorum, found themselves in the course of nature, as I found myself, the prey to a secret but uncontrollable urge towards early marriage. Emerging at last as the certified triumphs of the university process, missing

immediate promotion to orthodox academic posts and finding no other employment open to them except teaching at
schools, in which they were at a great disadvantage because
of their feebly developed skill at games, the offer from Briggs
of a secure three or four hundred pounds a year and probably more, seemed like the opening of the gates of Paradise
with Eve just inside. Hastily selecting wives and suitable
furniture for a villa, they entered the University Correspondence organization, and found it extremely difficult
thereafter to return to legitimate academic courses. For
there can be no denying that at the outset both the University Correspondence College and the Tutorial College had
an extremely piratical air and awakened the perplexed
suspicion and hostility of more respectably constituted
educational organizations to a very grave extent. I was
never under any illusion that my classes would open up a
way of return for me to genuine scientific work and my spirit
resounded richly to this piratical note.

The success of these classes of ours in satisfying the
biological requirements of the examiners in London University without incurring any serious knowledge of biology,
was great and rapid. We drew away a swarm of medical
students from the rather otiose hospital teaching in biology,
we got a number of ambitious teachers, engineering and
technical students who wanted the B.Sc. degree, and so
forth, and in the school holidays we packed our long black-
boarded room with the cream of the elementary teachers up
from the country, already B.A.'s, and taking an intensive
course in order to add B.Sc. to their caudal adornments and
their qualifications for a headmastership. We passed them
neatly and surely. In one year, the entire first class in Preliminary Scientific consisted of my men ; we had so raised
the examinee standard, that all the papers from other
competing institutions were pushed into the second class.

Harley Street is still dotted with men who found us useful in helping them over an unreasonable obstacle, and I am continually meeting with the victim-beneficiaries of my smudgy uncomplimentary corrections and my sleight of hand demonstrations. Lord Horder was one, the late Rt. Hon. E. S. Montagu, the Secretary of State for India (1917–22) another. We put all sorts of competing coaches out of business. One of those for whom we made life harder was Dr. Aveling, the son-in-law of old Karl Marx, at Highgate, and I suppose I contributed, unaware of what I was doing, to the difficulties my old friend A. V. Jennings encountered in his efforts to establish a private laboratory of his own.

At various times I have thought of making a large rambling novel out of William Briggs and his creations ; *Mr. Miggs and the Mind of the World,* or some such title. There were many technical difficulties in the way, but the more serious one lay in the uniqueness of his effort. It would have needed to be recognizably him and his staff because there was nothing else in the world like them. And, quite apart from the probability of blundering into libel, there was the impossibility of varying the personalities and relationships sufficiently to alleviate a touch of personal cruelty to the tutors and so forth in the foreground. These of course could be invented, but whatever one invented, that type of reader who insists upon reading between the lines would say " that is old X " or " that is Mrs. Y. Now we know about her." Which is enormously regrettable, because the whole Briggs adventure from start to finish, done on a big canvas and with an ample background of education ministries and immensely dignified university personages and authorities, is fraught with comedy of the finest sort. Apart from the endless quaintness of the detail there is the absurdity of the whole thing. That general absurdity, at least, we can glance at here.

At one pole of the business, you have the remote persons

and wills and forces which are presumably seeking or tending to produce a soundly educated community. That, if
you will, is the spirit in things which makes for the modern
world-state, that is the something not ourselves that makes
for righteousness, or—the dawning common sense of mankind. At that pole it is realized that in the new activities of
biological science there is illumination and inspiration of a
very high order. Thence comes a real drive and effort to
bring this powerful new knowledge into effective relation to
as much of the general mind as can be reached by formal
teaching.

But this drive towards biological education has to work
not only against passive resistances, but also against a great
multitude of common desires, impulses and activities, that
are not so much plainly antagonistic as running counter to
the creative power. First the new subject has to establish its
claim to a leading place in education. It is claiming space
in a curriculum already occupied. Everyone in authority
who as yet knows nothing about it, and everyone teaching a
subject already established and already suffering from the
progressive overloading of curricula, will resist its claims.
When they cannot exclude it altogether they will try compromises, they will try to cut down the share of time and
equipment conceded to it, to a minimum.

They will accuse the new subject of being " revolutionary "
and they will do so with perfect justice. Every new subject
involves a change in the general attitude. Biology was and
is a particularly aggressive and revolutionary subject, and
that is why so many of us are urgent to make it a basal and
primary subject in a new education. But in order to attain
their ends many of the advocates of the innovation, minimize
its revolutionary quality. To minimize that is to minimize
its value. So they are led to consent to an emasculated
syllabus from which all " controversial matters " are

excluded by agreement. In our biological syllabus for instance there was not a word about evolution or the ecological interplay of species and varieties. Biology had indeed been introduced to the London University examination, rather like a ram brought into a flock of sheep to improve the breed, but under protest and only on the strictest understanding and with the most drastic precautions that there should be no breach of chastity.

The fact that biology as we examination-ruled teachers knew it, was a severely *blinkered* subject, might not in itself have prevented our introducing scientific habits of interrogation and verification to our students, if we had had any sort of linkage with, or intelligent backing from, the men who were directly carrying on the living science and who were also the university examiners. But we were thrust out of touch with them. We never got to them, though we certainly got at them.

It is not always the professors, experts and researchers in a field of human interest who are the best and most trustworthy teachers of that subject to the common man. This is a point excessively ignored by men of science. They do not realize their specialized limitations. They think that writing and teaching come by nature. They do not understand that science is something far greater than the community of scientific men. It is a culture and not a club. The Royal Society resists the admission that there is any science of public education or social psychology whatever, and contemporary economists assembled at the British Association are still reluctant to admit the possibility of a scientific planning of public affairs.

Of all that I may write later. But here it has to be recorded that biology, having got its foot into the door of the university education, was wedged at that. It was represented only by a syllabus which presented a sort of sterilized abbreviation of the first half year of the exemplary biological course of Professor Huxley at Kensington. It began and ended with the comparative anatomy of a few chosen animal and vegetable types. It was linked with no other subject. Such reflection as it threw upon the problems of life was by implication. The illuminating structural identities and contrasts between the vertebrated types, were the most suggestive points to seek, and such real teaching of biological generalizations as was possible in my classes, was done in casual conversation while I and my assistant went round the dissections. In spite of such moments, the fact remains that when we had done with the majority of our students and sent them up for their inevitable passes, they knew indeed how to dissect out the ovary of an earthworm, the pedal ganglion of a mussel or the recurrent laryngeal nerve of a rabbit, and how to draw a passable diagram of the alimentary canal of a frog or the bones of its pelvic girdle or the homologies of the angiosperm oophore, but beyond these simple tricks they knew nothing whatever of biology.

My realization of what I was doing during my three years with Briggs was gradual. The requirements for the diplomas of L.C.P. and F.C.P. were not very exacting, but they involved a certain amount of reading in educational theory and history ; I had to prepare a short thesis on Froebel for the former and on Comenius for the latter ; and I presently added to my income by writing, in conjunction with a colleague on Briggs' staff, Walter Low, who was, until his untimely death in 1895, my very close friend, most of a monthly publication called the *Educational Times*. For the *Educational Times* I reviewed practically every work upon education that was being published at that time. Educational theory was forced upon me. This naturally set me asking over again, what I had already asked myself rather ineffectively during my time at Henley House School : " What

on earth am I really up to here? Why am I giving these
particular lessons in this particular way? If human society
is anything more than a fit of collective insanity in the
animal kingdom, what *is* teaching for?"

At intervals, but persistently, I have been working out the
answer to that all my life, and it will play an increasing rôle
in the story to follow.

Later on, having perhaps that early *Textbook of Biology*,
already alluded to, on my conscience, I exerted myself
to create a real textbook of biology for the reading and
use of intelligent people. I got Julian Huxley and my
eldest son Gip, both very sound and aggressive teachers of
biology, to combine with me in setting down as plainly and
clearly as we could everything that an educated man—to be
an educated man—ought to know about biological science.
This is the *Science of Life* (1929). It really does cover the
ground of the subject, and I believe that to have it read
properly, to control its reading by test writing and examination, and to substantiate it by a certain amount of museum
work and demonstrations, would come much nearer to the
effective teaching in general biology which is necessary for
any intelligent approach to the world, than anything of
the sort that is so far being done by any university. Other
interests would arrange themselves in relation to it. . . .

But I am moving ahead of my story. The main moral I
would draw from this brief account of these two remarkable growths upon the London University, the University
Correspondence College and the Tutorial College, is this:
that the progressive spirit must not only ask for education
but see that he gets it. And seeing that you get it is the real
job. We did not so much exploit London University as
expose it. The unsoundness was already there. We were its
reductio ad absurdum. The new expanded educational system
was not yet giving a real education at all, and Briggs' widely

advertised and ever growing lists of graduated examinees merely stripped the state of affairs down to its fundamental bareness.

Could the organization of this correspondence and extra-collegiate teaching have been made, could it even yet be made, of real educational use to the community ? I believe it could. It was the dream of Briggs' later years to be formally incorporated in the English university system. I believe the defects of our tuition were and are not so much in the tuition itself as in the indolence and slovenly incompetence of the University examiners and in the lack of full and able direction in the university syllabuses. There is nothing inherently un-desirable in the direction and testing of reading by corres-pondence, and nothing harmful in intelligent examining. But, as it was, we were, with the greatest energy and gravity, just missing the goal. We went beside the mark. The only results we produced were examination results which merely looked like the real thing. In the true spirit of an age of individual-istic competition, we were selling wooden nutmegs or um-brellas that wouldn't open, or brass sovereigns or a patent food without any nourishment in it, or whatever other image you like for an unsound delivery of goods. And our circumstances almost insisted upon that unsound delivery. We could not have existed except as teachers who did not teach, but pass.

§ 6

COLLAPSE INTO LITERARY JOURNALISM
(1893–1894)

THE FIRST PHASE of all my resistances to the world about me has been derision. I suppose I gathered my courage in that way for more definite revolt. And now I began to be ironical and sarcastic about this job by which I earned my living and sustained my household. The loss of genuine keenness about my teaching, and a corresponding release of facetiousness brightened my style in the *Educational Times*, and presently Briggs asked me to edit (at so many hours per number) a little advertising and intercommunicating periodical of his own, *The University Correspondent*.

Both Walter Low and I were very sarcastic young men and we had excellent reason so to be. The *Educational Times* was the property of the College of Preceptors. It paid Low £50 a year as editor and another £50 a year for contributors. He and I found it convenient that I should be the contributors—all of them. It saved him a great deal of correspondence. He was older and more experienced in newspaper matters than I, and I learnt a good deal of journalistic *savoir faire* from him. I acquired dexterity in swinging into a subject and a variety of useful phrases and methods of reviewing. We went about together, prowling about London, two passably respectable but not at all glossy young men, with hungry side glances at its abounding prosperity, sharpening our wits with talk. I was not so flimsy as I had been; I was beginning to look more compact and substantial. Low was tall and dark, not the Jew of convention and caricature, the ambitious and not the acquisitive sort, mystical and deliberate. He had an extensive knowledge of foreign languages and contemporary literature. He knew vastly more about current political issues than I did. We argued endlessly about the Jewish question, upon which he sought continually to enlighten me. But I have always refused to be enlightened and sympathetic about the Jewish question. From my cosmopolitan standpoint it is a question that ought not to exist. So, though we never quarrelled, we had some lively passages and if we convinced each other of nothing we considerably instructed each other.

Walter Low was one of a numerous and interesting family

which came to England, I think from Hungary, after the political disturbances of '48. His father prospered at first and then lost his business flair without losing his enterprise; and so the family fortunes were dissipated. Consequently the elder children had greater advantages than the younger. Sidney and Maurice both went to Oxford, became eminent journalists and ended with knighthoods. One of the sisters married well, and an elder one, Frances, became a prominent journalist. She wrote particularly in a ladies' paper called the *Queen* and scolded the girl of the period—with the usual absence of result. The younger members of the family had to fight for education by winning scholarships. The youngest sister, Barbara, is a psychoanalyst and has written an excellent little book on her subject. Walter's education fell into the trough of the family depression and instead of going to Oxford or Cambridge he worked in London and took a London M.A. degree, with exceptional distinction in foreign languages. The difficulties he had experienced gave him much the same discontented and disadvantaged feeling about life that pervaded my thoughts. We were in our twenties now and still getting nowhere. It wasn't that we were failing to climb the ladder of success. We had an exasperating realization that we could not even get our feet on the ladder of success. It had been put out of our reach.

We had both toiled hard for outside university distinctions and we found they had led us into nothing but this fundamentally unsatisfactory coaching. We had both worked strenuously at writing and discovered that the more we learnt of that elusive art the less satisfaction we derived from the writing we did, because of the haste with which we had to do it and sell it. Both of us, following some shy dream of sensuous loveliness and tender intimacy, had married and become householders, and neither for our wives nor for ourselves, was married life, upon restricted means, fulfilling the imaginations that romance and music had aroused in us. At the back of our minds was a vague feeling that we would like to begin life all over again and begin it differently; but although this feeling may have coloured our subconsciousness and certainly deflected our behaviour, it found no more definite expression. We did not own up to it. We scoffed and assumed a confident air.

My guiding destiny was presently to wrench me round into a new beginning again, but Walter Low never got away to good fortune. He caught a cold, neglected it and died of pneumonia in 1895. He left a widow who presently married again, and three bright little daughters. One of them, Ivy, wrote two quite good short novels in her teens, *Growing Pains*, and *The Questing Beast*, and then married a young Russian exile and conspirator named Litvinoff, who is now the very able Foreign Minister of the Russian government. We met at my home at Grasse and afterwards in London, in the spring of 1933, and Ivy talked with great affection and understanding about her father.

I did what I could to stifle my fundamental dissatisfaction with life during this period as a correspondence tutor. There was no one about me whom by any stretch of injustice I could blame for the insufficiencies of my experience, and I tried not to grumble about them even to myself. My correspondence fell away ; I had quite enough correspondence without writing personal letters. The zest may have gone out of my interest in myself and there is little or no record of the moods of this time. But between myself and Low there was a considerable mute understanding. Under the influence of his efforts I was beginning to write again in any scraps of time I could snatch from direct money-earning. I was resuming my general criticism of life. I had already had one curious little gleam of success. In the winter of 1890–91 after taking my degree, I had broken down and had a

*again, illness
brief a
break*

hæmorrhage, and Dr. Collins—who believed steadfastly in my ultimate recovery—had got me nearly a month's holiday at Up Park. This had given me a period of intellectual leisureliness in which my mind could play with an idea for days on end, and I wrote a paper *The Rediscovery of the Unique* which was printed by Frank Harris in the *Fortnightly Review* (July 1891). I have already mentioned this paper in § 2 of Chapter V, in my account of the development of my conception of the physical universe. This success whetted my appetite for print and I sent Harris a further article, the *Universe Rigid*, which he packed off to the printers at once and only read when he got it in proof. He found it incomprehensible and his immediate staff found it incomprehensible. This is not surprising, since it was a laboured and ill-written description of a four dimensional space-time universe, and that sort of thing was still far away from the monthly reviews in 1891. " Great *Gahd* ! " cried Harris, " What's the fellow up to ? " and summoned me to the office.

I found his summons disconcerting. My below-stairs training reinforced the spirit of the times on me, and insisted that I should visit him in proper formal costume. I imagined I must wear a morning coat and a silk hat and carry an umbrella. It was impossible I should enter the presence of a Great Editor in any other guise. My aunt Mary and I inspected these vitally important articles. The umbrella, tightly rolled and with a new elastic band, was not so bad, provided it had not to be opened ; but the silk hat was extremely discouraging. It was very fluffy and defaced and, as I now perceived for the first time, a little brownish in places. The summons was urgent and there was no time to get it ironed. We brushed it with a hard brush and then with a soft one and wiped it round again and again with a silk handkerchief. The nap remained unsubdued. Then, against the remonstrances of my aunt Mary, I wetted it with a sponge and then brushed. That seemed to do the trick. My aunt's attempt to restrain me had ruffled and delayed me a little, but I hurried out, damply glossy, to the great encounter, my début in the world of letters.

Harris kept me waiting in the packing office downstairs for nearly half an hour before he would see me. This ruffled me still more. At last I was shown up to a room that seemed to me enormous, in the midst of which was a long table at which the great man was sitting. At the ends were a young man, whom I was afterwards to know as Blanchamp, and a very refined-looking old gentleman named Silk who was Harris's private secretary. Harris silently motioned me to a chair opposite himself.

He was a square-headed individual with very black hair parted in the middle and brushed fiercely back. His eyes as they met my shabby and shrinking form became intimidatory. He had a blunt nose over a vast black upturned moustache, from beneath which came a deep voice of exceptional power. He seemed to me to be of extraordinary size, though that was a mere illusion ; but he was certainly formidable. " And it was *you* sent me this Universe R-R-Rigid ! " he roared.

I got across to the table somehow, sat down and disposed myself for a conversation. I was depleted and breathless. I placed my umbrella and hat on the table before me and realized then for the first time that my aunt Mary had been right about that wetting. It had become a disgraceful hat, an insult. The damp gloss had gone. The nap was drying irregularly and standing up in little tufts all over. It was not simply a shabby top hat ; it was an improper top hat. I stared at it. Harris stared at it. Blanchamp and Silk had evidently never seen such a hat. With an effort we came to the business in hand.

"You sent me this Universe Gur-R-R-Rigid," said Harris, picking up his cue after the pause.

He caught up a proof beside him and tossed it across the table. "Dear Gahd! I can't understand six words of it. What do you *mean* by it? For Gahd's sake tell me what it is all *about*? What's the sense of it? What are you trying to *say*?"

I couldn't stand up to him—and my hat. I couldn't for a moment adopt the tone and style of a bright young man of science. There was my hat tacitly revealing the sort of chap I was. I couldn't find words. Blanchamp and Silk with their chins resting on their hands, turned back from the hat to me, in gloomy silent accusation.

"Tell me what you *think* it's about?" roared Harris, growing more merciless with my embarrassment, and rapping the proof with the back of his considerable hand. He was enjoying himself.

"Well, you see——" I said.

"I don't see," said Harris. "That's just what I don't do."

"The idea," I said, "the idea——"

Harris became menacingly silent, patiently attentive.

"If you consider time is space like, then—— I mean if you treat it like a fourth dimension like, well then you see..."

"*Gahd*, the way I've been let in!" injected Harris in an aside to Gahd

"I can't use it," said Harris at the culmination of the interview. "We'll have to disperse the type again,"—and the vision I had had of a series of profound but brilliant articles about fundamental ideas, that would make a reputation for me, vanished. My departure from that room has been mercifully obliterated from my memory. But as soon as I got alone with it in my bedroom in Fitzroy Road, I smashed up that hat finally. To the great distress of my aunt Mary. And the effect of that encounter was to prevent my writing anything ambitious again, for a year or more. If I did, I might get into the presence of another editor, and clearly that was far worse than having one's MS. returned. It needed all the encouragement and rivalry of Walter Low to bring me back to articles once more and even then I confined myself mainly to the ill-paid and consequently reasonably accessible educational papers. They paid so badly that their editors had no desire whatever to look their contributors in the face.

Harris broke up the type of that second article and it is lost, but one or two people, Oscar Wilde was one, so praised to him the *Rediscovery of the Unique*, that he may have had afterthoughts about the merits of the rejected stuff. At any rate, when in 1894 he became proprietor editor of the *Saturday Review* and reorganized its staff, he remembered and wrote to me and I became one of his regular contributors.

But before then there had been some violent convulsions in my affairs. That humorous, that almost facetious Destiny that rules my life, seems to have resented the possibility that I might settle down in the position of one of Briggs' married, prize tutors, with occasional lapses into journalism and aspiration, and proceeded to knock my solidifying world to pieces again with characteristic emphasis.

Its course of action was threefold. It made its attack in three phases. First it concentrated the diffused discontent and self-criticism in my life into an acute emotional situation. I think I have already made plain how incompatible was my outlook of things from that of my wife. I want to make certain aspects of that relationship very clear. There is a traditional disposition to import blame or sympathy into every breach between a man and a woman. The people who tell the story about them say that he was false to her or that she was unworthy of him or that he or she made no effort and so forth and so on. But in most breaches between men and women, the want of harmony was there from the beginning and the atmosphere of a conflict and moral compulsions is imposed upon them by laws and customs that exact an impossibly stereotyped universality of behaviour from a world of unique personalities. My cousin and I had been thrown closely together by the accidents of life, we had been honest allies and we liked and admired innumerable things in each other. That we should marry had seemed the logical outcome of our situation. We both wanted now to be honest mates and adapt ourselves to each other completely. We were both perplexed and distressed by our failure to do that. We were in love with each other, quite honestly and simply desirous of being " everything " to each other. But there was an unalterable difference not only in our mental equipment and habits, but in our nervous reactions. I felt and acted swiftly and variously and at times very loosely and superficially, in the acutest contrast to her gentler and steadier flow. There was no contact nor comparison between our imaginative worlds, but within her range her quality was simpler and nobler than mine. If we had not been under the obligation of our marriage and our sentimental bias to agree in a hundred judgments and act together upon some common interpretation of life, all would have been well with us. But that need for a community of objective was the impossible condition which separated us.

The ideas which made me more and more discontented with the cramming of examinees by which we lived, were outside her world. She could not understand why I mocked and fretted perpetually at Briggs' grave and industrious organization of tutoring, because she had no inkling of the ultimate futility of the whole process. Examinations to her were like alarming but edible wild animals, they were in the order of nature, and it was my business as the man to go out and overcome them and bring back the proceeds. I on the other hand thought they were distortions of an educational process for which I felt dimly responsible. Mentally she lived inside a system, and I was not only in the system but also consciously and responsibly a part of that system in which I lived. She said, with perfect justice, that Briggs had always treated me very fairly and that I ought not to make fun of him. In her gentle but obstinate way she " stood up for him " when I talked about him. But indeed we brought in such different data that with regard to everyone in our world, her friends and my friends, we had hardly a judgment in common. She was equally unable to see why some issues of the *University Correspondent* satisfied me and others overwhelmed me with strain and fury because they wouldn't come right by certain impossible standards of my own. Why did I sit at my desk getting more and more put out by my work, while my dinner was getting cold ? She thought I " fussed about little things " too much. She was perplexed, seeing how much I had to do, that I should want to do quite other writing besides. And again it seemed to her on the verge of unreason that I could fly off from something in the newspaper to scorn, bitterness and denunciation. I can still see her dear brown eyes dismayed at some uncontrollable outburst. Throughout our married life, with no sense of personal antagonism, unconsciously, she became the gently firm champion of all that I felt was suppressing me. Conversation between us died away as topic after topic ceased to be a neutral topic. It shrank to occasional jests and endearments or to small immediate things ; to the sweet-peas in the garden or the gift of a kitten. My unaccountable irritability was a perpetual threat to our peace.

Meanwhile I talked outside my home and began to find an increasing interest in the suggestions of personality in the girls and women who flitted across the background of my restless, toilsome little world. Then it was that my Destiny saw fit to bring a grave little figure into my life who was to be its ruling influence and support throughout all my most active years. When I came into my laboratory to meet the new students who were assembling for the afternoon class of 1892–93 I found two exceptionally charming young women making friends at the end table. One of them was a certain Adeline Roberts, so dazzlingly pretty and so essentially serious, that she never in all her life had time to fall in love with a man before he was in a state of urgent and undignified protestation at her feet. So that she is still Adeline Roberts, M.D., L.C.C., and a soundly conservative influence in the affairs of the county of London. The other, Amy Catherine Robbins, was a more fragile figure, with very delicate features, very fair hair and very brown eyes. She was dressed in mourning, for her father had been quite recently killed in a railway accident, and she wanted to get the London B.Sc. degree before she took up high school teaching.

If either of these young ladies had joined my class alone I should probably never have become very intimate with either. It would not have been within my range of possibility to single out any particular student for more than a due meed of instruction. It would have been " conspicuous." But with two students capable of asking intelligent questions, it was the most natural thing in the world to put a stool between them, sit down instructively, and let these questions expand. They were both in a phase of mental formation and student curiosity, they were both reading widely, and it was the most natural thing in the world that comparative anatomy should lead to evolutionary theory and that again point the way to theological questions and social themes. They revived the discursive interests of my Kensington days. The disposition of Adeline Roberts was towards orthodoxy ; her mind had been built upon an unshaken and wholly accepted Christian faith ; Catherine Robbins had read more widely and had a bolder curiosity. She was breaking away from the tepid, shallow, sentimental Church of England Christianity in which she had been brought up. The snatches of talk for four or five minutes at a stretch that were possible during the class session were presently not enough for us, and we developed a habit of meeting early and going on talking after the two hours of rigorous biology were over. Little Miss Robbins was the more acutely interested and she was generally more punctually in advance of her time than her friend, so that we two became a duologue masked as a three-cornered friendship.

This was a new outlet for my imagination. I was under no necessity here of assuming the cynical tone I adopted with Walter Low, and I could talk of my ideas and ambitions more freely than I had ever done before. I could release old mental accumulations that had been out of action since my student phase had ended. I posed as a man of promise and effort and, as I posed, I began to believe in my pose. I cannot now retrace the easy steps through interest to intimate affection. We lent each other books ; we exchanged notes ; we contrived to walk together once or twice and to have tea together. It was a friendship that assured itself with the most perfect insincerity that it meant to go no further, and it kept on going further.

It came to me quite suddenly one night that I wanted the sort of life that Amy Catherine Robbins symbolized for me and that my present life was unendurable. That was the realization of a state of affairs that had been accumulating below the level of consciousness for some time. It did not in the least prevent that present life continuing. And the sexual element in this shift of desire was very small.

I became profoundly preoccupied with this realization of a better companionship. I did not know how to state my situation, even to myself. I did not clearly understand the fundamentals of my trouble. I tried over all sorts of explanations for this sudden sense of insufficiency in my cousin, whom nevertheless I still loved with pride, proprietorship and jealousy, and this distressing and overpowering desire to be together with a new companion. My habitual disposition to respect an obligation, to accept my immediate world and respond to its urgencies and imperatives was very strong. But almost equally strong was another system of dispositions not so immediate, but begotten of reading and thought and discussion, which denied the final claim of these immediate imperatives to control and shape my life, a system of dispositions which conformed to a code of right and wrong and duties—and excuses, that could at times run absolutely counter to the primary set. Seen in the perspective of forty-five years it is all clear enough. Indeed the primary theme of this autobiography is this conflict between the primary and the secondary values of life, and here it approached an acute phase. But I had still to realize that. I found myself divided against myself, contradicting myself, saying something that seemed on one day to be a revelation of the profoundest truth and the next day a feat of humbug. I had become inexplicable even on my own terms, and my humour and expressiveness had deserted me.

Every convention required that I should regard the business as a simple choice between two personalities, and I had not the acuteness to see through that at the time. The formula imposed upon my mind was that I had been " mistaken " in regarding myself as loving Isabel, which was not in the least true, and that now I had found my " true affinity " and fallen in love with her, which again was a misstatement. My sub-conscious intelligence was protesting against this simplification but it never struggled up to explicitness.

But I think it will be more convenient to postpone the

reference to this 'primary theme' of his autobiography

dissection of these emotional perplexities for another chapter and to go on here with the odd tangle of associated accidents which now in little more than a year transformed me from an industrious tutor into an ambitious writer. My sentimental education is a story by itself and it shall have a chapter to itself.

Having brought me to this phase of fluctuation between two conflicting streams of motive, my peculiar Destiny set itself by a series of decisive blows to change all the circumstances about me. The precarious hold of my family upon a living had already been loosened in the case both of my father, who was in that cottage at Nyewoods earning nothing, and of my brother, who was with him repairing and trading watches on a small scale. Now it was that Miss Fetherstonhaugh rebelled against my mother's increasing deafness and inefficiency and dismissed her, and almost simultaneously, my brother Freddy, who had seemed safely established in the confidence of his firm at Wokingham, discovered that he was presently to be replaced in his job by a son of his employer.

His heart burned within him. He had been happy at Wokingham and satisfied with himself for some years ; he had saved perhaps a hundred pounds, and his head spun with schemes of getting in a little more capital and credit and setting up for himself in the town and—just showing them. He consulted me. I found myself forced into the position of head of the family. My mother took refuge with me in February and I learn from an undated letter preserved by my brother Frank, that I actually went down to Wokingham, a trip I have completely forgotten, probably in the early spring, to consider the prospects of Wells Bros. Drapers (and Watchmakers) there. I did not find those prospects very bright.

I had none of the Bonaparte-Northcliffe disposition to

control and use my family. My impression is that I was hasty, harsh and stupid about all this tangle and almost uncouthly regardless of the humiliations and distressed desires involved therein, I seem to have experimented with my father and mother, possibly at my mother's suggestion, in giving them sheets of lessons to copy out. Poor dears, they were about as qualified to do that properly, as they were to make translations from Sanscrit. I also discover, in letters my brother Freddy has kept, that I wanted him to turn from drapery and try his luck for an art scholarship at South Kensington. There were various unstable plans for partnerships and business enterprises that vanished as they came, like summer snow. In addition to all the other little jobs I had in hand I seem at that time to have undertaken to organize, on the appearance of one or two possible examinees, a special course in geology for the London degree examination. This in itself was a complicated task needing close attention, reading and a balanced judgment. I never carried it out. Freddy was dislodged from Wokingham sometime in April or May. By that time my mother had gone to join my father and my brother Frank at Nyewoods and Freddy occupied the spare bedroom at Haldon Road, went into London daily, dividing his time there between the dismal pursuit of crib-hunting and, with a diminishing hopefulness, enquiries about the possibility of setting up in business for himself with practically no capital at all. Upon reflection he decided he could not work in partnership with brother Frank and it became clearer and clearer to us both that with so small a capital as we possessed, it would be impossible to get goods at proper wholesale prices. We should fall into the hands of intermediaries who specialize in eating up the hopeful beginnings of would-be small retailers. We were both very innocent about finance but not so innocent as all that.

I still have my old bank-books. At the beginning of

1893 I opened the account already noted at the Wandsworth Branch of what is now the Westminster Bank, and from the first of these little volumes which presently grow larger and fatter, I learn that in that year I earned £380 13s. 7d. My quarterly balance was usually round about £50. At the end of the year however it fell to £25 15s. 1d. A pound meant more then than it does now, but manifestly the fortunes of the Wells family were still being carried within a very narrow margin of safety. I seem to have paid out cheques to various Wellses, identities now untraceable, to the amount of £109. Most, if not all of this, probably went to my parents at Nyewoods.

One evening I gave a couple of hours to my new geological aspirant. I have quite forgotten him now, but apparently I introduced him to a few typical fossils. Where I procured these fossils, I do not know, but possibly they were hired. At any rate I found myself about nine or ten at night hurrying down the slope of Villiers Street to Charing Cross Underground Station, with a heavy bag of specimens. I was seized by a fit of coughing. Once more I tasted blood and felt the dismay that had become associated with it and when I had got into the train I pulled out my handkerchief and found it stained brightly scarlet. I coughed alone in the dingy compartment and tried not to cough, sitting very still and telling myself it was nothing very much, until at last I got to Putney Bridge. Then it had stopped. I was hungry when I got home and as I did not want to be sent to bed forthwith, I hid my tell-tale handkerchief and would not even look at it myself because I wanted to believe that I had coughed up nothing but a little discoloured phlegm, and I made a hearty supper. It was unendurable to think that I was to have yet another relapse, that I should have to stop work again. I got to bed all right. At three o'clock in the morning I was trying for dear life not to cough. But this time the blood came and came and seemed resolved to choke me for good and all. This was no skirmish ; this was a grand attack.

I remember the candle-lit room, the dawn breaking through presently, my wife and my aunt in nightgowns and dressing-gowns, the doctor hastily summoned and attention focussed about a basin in which there was blood and blood and more blood. Sponge-bags of ice were presently adjusted to my chest but I kept on disarranging them to sit up for a further bout of coughing. I suppose I was extremely near death that night, but I remember only my irritation at the thought that this would prevent my giving a lecture I had engaged myself to give on the morrow. The blood stopped before I did. I was presently spread out under my ice-bags, still and hardly breathing, but alive.

When I woke up after an indefinite interval it was as if all bothers and urgencies had been washed out of my brain. I was pleasantly weary and tranquil, the centre of a small attentive world. I had to starve for a week except for a spoonful or so of that excellent stimulant, Valentine's Extract. Much the same beautiful irresponsibility descended upon me, as came to many of the men who were sent out of the Great War to hospitals or England. There was nothing more for me to do, nothing I could possibly attend to and I didn't care a rap. I had got out of my struggle with honour and no one could ask me to carry on with those classes any more. I was quit of them. I might write or I might die. It didn't matter. The crowning event of this phase of my life came after seven days, when I was given a thin slice of bread and butter.

Within a day or so of this disaster I was writing heroically indistinct pencil notes to my friends and having a fine time of it. " I almost sent in p.p.c. cards on Thursday morning, but it occurred to me in time that they were out of fashion "

—that was the style of it. " No more teaching for me for ever," I write to Miss Healey. Sympathetic responses came to hand. Adeline Roberts, honestly appalled at my situation, felt it her duty to write me a letter, a most kind and affectionate letter of religious exhortation. I do not remember how I answered her, but it was something in the manner of a Cockney Voltaire. I'm sorry for that to this day. Dr. Collins heard of my plight and wrote also. I detected a helpful motive and wrote among other things to assure him that I had " reserves " for a year or so.

As I grew stronger I found myself exceptionally clearheaded and steady-minded. I amused myself in my convalescence by playing draughts and chess with brother Fred. Hitherto he had always been the better player and I had been hasty and inaccurate. Now for a time I found I saw all round him and he hadn't a chance with me. And suddenly I grasped the essentials of his problem. There came a demand from South Africa for an assistant, the rate of pay sounded very good in comparison with English salaries, and he was half alarmed and half attracted by the proposal. This was the very thing for him. He was honest, sober, decent and pleasant, he was trustworthy to the superlative degree and he lacked the sort of push, smartness and self assertion needed to make any sort of business success in England. In the colonies shop assistants do not run as straight or as steadily as they are compelled to do at home, they feel the breath of opportunity and the lure of personal freedom, so that out there his assets of steadiness and trustworthiness would be a precious commodity, and therefore I determined he must go. I had to overbear a strong sentimental resistance on the part of my mother, but Freddy was greatly sustained by my agreement with him, and in a week 'or so the engagement was made and the adventurer was buying his outfit and packing for the Cape,—to prosper, to acquire property and at last to return to England on the verge of sixty " comfortably off," to marry a first cousin on our maternal side, and present me with my one and only niece. With Freddy thus provided for and having undertaken to carry a share of the expenses of Nyewoods so soon as his first money came in, my mind was liberated to go into the details of my own problem.

I was not without a solution. There had already been a set-back to my earning power in the middle of 1891, when after a lesser hæmorrhage I had proposed to throw up my class teaching with Briggs. At that time he had found no properly qualified substitute and I had taken on the class work again after a rest. My classes had grown and multiplied steadily since then and we had already added a permanent assistant, J. M. Lowson, a very much better botanist than I, and a loyal and pleasant colleague. We arranged for my friend and former fellow student A. M. Davies, now a distinguished geologist, to relieve me of the rest of the class teaching, while my name remained on Briggs' glittering list of first-class honours men as the biological tutor, and I carried on with the correspondence work and undertook a textbook of geography that was never completed. Fate was pushing me to the writing-desk in spite of myself. I decided that henceforth I must reckon class teaching in London as outside the range of my possibilities and so we were free to move out of town to some more open and healthy situation. But before doing that we resolved, as my little aunt was now also in rather shaky health, to take a fortnight's holiday, all three of us, and pick up our strength at Eastbourne.

I see I drew a cheque for £30, payable to " self " in May, and I have no doubt this gigantic withdrawal represents that Eastbourne expedition.

(As I look over these yellowing old bank-books I see close to that another item : May 19th Gregory £10. It

clues from the old bank-books

recalls one of the brightest incidents in my life and I cannot
omit it here. My old fellow student R. A. Gregory was in a
tighter corner just then even than I was ; he had no ready
money at all and I lent him that ! (What courage and confidence we had in those days!) In a week or so he had paid
it back to me. Never in all my days since has anyone returned me a borrowed fiver or tenner, except Gregory.
And after that he and I put our heads together and arranged
to collaborate in a small but useful cram-book to be called
Honours Physiography, which we sold outright to a publisher
for £20—which we shared, fifty-fifty.

When I had been at Eastbourne for two or three days,
I hit quite by accident upon the true path to successful
free-lance journalism. I found the hidden secret in a book by
J. M. Barrie, called *When a Man's Single*. Let me quote the
precious words through which I found salvation. " You
beginners," said the sage Rorrison, " seem able to write
nothing but your views on politics, and your reflections on
art, and your theories of life, which you sometimes even
think original. Editors won't have that, because their readers
don't want it. . . . You see this pipe here ? Simms saw me
mending it with sealing-wax one day, and two days afterwards there was an article about it in the *Scalping Knife*.
When I went off for my holidays last summer I asked him
to look in here occasionally and turn a new cheese which had
been sent me from the country. Of course he forgot to do it,
and I denounced him on my return for not keeping his
solemn promise, so he revenged himself by publishing an
article entitled ' Rorrison's Oil-Painting.' In this it was
explained that just before Rorrison went off for a holiday
he got a present of an oil-painting. Remembering when he
had got to Paris that the painting, which had come to him
wet from the easel, had been left lying on his table, he
telegraphed to the writer to have it put away out of reach of

dust and the cat. The writer promised to do so, but when Rorrison returned he found the picture lying just where he left it. He rushed off to his friend's room to upbraid him, and did it so effectually that the friend says in his article, ' I will never do a good turn for Rorrison again ! ' "

" But why," asked Rob, " did he turn the cheese into an oil-painting ? "

" Ah, there you have the journalistic instinct again. You see a cheese is too plebeian a thing to form the subject of an article in the *Scalping Knife*, so Simms made a painting of it. He has had my Chinese umbrella from several points of view in three different papers. When I play on his piano I put scraps of paper on the notes to guide me, and he made his three guineas out of that. Once I challenged him to write an article on a straw that was sticking to the sill of my window, and it was one of the most interesting things he ever did. Then there was the box of old clothes and other odds and ends that he promised to store for me when I changed my rooms. He sold the lot to a hawker for a pair of flower-pots, and wrote an article on the transaction. Subsequently he had another article on the flower-pots ; and when I appeared to claim my belongings he got a third article out of that."

Why had I never thought in that way before ? For years I had been seeking rare and precious topics. *Rediscovery of the Unique ! Universe Rigid !* The more I was rejected the higher my shots had flown. All the time I had been shooting over the target. All I had to do was to lower my aim—and hit.

I did lower my aim and by extraordinary good fortune I hit at once. My friendly Destiny had everything ready for me. It had arranged that an American millionaire, Mr. W. W. Astor, not very well informed about the journalistic traditions of Fleet Street, should establish himself in London and buy the *Pall Mall Gazette*. As soon as the transaction was completed he called the Editor to him, and instructed him to change his politics. The Editor and most of the staff resigned, to the extreme surprise of Mr. Astor who, casting about for an immediate successor and meeting at dinner a handsome and agreeable young man, Harry Cust, heir to the Earl of Brownlow, whose knowledge of literature and the world were as manifest as his manners were charming, offered him the vacant editorship, then and there. Cust was a friend of W. E. Henley, the editor of the small, bright and combative *National Observer*, and to him he went for advice and help. A staff was assembled on which experienced journalists mingled with writers of an acuter literary sensibility, and in the highest of spirits and with a fine regardlessness of expenditure—for was not Astor notoriously a multi-millionaire—Cust set out to make the *Pall Mall Gazette* the most brilliant of recorded papers. Large and extravagant offices were secured in the West End near Leicester Square. Everyone available in Cust's social circle and Henley's literary world, was invoked to help, advise, criticize. Among other strange rules in the office was one that no contribution offered should go unread. The rate of pay was exceptionally good for the time, and there was less space devoted to news and politics and more to literary matter than in any other evening paper.

Quite unaware of this burgeoning of generous intentions within the cold resistances of the London press, I lay in the kindly sunshine beneath the white headland of Beachy Head and read my Barrie. Reading him in the nick of time. How easy he made it seem ! I fell into a pleasant meditation. I reflected that directly one forgot how confoundedly serious life could be, it did become confoundedly amusing. For instance those other people on the beach. . . .

I returned to my lodgings with the substance of an article

On Staying at the Seaside scribbled on the back of a letter and on its envelope. My cousin Bertha Williams at Windsor was a typist and I sent the stuff for her to typewrite. Then I posted this to the *Pall Mall Gazette* and received a proof almost by return. I was already busy on a second article which was also accepted. Next I dug up a facetious paper I had written for the *Science Schools Journal* long ago, and rewrote it as *The Man of the Year Million*. This appeared later in the *Pall Mall Budget*. It was illustrated there and someone in *Punch* was amused by it and quoted it and gave another illustration. I had been learning the business of writing lightly and brightly for years without understanding that I was serving an apprenticeship. The *Science Schools Journal*, the *University Correspondent*, the *Educational Times*, the *Journal of Education*, had been, so to speak, my exercise books, and my endless letters to such appreciative friends as Elizabeth Healey and even my talks to quick-witted associates like Walter Low, had been releasing me from the restricted vocabulary of my boyhood, sharpening my phrasing and developing skill in expression. At last I found myself with the knack of it.

I do not now recall the order of the various sketches, dialogues and essays I produced in that opening year of journalism. They came pouring out. Some of the best of them are to be found collected in two books, still to be bought, *Certain Personal Matters* and *Select Conversations with an Uncle*. Much of that stuff was good enough to print but not worth reprinting. Barrie was entertained by one of these articles and asked Cust who had written it. When Cust expressed his approval of my work to me and demanded more, I asked him to let me have some reviewing and routine work to eke out my income when I was not in the mood to invent, and he agreed. Books for review came to hand. . . .

In a couple of months I was earning more money than I had ever done in my class-teaching days. It was absurd.

I forgot all the tragedy of my invalidism and in August in a mood of returning confidence, we moved to a house my wife had found in Sutton, 4 Cumnor Place. Nyewoods read the articles, heard of the monthly cheques, participated, rejoiced and was glad. Editors of other papers began to write to me. I still went on with correspondence tuition, my text-book of geography and my collaboration with Gregory.

I lived at Sutton until after Christmas, when as I will tell more fully in the next chapter, I left my cousin. We parted and Catherine Robbins joined me in London, in lodgings at 7 Mornington Place (January 1894). She was reading and making notes for her B.Sc. degree and we scribbled side by side in our front room on the ground floor, prowled about London in search of stuff for articles and had a very happy time together.

I continued to write with excitement and industry, I found ideas came to hand more and more readily, and now the return of a manuscript was becoming rare. Editors were beginning to look out for me and I was learning what would suit them. But the particulars of these journeyman years I will deal with later. Here I will give only the testimony of my little bank-books to show how the financial pressure upon me was relieved and overcome. In 1893 I had made £380 13s. 7d. and it had been extremely difficult to keep things going. I seem to have carried off Catherine Robbins on a gross capital of less than £100. In 1894 I earned £583 17s. 7d. ; in 1895 £792 2s. 5d. and in 1896 £1,056 7s. 9d. Every year for a number of years my income went on expanding in this fashion. I was able to put Nyewoods on a satisfactory basis with regular payments, pay off all the costs of my divorce, pay a punctual alimony to Isabel, indulge comfortably in such diminishing bouts of ill health as still lay ahead of me, accumulate a growing surplus and presently build a home and beget children. I was able to

move my father and mother and brother from Nyewoods
to a better house at Liss, Roseneath, in 1896 and afterwards
buy it for them. My wilder flounderings with material
fortune were over ; my Destiny seemed satisfied with my
further progress and there were no more disastrous but
salutary kickings into fresh positions and wider opportunities. The last cardinal turning point on the road to
fortune had been marked by that mouthful of blood in
Villiers Street on the way down to Charing Cross.

§ 7

Exhibits in Evidence

THIS I THINK IS THE PLACE for various documents,
mostly letters written between 1890 and 1900, which give
the tone and quality of my relations to my family and to one
or two other people who were playing an important part in
my life at that period. I have had to pick them out from
a very considerable heap of material. One of the most
difficult things in my task of relating the development of
an ordinary brain during what I believe to be a very
crucial phase in human history, has been to select. I doubt
if anybody reads collections of So and So's letters right
through and I doubt if many readers will go through this
section closely. Yet these scribbles set down for some particular recipient without the remotest idea of publication and
subsequent judgment, do, I think, catch some subtle phases
in mental transition. A few sheets I have had reproduced
in reduced facsimile, to get the still puerile flavour of the
handwriting and the still puerile habit of facetious sketch-
ing. The rest have been transcribed and are given in small
print. As we used to say in our correspondence tuition : it is

not absolutely essential that this material should be read. They are for expansion and confirmation of what has been related already. I wish I could have had all of them done in facsimile. The browning old sheets have a reality and veracity impossible to convey in any other fashion. They add very few new facts ; they are living substance rather than record ; there they are.

These letters are full of the little jokes and allusions of a reluctantly dispersing household. None of us realized how we were drifting apart, each one of us to new associations that the other would never share. There is a sort of " listen to my wonders " in these letters which I find now just a little pathetic, the desire to make the most of any little success ; behind the apparent egotism and vanity is a living desire to keep up the old closeness of interest and the old intimacy of humour. That impulse fades out steadily, and in still later correspondence it has gone almost completely. The funny little inept sketches become rare and die out at last—cropping up finally only when Christmas or a birthday revives the fading family spirit. In the end the last umbilical threads are severed and hardly anything remains but a friendly memory of those vanished ties.

I suppose every biography, if fully told, would reveal this early predominance of home affections and the successive weakening out and subordination of one strand of sympathy after another, as new ones replaced them. It is clear that up to my thirtieth year there was still a very powerful web of feeling between me and the scattered remains of my home group. I was at least half way through life before my emotional release from that original matrix was completed. That, I think, must be the normal way of the individual life. It is a pilgrimage from familiarity to loneliness. I doubt whether any subsequent association systems, the dependences upon those persons and groups

again, the ' normal way '

to whom we turn to replace that confirmation and reassurance our families gave us in the beginning, have ever the same influence over us that our primary audience exercised. It is not that we break away but that we are broken away. We cling to friendships, social circles, cliques, clubs, movements, societies, parties, descendants : but for all our clinging we are forced towards the open. We lose the trick of easy clinging. In the long run, if we live long enough, we find ourselves standing alone, grown up at last altogether, in the face of the universe and life—and what remains to us of death.

The strongest secondary system of reference I ever developed was to my second wife, the moral background of half my life. For long years it seemed as though many things had not completely happened until I had told her of them. And even now, although she has been dead for seven years I find myself thinking " This would amuse Jane." I write a bit of a letter in my head or I think of a " picshua," before I remember.

Many of these letters were undated. These I have given an approximate date in italics in square brackets. I have corrected some of the dating by Ephgrave's useful calendar.

College of Preceptors,
Bloomsbury Square, W.C.
July 5th, 1890.

DEAR OLD FRED,

Just a line to mention the fact that you *have* a brother in London to whom your memory is a precious possession and *wild flowers very acceptable.*[1] Dog daisies, dandelions, violets, in fact anything in that way, the meanest flower that blows— a LARGE box.

I hope you keep healthy and happy. I am overworked of course, but my appetite is still unimpaired and while that lasts, I will keep happy.

" Our jokes are little but our hearts are great."

Tennison

Believe me,
Very respectfully yours,

BERTIE.

What is this ? Why do the people in the tram car shrink from his presence ? Why, in this hot weather sit there in a heap together ? Can it be—Satan ? Or the Hangman ? Or the Whitechapel Murder(er) ? No—it is none of these things. It is simply a young biological demonstrator who has been dissecting with a large class that particular form of life known as the Dog Fish (scylla canicula). He STINKS.

[1] I wanted these flowers for teaching botany in Milne's school.

What is this?

Why is this world so... is the an always tragic?
Or is it anyway?

Why do people... We train our shrink from the features?
Can it be — Satan?
Or Wonderful eyed monster?

No — this name of these things. It is simply a young biological demonstration which has been descending with a large class thus has fallen from the realm of life known as the Dog fish (Scyllis caniculus). He STINKS.

46, Fitzroy Road, N.W.

Monday 15/6/90 [? *91*]

DEAR G. V.,

I have sent you your glasses—they were done long ago but I could not forward them on account of my illness—they were forgotten in fact.

I had influenza about three weeks ago, and congestion of the right lung on the top of it. I have had to resign my class work with Briggs, and so I am—now that I am a little stronger again—hunting round for work to do at home.

I wrote to mother four or five days ago but she has not answered my letter.

It is no good going into the details of the disaster. It is a smash. Still living is not so impossible now as it would be if I had not a degree. My thing is to come on in the next *Fortnightly* and if they send me copies I will send one to you. The editor has written for me to call on him, about a second paper they have taken and perhaps there is something in that.[1]

Faithfully your son,

BERTIE.

I have had to pay a substitute for all my classes.

Marriage postponed—for ever ?

[1] What there was in that has already been told. See p. 356.

Wednesday
evening.

Dear Mother

You draw a doubtless familiar figure
above, keeping his 26th birthday. In the background are
bookshelves recently erected by your eldest, who came
up here Thursday & has been doing things like
that ever since.   He has laid hands upon

Wednesday evening.
[*Sep. 21st, 1892.*]

DEAR MOTHER,

You observe a doubtless familiar figure above, keeping his
26th birthday. In the background are bookshelves recently
erected by your eldest, who came up here Thursday and has
been doing things like that ever since. He has laid hands
upon all the available reading in the house and seems to be
going at it six books at a time. Isabel is at work doing
some—— (The rest of the letter is not to be found.)

[*January ? 1893.*]

DEAR FRED,

Of course mother can come here and live with us. She will not be happy, however, if Nyewoods is not kept on. If I keep her will you contribute 3/– a week or 12/– a month to that concern. I propose to leave things entirely in Frank's hands there and to pay all money to him. If you will do this I will see to all the rest myself. Let me hear. Very busy—excuse more.

BUSS.

You stick where you are, my boy, and don't let this little affair upset you.

Write and tell mother to come straight here, bag and baggage, and assure her it will be all right with the G.V.

May 22 (?) 1893

MY DEAR MISS ROBBINS,

When we made our small jokes on Wednesday afternoon anent the possible courses a shy man desperate at the imminence of a party might adopt, we did not realize that the Great Arch Humorist also meant to have his joke in the matter. For my own part I was so disgusted, when I woke in the dismal time before dawn on Thursday morning, to find myself the butt of *His* witticism, that I almost left this earthly joking ground in a huff. However by midday on Thursday, what with ice and opium pills, and this soothing bitterness and that, my wife and the doctor calmed the internal eruption of the joker outjoked, and since that I have been lying on my back, moody but recovering. I *must* say this for chest diseases ; they leave one remarkably cheerful, they do not hurt at all and they clear the mind like strong tea. My poor wife has had all the pain of this affair, bodily and mental, fatigue and fear. For my share I shall take all the sympathy and credit.

It was very kind of you to call this morning but my wife would have liked to have seen you. Next week—if I do not go to pieces again—I expect I shall be coming downstairs, and a visitor who would talk to me and take little in return, would be a charity. Will you thank Miss Roberts for the letter of condolence which—quite contrary, as she must be aware, to all etiquette, following your bad example—she wrote to my wife.

I guess class teaching is over for me for good, and that whether I like it or not, I must write for a living now.

With best wishes,
Yours very faithfully,
H. G. WELLS.

[May 26th, 1893.]
Thursday.

OFFICIAL BULLETIN

Mr. Wells tasted meat for the first time since Wednesday the 17th, yesterday, he also turned over on his side and sat up with assistance—cheerful. No recurrence of symptoms of hæmorrhage, no fever. Slept well. To-day stronger. Has eaten an egg, some boiled mutton, and other trifles. Pulse quiet, no fever or inflammation. No blood or clot expectorated now for eighty-five hours. Much stronger, able to sit up and turn about without help. *Getting a trifle troublesome.* Insists on writing letters in ink to everybody he knows—quilt spoilt and two sheets ditto—also in preference to tingling little bell, upsets table when he wishes to call attendance—also wants books to read and if those procured are not to his taste throws them at nurse—also plays Freddy at draughts and insists upon winning. Hopes are entertained that he may get up by Saturday. No definite plans. Possibly a month at Ventnor, and then if practicable remove from London.

It is particularly requested that in all letters of condolence it shall *not* be remarked that it may be for the best after all.

28, Haldon Road,
Wandsworth, S.W.
May 26th, 93.

My dear Miss Robbins,

Your unworthy teacher of biology is still—poor fellow—keeping recumbent, though he knows his ceiling pretty well by this time, but no doubt he is a-healing and by Saturday he will be, he hopes, put out in the front parlour in the afternoon. But he will be an ill thing to see, lank and unshaven and with the cares of this world growing up to choke him as he sprouts out of his bed. However that is your affair, only you must not make it a matter of mockery.

During my various illnesses I have derived much innocent amusement from letters of condolence but your Vice Principal Briggs thing capped it with a brief note written out by Miss Thomas and signed,

John Briggs,
S. T.

After that I can believe the story of the typewritten love letter signed by a pardonable slip of the pen, Holroyd, Barker and Smith.

Remember me kindly to Miss Roberts and Miss Taylor, especially Miss Roberts. Tell the girl not to trifle with Bronchitis, whatever other giddiness she may be guilty of. And believe me

Yours very faithfully,

H. G. Wells.

P.S. I think he will not be fit to see you before Sunday but I will write you before then.

Yours faithfully,

I. M. W.

28 Haldon Rd
Wandsworth
S.W.
May 26 93

My dear Miss Robbins.

Your unworthy teacher of Biology is still — poor fellow — keeping recumbent, though he knows his ceiling pretty well by this time but no doubt he is a healing & by Saturday he will be, he hopes, put out in the front parlour in the afternoon But he will be an ill

6, New Cottages,
Meads Road.
Eastbourne.
Tuesday.

MY DEAR MISS ROBBINS,

Your humble servant has been at this gay place now for eight long days. He has been led out daily to an extremely stony beach and there spread out in the sun for three, four or five hours as it might be, and he has there inhaled sea air into such lung as Providence has spared him, sea air mingled with the taint of such crabs as have gone recently from here to that bourne from which no traveller returns. His evenings have passed in the marking of examination papers and correspondence tuiting, and his nights in uneasy meditations on Death and the Future Life, and Hope and Indeterminate Equations. Moreover I have sorrowed greatly over Miss Roberts. When I was near the lowest point of my illness she sent me a wicked book by some evangelist—a word I have long used as a curse—about how that Huxley will not look his (the evangelist's) substitutes for arguments in the face, how that geology supports the book of Genesis (which is a lie) how that the gospel of St. Mark was written before A.D. 38 (which is idiotic) and all those dismal things. Egged on by this wicked book I wrote two letters to Miss Roberts blaspheming her gods, saying I knew God was a gentleman and could not possibly have any connexion with her evangelist and the like painful things. I am sorry now because I certainly was uncivil, but this particular form of Religion arouses all the latent 'Arry in my composition. But I know Miss Roberts will never approve of me any more.

This Providence has seen fit to increase the tale of my wife's troubles by sending her mother very ill. Of the two she is much worse than I am now, and I am still in a hectic unstable condition. A more serious man than myself would be horribly miserable at his inability to play his part of man in all these troubles. Everything is pressing on my wife's shoulders now, and I dare not exert myself to help for fear I shall give her a greater trouble still.

I sincerely hope you are working hard for your examination. I shall take anything but a first class pass very much to heart, so that I hope you will out of consideration for a poor suffering soul who must not be depressed by any means, do your best. I am looking forward to visiting Red Lion Square next week and seeing you again and conversing diversely with you.

Very faithfully yours,

H. G. WELLS.

Concerning literature to which you would have directed me, I have done nothing. One dismal article full of jocularities like the rattling of peas in a bladder has seen the light in the *Globe*. Moreover I tried a short story for *Black and White*, which impressed me when I had done it as being unaccountably feminine and acid—much what a masculine old maid would write. What *Black and White* thinks of it I do not know. I think my mind stagnates. It is blocked up with a lot of things. I shall come and talk to you a long time I think and deliver myself.

MY DEAR FREDDIE,

I have nothing to tell you except to keep your courage up and work hard and bear in mind that there are plenty of sympathetic friends over here anxious to hear about you whenever you can write. Things are going very evenly with us. We have not found a house yet, but we have hardly hunted for it. I have been and am very busy. I have almost written my share of Gregory and Wells' Honours Physiography which I arranged for a day or two before you sailed and a lot of small coachings jobs have dropped in for me, and next week (which will be about the time of your landing at Cape Town) I shall be sitting in glory above my roomful of candidates.

Izzums sends her love to you, Mummie is writing to you herewith.

With love from us all and best wishes

Your very affte brother

BUSSUMS.

The "roomful of candidates" refers to either some London University or College of Preceptors examination at which I earned a guinea or so as invigilator. My mother seems to have visited me in London again after my brother's departure. The four figures in the illustration are myself, my mother, my Aunt Mary and my cousin Isabel.

My dear Freddie

    I have nothing to tell you except to keep your courage up & work hard & bear in mind that there are plenty of sympathetic friends over here anxious to hear about you whenever you can write. Things are going very evenly with us. We have not found a home yet, but we have hardly hunted for it. I have been & am very busy. I have almost written my share of Gregory & Wells' Honours Physiography which I arranged for a day or two before you sailed & a lot of small coachings jobs have dropped in for me, and next week (which will be about the time of your landing at Cape Town) I shall be rolling in glory alone my room full of candidates

I thinks sends her love & your Mammma is writing to you herewith.

O for the touch of a vanished hand & the sound of a voice that is still

With love from us all & best wishes
Yours affte brother
Bussums.

[No date of entry, probably early August 1893.]

4, Cumnor Place, Sutton.

DEAR MISS ROBBINS,

I am in the tail end of the stream of congratulations, but I am happy to say I was the first person not in the confidence of the university to see that you were in the first division. And our Adeline has passed in Biology, she and her riotous school of boys, or at least Wells and Johns. Miss Saunders is in the second class, and one Miss Knight—you will remember a romantic young thing with expressive dark eyes, is, I am very sorry to see, missing.

Everyone will be in superlatives about this success of yours but as a matter of fact it is a mere beginning and not at all beyond my expectation. I should have been secretly disappointed if anything else had happened. You must not touch degree grinding for two or three years yet, though it is time for you to select your subjects. You must take an honours degree—that is a mere debt you owe your disinterested teachers.

This choice of degree subjects is a very serious one, and one you ought to make now. For mental greatness—such as mine—you must attack the biological group. I sincerely regard mathematics as on a lower level intellectually than biology. On the other hand you have done enough in mathematics to show you can get to brilliant things in that direction, while your biology is a brief growth of one year. However we must talk over this when you return. It will of course affect your attack upon South Kensington very considerably. I am glad your visit is to last another week. Putney for the last three days has been a melancholy oven. However I hope you will return before we leave here, because I would very much like to deal with this matter of the future at a greater length than is possible in a letter.

My wife sends her sincerest congratulations on your success. How did Painter get on? They have let me sign an article in the *Pall Mall Gazette*, by the bye, and signed articles in dailies is a distinct advance for a poor wretch like me.

Very faithfully yours,

H. G. WELLS.

[*November ? 1893*]

4, Cumnor Place,
Sutton.

MY DEAR FREDDIE,

I suppose, if I write to you now, this letter will reach you about Christmas time, and I daresay you will like to have our good wishes in season, even if we have to send them off unseasonably early to reach you. But over here already we are beginning to think of Christmas, there is a hard frost to-day and the roads are all hard, and last Sunday there was the first fall of snow. All the bookstalls are bright with the Christmas numbers of the magazines, and the London shops are getting brilliant with cards and presents. My two books[1] have been published now, and I have been writing articles for all kinds of publications since you left. The stories I wrote do not seem to be a great success but I have found a good market for chatty articles, and I am doing more and more of these. I had a cheque of £14 13s. from the *Pall Mall Gazette* the day before yesterday for *one month's* contributions. Not bad is it? But that may be a lucky month. However I am not drawing upon my small savings, thank goodness, and I am keeping indoors, and I think pulling round steadily. How are things going with you? I hope everything glides along, and that you are striking root in South Africa. Do you ever play draughts or chess? If so I hope you are improving, for your play with me was simply abominable.

Isabel and Mummie and the Cat are well, and we find ourselves very comfortable in our new home. We are only about twenty minutes walk from the downs, and we can go by Banstead and Epsom to Dorking over them all the way. We have had a lot of Sutton people call upon us, so that we already feel much more at home than we did in Putney, where the London custom of ignoring your neighbour is in fashion.

I have not been to see either Father or Mother since you left us but I daresay I shall run down there some of these days. I judge they are all right. Neither have I seen Frank now for some months.

I think now I am almost at the end of my news. It is not a

[1] The Textbooks of Biology.

very eventful record, but as someone has written, we are happiest when we have least history. Things have been going easily with us, and so I hope they may continue.

With very many wishes for a happy Christmas and a prosperous New Year.

> Believe me my dear Freddie
> > Your very affectionate Brother
> > > THE BUSSWHACKER.

Isabel and Auntie send their love.

> > > 4, Cumnor Place,
> > > Sutton.
> > > Dec. 15th, 1893.

MY DEAR MOTHER,

I had hoped to run down to Rogate for a day or so before Xmas to settle my accounts with father and to wish you all a pleasant time, but I am afraid it will scarcely be possible now, so I am sending a little cheque (payable to father) to pay for what he has done for me and the balance I hope *you* will dispense in making things festive on the great anniversary. As Frank has possibly told you I am still contriving to make both ends meet by writing articles. There are two more when the previous ones are returned. Did the G.V. notice that *To-day* had a note and sketch about my million year man ?

I and Isabel are going off this afternoon to stop with Mrs. Robbins at Putney until Monday—you will remember Miss Robbins who came to tea one Sunday—and we are going to a concert to-night with them. My cold and so on it is needless to say are better, or I should not be doing this.

We are looking forward to Frank's visit directly after Christmas.

> With love from all.
> > Believe me dear Mother
> > > Your affectionate Son
> > > > BERTIE.

It is not all jam this book writing. Part II of my Biology has been slashed up most cruelly in this week's *Nature* in a review.

7, Mornington Place,
N.W.
Feb. 8th, 1894.

MY DEAR MOTHER,

Do not be anxious about me. This trouble of ours is unavoidable, but I really do not care to go into details. Isabel and I have separated and she is at Hampstead and I am here. The separation is almost entirely my fault. I am with very nice people here and very busy. Yesterday I went over a microscope factory for an article for the *Pall Mall Gazette* similar to the one I sent a proof of to the G.V. Did I tell you that they had made me one of their reviewers? I keep very well, no cough in the morning or any of those troubles. I hope Frank will run up soon to see me and re-assure you. Let me know when he is coming as sometimes I am away all day. Love to the G.V. I will see to that Zoology soon. Ask him to send a letter card to Ellerington saying that no more B.Sc. Zoology will be sent for four weeks to give him an opportunity of getting the work up to date.

                    Your loving son

                                        BERTIE.

Will Father send me one copy each of the scheme for Zoology and for Biology and of the last lesson and test he has of each of those courses, please?

Tusculum Villa,
Sevenoaks, KENT.
August 10th, 94.

MY DEAR FATHER,

I had intended to come along this week but more delays have arisen and so I suppose I had better fill up the gap with a letter. I thought Frank who came up to see me a few weeks ago would have explained affairs to you. The matter is extremely simple. Last January I ran away with a young lady student of mine to London. It's not a bit of good dilating on that matter because the mischief is done and what remains now is to get affairs straight again. Isabel left the house at Sutton and went to Hampstead where she is now living (at my expense) and she has now got through about half the necessary divorce proceedings against me. I expect to be divorced early next year and then I shall marry Miss Robbins.

The house at Sutton the landlord took off my hands upon my paying the rent up to June. Since then I have been in apartments with Miss Robbins (passing as my wife) but now Mrs. Robbins has joined us. She owns a house at Putney and has let that now on a twenty one years lease at a rent of £90. We think of taking a house down here—as we are not very comfortable in apartments—and settling down. My wife will take her degree of B.Sc. (of which one examination still remains) and go on with me with literary work.

About my work. The *P.M.G.* is still my bread and cheese. I do from six to ten columns a month and get two guineas a column. I have been doing work for Briggs that brings in about £60 a year but it takes too much time and I am resigning that. I am also dropping the *Journal of Education* which comes to about £12 a year and takes nearly a day a month. I do *Educational Times* work from 2 to 5 or more cols. a month at half a guinea col. and in addition drop articles at *Black and White* and the *National Observer*, when I get the time free. Then there are short stories which are difficult to plant at present, but I expect this series in *P. M. Budget* will get my name up. They are paid at a slightly higher rate than articles but are much more profitable in the end because they can be republished as a book. Besides this I have been writing a longer thing on spec and have been treating through an agent to get some of my *P.M.G.* articles published as a book.

I think that is a pretty complete statement of my affairs. Naturally things are a little tight with me at present as the divorce business is heavy but after that bill is settled I see no reason why things should not go easily with all of us. I shall have to pay Isabel £100 a year or more, but my income by hook or by crook can always be brought up to £350 and it may be more in future. Mrs. Robbins is going to raise the ready money for our furniture by a small mortgage on her house and the interest on that with the ground rent will come to £30 out of her £90. Still I don't expect to be pinched

and I have no doubt that I shall be able to do my filial duty
by mother and yourself all right.

My health hasn't given me any trouble, save for one cold
and a bit of overwork this year.

Give my love to mother and believe me,

Yours ever,
BERTIE.

Of course I want you to hand this to mother to read as well.
Mother will remember Miss Robbins—she came to tea one
Sunday afternoon.

The letting of Mrs. Robbins' house was not a success.
Her tenant did not pay his rent and " flitted " at night
with his furniture. The house was then sold and the money
invested.

12, Mornington Road, N.W.

5/12/94.

MY DEAR LITTLE MOTHER,

I'm anticipating Christmas and sending you a little present (I wish it could be larger). I'm keeping very well this Christmas and at about the same level of prosperity. I don't do so much for the *P.M.G.* but I do stuff for the *Saturday* which is rather better pay and I have some hope of the *New Review*. . . .

This day week I'm giving my lecture at the Coll of Preceptors. There's nothing settled about any of my books yet but I think there will be two if not three in March.

Let me hear all about you. Have you heard from Fred ?

Yours ever affectionately

BERTIE.

Little Bertie writing away for dear life to get little things for all his little people sends his love to Little Clock Man and Little Daddy and Little Mother.

Little Bertie wishing away for dear
life to get little things for all his
little People   sends his love to
Little Clock Man & Little Daddy &
Little Mother.

12, Mornington Road, N.W.
5/2/95.

MY DEAR FATHER AND MOTHER,

Thanks very much for your letters in the last few days. It's very kind of the Father to say £40 a year will do to go on with. However I think I can manage £60, though just now is a tight time. Take £10 of the £15 to go on with and put £5 by for next quarter, say, as an experiment. You know the method is to put the cheque I send into the Savings bank—which will take cheques now—and draw out whatever you want as you want it. Later on I hope to do better things for you if I can only get hold of a little money. It's a dream of mine to get you into rather a better house, either by buying one or leasing it but that can't happen this year and may never happen. Whatever success I have, you are responsible for the beginnings of it. However hard up you were when I was a youngster you let me have paper and pencils, books from the Institute and so forth and if I haven't my mother to thank for my imagination and my father for skill, where did I get these qualities?

Believe me my dear Parents

Your very affectionate son

BERTIE.

12, Mornington Rd, N.W.
Sunday October 13th. (1895)

MY DEAR MOTHER,

Just a line to tell you that I am back with my old landlady here for three weeks (getting married). We've been up about a week. My last book seems a hit—everyone has heard of it —and all kinds of people seem disposed to make much of me. I've told nobody scarcely that we were coming up and already I'm invited out to-night and every night next week except Monday and Friday. I've had letters too from four publishing firms asking for the offer of my next book but I shall, I think, stick to my first connexion. It's rather pleasant to find oneself something in the world after all the years of trying and disappointment.

What is Fred's address at Johannesburg? I'm rather anxious to know. I sent a copy of the "Wonderful Visit" to him just before I had your letter, addressed to Messrs Garlick. I'd like to know all about him. There's no doubt that country is rising at an immense pace. I know one of the bank managers there and might be able to help Fred through him. He was my colleague at Milne's school. He's a Scotchman and bound to die rich, a long headed friendly man who might—if he chose—put Fred up to a lot of good tips. His name is Johnston. I'm getting his address from Milne.

Love to the Dad and Frank.

Your very affectionate son,

BERTIE.

Lynton, Maybury Rd.,
Woking, Surrey.
Friday, Jan. 24th, 1896.

MY DEAR LITTLE BROTHER AT THE SEAT OF WAR,

How goes it with you? For a day or two in the new year, while Jameson was astonishing the world, I was seriously anxious about your safety, and I should have cabled to know if all was well, had not the wires been choked with graver matter. I suppose we shall soon have a lengthy and vivid account of the whole business from you. Here things have been of the liveliest, war rumours, all the Music Halls busy with songs insulting the German Emperor, fleets being manned, and nobody free to attend to the works of a poor struggling author from Lands End to John o' Groats. Consequently a book I was to have published hasn't been published, and won't be until March. You see how far reaching your Uitlander bothers are?

I'm going on very well altogether. I made between five

and six hundred last year, and expect to make more rather than less, this year. I've married and ended all those troubles, and I've just taken a pretty little house at Liss with seven decent rooms and a garden and things all comfortable for the old folks. They are moving in next week. Frank is to expand his watchmaking business and altogether I think things are on the move towards comfort. I was down there about Christmas time and all three seemed very well and jolly. Frank's business seems picking up. The new home is one of a dozen or so decent little houses, and within comfortable reach of a church.

I'm riding a bicycle now and went a few weeks ago to a place called Odiham, which may perhaps awaken old memories.

Since I wrote the above I've received your letter. I'm glad to find you're all right. As you say, the Invasion was a Capitalistic enterprise, though Jameson himself is a gallant man enough. But the Transvaal has no business to intrigue with Germany for all that. Do you see any papers now? There's usually something about me in the *Review of Reviews*.

Go and see Johnston if you possibly can. He's a first rate man you'll find. Some of these days I must come and see you out there. I hope your getting on all right with the Dutch language and your business. What are the chances of opening for yourself out there? I should think that if you could pick up Dutch and master the habits and requirements, you'd have a better chance than you had in this crowded country. Don't dream of any speculation in gold mines or that kind of thing. Stick tight to your savings. If you want to invest trust old Johnston. He's a first rate, square headed, thoroughly honest man. What do you think of your move out of England? It wasn't so bad for you altogether—was it?

However time slips by. I've got to write a story before next week for a new monthly magazine, so I mustn't write any more now to you.

With kindest regards
Your very affectionate Brother
THE BUSSWHACKER.

[*July : 1896*]

Brosley.

Illustrated letter.

This does not represent a Dutchman but an elderly
gentleman of distinguished manners who has recently been
staying at Heatherlea, Worcester Park, Surrey. He plays
chess with considerable skill, draughts and whist—croquet
he learnt rapidly—and he answers to the names of
"Gov'ner" "Dad" or the "Old Man" with equal facility.
When returning to Liss he took away all the tobacco and
a box of Brosley clay pipes. In the place of him a short lady
of pleasing demeanour is shortly expected (as per accompanying illustration). She will probably be here on the
birthday of her middle and favourite son, whom she speaks
of variously as " Freddy " " Fezzy " " Fizzums " and
" Master Freddie." Needless to say his health will be drunk
on that anniversary both at Liss and Heatherlea with the
warmest feelings. This person (illustration) it is scarcely
necessary to explain is your long lost brother Buss. You will
observe that he has with growing years and prosperity
developed—a projection which he keeps in bounds only by
the most strenuous bicycle riding. He rejoices to say that
things go very well with him, books selling cheerfully and so
forth, in spite of the Jubilee. And speaking of the Jubilee
he saw nothing of it whatever, except that he went to
see the ironclads—hundreds of 'em lying all along Spithead
and the Solent for miles and miles and miles.—He went
round the show twice in a steamboat accompanied by
🖝 that chap ! And while he was going round the King
of Siam in his yacht came out of Portsmouth Harbour
and every blessed ironclad let off a gun (illustration). This
is a sort of Birthday card really. I've heard from mother
once or twice that things were going very well with you and
I was very glad to get your own letter. May your good luck
keep on for you deserve it richly. Many happy returns of the
day and a light heart to you, old boy !

From Buss.

, clay pipes .   In the place of his
lady of pleasing demeanour as shown
per accompanying illustration)
will be here on the birthdays
speaks of various as " Freddy "
his worthy health will be drunk on that auspicious
days .   This person
my lost brother Buss. You
can perhaps declared
into any of the most strenuous
things go very well with him

... the shore ... in a steamboat ... a ...
And while he was ... the King of Siam.
Portsmouth Harbour & my blessed uncle.

This is a sort of Birthday Carnival.

... of the Jubilee. And speaking of the Jubilee I
went to see the ironclads — hundreds of them ...
& miles & miles — He went
... That chap!
... yacht — came out of
let off a gun

Heatherlea, Worcester Park.
New Year's Eve. 1896.

MY DEAR LITTLE BRUZZER FREDDY,

I had your funny card for which, Bruzzer Freddy, there was one and a penny to pay ! but I would have cheerfully paid much more than that rather than not have had it. And as it is New Year's Eve and I have been thinking over the past year and all that has happened, I don't think I can do better than write this letter to you before the New Year begins. And to begin with myself, I have been still on the rise of fortune's wave this year, and it seems as though I must certainly go on to still larger successes and gains next for my name still spreads abroad, and people I have never seen, some from Chicago, one from Cape Town, and one from far up the Yung Tse Kiang in China, write and tell me they find my books pleasant. So far it has meant more fame than money to me, but I hope next year that the gilt edge will come to my successes. This year I have made between eight hundred and a thousand and next year it will be more and after that still more, and then I hope to put in operation little plans I have. You know the old people are now pretty comfortable at Liss, and Frank's business really seems on the move. There were two packing cases of clocks and things in the passage of the house when I went down there yesterday. And next year I hope to be able (though I don't want him to know yet for fear of disappointment) to put him firmly on his legs. I think it will be possible to get him into a shop in a good position in Liss, and to let the old folks have a better cottage than they are in at present. But you know the old maxim—hasten slowly. I want everything safe and straight first. Then when Frank is a really efficient citizen again—we shall be seeing you back I expect, brown and strong I hope and with a little something in your pocket. And then we must see whether at Wokingham or Petersfield or some such place, it won't be possible for you to start with fair prospects. Eigh ? The little old lady is rosy and active—fit for twenty years I shouldn't wonder, and before that time perhaps she will see all three of us flourishing in our own homes, and as cheerful as can be. The old man too is none so dusty a chap when you get him on the right side—and he seems hale enough for a century. So that this New Year's Eve I feel uncommonly cheerful and hopeful, not only for myself but for the whole blessed family of us.

Good luck Bruzzer Freddy

Yours ever,

H. G. BUSSWHACKER.

I don't know if you see *Pearson's Magazine* out there—in April next a long story of mine will begin and go on until December, and I expect great things of it. *Pearson's Magazine* mind !—not *Pearson's Weekly*.

Remember me kindly to Johnston who's a nice old chap isn't he ? When is he coming over ? If ever he comes I shall expect him to come and stop here for a time to gossip about old times.

Look out for the *Saturday Review* if you get a chance of seeing it. You will see among the reviews every week now H. G. W. which is me.

And don't forget to write to a chap and tell him all about yourself.

Beach Cottage,

Granville Road.

December 18th, 98.

MY DEAR FATHER,

I've been meaning to write to you all this past week and tell you about the work in hand. I don't know anything about the *Bookman* paragraph of which you speak—could I see it ? Possibly Nicol got hold of something through Barrie (who came to see us). But the paragraphs in the *Academy* were written by Hind the editor after a visit here in which we talked about our work. The serial about the year 2100 will appear very soon now in the *Graphic* with coloured illustrations. I've altered it a good deal for the book, which will be published in April or May by Harper Bros., and then this long silence of a year and more will be over. It's rather in the vein of the *Time Machine* but ever so much larger in every way. I don't think people will have forgotten me in the interval. The old books keep on selling— each at the rate of four to six copies a week bringing in little cheques for five pounds or so for the half year. The other book the *Academy* spoke of, is now being put on the market by Pinker, it's a sentimental story in rather a new style, and I think he has offered it to *Harper's Magazine*. It's called *Love and Mr. Lewisham*. I'm also under a contract to do stories for the *Strand Magazine* but I don't like the job. It's like talking to fools, you can't let yourself go or they won't understand. If you send them anything a bit novel they are afraid their readers won't understand. Two stories they have had, I consider bosh, but they liked them tremendously. Another I have recently done they don't like although it is an admirable story. So that will go elsewhere. Just now I am writing rather hard—though this is between ourselves—at a comic novel rather on the old fashioned Dickens line, a lot of entertaining characters doing ordinary things.[1] I keep better here than I've been since I was at South Kensington and get good work out of myself every day. There are more ideas in a day here than in a week of Worcester Park.

Amy wants me to say there is a Turkey at Shoolbreds simply gobbling to get at you, and it has some minor luggage under its wing. Our love to you all. Perhaps we may travel your way next Spring. It seems ages since I saw you. Best wishes for a Merry Christmas,

Yours ever,

BERTIE.

Our Fat Cat has fled. Break it gently to Frank.
No colds I hope?
No trouble with that liver?

(A little sketch shows a turkey *en route* for Nyewoods.)

Arnold House,
Sandgate,
Kent.
June 7th, 1900.

MY DEAR LITTLE MOTHER,

As it is so near quarter day I am sending you on £15 and I hope that in another week I shall see you. It was

---

[1] *Kipps.*

very jolly was it not? getting that letter from Fred and by this time I daresay he is reading all the letters you have been writing him since the war began. What a budget it will be for him!

But I don't like to hear you have "put by" £5. I don't want you to go pinching and saving out of the money I send you. It isn't any too much anyhow and you ought to spend it all upon things to make life pleasant.

I am sending you a first review of *Love and Mr. Lewisham*. They have sold 1,600 copies in England and 2,500 in the colonies before publication, and I think the book is almost certain to beat any previous book I have written in the matter of sales.

Give my love to Father and Frank. And believe me

Your very affectionate son,

BERTIE.

There survive scores of such letters, but these samples I think give the quality of all of them and my texture at that time. As I look over them I seem to realize for the first time the devitalization of relationship that seems to be an inevitable consequence of an ever widening divergence of experiences, associations and standards. And in turning over the pages of the *Saturday Review* (1894–97) in an attempt to identify all my contributions, I found a queer little intimation that this loss of dearness and nearness was troubling my mind at the time. It has never been reprinted and I think it may very well come in as a rider to these letters. It embalms a mood of over-work and doubt. There is real nostalgia for the close warmth of the Family peeping out in it, and an exaggerated sense of dislocation. Those forebodings of social isolation and inaccessible intimacies have not been justified. I was gradually learning an art, which I will call the Art of Modus Vivendi—not quite the same thing as Arnold Bennett's "Savoir Faire," but a very similarly necessitated accomplishment. I cannot complain of the share of friends and lovers life has given me or pose even to this day as a lonesome man. And though I missed horsemanship and good sound flannelled sport, most of what are called the good things of life, got to me in time.

" EXCELSIOR

" To rise in the world, in spite of popular illusions, is by no means an unmixed blessing. The young proletarian, playing happily in his native gutter, scarcely realizes this. So soon as he begins to think at all about himself, his teachers begin the evil lesson of ambition ; he lifts his eyes to the distant peaks, and the sun is bright upon them and they seem very fair. The garrulous Smiles comes his way with his stories of men who have " got on "—without a word of warning against the sorrows of success. No one warns him of the penalties. Every one speaks of climbing as though it were bliss unspeakable. And so the young proletarian, finding his limbs are stout and the strength is in him, starts confidently enough, by the way of book or barter as his tastes incline.

" Let the epic Smiles tell of the career of those who win. Let no one tell of those who fall, who drop by the way with bodies enfeebled by overstudy, underfed, who are lost amidst the mountain fogs of commercial morality. Our concern is with those who win, to whom a day comes when they can see their schoolmates far below them, still paddling happily in the gutter, can look down on venerable heads to which they once looked up, and, turning the other way, behold the Promised Land. One might think it would be all exultation, this Nebo incident, the happiest of all possible positions in the sad life of man. It may be even, that the man from below tells himself as much. And then he looks round for some sympathetic participator.

" With that he discovers, though perhaps not all at once,

the peculiar discomfort of worldly success. In his new stratum he finds pleasant people enough, people who were born in that station, educated to keep in it, and who regard it— perhaps correctly—as properly their own. To them he is an intruder, and largely inexplicable. He knows that any allusion to that steep pathway of broken heads over which he has clambered—for all human success is relative, and if one man rises some other must fall—and which he has found such excitement in ascending, any such allusion he knows will be the mental equivalent to putting his thumbs in the armholes of his waistcoat. Usually the man from below has a more than average brain, and is sensitive enough to keep his Most Interesting Topic, his Life, to himself. He knows, too, the legend of the Bounder, knows that these people credit all men who rise from his class with an aggressive ostentation, with hair-oil and at least one massive gold chain if not two, besides a complete inversion of the normal aspirate. He imagines that people expect breaches of their particular laws, and he knows, too, that there is some ground for that expectation. He blunders at times from sheer watchfulness.

"You begin to perceive the hair-shirt. To speak in the tongue of Herbert Spencer, the man from below is not adapted to his environment. That is not all ; he is adapted to no environment. Though the language of the people of the new stratum is not his mother tongue, though their manners and customs fit him like a slop suit, he has acquired just enough of these things to be equally out of his element below. He is a kind of social miscellany, a book of short stories, a volume of reminiscences of People I have Met. And that friend, that dear friend, who is the salt of life, with whom he may let his mind run free, whose prejudices are the same, whose habits coincide—the man from below knows him not. There was A in the pound a week stage, 'tis true, and B at the three hundred phase, and C in the early thousands ; but in some mysterious way they were all aggrieved. A time came when each remarked in a tone that rang false, " You're getting such a Swell now, you know," and he saw a new light in the erstwhile friendly eye, and therewith yawned a gulf. His friends are not life companions but epochs, influences. And he has worse troubles. One of two things happens to the man from below in his marrying. Either he marries early some one down below there, and she cannot keep pace with him, or he marries late up above— some one very charming and young, and he cannot keep pace with her.

" For by the time he has risen to his highest stratum, and donned the stiffest, prickliest hair-shirt of all, the man from below begins to feel old. He has never been a youth at that level, and he does not know how to begin. The perennial youthfulness of your retired general—who is perhaps half his age again—appals him. You see him watching cricket in a puzzled way—he had no time for cricket—or hanging over the railings of Rotten Row (in an attitude that he feels instinctively is a little incorrect), and staring at the hand-some, healthy, well-dressed people who ride by. Theirs is the earth. *His* means for horse exercise came when his nerve for it had gone. The wine of life does not wait. After all the man he has ousted had drunk the best of the cup. For the conqueror, the dregs.

" That is the disillusionment of the successful proletarian. Better a little grocery, a life of sordid anxiety, love, and a tumult of children, than this Dead Sea fruit of success. It is fun to struggle, but tragedy to win. Happy is the poor man who clutches that prize in the grip of death and never sees it crumble in his hand."

To which betrayal of a mood I add thirty-nine years later only one word : " Nonsense."

But let me get on with my story which this exhibition of documents has delayed. This divorce put me askew to the usages and institutions of my times in a very elementary, provocative and stimulating way. It affected my attempts at fiction and my social and political reactions profoundly and I must do my best now to dissect out the complex of motives and suggestions that was determining my conduct at this crucial phase.